JUDGE

Books of the Infinite #2

Judge

R. J. Larson

BethanyHouse
a division of Baker Publishing Group
Minneapolis, Minnesota

Published by Bethany House Publishers
11400 Hampshire Avenue South
Bloomington, Minnesota 55438
www.bethanyhouse.com

Bethany House Publishers is a division of
Baker Publishing Group, Grand Rapids, Michigan

Printed in the United States of America

Library of Congress Cataloging-in-Publication Data

Larson, R. J.
Judge / R.J. Larson.
p. cm. — (Books of the Infinite ; 2)
ISBN 978-0-7642-0972-7 (pbk.)
I. Title.
PS3602.A8343J84 2012
813′.6—dc23 2012028886

This is a work of fiction. Names, characters, incidents, and dialogues are products of the author's imagination and are not to be construed as real. Any resemblance to actual events or persons, living or dead, is entirely coincidental.

Cover design by Wes Youssi/M.80 Design
Cover photography by Steve Gardner, PixelWorks Studio, Inc.

12 13 14 15 16 17 18 7 6 5 4 3 2 1

To all adventurers
who wish an epic destroyer would
follow them home.

CHARACTER LIST

Kien Lantec **Kee**-en **Lan**-tek\ Military judge-advocate for the Tracelands

Ela Roeh **El**-ah **Roe**-eh\ Prophet of Parne

Ara Lantec **Are**-ah **Lan**-tek\ Rade Lantec's wife, Kien's mother

General Rol \Rawl\ The Tracelands' General of the Army

Tamri Het **Tam**-ree Het\ Citizen of Munra, Siphra

Tzana Roeh **Tsaw**-nah **Roe**-eh\ Ela's sister

Beka Thel **Bek**-ah Thell\ Jon Thel's wife, Kien's sister

Jon Thel \Jon Thell\ A Tracelands military commander, Beka's husband

Rade Lantec \Raid **Lan**-tek\ Kien's father, the Tracelands' preeminent statesman

Ruestock **Roo**-stock\ Exiled former Siphran ambassador to the Tracelands

Tsir Aun \Sir **Awn**\ Istgard's prime minister, Tek Lara's husband

Bel-Tygeon \Bell-**Ty**-jee-on\ King of Belaal

Akabe Garric \Ah-**cabe Gair**-rick\ Former Siphran rebel, the Infinite's chosen king of Siphra

Zade Chacen **Zaid Chase**-en\ Parne's deposed chief priest

Sius Chacen **See**-es **Chase**-en\ Elder son of Zade Chacen

Za'af Chacen **Zay**-aff **Chase**-en\ Second son of Zade Chacen

Dan Roeh \Dan **Roe**-eh\ Ela's father

Kalme Roeh **Call**-may **Roe**-eh\ Ela's mother

Ninus **Nine**-es\ King of the island-city Adar-iyr

Matron Prill \prill\ Ela's chaperone

Ishvah Nesac \Ish-**vaw** **Ness**-ak\ The Infinite's chosen chief priest of Parne

Siyrsun **Seer**-sun\ Belaal's General of the Army

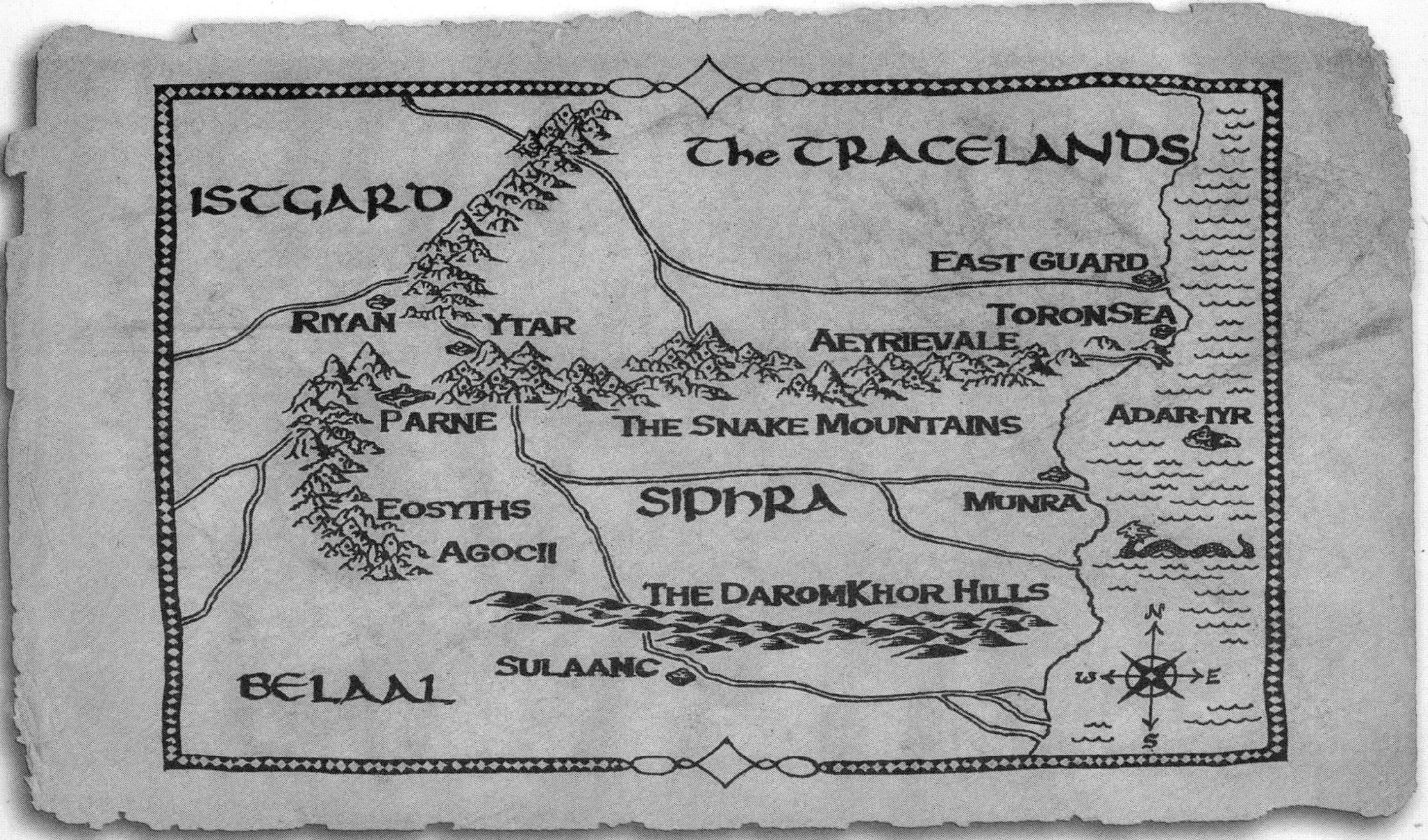
The TRACELANDS
ISTGARD
EAST GUARD
TORONSEA
RIYAN
YTAR
AEYRIEVALE
PARNE
THE SNAKE MOUNTAINS
ADAR-IYR
SIPHRA
MUNRA
EOSYTHS
AGOCII
THE DAROMKHOR HILLS
SULAANC
BELAAL
N
W
E
S

✦ I ✦

Kien Lantec lifted his chin, pressed his fingers against his wet skin, and then swept the razor up his throat—just as the Infinite's voice resonated within his thoughts.

You will go to ToronSea.

"Ow!" Jolted by the voice, Kien gasped as the blade pierced his skin. He dropped the razor and leaped backward as it clattered on the tiled floor, threatening his bare toes. Hearing from one's Creator evidently involved undreamed-of risks. Not to mention worrisome symptoms that included sweating, tremors, and an unnervingly rapid heart rate. Kien exhaled and thumped a clammy fist against his heart. Steady.

ToronSea? Why? He'd just returned home on military leave. His first leave! And ToronSea was at the edge of nowhere, governed by a pack of argumentative antisocials who were supposed to be civilized Tracelanders. Controlling himself, Kien smudged some powdered balm against the bloodied nick beneath his jaw. "Go to ToronSea?"

You will warn My faithful in ToronSea of My displeasure because they are beguiled by certain Siphran worshipers of Atea. Tell the one who speaks for them that he must be faithful to Me and seek My will. You must also speak to certain deceived ones who love Atea. Tell them only that I see their failings and seek their hearts. The wise will hear Me.

Worshipers of Atea. Weren't they given over to disturbing little quirks like divination through watching the death throes of victims in ritual strangulations? Kien hoped the oft-repeated stories were unfounded. He didn't relish being the target of a divination ritual. "But, Infinite, I'm not a prophet. I'm a—"

Are you My servant?

Defeated before he'd begun. "Yes. I am your servant." Kien meant every word of his pledge, but he didn't have to feel comfortable about it, did he? He moistened his lips. "Am I no longer training to be a military judge?"

Waiting silence answered. Kien exhaled, retrieved his razor, and tried to ask an answerable question. "Should I depart today?"

Yes.

"Will I survive?"

More Omnipotent silence. Survival, evidently, shouldn't be his first consideration. "Fine. I'll finish shaving, then organize a few details and gather my gear. Will one knapsack suffice?"

He paused. Nothing. It seemed he must answer most of his own questions. And he had plenty to ask. For example, why wasn't the Infinite sending His true prophet, Ela of Parne, to confront ToronSea? No, sending Ela into any situation where her life might be endangered was completely unacceptable. For Ela's sake, Kien would go to ToronSea himself.

Ela . . . Kien grinned into his polished metal mirror and finished shaving. He now had an ideal excuse to visit the most captivating person in East Guard. No doubt Ela would—

"Kien?" His mother's voice echoed up the stairwell steps to his tower room. "*Keee*-en!"

He hurriedly wiped his face and smoothed his tunic before opening the door. Ara Lantec marched up the last few spiraling stone steps and stopped on the landing. Cool gray eyes narrowed, she folded her elegant arms and glared, her usually serene face a study of restrained maternal fury. "Your destroyer is eating my garden! My *whole* garden! Unless you can control that monster, your father will have him shot by archers, then butchered and stewed!"

Kien saw six months of military wages vanish, consumed by a gargantuan warhorse's gluttony. "Sorry. I'll pay for the damages."

Ara seethed. "Paying for my garden won't help me this evening. My reception is ruined!"

He wasn't about to offer advice for saving his mother's reception—a gathering of the Tracelands' most elite women. Wives of members of the Grand Assembly. And their daughters, whom Kien devoutly hoped to escape. No doubt his parents would be planning his wedding the instant he smiled at one of those spoiled girls. Kien kissed his mother's perfectly arranged dark hair, hoping to soothe her. She scowled.

Barefoot, he started down the stairs. "Don't worry. You'll be rid of me and the destroyer by midday. I'm leaving on an assignment."

"What? You've just returned after six months of duty."

"It's an emergency." And that emergency looked positively inviting compared to his mother's wrath—not to mention her reception. Several steps down, he hesitated and looked up. "Anyway, I thought you wanted me gone."

"No, I simply want you to *kill* that destroyer!"

"Oh, sure." Kien hoped she hadn't caught his sarcasm. Chaining the beast, not killing it, would have to suffice. Kien rushed down the spiraling stone steps and charged through the stairwell's open doorway, into the adjoining hall. "Scythe!"

He found the black monster-horse in Mother's formal garden, dwarfing a crimson stand of miniature spice trees, crunching down leaf after expensive leaf. The massive creature turned his rump toward Kien and flicked his long black tail.

Kien growled. "I know you heard me. Don't you dare turn away!"

Scythe swung his big head around, irritable, still chewing. Kien glared and grabbed his halter. "Not another bite! Your morning meal is finished. Move. Now. *Obey.*"

At least destroyers heeded *obey*—though the command never improved their attitudes. The oversized brute grumbled as Kien led him toward the stable. To gain his cooperation, Kien said,

"Let me make myself presentable, then we'll visit General Rol. And Ela."

Scythe's big ears perked. "Ela," Kien repeated, knowing she was this beast's greatest weakness. Kien's as well. "I'm sure she has six months' worth of shrubs for you to devour."

He continued to talk of Ela as he reluctantly chained Scythe to an iron ring embedded in stone within the stable yard. "Wait. I'll return." He'd won this round. With the destroyer at least.

His mother and the Infinite were different matters entirely.

Visions of ToronSea's Ateans and their brutal divination rituals overtook his thoughts.

Kien hoped he would survive.

✦ ✦ ✦

Seated on a woven mat near the ancient stone ruins of the Infinite's temple, Ela Roeh, prophet of Parne, shifted in place and studied her scholars.

Five young ladies sat before her, decorously clad in pastel tunics and soft mantles. Wielding reed pens over their wax writing tablets, they bowed their fashionable curl-crowned heads in the early-autumn sunlight and wrote this morning's lesson.

How troublesome to realize her students were all near her own age. In spirit, Ela felt older than eighteen. But surely not older than her dear eightyish chaperone. Ela slid a glance toward Tamri Het, a Siphran who'd followed Ela to the Tracelands after Siphra's revolution seven months past. Seated nearby on a cushion, Tamri looked utterly harmless with her veiled silver hair-braids and embroidery. Who would ever believe this great-grandmother was a mob-inciting revolutionary who'd helped to topple Siphra's previous king from his throne? Particularly now, as she hummed like a girl, her veils fluttering in the light breeze . . .

Hmm. Perhaps, in spirit, Ela *was* older than Tamri. Not that it mattered.

Old-spirited or not, all prophets of Parne died young. Ela

chewed her lower lip. Surely her death would serve the Infinite's purpose. But when?

Tzana, Ela's fragile little sister, crept onto the mat, her small, prematurely aged face wrinkled both with concern and with her incurable condition. "You look sad," Tzana whispered.

Bending, Ela returned the whisper. "I'm not." However, she was restless. Ela tucked back one of Tzana's sparse curls and willed herself to relax. Tzana huddled beneath Ela's arm and shivered until Ela snuggled her close. The little girl disliked the cooler autumn air. Ela couldn't blame her. Tzana was accustomed to Parne's warmer climate, which was more soothing to her arthritis than these damp ocean-borne breezes. Tonight, Ela decided, she must prepare more ointment to ease Tzana's aching joints.

Another whisper lifted—this time from among her students.

"Finished!" Beka Thel, Kien's sister, set down her pen and tablet with a delicate click. Beka was as clever as her brother. And equally charming. Warm brown eyes sparkling, Beka threw Ela a mischievous smile so like Kien's that Ela sighed. Kien . . .

She returned Beka's smile. But as they waited for the other four girls to finish their work, Ela scolded herself inwardly. She mustn't think of Kien. Why torment herself? Yet she thought of him constantly. *Not* proper musings for a prophet. It was better to consider the Infinite.

Ela closed her eyes and offered silent worship to her beloved Creator. Until agitation permeated her thoughts. Dark, unsteadying fear. Why?

Infinite?

Silence. Yet she perceived His Spirit hovering near. Determined, Ela closed her eyes, focused on her prayer, and on the Infinite. He might not answer whenever it pleased her, but He did answer. She simply needed to persist, then accept His decisions.

Infinite, what is Your will?

Before Ela could gasp, a vision swept over her like a cloak and sucked her spirit into a whirlwind. Ela trembled as she recognized her surroundings. She was home in the city-state of Parne, standing atop the guard's stone lookout shelter on Parne's soaring city wall. Too high! Dizzied, she fixed her thoughts on breathing and enduring the vision's torment. Infinite!

Child of dust, the Infinite murmured, *what do you see?*

Scared to look down, Ela fixed her gaze on the western horizon. On a terrifyingly huge mirage-like image, spreading from north to south. Barely able to squeak out the words, Ela whispered, "I see a giant cauldron in the sky . . . pouring boiling liquid toward Parne."

Home. About to be destroyed.

As Ela tried to gather her wits, her Creator said, *My people, whom I love, have forsaken me! They burn incense to other gods, and they worship idols made by their own hands.*

"No. . . ."

They seek other souls to lead into eternal torment! Therefore disaster is about to overtake Parne and all who live there.

"No!" All who live there? Father. Mother. Ela's baby brother. Where was Tzana? Ela's arms and legs felt weighted now, as if turned to stone. Impossible to reach Tzana. Though she heard her sister calling her from a distance. Nightmarish images came to life behind her eyelids and within her thoughts. The vision expanded with such force, such an inundation of faces, whisperings, and terrors, that Ela screamed. Falling from the lookout—

Darkness, thicker than she'd ever known, drew her soul beneath the ground, entombing her alive. As she clawed at dank walls within her vision and inhaled the stomach-churning stench of death, the Infinite said, *Prepare yourself.*

The vision's agony closed in tight, crushing her. Desperate to save her family, and Parne, Ela fought for consciousness and failed.

✦ 2 ✦

Scythe groused in deep-throated rumbles as Kien halted him before General Rol's sprawling low-walled home. Ignoring his steed's complaints, Kien descended and chained the twitching beast to the legally required destroyer restraint—a massive half-buried block of stone with two huge metal rings. Though he understood a chaining stone's intended purpose, Kien was aggravated whenever he saw one.

How kind of the Tracelands' Grand Assembly, and Father, to legislate such expensive measures for the country's newly acquired destroyers. Bound as they were by so many civil regulations, destroyers were now guaranteed to cost more than an ordinary landowner could afford. Worse, the chaining blocks did nothing to soothe the belligerent temperaments of the powerful beasts.

Ironically, if a destroyer's owner commanded his beast to wait, the creature would wait through eternity. Food or no food. No chaining block needed.

Kien reached up and patted Scythe's glossy black neck. "Wait. I won't be long—the general needs to know why I'll be gone. Don't eat anything or anyone while I'm inside."

The destroyer's eyes glinted, and he huffed. Suppressed rage? Thwarted appetite? Kien didn't want to know. He entered the general's residence, was recognized by a servant, welcomed, and shown to General Rol's meeting chamber.

"Lantec!" The general looked up from his seat behind a broad, cluttered table. His silver hair and his heavy tunic were rumpled, but his thin, stern face was death-serious. "I was about to send for you." He cleared his throat and narrowed his piercing brown eyes. "Turn in your sword."

Involuntarily, Kien gripped his military sword's hilt. "With respect, sir, what have I done to deserve . . . ?"

The general cut off his question with an upraised hand. "You have failed to meet current regulations." Rol motioned impatiently. "Your sword!"

Kien complied, unbuckling his sword-belt and lifting the baldric off his shoulder. He was being thrown out of the military after his first tour of official service. How would he explain this to his parents? But even as he placed his sword and its matched scabbard on the table, Kien's thoughts sped toward possible explanations and additional career options for his future. If the military had dropped him so swiftly and unfairly, then—

General Rol opened a long wooden case, lifted a sword from it, and walked around the table to stare Kien in the eyes. "*Now* you meet current regulations."

Kien looked down at the newly issued sword and laughed. Apparently only his sword was being removed from service. This new Azurnite weapon, with its magnificent blue water-patterned blade, was well worth enduring the general's prank. Only the wealthiest citizens in East Guard possessed these extraordinary weapons. Until now. "I'm not dishonorably cast out?"

"No." Rol grinned like a boy. "The first shipment of swords was delivered this morning. Had you duped, didn't I?"

"Yes, sir, you did." Good thing he hadn't unleashed a tirade upon the general.

"Well, arm yourself, soldier! If I had the time, I'd challenge you to a bout."

"I regret your lack of time, sir." Kien hid a smile as he angled the new black baldric over his shoulder, then swiftly doubled the long belt around his waist. Fortunately, Rol was too engrossed with the new weapons to notice Kien's grin.

"These swords, combined with our nearly exclusive possession of destroyers, makes the Tracelands *the* dominant force. No other country can match us! Not Istgard, not Siphra, nor Belaal."

"Undoubtedly, you're right," Kien agreed. But possessing the strongest military would guarantee problems, such as envy and conspiracies hatched by other countries. Kien shook away his concerns. "With respect, sir, please give me your word that you intend to 'fail' your other staff members as well."

"I intend to 'fail' my entire staff and all my commanders. One by one." The general rubbed his hands together, scheming. "I forbid you to say anything to the others."

"I'll be silent as the dead," Kien promised. He suppressed a sudden chill as he fastened his new black-bound scabbard onto the belt. What if he *was* a prophet and had just foretold his own demise? "Actually, sir, I won't be here to ruin the fun or to enjoy it. I'm leaving for ToronSea this afternoon."

"ToronSea—that barnacle on a rock? Whatever for?"

"At the Infinite's command. I'm supposed to seek the Infinite's followers there and correct them. And I'm told I'll need to warn some Ateans in the vicinity to seek the Infinite."

Rol frowned. "The Infinite, eh?" While the general had never professed belief in his Creator, he didn't deny the Infinite's existence. "Not that I'm questioning matters, but isn't this Ela of Parne's role? She's the prophet and messenger, my boy—the little kingdom-shaker. Or have you turned prophet as well?"

"I hope not."

"Good. I hope not either. I commissioned you for military duty. Your job is to negotiate treaties with our foes and our allies! And to represent the legal interests of our enlisted men. *Not* to dabble in soothsaying. Is that understood?"

Soothsaying? Kien wasn't entirely sure he liked that designation. "Understood, sir."

Rol lifted a silver eyebrow and stared at Kien's jaw. "Did you cut yourself with a razor?"

A tinge of heat swept Kien's face. He focused on sliding the new sword into its scabbard. "Yes, General. I was interrupted while shaving."

"You worry me, Lantec. I ought to confiscate that sword until I'm certain you can handle it. How long will you be gone?"

"About five days." Kien hoped the estimate was realistic. Six weeks was the extent of his military leave. If he spent almost two days' travel each way and one day in ToronSea itself, he could look forward to almost five weeks of courting Ela. With enough time to practice bow-hunting and racing destroyers with his brother-in-law, Jon.

The general's voice quieted. "This won't involve a local revolt or other such commotion, will it?"

"I . . . don't know," Kien admitted. "I haven't received much information beyond orders to depart today."

"A need-to-know basis, eh?"

"Not even that much, sir."

"Not good." The general puffed out a breath. "I've heard reports of trouble around ToronSea. Robberies and such. Are you certain there's no chance of military involvement? Do I need to cancel your leave?"

"Yes, sir. And no, sir!"

"Hmph. I'm denying all knowledge of this if the worst happens, Lantec. Fair warning."

"Fairly warned, General."

"And don't lose your sword. Otherwise, you'll be in chains when we catch you."

Chains? Memories resurfaced of his months as a political prisoner in Istgard, the Tracelands' neighboring country to the west. Kien shuddered. Before suffering imprisonment again, he would run—or fight. "Agreed, sir." Did this mean the general had granted unofficial permission for Kien to take the Azurnite sword with him to ToronSea? Well, he hadn't explicitly forbidden

Kien to take the sword. Another unarticulated command from a superior. Splendid.

Rol's suddenly dour expression reflected Kien's own dissatisfaction. "Keep me informed of events in ToronSea. Discreetly. We can't have our own citizens taking offense, eh?"

"No, sir." Kien bowed and took leave.

Outside, Scythe was clomping in agitated circles around the huge chaining block. He halted and stomped as if urging haste. Kien released Scythe's chain and latched it to the beast's huge leather war collar. "Easy. We'll visit Ela now."

Climbing the war collar's narrow rungs, Kien seated himself on Scythe's quilt-padded back. The instant Kien shoved his booted feet into the collar's footholds and gathered the reins, his destroyer charged ahead like an arrow shot from a bow.

"Hey!" Kien gripped a handhold on the war collar and caught his breath. At this speed, the beast would trample someone in East Guard's streets. He tightened the reins. "Scythe, what's your problem? Slow down!"

The destroyer didn't respond. His hoofbeats thundered through the streets and echoed off the stately pillared public buildings with such force that Kien's ears rang. On the stone-paved street ahead, citizens shrieked and scattered in justifiable fear for their lives. A black-robed scholar tripped, but managed to scramble out of Scythe's path.

Seeing civil lawsuits and fines in the making, Kien bellowed, "*Walk!*"

Scythe walked, but he trembled and groaned. Clearly his agitation indicated more than simple fury at being chained during Kien's visit with the general. Only one thing could throw a destroyer into such emotional turmoil—a master in danger. As current master, Kien was certainly shaken but not in much physical danger. Therefore, Scythe's other master must be suffering. Perhaps dying. Sweat lifted on Kien's skin. "Ela!"

Gritting his teeth, Kien held the destroyer to a reasonable pace through the city of East Guard. But as they approached

Temple Hill's broad wood-shaded slopes—beyond the city's jurisdiction—he leaned forward, braced himself, and gave the huge horse free rein along the dirt road. "No trampling anyone. Go!"

Trees shivered and swayed into a blur as Scythe bolted up the hillside road. Breathing in massive gusts, the warhorse crested Temple Hill and dashed into its broad clearing, slowing only when he rounded the temple's ruins. A cluster of girls screeched and scattered from a mat in the sunlit grass, leaving four figures in Scythe's path. Kien called to the destroyer, "Walk!"

Scythe growled, but obeyed.

Studying the four ladies ahead, Kien immediately recognized his sister, Beka, with Ela's diminutive sister, Tzana, and Ela's spry self-appointed chaperone, Tamri Het. All three were kneeling beside Ela, who lay curled up on the mat.

Ela . . . As Kien dismounted, Scythe cautiously nuzzled Ela's ashen face.

Crouching next to his sister, Kien asked, "What happened?"

Beka's eyes brimmed with tears. "She lost all color, then whispered to herself and fainted. But before fainting, she screamed. Oh, Kien, I've never heard such a scream!"

Tzana rubbed a gnarled little hand over her sister's arm as if trying to coax Ela awake. "She'll wake up soon, I think."

Kien pressed his fingertips against Ela's cold wrist. The slightest pulse imaginable threaded beneath his touch. Ela's eyes flickered beneath her eyelids. Kien unpinned his cloak and—as Scythe grunted approval—he draped the warm fabric over Ela. He didn't like her deathly pallor, or the chill of her skin. But at least he knew what had knocked her unconscious. "She's inside a vision. Though I've never seen one hit her with such force."

The other girls were returning now, casting wary, tearful glances at Scythe. "He won't hurt you," Kien promised. "He's worried about Ela."

"As if we're not?" one of the girls sniffed, just a hint of indignation edging her voice.

Alarmed by the girl's tone, Kien eyed her. Recognized her.

Lovely and spoiled Xiana Iscove. With Nia Rol—the general's daughter. Kien suppressed a wince. Wonderful. If Ela wasn't in such torment, he would run. A battlefield was more enticing. His parents wanted him to marry one of these girls.

Never. Wouldn't happen. Not even if Ela's lessons and exemplary character improved her students tenfold.

He kept his gaze on Ela and waited, praying aloud. "Infinite, restore her, please."

One of Ela's hands rested just outside the cloak's dark edge. As Kien started to tuck his cloak around those limp fingers, a blue-white light flashed within her bloodless palm and took the shape of a thin, iridescent, weathered vinewood staff.

Kien stared. The prophet's branch—Ela's insignia. He'd seen the branch transform itself before, but he didn't know the sacred object could simply materialize from nothing. Amazing . . .

The branch's glow intensified, exuding warmth. To Kien's relief, Ela clenched the branch fiercely, gasped, and opened her eyes. One of her younger students burst into tears.

Ignoring the commotion, Kien leaned forward. "Ela?"

✦ ✦ ✦

Ela blinked and took another breath. No. She didn't want to live. Not if living meant facing Parne. She shut her eyes tight and willed herself to perish.

"Ela?" Kien's voice beckoned, low and so concerned that Ela's longing to die faded. For now at least. Was Kien here? She feared opening her eyes. Kien might vanish. Then the vision of Parne would reappear.

Warm, soggy destroyer breath wafted over Ela's cheek, followed by the light grazing nudge of an equine muzzle. Scythe . . . Pet.

The destroyer licked her cheek and throat, his wet tongue so raspy that Ela raised a defensive hand. "Pet," she mumbled, eyes still closed, "No licking." Destroyer drool. Ick. At least his breath was sweet. Like flower petals. And warm tree sap. She concentrated on petals and tree sap. More tolerable than her vision of Parne's ruin. Smoothing the destroyer's soft muzzle, she asked, "What have you been eating?"

"My mother's garden," Kien said, also real.

Ela looked up at him—his beautiful gray eyes. Appealing lips. No-no. Not prophet-like, allowing herself to be captivated by his handsome face and charming soul. Think of something else. Yes. Scythe had feasted in Ara Lantec's perfect garden. "The whole garden?"

"Every petal and leaf. With the exception of five spice-gum trees."

"Oh, Pet!" Tzana scolded Scythe, disappointment weighing her little-girl voice. "You ate *all* the flowers?"

"All of Mother's flowers?" Beka asked, horrified.

Scythe gave a trifling sniff and looked away. At any other time, Ela might have laughed.

Kien scowled at the destroyer. "Naturally you're unconcerned, you monster. You aren't paying for the damage. *Are* you?"

Trying to be hopeful about the garden at least, Ela sat up. Her senses wavered, forcing her to support herself with the branch. "Perhaps Pet . . . Scythe . . . simply gave all the plants a severe pruning and everything will be even lovelier next spring."

"Trampled and splintered plants aren't pruned." Kien leaned forward, turning grim. "And you, Parnian, are avoiding a subject we actually want to discuss. What did you see in your vision?"

Xiana Iscove's bored expression brightened. "Yes, please tell us!"

Aware of the listening girls, Ela touched her sister's frail shoulder. "Tzana, could you bring me something warm to drink, please?" Just remembering the vision chilled her, despite Kien's heavy cloak.

Beside Tzana, Tamri said, "What am I thinking? Naturally, you'd need something warm to drink after such a shock. We'll hurry. Tzana dear, come help me." The older woman stood, so nimble that Ela envied her. What was it like to be eighty? *Truly* eighty. She could only wonder. She'd never experience old age for herself.

"Thank you, Tamri." The instant Tzana was beyond earshot, Ela said softly, "Parne is now in open rebellion against the Infinite and has been judged. I need to warn my family and friends—and anyone who will listen. Perhaps they'll survive."

All five girls stared at her, incredulous. Beka frowned, her long-lashed brown eyes narrowing. "Survive what?"

"The siege."

"A siege?" Kien's expression turned cold. Soldierly. "When? And besieged by whom?"

"In one month. The country of Belaal will bring its army against Parne first, with two allied tribal nations—the Agocii and the Eosyths—seeking control of Parne's wealth and resources. They'll be followed by the countries of Istgard and Siphra, with a smaller force from the Tracelands, all hoping to defeat Belaal."

"Istgard? And Siphra!" Kien shook his head. "No. You must be mistaken. Belaal and its neighboring tribes, I understand—they're constantly creating turmoil, north and south. But not Istgard and Siphra. They're our allies! We'd *know*!"

Kien doubted her? How dare he! Just what she didn't need. Ela tugged his cloak from her shoulders and wadded it into his arms, not caring if she died of the cold. She'd have to face death anyway. "Yes, Istgard and Siphra! They'll want to protect their own interests during the siege, as will the Tracelands."

Scythe nudged Kien and whickered concerned-destroyer noises.

Kien shoved the warhorse's muzzle away. "Ela, Istgard and Siphra have *no* interests in Parne! Why would they? If I'd—"

As if Parne was nothing? Oh! "They *do*! Istgard and Siphra must protect their own borders, particularly if Belaal acquires more gold and weapons to support its attacks! I notice you're not very concerned about the Tracelands' involvement!" Why was he arguing with her?

Nia Rol gasped, making Ela look at her. "Father would have

said something, I'm sure, if we were planning to invade Parne. . . . Not that I listen to everything, mind you, but . . ."

When Nia's half-coherent protest faded, Kien said, "I'm not concerned about the Tracelands, because if our allies are involved in *any* military action, then of course we'll support them." He hesitated. "Are you telling me that you're going to Parne, knowing it'll be under siege? Ela, I forbid it!"

"No you don't!" She wanted to wallop him with the branch. Who did he think he was? Didn't she have enough trouble without his misguided interference? Pet bumped her, exhaling an anxious rumble. Ela leaned away from him and scowled at Kien. "I'm Parne's prophet. I have to go, whether or not *you* approve."

"Ela—!"

"Kien!" She stood. Swayed.

Kien jumped to his feet and grabbed her arm. She shook him off. "Stop!"

"No. Listen to me! You don't need to—"

"You listen!" As Ela aimed the branch at Kien, the destroyer stamped and snorted as if prepared for battle—then nosed his way between them. Ela cried, "Pet, *move*! I want to beat your master!"

The destroyer groaned and stood his ground.

3

Ela wanted to beat him? Kien scowled, stepping backward as Scythe muscled him away and then halted, blocking Kien from Ela. Didn't Ela realize he was concerned for her safety? If she would just listen to his suggestions!

Beside Kien, Beka grabbed his sleeve. "Look, you've upset your destroyer."

"He started *my* morning by upsetting me," Kien argued. He shoved at the destroyer's huge black shoulder. "Move, you lummox!" Naturally, the beast didn't budge. But his powerful muscles were twitching. Wildly. Adopting a calmer tone, Kien called out, "Ela, he seems certain you want to injure me. Do you?"

"Trust your destroyer!" Ela yelled. "You've basically said I don't know what I'm talking about!" To Scythe, she said, "Pet, never mind. You stand right where you are!"

The giant horse shut his eyes and groaned again. Probably because she'd called him *Pet*.

Unseen, some of Ela's students were now giggling. Xiana's too-cheerful voice cooed, "Oh, beat him a little, Ela. He deserves it!"

Kien fumed. Was Xiana referring to Scythe, or to him?

Beka tugged at Kien's sleeve, clearly irked. "You two cannot give your destroyer conflicting orders. You'll drive him insane!"

Kien opened his mouth to snap a reply at his sister, then paused. She was right. And Ela was right. But that didn't make him wrong. His training in diplomacy took hold. Kien sat down, looked past the destroyer's immense black hooves and legs, and studied the opposition. Ela's face wasn't visible, but he saw her fingers restlessly tapping the branch. Then she aimed a fierce kick at a fold on the mat. Bad-tempered little prophet. With pretty feet. At least she seemed mostly recovered from her vision.

Keeping his voice reasonable, he called, "Ela, I'm leaving for ToronSea this afternoon, and I'd prefer to depart with blessings from the prophet of Parne."

Ela's hands and feet stilled. She thumped the branch against the mat and bent to stare at him. "ToronSea? But . . . why? You've just returned home!"

She sounded like his mother. She'd miss him. Kien grinned. "You're the prophet. You tell me."

Ela sat down and shut her eyes, evidently questioning the Infinite. Her students sat on either side of her, whispering, then smiling at him and Beka from their side of the destroyer.

Beka sat next to Kien and hissed, "What's this about ToronSea?"

"Listen," he muttered. "You won't believe it."

Apparently finished communing with the Infinite, Ela opened her dark eyes and stared at him, horror-struck. "You're being sent to ToronSea in my place. Because I'm going to Parne."

"So it would seem."

"But . . . we don't know what you'll be facing!" Whatever color she'd recovered faded.

Kien realized she didn't like it one bit that he would confront danger on the Infinite's behalf. He wanted to say, *Now you understand how I feel about you being caught in a siege.* But tormenting Ela wouldn't gain the answers he sought. "I only know that I'm leaving today. Any advice for a temporary prophet?"

Her voice distant, shaken, she simply said, "You must obey the Infinite."

"That's the reason I'm going," Kien pointed out. He instantly regretted his challenging tone, half expecting to see Ela fling the branch at him like a javelin.

Instead, she rubbed a hand over her face, seeming dangerously close to tears. Worse than a makeshift javelin, as far as Kien was concerned. Could she be overwhelmed by fear for him? It *was* pleasant to think Ela loved him enough to be distraught.

After a pause, she looked up, addressing the destroyer. "Dear rascal, you can move now. We're finished quarreling."

The destroyer ambled away, but lingered at the closest clumps of shrubs, still watching.

Tzana returned, carrying Ela's rough mantle. Tamri followed with a ceramic goblet of steaming liquid. Ela wrapped herself in the mantle, then nestled Tzana in her lap. She thanked Tamri and accepted the goblet, but made no effort to drink. Kien wished she would. She looked almost lifeless.

Ela watched him instead, looking as if she wanted to speak but no longer had the strength. He nudged Beka toward Ela, then joined their circle. Settling himself, Kien studied Ela. If only they were married. He could hold her. Comfort her. Instead, as a mere friend and erstwhile suitor, he had to be content with ridiculous formalities and tame questions. "You look as if you want to tell me something. What is it?"

"You're about to be tested." Her low, somber prophet voice. Warning him. Raising the hairs along his scalp. "Obey the Infinite. Don't stray from the tasks He's given you."

Now she sipped from the clay goblet. Kien waited for her to say more. She didn't. "That's all?" So much for Ela loving him enough to be distraught. "Those are my complete instructions?"

The faintest sad hint of a smile lit her big brown eyes. "Shall I repeat them?"

Xiana tittered. Nia fluttered her lashes.

Kien grimaced. "No, thank you. I'll repeat them to you instead. I'm about to be tested. Obey the Infinite. Don't stray from the task He's given me—which is ToronSea. *Which*, incidentally, has been swayed by Atea-worshipers from Siphra who may not react cordially to my news, and I risk ritual strangulation. Did I remember everything?"

"Yes." Her weak smile had already faded. She set down the goblet and rocked Tzana as if the little girl were a baby. Before Kien could persist in questioning her, General Rol's personal chariot, driven by his ancient household charioteer, clattered around the clearing, its little horse becoming skittish at Scythe's monstrous presence.

Accompanied by Xiana Iscove, Nia stood and smiled. "Safe journey, Kien. I mean . . . return home soon. Ela, thank you. Rather, I'll see you later, maybe. . . ."

Xiana sang out, "Come, Nia, that's enough, dear!" She aimed a dart of a smile at Kien. "It's a pity we won't see you at your mother's reception tonight, Kien. We'll miss you."

He grinned, pleased they were departing. "My apologies. I hope you enjoy your evening."

Another chariot rattled alongside the ruins to retrieve two more students—a pair of twin-like sisters who, in Kien's opinion, seemed dazed and glad to leave. Only Beka remained, and she sat quietly with Ela. Kien glanced up at the sky. Midmorning. He still had time. "Ela, I don't intend to quarrel, but I need information. If you can't tell me anything more about ToronSea, then tell me why Belaal would attack Parne. Remote as Parne is, what could Belaal gain?"

"Gems. Gold, which they've promised to the Agocii and Eosyths. And, most of all, new ores for dangerous weapons."

"Ores similar to the ones we use for Azurnite?"

She shook her head. "I wish they were Azurnite." Her gaze rested on his sword, concealed in its black military scabbard. "May we see your new sword?"

"You knew I would receive it?"

"Yes . . ." She seemed ready to say more, but hushed, sad-eyed.

Wondering at her wistfulness, Kien slid the exquisite blue sword from its scabbard. The early-autumn sunlight shimmered and danced against the blade, showing off the metal's rich forged pattern of dark blue and deepest gray waves.

Tzana scrambled from Ela's lap and plunked herself down

beside Kien. She crooned over the sword, "Ooooo . . . it's so pretty. I wish I could have one."

Kien smiled at her fragile old-woman features, wishing she could indeed have an Azurnite sword. It would mean she had the strength to carry a sword—or anything of a similar weight. It would mean that Tzana was healthy. The proper size and height for a near-adolescent girl. She had such spirit. . . .

Ela sighed shakily. "I saw you with this sword. I'm glad you have it."

Kien eyed her. No, she wasn't entirely glad.

Ela looked away, but not quickly enough to hide the glitter of tears. Beka hugged Ela. "Don't be upset! Everything will be fine—you'll see."

"I *have* seen." Ela mopped her face with her coarse mantle, then patted Beka. "It won't be fine. But thank you."

Kien couldn't endure her misery. He slipped the sword into its scabbard, crossed the space between them, and sat beside Ela. Tamri Het joined them, wringing her embroidery between her aged fingers. "Is there anything we can do, Ela-girl?"

"Pray. For all of us." Ela's gaze turned distant, pained and frightened, as if absorbed in some nightmare. "And for Parne."

On impulse, Kien wrapped an arm around her in sympathy. Ela didn't ward him off, which was alarming. Usually improprieties provoked her to feistiness. Now, however, she looked defeated. Kien jostled Ela gently. "Why are you so scared? You've faced equally dire situations before. You can manage this one."

She remained silent, and Kien continued. "Is there a chance the Infinite might forgive Parne?"

"Forgive Parne for what?" Tzana demanded.

"For turning against Him, though they know better," Ela murmured. To Kien, she said, "The Infinite is always willing to forgive—if offenders truly regret their offenses and change their hearts." Ela looked Kien in the eyes. "I'm not concerned with Parne alone. Please . . . don't stray from the Infinite's plans."

"I won't. Is there anything else you'd like to discuss?" He

watched her, hoping for details or some encouragement regarding their respective missions. And, perhaps, their future.

She shrugged, on the verge of crying. Had she seen what would happen in ToronSea? Kien said, "Let's walk a bit."

Tamri Het shot him a fierce look. "Sir, you remain where I can see you."

Kien didn't have to become a prophet to see Tamri running him through with his own sword if he misbehaved. "Yes, ma'am."

He helped Ela to stand, then set a slow pace. Despite her earlier temper, she was still ashen. Kien wished he could carry her. Cuddle her until she'd recovered. Tamri *would* kill him. He wasn't sure about Ela. Opting for a slightly safer alternative, Kien led Ela to the stone base of a fallen pillar, made her sit down, then sat beside her. He enfolded her cold hands in his, rubbing warmth into her fingers. "Ela, when the bravest person I know is in tears, I'm worried."

She glanced away. "I wouldn't be so weepy if you weren't being so sympathetic."

Meaning she felt safe enough to be vulnerable with him? "I'm taking that as a compliment."

"I should have known you would."

"Should have?" Kien couldn't resist teasing her. "Not much of a prophet today, are you?"

She sniffled noisily, but gave him a fierce nudge. "I'm never much of a prophet where you're concerned. You know that."

"Yes. And I've wondered why. Perhaps it's because our futures are so closely intertwined." Wait. Had he sounded too suggestive?

Ela's dark eyes went huge. She blinked at him, then reddened. Adorable. Kien grinned. Obviously, he couldn't kiss her, but . . . He leaned down until he could feel the warmth of her blush and inhale the scent of her skin. "I see the perfection of my theory has left you speechless."

She returned his stare for a lingering breath of time, then managed, "You don't give up, do you?"

"Not while we're both alive."

Ela leaned away slightly—not enough to convince Kien she was upset with him. "You need a new theory."

"No. I'm pleased with the one I've just developed."

"I'll disprove your premise in Parne. I doubt I'll survive."

"But you aren't sure," he argued.

She looked away. "In my vision, I was entombed. Surrounded by the stench of death." Her hands went cold again, and her lovely blush faded to the ghastly pallor induced by her vision. Deathlike. Particularly now, as she shut her eyes and retreated into silence.

If Ela hadn't just foreseen her own demise, Kien feared he had. Sickened, he began to pray.

✦ ✦ ✦

"What were you studying?" Kien asked as he walked with Beka down Temple Hill's shaded dirt road. He needed a distraction. Something lighthearted. A cheerful discussion to make him forget his fears for Ela. Not to mention Scythe's testiness at his departure. He hoped the destroyer wouldn't uproot every tree on Temple Hill in a fit of resentment.

While Kien would have welcomed Scythe's presence in ToronSea, Ela's situation in Parne was more dangerous, and more distant. She could ride the destroyer to Parne. And Scythe would protect her on the journey. As would the Infinite, he prayed. Kien pushed back his fears for Ela and concentrated on Beka, who was answering his question.

Unsmiling, Beka said, "We're studying one of the Books of the Infinite. *Wisdom*. Do you think it will help?"

"Those who have wisdom are always eager for more. Those who need wisdom rarely gain it."

"And, often, those who have wisdom need to use it!" Beka snapped.

"Meaning what?" Kien raised an eyebrow at his sister. "That sounded like an attack."

"It was. And is." Beka mimicked his lifted eyebrow. "You and

Ela love each other. Genuinely love each other. My friends have all recognized it." She stopped on the road's edge. "I say you two should marry."

"Instantaneously? As you married Jon?"

His sister turned pink and huffed. "Our marriage *wasn't* instantaneous. I've loved Jon for most of my life, as he's loved me. You're changing the subject."

Kien's throat tightened. "Some subjects are best left alone."

"And some subjects are too important not to discuss. Marry her, Kien! Today. Twist Father's arm for special permission. Twist Ela's arm—nicely."

Did Beka know what a wound she was opening? Kien listened to his boots crunching against the gritty dirt road as he and Beka resumed walking. The decision was Ela's, actually. But he wasn't about to twist her arm, as Beka had urged. Not yet, anyway.

At last, protective of Ela, he said, "We can't marry. Imagine the two of us together. Today, for example. Ela's been sent to Parne. I've been sent to ToronSea. One or both of us could die." The strain in his throat worsened. His voice rasped. "What if we marry and have children? They'd be orphaned."

His sister was quiet for about ten paces. "Jon and I would cherish your children while you're gone. You know we would."

"Thank you, but that doesn't help."

"Even so, it's true. We'd protect your children." Then, as if summoning courage, Beka blurted out, "Jon and I have been married for seven months, and I'm still not pregnant! We—"

Kien flung up a hand. "Stop! Spare me the details—I don't want to hear."

"Well . . ." Beka quavered, "we've w-wanted babies. . . ."

"Beka!" He softened his scolding with a fond shake. "Hush. You'll be wonderful parents. Just allow me to be a proud, ignorant uncle, and we'll leave it at that." If he survived ToronSea.

Her lower lip was out. "I suppose I don't blame you for being grouchy."

"Grouchy doesn't begin to describe my mood."

"You're worried about Ela."

Surprise. "Yes."

Beka kicked at a pebble. "Jon and I could accompany her to Parne. We've been eager to travel with our destroyers, and she'll have Scythe, so it's ideal."

Kien linked an arm with his little sister's. "It's not ideal. There's going to be a siege."

"We'll leave before then," Beka promised. "And you'd feel better, wouldn't you?"

"I might." But only a hint. Certainly not enough to make a dent in his fears for Ela. Plus now he'd fret about Beka and Jon's safety while they were in Parne.

They marched into East Guard and tramped through its main streets to the quiet residential area Beka and Jon called home. Though a long walk, it did little to settle Kien's nerves.

The instant they passed through the stone-arched gate leading to Jon and Beka's huge private courtyard, Commander Jon Thel bounded out of the house, grinning, while armed with his new Azurnite sword. Smiling, Beka kissed her husband's cheek. "Dearest, cancel your military leave. We're traveling to Parne."

Jon's dark eyebrows rushed together. "What?" He glanced at Kien for clarification.

Kien punched his brother-in-law's shoulder. "Good luck with the siege—and enjoy your new sword. I'm leaving for ToronSea. I hope to rejoin you within a few weeks—and find some way to assist Ela."

"What?!" Jon yelled after him, "Hold on, Kien!"

Kien pretended to walk off. But then—as Jon bellowed again—he turned around. No doubt Beka would invite him to share a meal while they talked. And they needed to talk.

Surely the Infinite was testing their loyalties to Him, sending them all on hazardous missions with virtually no information. In silence, Kien begged his Creator, *Be with us!*

✦ 4 ✦

In Kien's tower room, Father stared as if Kien had grown a second nose. "Siege?"

Kien almost chuckled despite his bad mood. Rade Lantec, preeminent member of the Grand Assembly, prided himself on his network of spies. Well, they'd clearly failed him here.

"Ridiculous!" Rade protested. "The Tracelands has nothing to do with Parne. Or Belaal!"

"Ela said new ores have been discovered in Parne. Ores that can be used to create weapons. Ores dangerous enough that Belaal is preparing to attack Parne for them, while Istgard and Siphra will fight to protect their own interests."

Garbed in a comfortable tunic, boots, and a cloak, Kien buckled a dagger onto his sword-belt. After checking his sword, he gathered a spare tunic, sandals, a small tarp, a cooking pot, his flint and metal fire kit, fishing net, and packets of dried fruits and meats, and shoved them into his knapsack. "The Infinite will allow Parne to fall."

"The Infinite." Rade pursed his lips and looked up at the tower's roof beams.

Kien ignored his father's disdain. Though Rade and Ara Lantec refused to believe in the Infinite, Kien hoped to eventually change their minds. Finished packing his gear, he pulled about a third of the coins from his pay bag, dropped them into the pouch slung from his belt, and handed his father the balance. "I promised Mother I'd make restitution for the damage to her garden. Here's the initial payment."

Rade blustered, "We don't need your money!"

"It's a matter of honor, sir. Have you seen the garden?"

"Of course not. Your mother ordered it curtained off for this evening. Did you get rid of that destroyer?" Rade looked hopeful, not quite managing to disguise his loathing for Scythe.

"I've left Scythe with Ela. She'll ride him to Parne."

"Oh. Well. I wish them a good journey."

And glad to see them go, Kien knew. He slung a waterskin over his shoulder, then landed a fist on Father's shoulder and gave him a ferocious hug in farewell.

Rade thumped Kien's back. "Let's go find your mother."

Downstairs, Kien halted Mother's reception preparations just long enough to kiss her and murmur, "I'm sorry. Father has my first payment for repairs to the garden. I hope to see you in a week or so. Until then, be safe."

Ara's big gray eyes misted. "*You* be safe, dear. I'm sorry I lost my temper this morning."

He grinned. "After seeing the garden, I thought you restrained yourself admirably."

Mother hugged him tight. "Oh, my boy, I miss you already!"

"I miss you too." He gave her a final hug and another kiss. Before she could add to the ruin of his day with sobs, Kien fled outside to the stables.

He approached the low, long stone building and looked over the selection of Lantec horses. Handsome creatures, every one. But even the best was nothing compared to Scythe. "C'mon, you mouse," he muttered to the sturdiest beast. "You'll have to do."

A year ago, Kien would have been overjoyed at the thought of escaping one of his mother's parties by way of a week-long jaunt on a horse. But now, as Kien rode through East Guard, the horse's puny snufflings and the minuscule clipping sounds of its hooves against the street pavings made the notion ridiculous.

Really, he must pity the horse, who was—after all—one of the Infinite's creations.

The thought didn't help.

As he turned the beast south onto the coast road, Kien studied the cliffs on his right. He could see the ruins above on Temple Hill. Was Ela watching him depart?

How could he leave her to face Parne alone? Surely there was something he could do to ease her situation. Remembering her deathly pallor, and her tears, Kien shut his eyes.

You are about to be tested, she'd said.

In what way? He'd been given no instructions whatsoever. Was he supposed to be tested for his willingness to warn a town full of obtuse Tracelanders against spiritual corruption? Was his courage being measured? His love for Ela? Or perhaps his good judgment was being tested. What about his abilities as a military judge? Might they be the true focus of this test? If so, which situation was more critical? ToronSea or Parne?

Besides, what if ToronSea's citizens ignored his warnings? Would he be blamed? Kien scowled, puzzling out his options.

You must obey the Infinite, Ela's voice whispered in his thoughts.

Fine. He would go to ToronSea. But then he had to help Ela.

Wasn't ToronSea on Siphra's border? Kien would use his connections in Siphra. He'd hunted with the rebel Akabe "of no other name" before the young man became king of Siphra. Despite his now-regal status, Akabe would certainly remember Kien and grant him an audience.

An uncomfortable shiver slid upward along Kien's backbone. Doubt nudged his conscience.

Would it be wrong of him to somehow interfere in Parne?

No. He refused to think of it.

He would ride this pathetic little horse to Siphra the instant he finished with ToronSea.

✦ ✦ ✦

Holding the branch, Ela watched General Rol turn loose his destroyer in the clearing. The destroyer, Flame, a striking but fierce creature Ela had always admired, immediately charged into the woods.

To eat, Ela hoped. Not to fight with Scythe. Nor to pester Tzana and her little friends—girls who frequently visited from the dwellings scattered over Temple Hill's lower slopes.

The general greeted Ela with a smile and an air of concern. "You frightened my daughter this morning, Prophet. Are you well enough now to talk?"

"Yes, sir. I'm sorry Nia was upset."

"It doesn't take much to alarm her," Rol muttered.

Protective of her student, Ela said, "Nia is a tenderhearted girl with a lovely soul. I'm grateful I've had the chance to study with her." She led the general to the mat where she'd conducted the morning's class. "You wish to discuss Parne."

"You are blessed with perfect insight as usual." The general nodded at Tamri Het, who marched over to Ela.

Her normally pleasant face set in stern lines, Tamri warned, "General, do not upset my girl."

"Doing your duty, eh, Het?"

Ela frowned at the pair. Why did they dislike each other? Was it because Tamri was Siphran and General Rol didn't trust her? "General, please sit down."

He sat, but rested one hand on his sword's hilt. As if certain Tamri was half monster and wholly venomous. "Now, Ela." Rol's tone turned fatherly. "Tell me about Parne. What's all this fuss?"

"The Parnians have chosen disaster." Ela tried to convey facts without allowing emotions to overwhelm her. Without allowing the vision to reemerge. "After I left home, the Infinite's enemies within Parne shunned Him and began to openly worship Siphra's goddess Atea, enticing others to do the same—as they've secretly done for generations." Infinite! How had she been so blind? Ela struggled to quell her frustrations and fears. "Parne also initiated trade with Belaal and foolishly gave them samples of new ores they found while repairing Parne's walls."

"Ores for new weapons," Rol observed. "Yes. Nia told me. Do you know anything about these new ores?"

"They aren't Azurnite," Ela said, nodding at the general's new sword. "One of the ores is yellow and has poisonous characteristics. Merely handling the ore without gloves can cause ulcerations. Weapons forged with an alloy of this ore are softer than Azurnite, but they inflict wounds that won't heal."

"Causing a slow kill after the initial wound?" The Tracelands' general fumed. "We can only hope the fools cut themselves with their own weapons."

Ela waited. When Rol looked her in the eyes, she said, "The second ore is silvery. Powdered and mixed with wax, it can be ignited with oiled tapers, resulting in an uncontrollable fireburst. One ignited 'brick' can burn a small building." She allowed the general to ponder this horror, then added, "Also, Belaal has recently learned that Parne's temple is filled with gold."

"Huh. Gold alone is enough to tempt Belaal and its allies."

"Perhaps. But the thought of Belaal controlling those ores will be enough to alarm Istgard and Siphra. And, unless Parne repents of its self-destructive ways, the Infinite will allow the city to fall. Otherwise, countless future souls will be lost—souls He loves even now."

Somber, the general said, "Naturally, you feel you must travel to Parne. Sounds like a thankless task." He sighed. "I am so sorry. Do you need weapons? Unofficially, of course."

Ela allowed herself a humorless chuckle and settled the branch in the crook of an elbow. "No, sir. But thank you. The Infinite provides my weapons."

"As you wish." Rol's expression eased a bit. "Commander Thel and his wife have asked to see you safely to Parne. If the situation becomes critical, I will ask the Grand Assembly to appoint him as our envoy and oversee matters."

He paused, as if expecting Ela to be surprised. She smiled. "Thank you, General."

"Hmph. Of course. In addition, I am sending several crates of courier birds with Commander Thel. I ordered him, and I am asking you, to use them wisely. Keep us informed."

"Again, thank you, sir."

He didn't reply. Instead, he glanced over the Temple Hill site. The ruins. The orchard. And the stone bluff beyond, which sheltered Ela's temporary residence—an entry tunnel leading to a stone chamber carved within the high bluff. "Who will watch this place while you're gone?"

"I will, sir." Tamri plainly dared him to disagree.

Rol made a face. "Aha. I'll see that the locals do not interfere with you." Before Ela could decide whether his statement required thanks or a gentle rebuke, he gazed at the ruins. "My daughter and I hope to see the Infinite's Temple restored to East Guard within a few years. It will be a sight to behold!"

A fragment of a vision emerged in Ela's thoughts: the temple rebuilt. Pristine, majestic, and honored on this hill. "*That* will be a joy, indeed!" Sadly, she would probably see it only in her vision.

✦ ✦ ✦

"Do the writings go or stay?" Tamri asked.

Ela glanced across the stone chamber at its trove of precious writings. Neatly categorized, gem-studded ivory plaques shimmered at Ela from their stone niches carved within the chamber's walls. An ancient collection of the Sacred Book of the Infinite. "They'll stay. They belong to the Tracelands. Just be certain the researchers return them to the shelves—the grown scholars are worse than the children." She would miss studying the Sacred Books.

And she would miss this quiet chamber. She'd felt safe here.

But safety would vanish the instant she started her journey.

As if to fill in the long silence, Tamri said, "My daughter will arrive from Munra within the week. We'll tend the place and keep watch over your scholars until you return."

"If I return," she reminded her elder. Crossing the chamber, Ela bent to hug Tamri's wiry shoulders. "If something happens to me, the Thels and Lantecs will return you safely to Munra. Until then, you'll continue to receive my weekly caretaker's stipend from the Tracelands." Ela paused to swallow the catch in her throat. "Tamri—you have been such a dear friend to me, and to Tzana. I pray the Infinite repays you with blessings a hundred times over."

Stubborn as any destroyer, Tamri refused to look at her. "I'll expect your return, prophet-girl."

"I pray you won't be disappointed."

✦ ✦ ✦

Scuffing her small booted feet, Tzana entered the stone chamber and sighed. Lower lip out, she gave Ela a pathetic look. "Can't we bring my friends?"

Glad to be distracted from her fears for Parne and Kien, Ela tied the last bundle of their gear and smiled at her little sister's dramatics. "I wish we could—I know it would make you happy. But Commander Thel and Beka cannot feed all the children from East Guard. And I'm sure your friends will miss their parents."

"I *have* missed Father and Mother," Tzana admitted.

"Well, you've been very good about not complaining." Ela slung a plump, slightly damp waterskin over her shoulder, then picked up her bundle and the branch, which gleamed at her subtly. "Come now. We're late. Let's bid everyone farewell."

"All right." Tzana trudged ahead of Ela, through the chamber door, and into the long entry tunnel leading outside.

A chorus of voices greeted them in the morning sunlight. Most were children calling to Tzana. Ela's heart squeezed with a small pang. Was she being cruel, taking Tzana from East Guard? How had her little sister made so many friends in six short months? Tzana's popularity was a marvel, considering East Guard's reputation for shunning people they called Unfortunates—children born with deformities or incurable afflictions like Tzana's aging disease.

Had the Infinite used Tzana to motivate the Tracelanders to reconsider their attitudes? Ela hoped so. As Tzana chattered with her friends, Ela traded farewells with her students.

Red-eyed, Nia Rol hugged Ela. "Father said you'll be in danger—I-I'm praying!"

"Thank you. I need your prayers." She returned the trembling girl's hug. "Study hard, pray, and be strong. The Infinite will bless you!"

Mute, Nia nodded and turned away to dry her eyes.

Several black-robed scholars greeted Ela more formally. The eldest scholar scanned Ela critically, head to toe, then relaxed. Hints of his thoughts, conveyed by the Infinite, made Ela smile. "Don't worry," she told the man. "The Infinite's Sacred Books are in the stone chamber, with copies of all my notes. Just warn everyone not to invite disaster upon themselves by removing the tablets. They belong to the Tracelands. And to the Infinite."

"As you say." The eldest scholar harrumphed and brushed nonexistent dust from his black sleeve. "Er . . . What sort of disaster?"

Ela shrugged and studied the branch. Mesmerizing tendrils of light and heat seeped from the aged vinewood. "That's the Infinite's decision, isn't it? Hand rot. Blindness. Insanity—or all three, perhaps. But why should it matter? You won't take the writings."

"Oh. Certainly not!" His gaze fixed on the branch, the eldest scholar twitched. His subordinates agreed, mute, shaking their heads.

"I hope to see you again," Ela said, surprised to realize she meant the words. "However, if I don't return, I pray you'll continue to translate and distribute the Infinite's Sacred Word."

"I will," the youngest scholar promised. His brown eyes shining, he said, "This work has been the greatest honor of my life!"

"Short life," the eldest muttered.

The youngest grimaced.

Tamri Het tugged Ela's sleeve. "Commander Thel and his wife are waiting."

"Thank you, Tamri." She kissed her chaperone's cheek and fought down tears. "Dear friend, I pray the Infinite blesses you. Tzana! Climb onto Pet."

The glossy destroyer stomped a massive hoof and rumbled a warm, beckoning call. Tzana's little-girl laughter rose above her friends' chatter. "Oh, Pet, you're so bossy! I'm coming, I'm coming!"

Ela boosted her sister high onto the warhorse's back, then tied their gear and the branch to Pet's freshly cleaned and polished war collar. "You look wonderful," she told the destroyer. "Aren't you glad I brushed you?"

Pet huffed, but flicked his shining black tail.

"Show-off." Ela smiled. Grasping the war collar's ladderlike rungs, she climbed onto the destroyer and settled herself sideways on the rider's quilt, then gathered the reins.

Sitting astride in front of Ela, Tzana kicked her small booted feet against the collar. "You can go now!"

"Walk," Ela commanded beneath her breath.

The destroyer walked, but grumbled as Tzana leaned back to wave and blow kisses at her friends. Ela looped an arm around her sister and reassured Pet, "Don't worry. I have her."

He snorted.

Ela hoped the destroyer wouldn't fuss throughout the journey.

"Infinite," Ela whispered for perhaps the thousandth time, "What's happening to Kien?"

She didn't like the brooding feel of His silence.

When Ela reached the clearing's edge, Jon and Beka Thel, astride their destroyers, greeted her with smiles. Beka added a cheery, "Good morning!"

"Good morning." Tensed, Ela returned their smiles. Should she tell Beka of her fears for Kien? Looking up at the sky, she begged for wisdom. Infinite?

Child of dust, do you give Me the care of those you love?

Her Creator's challenge caught her off guard. Afraid to talk, lest Beka hear, she nodded. Yes. I do. At least . . . I'm trying. I know I must, but . . . Infinite? Is Kien safe?

When the silence continued, Ela bowed her head. "As You will."

✦ ✦ ✦

Rain pelted Kien's heavy hooded cloak, and gusts of wind spit the drops into his face. His poor horse was drenched, plodding through the puddles with a melancholic walk depressing to see. Almost two days with this animal hadn't raised Kien's opinion of it. "Do you have any fight at all?" Kien asked the beast.

An equine snuffle answered. The wearied steed splatted through another puddle. Pathetic.

"You'd probably die if I had to ride you through the night." Kien sighed and peered ahead. Surely they were approaching ToronSea.

Lights flickered in the evening's gloom, then vanished.

An instant later, something hammered Kien's shoulder, pitching him sideways. Before he could right himself and draw his sword, the stupid horse tossed him into the mud, and then fled.

Deep-throated yells filled Kien's ears. "You've done it! Catch 'im!"

Robbers! Kien scrambled to his feet, flung aside his cloak, and whipped out his sword.

✦ 5 ✦

Staring hard into the rainy dusk, Kien shifted his sword and called out, "I am Kien Lantec—Tracelands' judge-advocate to General Rol! Identify yourselves!"

This pack of miscreants didn't have to know he was in training. Let them think the entire army would be after them if he died.

Kien's challenge prompted less coherent sounds. Scuffling. And a splash. Followed by a boyish whine. "Ya don't havta take off m' ear!"

"We should!" a man's deep voice snarled. "Get up! Stop whimpering and catch that horse."

Three shadowed men emerged from the evening's gloom, every bit as rain-bedraggled as Kien. The smallest shadow emitted a beckoning whistle and scurried off in the direction of Kien's horse, while the taller forms lifted their hands. One man called, "Sir, no offense was intended. Let us explain, and we'll make whatever reparations you demand."

Kien approached them warily, leveling his sword to their throats. "Talk!"

The man obliged, hands still upraised, his voice low and sensible. "In the past few months we've been fighting off robbers. We've never had trouble with such until recently. The town's council agreed to form a night watch. Otris—that brainless louse!—was overeager and took aim at you."

"More than took aim," Kien snapped. "He struck me! What would have become of your town if I'd been trampled and killed for this Otris's stupidity? Crippling fines at the very least, with Otris slapped into chains!"

"Sorry, sir," the other shadowed form offered. "Might we step out of the rain and properly introduce ourselves?"

Tempted by the idea, Kien asked, "Can you manage introductions while keeping your hands lifted?"

"Suppose so," the first man agreed, his tone gloomy as the weather. "I'm Chully, he's Giff. Not the best welcome to ToronSea, sir. Our apologies. Follow us, please."

They slogged along the road in silence, until Otris's voice lifted in the distance, cheerful for a youth who'd nearly committed manslaughter. "I've the horse! What now?"

The second man yelled, "Put it in the stable and be sure it's rubbed down and covered. Then drag your worthless hide to the inn."

A public inn? Kien grimaced against the easing raindrops, hoping the place was clean. More lights came into view, framed by small windows in stone houses and stout, short towers. ToronSea would have looked cozy and welcoming if he hadn't been assaulted at the town's limits. Anyway, best to not enter a building with his sword drawn. No sense in provoking ill will before explanations had been made.

Keeping his movements slow and hushed, Kien slid his sword into its scabbard as the first man kicked at the door and called out, "Hey, lift the latch!"

Following a brief delay, the door creaked open. A low light shone from within, accompanied by convivial voices and the doorman's uproarious greeting, "Chully! Giff!" He slugged each man on the back. "What's wrong? The latch wasn't down. What're ya doin' with yer hands all upraised? A new dance, eh?" The doorman waggled his fingers and turned, shaking his rump.

"We'll dance all over you if you don't move," Chully snarled. "Your son is acting like his father again!"

"Otris?" The doorman blinked at Kien as he followed Chully and Giff into the warm firelit room. "Well, I don't see blood anywhere. Guess he's still alive."

"You might wish he weren't." Giff turned to face Kien, revealing ordinary features and a remorseful expression. "May we be seated, sir?"

"I believe so." Kien hung his dripping cloak on a peg near the door. An ache worked through his shoulder, tempting him to rub the bruised area and test his arm's range of motion. But not in front of the inn's half dozen other patrons. Normal-seeming people, it appeared. However, the most normal-seeming people could become animals, given certain provocations.

Evidently noticing that Kien had replaced his sword, Chully and Giff lowered their hands.

Chully motioned to tables and benches along one of the stone walls. "Anywhere here, sir. Please yourself. The place is quiet tonight."

Kien chose a table and sat facing the other tables. Chully and Giff settled on the benches opposite him. With cooperation from all parties concerned, Kien hoped to fulfill the Infinite's orders this evening and leave for Munra in the morning—he *must* speak with Akabe of Siphra as soon as possible. Before he could say a word, the doorman leaned on the table. "What's my Otris got to do with anything? Is he in trouble?"

"Probably not," Kien said. The two men opposite him visibly exhaled in unison, their expressions relaxing a bit. "However, I have a few questions for you all."

Giff wrinkled his nose. "I suppose we could answer them."

"I'm certain you can." The scent of food reached Kien now—aromatic enough to make his mouth water. "Does this inn serve meals to travelers?"

"One sixteen-noble or a Trace-bit buys a good meal," Chully said. "But it's fish stew and bread most evenings." He motioned to the nosy doorman. "Rit, you're buying this man's evening meal. Otris sling-stoned him off his horse. It's the least you can do."

Sling-stoned? Kien lifted his eyebrows, then hurriedly covered his surprise. A sling-throw, properly executed, should have broken his shoulder or stopped his heart. It seemed young Otris needed more practice with the weapon. Thank You, Infinite!

"The least I can do?" Rit let his mouth sag open, then protested, "The boy should pay, not me!"

Exasperation crossed both Chully and Giff's faces. Chully unlaced his coin pouch from his belt and upended the leather bag on the table. An assortment of Tracelandic and Siphran coins clinked onto the polished tabletop. "There! Take enough for three and order us each a bowl and a cup. Then leave us alone."

Rit grumbled. "Ya could've spoke a cup for me, seein' how I'm runnin' yer errands." But he ambled off, the coins in his fist.

Kien eyed the Siphran coins. Most likely they'd been brought into the Tracelands by Siphra's Atean faction. "I see you carry Siphran coins. I've heard ToronSea has accepted refugees after the Siphran crisis."

Chully shifted on the bench. "'The Siphran crisis.' A pretty way to say it, yes."

Giff glanced over his shoulder at the inn's other occupants, then gave Kien a frown. "You said you're a general's judge or some-such. Why are you here? What have we done that the military is interested in ToronSea?"

"The military isn't interested in ToronSea." Kien leaned forward. "The Infinite is."

Chully snorted. Giff stared. Rit returned with three steaming mugs and a grin. "There, y'are! Steeped char root with syrup. I'll bring our stew in a blink or three."

"Thank you." Kien chose a random mug and hoped it wasn't poisoned. He sipped, then set down the mug and waited. No burning. No throat-closing. No giddiness. He drank a bit more.

And he watched his reluctant hosts. Mentioning the Infinite had made them nervous. Chully drank. Giff cleared his throat. "What would *you*–with your military sword and your fine East Guard speech—know of the Infinite?"

"Enough to ride here at His command for almost two days in the rain, when I'd rather not, to speak to people I've never met."

Chully paused, holding his mug in midair. "Meaning us?"

Was the man going to throw the drink at him? "Do you follow the Infinite?"

"Some people have honor enough to follow the ancient ways," Giff muttered.

"And some don't," Chully added, with a scowl at Giff that threatened a clash.

Kien took another drink, evaluating his argumentative hosts. They seemed to be friends, though with a few unsettled quarrels. Not helpful. Perhaps he'd been too certain of finishing this business tonight. Even so, he must hurry matters. "If I need to speak to those leading the Infinite's faithful here in ToronSea, where would I go to find them?"

Giff remained silent. Chully thumped his now-emptied mug on the table. "Why?"

His patience thinning, Kien said, "Because they're being tempted to follow the ways of the Atea-worshipers from Siphra. The Infinite sent me to warn any strays that He is displeased."

Both men stared at him as if he were the bumbling Rit. Giff leaned forward. "You're claiming to speak for the Infinite?"

"Will you listen if I do?"

Chully laughed. "What if no one believes you?"

"That is *their* problem." Kien supposed it would be counterproductive to pull out his sword again. Though the impulse intensified as the irritating Rit trotted over, bearing a tray. With a flourish, Rit displayed four wooden bowls of thick stew, spoons, a round loaf of bread on a board skewered by a knife, and a slender clay pitcher. He thumped the bowls, spoons, and bread on the table and plopped himself on the bench beside Kien.

"So, my Otris dealt ya a wallop?" He chortled, seeming pleased by the thought.

"Yes. Fortunately, I've survived." Kien watched as Rit lifted the miniature pitcher and poured a golden stream of sauce over his stew and—without asking—over Kien's. Fermented, oily fish sauce by the smell of the stuff. Was it considered rude in ToronSea to refuse the local food? Kien stirred the sauce into his stew, then lifted a spoonful, hoping that hunger would make this mess edible. Not bad. Hearty. Flavorful and a bit salty.

Encouraged, he spoke to Chully and Giff again, determined to speed along his mission in order to seek help in Siphra for Ela. "I was also instructed to speak to certain refugees you've sheltered here."

Rit swallowed, then stuck his spoon into the stew, where it remained upright. "Why? Ya sound as if it's a bad thing that we've offered a home to th' poor Siphrans."

"Whether it's a bad thing or not depends on the Siphrans themselves, doesn't it?"

"Well, ye won't find 'em here tonight." Rit lifted his spoon. "They're at worship, with some from the town. Otris's taken by their ceremonies."

Chully was frowning. "Quite taken, it seems. I'd wager he's abandoned the night watch."

"Not that it matters," Giff added. "He's caused enough turmoil for one night."

Had Otris forgotten to tend Father's horse? Even if the poor beast couldn't match an eyelash to Scythe, it deserved a thorough grooming and proper food. Not to mention that all of Kien's gear was still tied to the creature. He swallowed the last of his stew, then stood and bowed his head slightly toward the others, taking leave. "Which way to the public stables?"

Chully grunted. "Four houses to the right, turn, then three buildings to the right."

"Thank you." Kien lifted his cloak from the peg near the door, flung it on, and hurried outside. The rain had departed, leaving a fog that misted his face and hair. Counting his way past the houses, then turning right, Kien rushed down the street and found the stables.

Worse, he found them unbarred and unattended. If Father's horse was missing—

Inside, an oil lamp barely glimmered within a stone niche high in one wall. Kien waited until his eyes had adjusted, then checked the stalls. Father's horse was in the third stall, evidently untouched and still bearing Kien's gear. Sighing with relief, he unburdened the creature, groomed it, then found water and hay. Good hay, he noted. Sweet scented and dry. Enough like East Guard's that he needn't fear colic, he was sure. A sick horse couldn't carry him to Siphra.

Finished with the horse, Kien shouldered his gear and trudged from the stable. Good thing Otris was honest. Or, more likely, distracted by the chance to escape night watch in favor of the Atean ceremonies.

The ceremonies. Was Otris in attendance?

Kien paused in the misty night, listening intently. Nothing. He walked farther into the town until remote chanting caught his attention. Repetitive, almost lulling rhythms echoing from a wooden slant-roofed structure, unlike the other stone structures in ToronSea. Surely these were the Ateans.

Kien glanced around. No one. And the mist would obscure anyone trying to see him from a distance. He placed his gear in the darkness beneath a tree, then crossed the clearing before the slant-roofed structure and studied its walls. Several narrow backlit ventilation slats gleamed just beneath the roof's edge, but there were no windows. To be expected.

Ritual strangulations demanded concealment.

Obviously, if he wished to halt any murderous rites, then he ought to approach the door as anyone else would. Thin slivers of light showed beneath the door and near its hinges. Kien focused on those slight gaps at the hinges. He crept up the stone steps and leaned down, shifting until he gained a fractional view of the hall's interior.

Lamps rimmed what he could see of the walls. As for the worshipers . . .

Granted, he saw no evidence of ritual strangulations being performed. But murder was, perhaps, the only thing Kien didn't glimpse within the hall.

As the pulse-beats of the chants intensified, some of the worshipers ran blades over their arms and chests, allowing blood to flow down their skin. Others were disrobing and indiscriminately reaching for partners. And there was young Otris, reveling in the midst of it all.

Kien winced and turned away from the door. This was Atean worship? An orgy of bloodletting and intimate intermingling?

Appealing rites, in the most primitive way. Provided one didn't, or couldn't, consider the potentially dire disease-sharing consequences of such licentious behavior. Shuddering, Kien hurried to collect his gear. He felt unclean, longing to scour those fragmented images from his eyes and his thoughts.

No wonder the Infinite had sent him here.

Tomorrow, he must deal with the Ateans. Lifting his knapsack, Kien gritted his teeth against the stabbing ache in his shoulder and against images of the worshipers capering through his thoughts.

How could he speak to those reprobates civilly with such dissolute images frolicking in his mind?

Impossible!

If the Ateans said or did anything offensive tomorrow, he would run them from ToronSea at sword point.

✦ 6 ✦

Seated outside the inn's benches in the early morning light, Kien watched Chully and Giff's bleary faces as he told them of the Atean rites. "Believe me, I know what I saw, and I wish I hadn't seen it. Otris was cavorting with them, unclothed." Both men flinched, clearly squeamish at the thought. Kien continued. "Who knows how many of your young people will be lured into this licentious behavior? The Ateans will corrupt this town—and others—if they remain."

Giff rubbed his hands down his unshaven face, then sighed. "We considered it an act of mercy to shelter them after everything they've suffered."

"You have only their word that they suffered. Did they appear to be starved, mentally tormented, or beaten when they arrived?"

"No," Giff muttered.

"Send them away!" Kien urged, impatient to be gone himself. "Those of you who follow the Infinite should have nothing to do with them."

Giff shook his head in apparent disbelief. Beside him Chully looked up at the gray skies, tight-lipped. After an instant of heavy silence, he said, "We'll consider what you've said."

"Don't *consider*. Take action!"

Now Chully glared. "Who are you to be rushing in here and telling us how to manage our town? What if I tell you that the citizens of ToronSea voted to allow these refugees to live here, eh? What if I tell you that we regard it as a point of honor to provide sanctuary as we've promised?"

"You were not in possession of all the facts," Kien argued. "What will happen to honor when all your citizens are disease-pocked and the Ateans have usurped control of your town and thrown you out?"

"They haven't yet!" Chully snapped. "And Tracelander you might be, but you aren't one of *us*, so back off and let us manage our own concerns!"

Not good enough. Kien growled. "Who is your mayor?"

Silent, Giff nodded toward Chully, who folded his big arms and lifted his chin.

Forcing down his frustration, Kien tried another angle. "Who leads the Infinite's followers in ToronSea?"

"My family," Giff admitted, as if the words cost him something. "But—" A hint of defiance crept into his voice. "From what I've heard all my life, we're the last of the Infinite's faithful in the Tracelands. No one else honors the ancient ways, and our gathering isn't much more than my own kindred. Which means the Ateans outnumber us. Moreover, we haven't found them to be dishonorable in their dealings with us."

Giff was siding with them? Undoubtedly beguiled by the Ateans' ways. Kien measured his words. "You'd allow them to remain, though they'll ultimately corrupt your town?"

As Giff shrugged vague agreement, Chully said, "Listen. You and the others from up north have no right to meddle in our affairs here. We say they stay unless they give us good reason to cast 'em out. Until then, Judge, leave us alone."

"If that's all you have to say, then I'll repeat my message to you, Giff, from the Infinite. He's displeased that you and some of His followers are beguiled by the Ateans. He reminds you to be faithful to Him and seek His will." Kien bowed to the men, knowing the motion was as sarcastic as his words. "By-your-leave, sirs."

Scowling, Kien strode toward the Ateans' stark sharp-roofed wooden hall. He would deliver the Infinite's message to the first Atean he saw, then return to the inn, gather his gear, and ride out of this place to seek help in Munra for Parne.

The Ateans' hall seemed unremarkable this morning, its edges softened in the gray mist, its newness already faintly weathered by the ocean's salt air. Laughter echoed toward Kien from within the building. An agreeable sound. But agreeable laughter or not, he wasn't about to set one foot inside that structure.

Kien leaned against a young tree in the green open space before the hall and watched, fingering the hilt of his Azurnite sword. The voices, men's and women's, lifted in idle-sounding chatter and amiable taunts. Soon, a man and a woman, both simply clad in flowing gray and green robes, stepped outside and headed for a nearby lean-to, which was filled with wood.

As they returned, arms full, Kien intercepted them at the hall's entry. The woman smiled at Kien and the man started to speak, but Kien aimed his warning at the pair like a verbal weapon. "The Infinite sees your failings and seeks your deluded hearts. If you're wise you will hear Him!"

They both gaped. Kien turned away. Done.

He marched toward the inn, determined to forget ToronSea. Stubborn, foolish . . . !

Turn right.

"What?"

The Infinite repeated the command in Kien's thoughts, calm and deliberate. *Turn right.*

Kien turned, baffled. Wasn't his designated task here finished? "Do you want me to walk down this lane?"

Yes.

Why? Kien strode along the designated road, a pleasant-seeming route of mist-veiled stone houses and towers, many edged by evergreens and moss. He hadn't realized ToronSea was so quaint and rustic. The farther he walked, the more Kien wished he had a better opinion of the place. It would have been an excellent vacation town.

Before long, the rhythmic liquid hiss and tumult of ocean waves crashing against rocks met Kien's ears. A brisk air current whipped his hair. "How far should I walk?"

He shouldn't have asked. An invisible hand gripped his unbruised shoulder and forced him onward. The sensation was akin to the day Father had caught Kien's three-year-old self dropping Mother's best dishes one-by-one for the pleasure of seeing and hearing them shatter on the kitchen's stone floor. But this was worse. The stern, invisible grip informed Kien that he'd be unable to cajole his Creator into excusing him as easily as he'd charmed Father.

Did you follow My orders?

Hadn't he? The unseen hand was propelling him onto a cliff. "I thought I did." Kien's own thoughts rebuked him now, like tattletale traitors: You acted as you pleased. You said what you thought and did more than you were commanded. You spoke in hatred and haste! You didn't consult your Creator! Your attitude was the same as any rebel's!

Despite the mist and the chill breeze, he began to sweat.

The Infinite gave him a scruff-of-the-neck shake. *Did you seek My direction before pronouncing your verdict upon* random *Ateans, Judge Kien?*

"No." He'd spoken to the wrong Ateans. . . .

Do you believe that you have a better understanding of mortals than their Creator? Can you see their souls, Judge? Do you perceive their hearts?

"No." Kien was within a foot's width of the cliff's edge now. The water below was visible despite the mist. Dark, angry waves foamed against the stones, dashing upward like living things striving to climb up that rocky wall. To snatch at him. Like claws. Actual seafoam claws. Kien felt his knees weaken, but the Infinite held him upright.

What is the proper sentence for one who has disobeyed Me?

In a whisper nearly drowned by the raging surf, Kien said, "I don't know."

Death!

The hand swept him off the cliff, casting him sideways, far into the mist.

When the breathtaking momentum of the Infinite's blow faded, a sickening wave of vertigo curdled his stomach, and he fell toward the hissing, raging sea. Kien gasped. Was this how he would die? Infinite! Forgive me. . . .

Dark waves rushed at him, seething.

He hit the water boots first. Brine bubbles swept over his face and into his nostrils as he sliced deep into the ocean. Above the surface, the clouds parted. The sun's glow suddenly pierced the waters . . . and illuminated an eye as large as Kien's head. An immense sea beast's silver iris, its dark pupil reflecting Kien. Seeing him. Perhaps considering him a meal.

Hit by sunlight, the monster's iris contracted in a flash, its pupil suddenly a thin slit of ominous black in a pale iridescent circle.

Jolted, Kien stared into that fearsome giant eye and resisted panic. Infinite?

No answer. His lungs constricting, Kien struggled backward in the water. Unfood-like, he hoped. Would wielding an Azurnite sword make him appear dangerous? Difficult to digest? At most, Kien guessed he could blind that colossal eye, and hack at one of those tough pectoral fins. Not enough to kill the creature. Even half blind and minus a bit of flesh, the beast could still swallow Kien whole.

And there was the risk of dropping the sword—he'd never recover it in this ocean.

Air. He needed air. Would he seem too much like prey if he worked toward the surface?

Cloak and boots dragging at him, Kien pushed upward, away from the beast. In the current below, the perverse creature swung about, aligned itself alarmingly beneath Kien's feet, and swept toward him.

No! Kien kicked, fighting to reach the surface. A shoal of slender crimson fish dashed around him, their panic mirroring his terror.

Below Kien, the beast opened its mouth. The cavernous yawning maw surged toward him, sucking him into darkness within the thud of a heartbeat. Mingling Kien with tiny flapping fish and a sludge of seaweed. Surrounding him with the beast's slippery interior—the horrific give of living muscle.

This is how he would die. . . . Smothered and digested within a sea monster's gullet.

Suffocating, Kien tugged at his sword. If he could somehow cut through the beast's belly—but the monster's guts tightened around Kien, constricting his arms.

A sickening downward plunge in his own belly told Kien the creature was swimming toward the ocean's floor. Away from air and light. And any hope of survival.

Ela had warned him to obey. Ela!

With the beast's descent, a crushing pressure clamped around Kien. Intensifying. Overwhelming him until he expelled his final breath in a scream.

Infinite!

Speckled lights danced behind his eyelids, then faded.

7

Straightening herself wearily on Pet's back, Ela looked ahead at the narrow, wild river valley. Tall, lush evergreens crowned gray rocky cliffs, which descended sharply to the rushing river below. And the hard-packed cliff road was widening—an indication that they were nearing the next overnight stop on their journey. The Tracelands' border city of Ytar.

Seeming to echo Ela's thoughts, Jon Thel looked over his black-cloaked shoulder to grin at Beka and Ela. "We'll be in Ytar before sunset!"

"Finally!" Beka exulted, patting her lovely destroyer's dark neck. "A bath and real food!"

"And sleep," Ela agreed. They'd need to rest before heading into the southern borderlands that separated the Tracelands from Istgard and Parne. Ela winced. She mustn't think about Parne. Tzana's head lolled against Ela, her small body limp as she dozed astride Pet. Ela snuggled her little sister closer. Pet's big ears perked, listening. He rumbled an alarm.

Infinite? Ela tugged the vinewood branch from its place on Pet's war collar and raised it to halt Jon's staff and servants, who trailed them on the road. Behind her, Jon's subordinate-commander, Selwin, had to rein in his destroyer. Beka's elegant destroyer squealed, and Jon's destroyer turned about and huffed, alert. Jon drew his Azurnite sword, holding it high, readied.

They all looked up at the low tree-fringed rock formations to their left.

A ragged figure hurtled from a shaded ledge onto Jon, knocking him off his destroyer, sending Jon's blue weapon over the cliff into the river below. Beka screamed. "Jon!"

Jon yelled and grappled with his assailant. Jon's destroyer, Savage, bit into the man's tattered garments, lifted him off Jon, and flung the howling offender over the cliff, into the river after Jon's sword. Jon scrambled to his feet. "Beka, wait here!" Yanking a short-sword from his destroyer's war collar, Jon turned and ran along the cliff road, evidently scanning the rocks below for his enemy.

Tzana awoke and squirmed. "What's happening?"

Pet stomped, gouging potholes into the road. He started to turn, but Ela restrained him, fearing he would plow into Beka's destroyer. "Halt!"

The destroyer groaned.

Behind them, Jon's servants bellowed as a motley throng leaped from the foliage above, wielding clubs and knives. Ela cried, "Infinite, stop them! Blind them!"

At once, the attackers fumbled, dropped their weapons, and yelled in sightless panic.

"Oh . . . !" The robbers *were* blinded! Could she truly call on the Infinite to create such calamity? Frightful power! She must be more careful. And yet . . . Infinite, it would have been helpful to know of this prophet-trait months ago!

By now Jon was running toward them again, but his attendants didn't need his assistance. Led by Selwin, they were beating the helpless men. Ela hesitated. Disgusting as these failed robbers were, she felt responsible for their safety. She'd prayed for them to be blinded, and now they were defenseless. If one of them died while debilitated, she'd be eaten with guilt. Reluctantly, Ela called out, "Stop beating them—they're blind! Find cords and tie them."

Pet's noises of ferocious complaint shifted to grumbling.

His expression cold with suppressed fury, Jon hurried to Beka. "Everyone seems safe for now, except the reprobate Savage threw over the edge—that cursed man made me lose my sword!" Jon swung at the air with a fist. Composing himself somewhat, he said, "I'll send others back to retrieve his body after we've dealt with these thugs. Beka, are you well?"

Beka faltered, "Um . . . yes . . . but what should we do now?"

Jon scowled at their prisoners. "We lead these criminals into Ytar, though I'm half ready to thrash them all. My sword—the military's Azurnite sword—is lost in the river! General Rol will lock me up for the remainder of my life."

Infinite? Ela appealed to their Creator. Could she retrieve Jon's sword? Images slid through her thoughts, stole her breath, and left her disgusted. This was more information than she'd cared to know. "Is this another test?" she demanded. If the Infinite *was* testing her self-control, she was on the verge of failing. "Ugh!"

"Ela?" Beka leaned toward Ela, alarmed. "You're not suffering another vision, are you?"

"Not a big one," Ela sniffed. "Just two small ones—the second *very* irritating." If only Kien were here. Praying, she descended from Pet, who gave her a dire glare, as if warning her not to leave him.

Tzana frowned at her, still sleep-grumpy. "Where're you going?"

"Down to the river—we won't be long. Stay with Pet." To emphasize her order, Ela gave her destroyer a low growl. "Wait."

Pet stomped. But he waited.

Beka also commanded her destroyer to wait, then dismounted to join Ela and Jon. Still disgusted, Ela shook her head. "You won't believe my vision!"

Jon looked sickened. "You've seen that I won't find my sword?"

His sword? "Yes. I mean—let's hurry." She'd cool off beside the river, then deal with her anger and its cause.

While they walked toward a lower portion of the riverbank, Beka cajoled her husband. "Jon, dear, with everything we've been through, I ought to have a sword."

"You don't know how to use one. You'd need lessons. Besides," he warned, "if we don't find mine, we'll be unable to buy you a needle, much less a sword."

They picked their way down the rock ledges and stepped onto the narrow riverbank. Ela stared out at the rapids, then at the cliffs above, gauging the proper location. "Where, exactly, did it fall? Here?"

Bleak, Jon eyed their destroyers above, aligned his steps near Ela's and nodded toward the river's center. "You're right. I'm sure it was there, more or less."

Ela threw her prophet's branch into the river.

Beka gasped. "Why did you do that? The branch was your insignia!"

"It's still my insignia. Look." She nodded at the water. Jon's sword popped up in the current, suddenly buoyant as a leaf. "Grab it!"

Jon whooped and bounded into the water, reaching for the sword, which glided into his hand, contrary to the river's flow. He clutched the silvery hilt and kissed its dazzling blue blade, then danced out of the river, making Beka laugh. "Infinite, bless You!"

Ela bowed her head, also thanking the Infinite. When she opened her eyes, the branch was floating directly in front of her at the river's edge. She lifted the precious vinewood from the current and stared. Not a drop of water on it. Useless to show Jon and Beka this marvel; they were kissing. Well, at least two members of their group were happy.

Now to deal with the second portion of her vision. Ela tucked up her tunic and used the branch for support as she hiked up the small rock incline, leaving Jon and Beka behind. On the hard-packed cliff road, Ela smoothed her garments and lifted her chin. "Behave," she ordered herself. She marched toward their small entourage.

"Are we leaving now?" Tzana demanded, looking down from the disgruntled Pet's back.

"We'll leave as soon as the Thels return," Ela promised. "Be patient, both of you."

She must take her own advice. Be patient. Self-controlled. As must Pet. Poor dear monster. Ela couldn't blame him for being upset. Obviously he feared she was in danger.

The eleven prisoners were sitting in a tattered, woebegone line at the edge of the road. Ela stopped directly in front of their renegade leader—a thin man, not quite as ragged as his followers, but definitely not as elegant as Ela remembered. Lord Ruestock. Siphra's former ambassador to the Tracelands, a spy, and her own pitiless abductor. Not to mention a lecher who made her feel unclean with his every glance. Shuddering, she snapped, "Ruestock!"

His blinded brown eyes widened. A sneering smile lifted his narrow face. Oily and fawning as Ela remembered, Ruestock crooned, "Ah, Ela. Parne's loveliest prophet! Really, your apparel was so dowdy I didn't recognize you in the least—when I could see you. It *is* you, my dear, am I right? I never forget a beautiful woman's voice."

Ela clenched her teeth and reminded herself not to kick a man she'd disabled. "I am not your 'dear'!" She half knelt to ensure he would hear her clearly. "Why did you imagine you'd be safe attacking us, particularly when we were riding destroyers?"

Ruestock sneered as if considering her question silly. "My orders were to attack the servants only, to snatch a few valuables and flee. Wylie, the fool who attacked your leader, disobeyed."

"Still, your action was inexcusable." Ela hardened her tone. "Our leader is Commander Thel, whose home you raided last year while abducting me."

Ruestock's scorn thinned. "*I* raided the Thels' home while abducting you?"

"Your hired thugs, then—don't mince matters!" Ela snapped. "The Infinite has given me authority to repay you for everything you've done. Tell me, sir, why should I allow you to live?"

8

Ela tightened her grip on Tzana and the reins. Pet grumbled, a low echoing threat that vibrated through Ela, and—she was sure—everyone traveling with them. Worse, the warhorse twitched violently, clearly longing to wreak havoc on Ela's irksome enemy. She smoothed Pet's massive neck. "Shh. We're approaching Ytar. I'll deal with matters there."

Beka leaned over her destroyer's war collar, catching Ela's attention. "Why does he keep making that awful noise?"

"He wants to crush Ruestock."

"Well . . ." Beka shrugged. "Doesn't everyone?"

"You're right."

"Of course I am."

They traded smiles. Riding ahead of them, Jon whistled sharply, signaling their approach to the Tracelands' most distant western border city, Ytar.

Slivers of memories pierced Ela's thoughts, causing pain. Her first vision as a prophet had dropped her into Ytar as a helpless witness to its earlier destruction during an attack from the now-vanquished neighboring kingdom of Istgard. She'd seen flames consuming Ytar's buildings. Citizens screaming, pleading for their lives . . . being hacked to death by Istgardian soldiers. She'd wailed and mourned with Ytar's people, suffering their terror.

But now Ytar's white outlines attested to its rapid recovery from death and ashes.

Ela leaned forward, scanning the small city in the afternoon light. Delicate spires of new buildings gleamed above a short white, bulky section of wall, evidently the beginning of a stone shell meant to encircle the city. Clashing styles hinted at recent architectural conflicts. Infinite?

A wisp-like image slid into Ela's thoughts, making her frown. "Jon?"

He turned, one dark eyebrow raised. "Yes?"

Ela tilted her head toward Ytar. "They've been quarreling with Istgard despite the peace treaty." A treaty Kien had composed while imprisoned in Istgard. "Have you heard any reports?"

"Not until this instant." Grim-faced, Jon glanced at the city, then back at Ela. "Will we suffer an extended stay here?"

"Yes. Unless we can persuade both sides to see reason—and I don't feel like being reasonable!" Much as Ela dreaded it, she was needed in Parne. If only Kien were here as a military judge, protecting his treaty.

"I wish Kien were here," Beka said, so plaintive, so near Ela's own thoughts that Ela nodded and blinked away frustrated tears.

"First," Jon spoke as if pondering aloud, "we deal with our living baggage, stash our gear, stable the horses, and eat. Then I'll investigate and decide if we must intervene."

The living baggage, Ruestock and his cohorts, were reassuringly meek as Jon's servants led them into Ytar's sparse new jail. Jon called the jailer to the prison gate and snapped, "I am Commander Jon Thel, here on official business. I require your full cooperation *and* an interrogation room—as soon as I've found quarters and stables for my staff and my family."

Family? Hmm. Ela almost smiled. Jon had evidently adopted her and Tzana.

The jailer scowled at the destroyers, the Thels' servants, and Beka, Ela, and Tzana—particularly Tzana—seeming ready to complain. Jon said, "This is Ela Roeh. Prophet of Parne."

The jailer exhaled, swallowed, and bowed. "Um. We're honored, Ela of Parne."

Infinite, she begged in silence, *give me wisdom. And patience.* Her headache eased. She smiled at the jailor. "Thank you, sir. Your name is . . . ?"

He squared his shoulders as if reporting for duty. "Amak."

"Thank you, Amak. Unfortunately, I must trouble you further. The former ambassador of Siphra is one of your prisoners, and I'll need to speak with him as soon as I've settled my sister in our quarters. I'd welcome your presence as a witness to our conversation."

"Of course." Eyes narrowed with distaste, Amak said, "Former ambassador, eh? He won't require pampering, will he?"

"None at all. He's suffered too much pampering already."

Jon looked over his shoulder at Ela. "General Rol would insist that I also witness your meeting with Ruestock—accompanied by my subordinate-commander."

"Witnesses will be welcomed," Ela murmured. Perhaps Ruestock would be more businesslike. Less blatant in flirting with her.

Jailor Amak interposed, "Am I permitted to bring in our local authorities?"

"Yes." Jon gave the man a glare evidently calculated to impress. "On behalf of the Tracelands, I require their attendance tonight. Send word to Ytar's council."

Beka sniffed as they rode away from the jail. "I'm all for seeing Ruestock punished, but if you two are dragging the city's council into this, then no doubt the meeting will last all night. *I* am bowing out. Tzana and I intend to rest and enjoy our evening."

A glowing smile lit Tzana's wearied little face. "Yeah!"

"Cowards," Jon teased. "Let's go find some food."

✦ ✦ ✦

The meeting hadn't even begun and already she was tired. Ela shifted the branch between her hands and watched Jon motion his subordinate-commander, Selwin, to sit at the jail's stark meeting-room table. Bruised from today's roadside battle and exuding bothersome self-importance, Selwin swaggered to the table, acting as Jon's scribe.

Would it be rude of her to verify the subordinate-commander's discretion? Undoubtedly. Ela bit her lip as Jailor Amak led the rope-bound Lord Ruestock inside. Amak bowed to Ela. "I supposed you wanted to speak with this one before the council arrives."

"Yes. Thank you," Ela murmured.

Jon addressed Selwin. "This part of the meeting is unofficial."

Grimacing, Selwin folded his hands on his traveling desk. "Yes, sir."

Ruestock sniffed. Disdain dripping from his every word, he said, "Ah, yes. An unofficial meeting. How convenient for you, that you might pretend no knowledge of it later, *good* sirs." And he uttered a soft curse.

Ela watched Jon's hands clench into fists. He said, "I remind you that a lady is present. Whatever your opinion of me and my men, you will guard your tongue for her sake."

"Mmm," Ruestock agreed. "The lovely prophet. Tragic that I cannot see her—quite unfair."

To end his complaints, Ela prayed aloud, "Infinite, please restore this man's sight."

Ruestock blinked, squinted, then recovered and smiled. "Ah, Ela. What a joy to see you! Pretty as ever." He swept her with a critical glance. "Despite your dreary attire."

Before Jon had the chance to lose his temper, Ela warned Ruestock, "The Infinite restored your sight, sir, but that can be reversed."

"My dear girl, I—"

"I am not your dear girl."

He affected hurt. "Are you not the least bit flattered by my sincere admiration?"

"No. Your sincerity means nothing. *You* are a sneaking, foul-minded, vicious—"

"Ah," Ruestock interrupted. "You're thinking of the past. I assure you, my actions were strictly impersonal. They—"

Despite her resolution to remain calm, Ela cried, "You threatened to kill my sister!"

Jon shifted one hand to his sword. "What? He threatened to kill Tzana?"

Ruestock's voice pitched higher now, in a genial-sounding protest. "What threat? It was nothing. A bluff against the little Unfortunate to gain your cooperation."

Ela wanted to strike him. "It was no bluff, sir. Admit the truth."

Expression hardening, the former nobleman said, "Well, it's unimportant now. My plans failed and the king is dead. Long live Siphra's new king, whose supporters confiscated my lands! And, because I'm neither lord nor ambassador, I'm reduced to roadside skirmishes to survive. Moreover, I'm in exile, which is not *entirely* my fault."

"Implying that I'm partly to blame?" Ela shook her head. "No. Accept responsibility for your actions. You're no longer an ambassador because you deserved to be ousted."

"Deserved? How dare—!"

"Control yourself," Ela warned. "If my destroyer believes I'm in danger, he'll come after you." Ruestock looked down, fury visible in the tensed line of his mouth. Ela continued. "Also, I must point out that, prophet or not, if *I* act according to my own will and make such errors in judgment as you've done, then the Infinite allows me to suffer the consequences. You are collecting the punishment you've earned."

"And what is my sentence?"

Ela hesitated. Ruestock began to wheedle, "Ela, Ela, you are too merciful and tenderhearted to declare me guilty without proof of any wrongdoing worthy of death."

He was right, regrettably. She studied the branch. It remained plain uncommunicative vinewood. Sighing, Ela gave up. "When the Ytarians release you, you'll go home to Siphra."

"Why? My lands have been confiscated by the new king's royal council."

"King Akabe is a reasonable man. Appeal to him for the restoration of your lands."

"Then what?" Ruestock argued. "He wouldn't trust me in any official capacity!"

"Trust can be earned, and your reputation can be restored—it's not too late. Meanwhile, learn to manage your province."

"Like a common overseer? My dear girl—"

She glared. Oh, he was making forgiveness a serious ordeal!

Ruestock exhaled gustily. "Excuse me. I cannot help myself, seeing your exquisite face."

Impossible man. Would forgiveness offer him a chance for true understanding of his Creator? Infinite? Silence compelled her toward mercy. "This will be your final reprieve. And before you argue your innocence, remember that men have died because of your schemes."

"An unjust accusation!"

"Is it? Do you wish me to recite the circumstances?"

Silent and unmistakably hostile, Ruestock shifted his gaze to the roof beams.

Jailor Amak cleared his throat. "Can you prove his guilt?"

Ela shook her head. "The dead weren't Tracelanders, sir, and I have no proof. The only thing you can punish him for is attempted robbery—yet he is Siphran."

The jailor and Jon both looked disappointed. A sharp tap on the door caused them to straighten. Members of the city's council filed in, men and women in long formal robes. As if eager to evade attention, Jailor Amak whisked Ruestock out and quietly closed the door.

Jon nodded to Selwin, who picked up his writing utensil, then Jon addressed the council. "Thank you for meeting on such short notice. The Tracelands appreciates your time. I am Commander Jon Thel, and this is Ela, Prophet of Parne."

Ela noticed their shifting gazes and stances. Like children

caught in wrongdoing. When Jon eyed her, prompting her silently, Ela asked, "Why are you endangering the Tracelands' treaty with Istgard by demanding more than the Istgardians can provide? They are restoring your city as agreed. But the wall—which is something Ytar should have built generations ago—did not exist during Istgard's attack. The Infinite demands an explanation. Why are you causing such trouble now?"

After an uncomfortable silence, a thin, officious councilwoman pursed her lips, then sniffed, "We believe they owe us a wall. We are thinking of our children."

His tone ice, Jon said, "You're being greedy. Your country negotiated with its new allies in mutual good faith. You accepted those terms—excellent terms! If you want a wall, you must give up at least half the new buildings. Or would you prefer to return all the money Istgard paid you in restitution?"

The council members began to squabble. Ela shut her eyes, foreseeing a long night.

A headache brought Kien into awareness. Pain. Absolute darkness. And the realization that he was drawing breath. Seaweed-scented breath, perhaps, but it was better than none. "Ugh." His arms and legs felt unbearably heavy. Dead.

Struggling to work life into his limbs, Kien twisted within his black confines. Nauseating rotten-fish stench surrounded him, and—from the slippery, taut feel of it—mucoused muscle. Still in the sea monster's gullet. Why was he even alive? "Infinite, why have You saved me?"

He'd deserved to die for his disobedience. Still deserved punishment. Yet now . . .

If the Infinite allowed him to live, he would fulfill his Creator's commands, whatever they might be. He would praise the Infinite to anyone who would listen. He would listen.

He would obey.

The monster lurched, its muscles tightening around Kien as

if the beast realized he was still alive and intended to crush him. The sea beast heaved, its surrounding muscles contracting with such force that Kien yelled—and regretted it amid a mouthful of seaweed-and-bile-tasting mucous. Before he could spit, the monster's muscles constricted again. Violently. Hurtling Kien through the beast's gullet and open jaws, shooting him like a projectile into blindingly brilliant morning light. And fresh air.

He landed face-down in hard-packed sand, earning a mouthful of grit. "Ugh!" Eyes watering, Kien spat out the sand and looked around, squinting. Breathing. Burning with pain from scalp to heel, but alive. Truly *alive*. He'd been heaved up on shore. Living vomit. Something he'd never aspired to be. But wasn't it better to be sea-monster vomit than sea-monster excrement? "Infinite . . . thank You!"

His voice was a croak. A rasping mockery of itself. He coughed, cleared his throat, then hacked mucous, his entire body screaming with the effort. Undeserving of existence. "Thank You!" Trembling, Kien prostrated himself on the sand and wept. "I failed! I deserved no mercy yet You pardoned me!" He felt his Creator's presence now, cloak-like and calming, surrounding him. Promising a new beginning. Divine and unmerited amnesty to a headstrong rebel. "Whatever You command, I will do! I am Your servant!"

As his eyes adjusted to the sun's brightness, Kien finally looked out at the ocean. The sea beast was thrashing amid the onrushing blue-green waves, working itself into deeper waters. A unique, beautiful creature . . . armored scales, crest, and fins shimmering in iridescent pearl hues. He watched the beast depart, marveling at their Creator's handiwork and His forgiveness.

Weakened by his ordeal, Kien dropped onto the sand, dragged his sea-infused cloak about himself, and shut his eyes. He blessed the Infinite again. Then dozed. Until a cackling voice called out, "Looks sun-fried an' near gutted to me!"

Sun-fried? Near gutted? Kien willed himself into alertness, fear making his heart pound. Surely he hadn't survived the digestive tract of a sea monster only to be attacked by ruffians.

Cautious, praying his movements were hidden by his cloak, Kien slid a hand along his belt. Yes, there was his dagger and the sword, both safe in their scabbards. Though he barely had strength to wield the dagger. He hoped the ruffian wasn't clever enough to perceive the truth.

In one desperate move, he flung aside his cloak and sat up, aiming his dagger at the source of the voice. "Stand back!"

A wizened old beachcomber, clad in a bunchy, stained linen tunic, skittered backward, scrawny arms upraised, his dark eyes bugged in fear. "Aw, no! We mean no harm."

"Keep it that way!" Kien growled.

The beachcomber fled, shoving a scrawny boy ahead of him. Fast for being so emaciated.

Kien paused, hit with remorse. Had he reacted too hastily—threatening the man when he should have sought their Creator's will? Infinite, I've already failed my resolutions! Forgive me. . . .

Kien slid his dagger into its sheath, then noticed his hands. Red. Wrinkled. Skin peeling like a molting reptile's, as if he'd been burned. No wonder he was in such pain. Horrified, Kien touched his face, his raw fingertips grazed areas of loosening flesh over his nose and cheeks.

So the old beachcomber's *sun-fried an' near gutted* observation was understandable. As was his fear. But the flesh beneath the molted surface seemed intact—though searingly tender. Truly, until his flesh healed . . . he was a freak.

Queasy, Kien inspected his gear. The various silvery metals on his new sword and the few coins in his pouch gleamed as if freshly polished. However, his leather scabbard and coin pouch looked faded, weatherworn, and waterlogged. As did his boots. Ah well. Once they dried, they'd be fine. For shoveling manure. Which was approximately what he smelled like right now.

He hauled himself to his feet, wincing at the gritty squish of liquid and sand in his boots. He could only imagine what his feet must look like. No, better not to imagine the feet.

Kien suspected a thorough dousing in water—even salt

water—was necessary. Obviously, sea-monster gut juices weren't healthful, and the thought of allowing them to dry on his skin and clothes sent a shudder down his spine. Trudging toward the waves, Kien checked for carnivorous aquatic creatures, then dropped into the surf, almost yelling at the water's vicious sting as it met with his raw skin. His flesh seemed ready to slide off his body. Which brought up another thought. Were his garments falling apart?

Kien inspected his frayed, fading cloak, and saw holes in his now-discolored tunic and leggings. His garments had been almost new when he left the Tracelands. Now he'd be mortified to give them to a beggar. No doubt his vagabond appearance offered the ultimate lesson in humility. "And well deserved," he told the Infinite. "Please forgive me if I forget and complain."

After diving beneath the waves for a final tormenting rinse, Kien hurried onshore. His stomach was growling now. Loudly.

He hoped his innards weren't peeling.

As he wrung out his cloak and drained his boots, trying to ignore his reptile-skinned feet, Kien looked around. Was that a city wall in the distance? "Infinite? Forgive me, but there's no one else to ask, since I've frightened the locals. . . . Where am I?"

Adar-iyr.

Adar-iyr? That thoroughly disreputable island-kingdom off the coast of Siphra? An island-kingdom filled with the dregs, the lowermost scrapings of mortal life, all of whom indulged—if the stories were true—in every sort of corruption. Murders and fleshly depravities worthy of any Atean enclave. Kien hesitated, suspecting bad news. "Will I travel home from here?"

No. I brought you to Adar-iyr to offer you another chance to obey My will.

Yes. He would obey, no matter what the Infinite requested. But curiosity nagged at him, accompanied by irrepressible wonderment. "You gave the sea beast directions?"

✦ ✦ ✦

Blaring trumpets woke Ela. As Tzana stirred beside her in the quilt-heaped bed, Ela hauled herself upright, straightened her robes, and stumbled to the window of their rented room. Shoving aside the wooden latch, she opened the shutter and blinked at ruddy dawnlight. Echoes of more trumpets vibrated through the air. A young man ran down the street, his voice raised in shrill panic. "Soldiers! Banners! Ytar is under attack!"

"Infinite!" Ela flung on her mantle, swooped up the blanketed Tzana, grabbed the branch, and rushed outside.

9

As Ela ran barefoot across the slab-paved street to Jon and Beka's lodgings, Tzana hugged her neck, demanding, "What's happening?"

"I don't know." Infinite? Any hints? Praying, Ela shifted Tzana and the branch in her arms and pounded on Jon and Beka's door until a vision sent her staggering into the wooden doorpost.

Beka, already garbed in her robes and boots, opened the door, grabbed Ela's arm, and hauled her and Tzana inside. "Ela! What's happening?"

"I just asked the Infinite the same thing." Ela pressed a hand to her aching head.

Finished buckling his sword, Jon leaned down to stare her in the eyes. "Obviously you've received the answer. Looks like a painful response. Is the situation serious?"

"Potentially. We must hurry."

While Jon donned his cloak, Beka frowned at Ela's bare feet like a dictatorial big sister. "Where are your boots?"

"I've no time to lace them on. You'll have to endure my rustic appearance."

"It seems I must."

Deep hoofbeat reverberations thundered from a distance, drumming through the walls, the noise making Ela wince. Tzana whooped in Ela's arms. "Pet's coming!"

Ela crossed to the window. "The destroyers have broken out of the stables—they're fetching us."

Jon muttered, "Yes. And I suppose we'll be billed for the stable doors." He marched outside.

Beka pinned a deep blue mantle around her shoulders, then joined Ela. "Ready."

They dashed into the street, just as all three destroyers rounded a far turn, looking half-wild. Fearful for Ytar's already panicked citizens, Ela raised the branch. "Walk, you three!"

Pet slowed at once, but Jon's rascal horse, Savage, rumbled in complaint, while Beka's elegant mare snorted angrily. Beka called, "Audacity! Stop fussing. Come here, and kneel!"

Audacity obliged, allowing Beka to climb onto her back, but she gave Ela a sidelong look, as if considering her a spoilsport.

Ela boosted Tzana onto Pet, who'd also knelt though he twitched with impatience. Beyond them, Jon vaulted onto Savage's back, then called to Ela, "Which way?"

"West, toward Istgard!" But she had no need to explain "west" to the destroyers. The instant Ela grasped Pet's mane, the monster warhorse stood and trotted down the street, his sonorous huffs chasing pedestrians out of their way. Savage and Audacity kept pace, in obvious agreement with Pet's sense of direction.

Jon yelled, "Trust destroyers to scent a conflict. Ela, where are we headed?"

"To meet the household of Istgard's new prime minister. Not a military force."

"But it's evidently been perceived as one, given all the uproar." Jon's expression tightened as if appalled by the confrontation's potentially awful outcome.

Equally horrified, Beka gasped, "Ytar will be at fault if the prime minister dies!"

Ela nodded. "Which is why we must prevent an attack."

They rode through Ytar's western district—a pristine collection of buildings, all recently rebuilt by Istgard's funds. Agitated citizens, mostly older men, women, and boys, streamed from

Ytar, carrying swords or pikes and congregating in the bordering field. Battle ready.

Across the field, Ela spied the prime minister's household. The riders had halted beneath their green and gold banners, seeming taken aback by the hostile crowd.

A chill of nerves prickled Ela's arms. She wouldn't die here, that much was certain. Her lot was cast in Parne. But knowing she would survive Istgard didn't guarantee that Ela and Tzana and the Thels would escape injury. Nor were the destroyers safe. The Istgardians, however, were most at risk, judging by threats snarled from amid the crowd.

A ruddy-faced woman brandished a rusted pike toward the visitors, her eyes burning with hatred. "They started this!"

"Murderers!" a young man yelled.

Tzana leaned back against Ela, her small voice clear and worried. "Why is everyone angry?"

"Because the people of Ytar believe something that isn't true," Ela said. "Pray that they don't behave even more foolishly."

Obedient, Tzana tucked down her chin and shut her eyes, praying.

Jon swept a look over the throng and called to Beka and Ela. "We split up and prevent them from advancing. Beka to the left, Ela to the right. Be careful, please!"

"Yes, dear," Beka answered, chin up and shoulders back. "Heed your own warning!"

While they rode out to confront the makeshift army, Ela breathed, "Infinite, please don't let anyone die." She edged the crowd and coaxed Pet into the open field to face the Ytarians. As Pet stomped and snorted equine threats, the branch sent out spirals of warmth and light. Hoping to convey calm authority, Ela lifted her voice. "I am Ela, Prophet of Parne. All of you, lower your weapons and disperse! Ytar is not being invaded. The warmongers who attacked you are dead—buried in your own fields. You are threatening a private household that intends only good!"

A burly man argued at the top of his lungs, "Good?" He spat. "They're from Istgard! And I say—"

At the front center of the crowd, Jon interrupted the man's tirade. "Use your brains! *Think!* You see the Istgard banners, yes, but where are their shields? They are not soldiers and have no plans to attack you! If you harm this family and its servants, you will disgrace the Tracelands and jeopardize your futures. All of you, lower your weapons and disperse!"

Their warnings—not to mention the branch's formidable glow and three irate destroyers—subdued the crowd. Some members of the makeshift army edged away.

His voice echoing, Jon continued. "Anyone foolish enough to advance will be arrested. *If* you survive our destroyers!" More would-be combatants retreated from the throng.

Over her shoulder, Ela glimpsed a solitary gray-cloaked rider on a destroyer, approaching from the Istgard party. With marvelous composure, the rider raised a broken pike with a banner of gold-edged white gossamer trailing from its shattered tip. The gossamer banner, obviously a woman's sacrificed veil, rippled in the breeze like a delicate testimony, avowing the visitors' peaceable intentions.

Seeming convinced by this feminine frippery, most of the Ytarians lowered their weapons and stared.

The dark-eyed, powerfully built Istgardian surveyed the throng without expression. When the last swords and pikes were lowered, his gaze finally rested on Ela. She exhaled gratefully, delighted to see him again. Istgard's prime minister was a most honorable man—as well as being her former guard, and one of the few people who'd protected Ela, Tzana, and Kien during their imprisonment in Istgard. "Tsir Aun!"

Dignified as ever, Tsir Aun said, "Parnian. I should have expected to see you in the midst of such commotion. Can you never stay out of trouble?"

"I'm not the one causing trouble," Ela argued, squelching a smile. "But you will, Prime Minister, if you dare insult me."

The prime minister allowed a trace of amusement to ease his stern, handsome features. "Indeed. If I insult *you*, my beloved wife will trouble me for the remainder of my short existence." He flicked a look at Jon. "May I address the welcoming committee?"

Jon coughed. "By all means, sir. But try not to provoke them further."

"Four destroyers can hold this pitiable army in check," Tsir Aun muttered. He slid the makeshift gossamer banner into a holder on his destroyer's intricate war collar, removed a scrolled parchment from his belt, and then commanded his destroyer. "Wrath, walk. No biting."

Wrath snorted and took a few steps toward the crowd.

The Ytarians backed away. At least twenty men and women turned and fled into the city. In the crook of Ela's arm, Tzana straightened and frowned. "That destroyer wouldn't really eat them. Why are they running?"

"They're not as brave as you," Ela said. "Hush now and listen to Tsir Aun."

Unhurried, Tsir Aun halted Wrath and lifted the scroll and his voice. "Good citizens of Ytar, I am Tsir Aun, Istgard's prime minister. This is your most recent list of complaints concerning our plans for rebuilding your city. I've traveled here because I wish to personally discuss this list with your council and reach a consensus before continuing the work."

Allowing his words time to sink in with his dumbfounded audience, the prime minister challenged, "Will you welcome me, and my wife and servants, and guarantee our safety as we inspect the buildings that have been completed?"

Ela waited. If the citizens of Ytar dared to argue now—

The thin, officious councilwoman who had dominated last night's meeting stepped forward, evidently unarmed, a pleasant smile gracing her narrow face. "Welcome, Prime Minister. I am Naia Vara, lead councilmember. I give you our word that you and your household will be safe in Ytar."

By the disgruntled looks cast toward Councilmember Vara,

Ela knew the lead council position had just been created by Vara herself. "Infinite," Ela complained beneath her breath, "the woman is a born instigator and power monger."

Tell her she will resign. Now.

Oh no. Her own father had never sounded so displeased. Ela quaked inwardly as the branch gleamed in white fire. She nudged Pet toward Naia Vara, who froze like a spied rabbit.

Pitying the woman, Ela said, "Naia Vara, the Infinite commands you to resign now. Go home. If you resist, your fellow council members will oust you. Viciously. Believe me."

Her eyes huge, fixed on the branch, Vara's color faded. Mute, as if she knew she'd pushed matters too far, the woman turned and scurried through the crowd. Glares followed her.

Taking advantage of Vara's unexpected retreat, Jon called out to the crowd, "Follow her example, all of you! Disperse! Immediately!" The crowd, though sullen, scattered.

Tsir Aun reined in his destroyer and caught Ela's attention, questioning her in a low voice. "Will negotiations proceed, or should we leave?"

"They will proceed." Ela smiled at her friend. "You have the Infinite's blessings, sir."

"Thank you for the reassurance." He returned her smile. "Ela, it's good to see you. I hope you and your companions stay long enough for us to visit—we must speak with you. My wife prayed for the chance to meet you again."

His wife. Lady Tek Lara, formerly of Istgard's royal family—and Ela's dear friend and benefactress during her imprisonment in Istgard last year. "I've prayed the same." Ela looked over her shoulder and laughed, seeing the prime minister's household approach in a clattering procession of light chariots and wagons. She handed the branch to Tzana and descended, using Pet's thick mane to slow her drop.

Tzana protested, "I want to go with you!"

"Wait and I'll bring Lara," Ela promised. Her bare feet sinking in the damp, aging grass, she ran to meet her friend.

Lara was already waiting outside her chariot, obviously pregnant and unable to hurry. She greeted Ela with a fierce hug. "Ela! I've been worried about you!"

Ela laughed, kissed Lara's cheek, then stepped back to admire her rounded waistline. "You look wonderful! Why are you worried about me? I'm in no more danger than usual."

Serious as ever, Lara didn't appreciate the joke. "Obviously my husband's had no chance to tell you about our recent dealings with Parne." Her soft brown eyes went huge as she gripped Ela's arm and they began to walk toward the others. "Ela, why would your father—your own father—be involved in illegal smuggling?"

10

While they knelt about the low table and shared their evening meal, Ela watched Tsir Aun move away from his wife, as if fearing the leather parcel in his hands would harm Lara and their unborn child. He untied the parcel's leather cords and placed it at the end of the table, revealing crystallized ores.

Obviously taking his cue from Tsir Aun, Jon caught Beka's hands, preventing her from touching the yellow and silver-gray stones. Beka protested, "I won't touch them, but I want to see what all the fuss is about. Really, Jon, let go of my hands and I'll be good. For now."

Tzana piped up, "I've never seen yellow rocks like those." She reached for the crystals.

"No! They're dangerous." Ela lifted her sister away. Tzana loved odd chunks of ore.

Ela settled Tzana beside her, then stared at the glistening stones. "Those are the types of ores I saw in my vision. The yellow one is poisonous in any form." She hesitated, hating to discuss the matter in front of Tzana. "But how is my father connected with contraband ore?"

Lara shook her head, clearly at a loss. "When our authorities found these ores being secretly sold in our capitol, in the middle of Riyan, we had to arrest the offenders. Our citizens became ill when they attempted to smelt the yellow ore. And after the silvered ore was crushed, the residue caused buildings to burn to the ground, killing several men."

Taking up her explanation, Tsir Aun said, "When we demanded information from the Parnian smugglers, they specifically named your father, Dan Roeh, as their supplier of contraband ore."

Reprobate Parnian liars! Ela clenched her hands into fists and paused. Be calm. Temper tantrums were unprophet-like. "My father is an ordinary workman. A stonecutter who maintains Parne's foundations and walls. He has studied stone formations around Parne, but he'd never require others to sell such ores on his behalf. Particularly knowing the ores are dangerous."

Jon and Beka, and Tsir Aun and Lara each cast her troubled glances. Did they suspect her father? Or her? Infinite, why?

"Nevertheless," Tsir Aun said, "your father was . . . named . . . and it is a concern."

He'd almost said *accused*, Ela was sure. In answer to her prayer, traces of a vision offered faces. And hatred. Hearing her own name hissed within the thoughts of others, Ela pressed her fingertips hard against the stabs in her head. "My enemies are attacking Father because of me."

Because of Me, the Infinite corrected.

"Because of the Infinite," Ela repeated, in perfect agreement with His statement. Hurting, she focused on the tiny bowls of brightly pickled vegetables, baskets of soft flat breads, autumn fruits, and a platter of fat herb-roasted partridges. The vision's residual pain faded, leaving Ela wearied.

Tzana huddled against Ela, her fragile body beset by tremors. "I want to go home—I need to see Father."

"Yes. Soon," Ela promised. She landed a soft kiss on Tzana's insubstantial curls, then tucked the little girl close to soothe her shivers. "We'll leave tomorrow. Until then, you should eat and rest." She offered her sister some fruit. Tzana ate.

Jon cleared his throat and spoke to Tsir Aun and Tek Lara. Polite, but defensive. "It makes sense that Ela's enemies would attack her father in an attempt to smear her good name. If her enemies convince others of this lie, then they've diminished Ela's authority."

"We agree," Lara said, with a glance at her husband, who nodded. "Ela, you will keep us informed, won't you?"

"Yes. Istgard will be informed." They deserved to know everything. She addressed Tsir Aun. "Prime Minister, within a few weeks, the country of Belaal will attack Parne from the south to gain control of these ores—and Parne's gold, which they've promised to share with the Agocii and Eosyth tribes."

Tsir Aun tensed, scorn crossing his bronzed features. "Belaal!" He hesitated. "If Belaal's god-king—that Bel-Tygeon—gains exclusive command over these ores, then devious as his mind is, he'd command that Belaal create a destructive arsenal to use against other countries."

Passing Beka a dish of pickled vegetables, Jon agreed. "If not an outright war, then the least Bel-Tygeon would do is threaten the Tracelands and Siphra to gain trade concessions. And lands."

"Bel-Tygeon won't be satisfied with such small victories for long," Tsir Aun said.

Lara frowned. "With our new government, he'd consider Istgard vulnerable." She gave Ela a pleading look that ought to have carried some blame. "Ela, can't you subdue Belaal and its king?"

"Parne's judgment comes first. Through Belaal and others." Ela put down the morsel of bread she'd taken, her appetite obliterated by thoughts of the coming siege.

Unaffected, Tsir Aun ate. Neatly. Between bites of herbed meat and bread, he said, "We cannot allow Belaal to control Parne and these ores. I'm sending the Tracelands and Siphra warnings as soon as we return to Istgard. If need be, we will go to war."

Beka cleared her throat in the silence that followed. As Jon nodded agreement, she said, "Unofficially, I promise you, the Tracelands is concerned and will send a force to join yours."

"Thank you." Lara studied Beka now, her expression fond. "You look so much like your brother—I'm surprised he's not here. How is Kien? Where is he?"

Jon chuckled. "The Infinite sent him off on a mission."

His dark eyebrows raised, Tsir Aun asked, "What type of mission?"

"I'm not entirely sure."

Sudden fear tightened Ela's stomach. She shut her eyes, praying for Kien.

✦ ✦ ✦

Ominously dark clouds dropped shroud-like over Adar-iyr's rooftops as Kien passed through the island-kingdom's main gate. Odd island weather. Covering his mouth and nose with the edge of his cloak, Kien entered Adar-iyr's filthy streets, his boots slipping in the fetid mud and waste heaped on the pavings. Didn't the authorities enforce sanitation regulations? The city's central gutter was blocked with . . . rotting corpses. Two bloated humans and one goat. The stench worked into Kien's nostrils, gagging him. So much for the cloak. He lowered his hand.

"Infinite," Kien muttered as his stomach churned in revolt, "thank You for not allowing me to eat." Steady. Given the situation, he must behave as a prophet and follow Ela's example. Warn offenders while trying to see them as the Infinite did, with concern for their souls.

He wove away from the gutter toward the buildings, still counting the corpses. Six now. Three human. Three animals . . . One, by appearances, had been carved up for roasts while still alive. No more than ten breaths within this stinking city and Kien had already counted at least eleven violations of the Tracelands' criminal codes.

"Ooo . . ." a feminine voice purred as an arm slipped around Kien's waist, chafing his raw skin so sharply that he wanted to yell. A young woman with sun-streaked brown hair clung to Kien, caressing him, and—between nervous glances at the forbidding clouds—taking liberties he'd allow no one. "Who are you, stranger? Never mind. You're not in a hurry, are you?"

Kien stepped away, frowning. Why would anyone touch him, rotted as he appeared?

She flung herself at him again. "Wait! My, but you're in a bad mood. Well, I can make you forget everything for a quarter-ninus."

Twelve violations. Thirteen if she'd stolen his coins. Fourteen if she continued to maul him against his will. Gritting his teeth, Kien unwound her arms from his waist.

She grabbed him again, painfully, revealing her desperation. "Please, sir!"

This was like trying to free himself from a many-tentacled creature—its arms continuously entwining him. Frustrated, Kien stared down into the young prostitute's eyes. He froze, shocked. She was so *young*! Obviously this girl's situation wasn't her fault. He removed her hands from his waist and held her wrists to keep the girl's attention—and some distance.

Remembering his divinely dictated guidelines—the twelve official words he'd be allowed while in this city—Kien spoke gently, hoping she recognized his concern. The Infinite's concern. "In twenty-one days, the Infinite will destroy Adar-iyr. Repent and be saved."

"What?" She stared at Kien as if he were insane.

"In twenty-one days—"

"You're teasing me." The girl pouted, her voice pathetic, her lower lip out as she looked up at him through her lashes. "Don't be mean."

Were those specks crawling through her hair *lice*? Kien held the girl off, repeating earnestly, "In twenty-one days, the Infinite will destroy Adar-iyr. Repent and be saved."

"Huh! Madman! Let go!" She ducked and tugged her hands from his. "Freak!"

A man leaned from the nearest doorway and snarled at Kien, "If you're not conducting business, move on!"

The man's hair was the same sun-streaked brown as the girl's. Was he the girl's panderer, selling his own daughter or his little sister to a peeling, blighted stranger? No doubt he was. Infinite? Did Adar-iyr have any laws at all? This poor girl had been defiled through her relative's greed! Kien eyed the man and struggled not to judge and condemn him with evidence unheard. "In twenty-one days, the Infinite will destroy Adar-iyr! Repent and be saved."

As the man stared, then cast a wary glance at the threateningly low sky, Kien turned his scruffy-booted heels in an about-face and marched down the cloud-darkened street. He checked his coin purse, still secured to his waist, silver drams intact. Amazing. He untied it, cinched his belt tight, then dropped his coin purse inside his tunic, where it would be safe. Unless someone gutted him, which was bound to happen.

Raising his voice, Kien yelled, "In twenty-one days, the Infinite will destroy Adar-iyr! Repent and be saved!"

Unless their Creator forgave all these miscreants. Infinite? Would You?

If they repent. Yes. And you are right to not judge them by your own mortal understanding.

He'd done something right? Thank You! Heartened by his Creator's approval, Kien clasped his sword's hilt and crossed the filthy, gloomy streets, praying with every step that he'd survive.

✦ ✦ ✦

Branch in hand, Ela waited in Ytar's council chamber.

Expressionless, Tsir Aun rolled up a signed agreement and spoke to Ytar's council. "Istgard has your oath, and you have Istgard's, according to our first agreement. The wall, as it stands, has been paid for by Istgard, but it is now returned to your care. Remember that we've contributed to its construction."

The eldest council member—a slight, weathered man with reflective gray eyes—nodded. "Agreed. Istgard has been fair enough."

Considering that Ytar's slaughtered dead couldn't be restored to life.

Ela almost heard the unspoken thought echo through the

chamber. “Remember,” Ela cautioned the council gently, “the Istgardians who dared to massacre your people are also dead. They paid for their crimes with their lives.”

“Speaking of crimes,” another council member intoned, her straight dark hair and long face as solemn as her voice, “do you intend to leave us with the care—the expensive care—of ten blind prisoners?”

Ruestock’s men. If they were blind for the remainder of their lives, they’d rob no more. And yet . . . An impulse of pity made Ela sigh. “Have them brought here. We’ll see if the Infinite is merciful to the undeserving.”

The prisoners soon arrived in a straggling line, bound together by ropes at their waists. Leading the miserable parade, Ruestock threw Ela a surly glance. His men stumbled after him, seeming exhausted, untidy, and drained of hope.

Ela bowed her head, praying, “Infinite, open the eyes of these men.”

The branch sent a burst of light through the blinded prisoners. They gasped and lifted their bound hands to their eyes. Several uttered choked sobs. The eldest councilman stood and looked from the prisoners to Ela. Recovering, he asked, “What must we do with them? Kill them?”

Her voice monotonously flat, the dark-haired councilwoman said, “It’s too expensive to feed and shelter so many prisoners.”

The eleven prisoners sucked in their breaths. Ruestock darted a silent plea at Ela.

Ela frowned. For all their promises of peace, were the Ytarians still consumed by thoughts of spilling blood for revenge? Even if the blood wasn’t Istgard’s?

As the council members began to argue, Ela said, “Send them home. If you’d captured these men in war with your own weapons, wouldn’t you spare them for the sake of your own honor? Don’t tempt the Infinite’s anger. Be sure these men leave the Tracelands. Safely.”

Ruestock gave Ela a smile she couldn’t quite decipher. “There’s our charming, tenderhearted prophet. Ela, my dear, you are a jewel."

Minding her temper, Ela said, "I am not your dear."

"You break my heart."

Did he have a heart to be broken? Ela wasn't about to ask the question aloud. Duty done, she left the council chamber. Surely she would never see Ruestock again.

Parne would consume her instead.

✦ ✦ ✦

Travel-wearied, Ela stopped Pet and dismounted before Parne's single iron-shielded, stone-edged gate. Why was the city closed in full daylight? Were the Parnians already aware of their dire situation? She helped Tzana off, checked that Jon and Beka had also dismounted, and then waved to the watchman above. "Let us in, please!"

He shouted down, "I've orders to never admit you, Prophet!"

Oh? She'd been named an enemy? Very well. Ela removed the branch from Pet's war collar and glared up at the guard. The branch blazed in fiery blue-white warning—and the Infinite's wrath. "The Infinite's orders surpass yours, sir! Will you open the gate?"

Silent, the guard crossed his arms over his chest and didn't budge.

"So be it!" Ela marched up to the gate and touched it with the branch. Deep metallic squeals answered. The gate lifted into darkness.

By now, Jon was beside her. He leaned forward to peer into the gate tunnel's blackness. "You're not serious. We're going in there?"

"You don't have to go with me."

"Of course I do. I'm under orders. But my concern is for the destroyers. Will they fit?"

"Certainly." Ela hesitated. "As long as they can navigate the turns."

"An unlit tunnel—with turns—for a city's gate?" Jon shook his head. "That's preposterous! What an ordeal for traders."

Despite her own nerves, Ela couldn't resist tormenting Kien's brother-in-law just a bit more. "Yes. And those turns are why traders call this the Murder Maze. It's agony to get through. But this gate was built over generations by a people who cared little for outsiders." By a people once glad to be separated from others for the Infinite's sake. No more. "Coming?"

Distinctly gloomy, Jon ordered his servants to set up camp for the night. While they obeyed, he snatched Savage's reins and Beka took charge of Audacity. Ela picked up Tzana and settled the little girl like a toddler onto her hip. Then she coaxed the stomping, snorting Pet to follow her into the blackness. Toward her enemies.

The gate lowered behind them with an ominous thud.

✦ II ✦

Could this island-kingdom be any worse? Halting in the street beneath the perpetually darkened skies, Kien watched a pack of tattered children beating each other bloody near a refuse heap, fighting as if their lives depended upon the garbage. Where were their parents?

A woman staggered from an arched stone gateway, spied the children, and yelled, "G'on! Leave 'em 'fore I rip out yer hair!" She descended on the urchins and scattered them with curses and thumps until only two remained. And those bloodied two cowered beneath her fists. She cursed again, then snarled, "Set the noon meal 'fore I boil yer 'nstead!"

Her ragged, scrawny offspring snatched rubbish from the heap and scuttled beyond her reach. With their meal, no doubt. Could he at least intercede for these children? Kien bellowed, "In eighteen days the Infinite will destroy Adar-iyr. Repent and be saved!"

Cursing again, the drunken woman grabbed a dirt clod from the heap and flung it at him.

Missed.

Her children hesitated, staring at Kien from the rugged stone archway, which framed a garbage-scattered yard. But when their mother pelted Kien with more curses and dirt clods, they fled. Good. Perhaps he'd saved the little ones from a dirt clod or two.

Infinite, protect them. Praying, Kien trudged on, turning from one narrow alley to another, seeking more wretches to warn of their doom.

Wait. Watch.

Infinite? Kien hesitated, the hairs along his neck and arms prickling in unease. Seeing two cloak-obscured forms duck behind a garbage heap in the chilly overcast street ahead, he half drew his Azurnite sword. Robbers? Be with me, Infinite, though I don't deserve—

One of the forms shifted, hiding behind the mountain of rubbish. But the second man charged Kien, lifting a sword and roaring an incoherent cry, like a man rushing to battle.

Kien waited. His attacker, muscular, with a deeply creased face, loped within striking distance and swung his sword in an undisciplined arc. Kien parried the blow with all his might.

Their blades collided, and the stranger's sword snapped against the deep blue-gray Azurnite, its broken tip ringing as it hit the nearest wall. The would-be thug gasped and stumbled backward, lifting his almost useless blade. Kien leveled the Azurnite with his assailant's chin. "In eighteen days, the Infinite will destroy Adar-iyr—repent and be saved!"

The man escaped behind the garbage heap, evidently meeting a fellow conspirator amid a flurry of curses and scuffling. Kien charged after them in time to hear a man's rough voice snarl, "Run! He's God-protected and mad!"

Mad? Kien halted. Well, if he wasn't insane yet, he could be soon, provoked by hunger, cold, fear, and fatigue. As for God-protected . . . yes.

Quiet, furtive footsteps on gritty pavement made Kien turn, sword readied.

The wizened old beachcomber who'd awakened Kien on his first day in Adar-iyr was sneaking across the narrow street. As if trying to escape Kien's notice. Evidently realizing he'd been caught, the aged man lifted his hands and quavered, "I'd thought t'was you, sea whelp. Don't kill old Hal!"

Sea whelp. Oh, what a dashing name. Despite his frustration, Kien shook his head, giving Hal a rueful grin, followed by the obligatory stern warning. "In eighteen days, the Infinite will destroy Adar-iyr. Repent and be saved."

The old man's eyes widened in the gloom. "You're serious as I feared. We're gonna die!" Moving his trembling hands protectively before his face, Hal backed off, then turned and ran.

Finally! Kien almost laughed. *Someone* had listened.

✦ ✦ ✦

The Murder Maze unwound before Ela in tortuous darkness, lit only by the branch's silver-blue glow. Aware of Beka and Jon following with their destroyers, Ela lifted her insignia as high as the ancient tunnel allowed. Each hide-scraping turn brought low grumbles of complaint from the destroyers and provoked Ela's sense of guilt. She shouldn't have subjected the destroyers to this. Nor Jon and Beka. But they wouldn't have allowed her and Tzana to proceed unaccompanied.

Tzana clung to Ela's neck and whispered, "I can't like this—it's scary as ever."

"Hold tight. We'll be outside before too long."

But leaving the oppressive tunnel would mean walking into the sunlit, pale-plastered warmth of Parne's myriad houses and courtyards: another darkness more malicious than the gloom stifling their senses now.

Shivering, Ela sucked in a breath. The tunnel's sluggish air lay so stagnant and heavy that a mineral taste lingered on her tongue. Panic pressed into her spirit, threatening to crush her courage. Everything she'd survived in the past nine or so months faded to nothingness. She was, once again, a girl facing Parne's authorities.

Infinite?

I am here.

Solace enfolded her like a warming mantle. Strengthening her. "Thank You."

"What?" Tzana whispered.

"I'm praying." Ela boosted her little sister higher. "You can pray, too, if you'd like. And think of Mother and Father waiting for us."

Behind them, Jon's destroyer grumbled in the dark. Audacity huffed. And Pet snuffled at Ela's hair-braid, startling her. Did the destroyers sense her hostile enemies waiting at the tunnel's opening? "Easy," Ela murmured.

Beka's anxious voice echoed against the stones. "How much farther?"

"Another turn or two. But before each of you walk out, wait until your eyes adjust to the light. Otherwise, you'll enter Parne blind."

Wary, Jon called, "Should we fear walking out blind?"

"Jon, they'll be after me, not you."

Dry as Parne's dust, Jon retorted, "We'd prefer to not be incidental casualties."

She wished she could laugh. "You'll leave before the siege, unharmed—you, Beka, and your household."

Pet grunted as they maneuvered the final turn. While she waited for her eyes to adjust, he nipped at Ela's mantle, tugging her backward a step, as if trying to prevent her from leaving the darkness. Her arms filled with Tzana and the branch, Ela looked up at the massive warhorse. "You sense them, don't you, dear rascal? Those who hate the Infinite, and me. Well, it's time to face Parne. Come, come." Ela led her destroyer into the open, sunlit public square.

And confronted a wall of watchmen, traders, and citizens, some glaring.

The watchman who'd refused her entry snarled in a clear attempt to protect himself against his perceived failure. "Why have you broken through the gate against my command?"

Feeling her little sister tremble, Ela ignored him. Rude man! When Beka and Jon emerged from the tunnel with their destroyers, she set Tzana on Parne's worn stone pavings. "Go stand with Beka."

Her small face pitiably wrinkled, Tzana argued, "But I want to go to Father and Mother."

"Father is coming—you'll see him soon." Ela kissed her sister's cheek, willing her to feel the Infinite's calm. His love. "But until Father arrives, please stand with Beka."

Chin down, her footsteps a mournful trudge, Tzana went to Beka and took her hand.

Beka hugged the little girl in welcome, then flicked her dark gaze at the furious watchman.

He repeated, "Why have you broken through the gate against my command?"

Behind Ela, Pet rumbled a deep threat, dangerously close to becoming Scythe. Ela touched her destroyer's powerful face. "Be still."

The destroyer snorted, then stilled.

Ela frowned at the watchman and raised her voice so the growing crowd could hear. "The Infinite opened the gate, then closed it behind us. So how have I harmed you, or Parne? And why would you refuse to allow me to visit my family—my city? Am I a criminal? If so, then arrest me!"

Shadows loomed behind the watchman now. Smoke-murky forms, their twisting movements indicating deliberate intelligent action. Sending malice toward her. Malice? Ela shook her head. Had she sensed aright? Were those dark-misted forms deceivers? Infinite?

Yes. Do not fear them, for they have no direct power over you, My servant. The Infinite's voice deepened with grief. *Yet their shadows reveal the Adversary's influence among My people.*

Wounded by His sorrow, Ela studied the deceivers. Lying shadow-servants of the immortal Adversary, who warred against the Infinite. . . . Yet the Adversary's shadows, however loathsome and unnerving, were equaled in nature by the mortals they'd deluded. Didn't the Book of Beginnings point out that every mortal heart leaned toward evil from childhood? Herself included. Such a humbling thought.

As Ela praised her beloved Creator, the deceivers shifted within the crowd, their hazy forms seeming to darken, conveying hostility against the Infinite. And against the people they'd deceived. Such as this watchman. She stared at the burly man, comprehending his uncertainty and his agitation, which was multiplied by the unseen wraiths lurking about his shoulders.

He recovered and sputtered, "Arrest you? I should! I—"

A man's rich, taunting voice overrode the watchman's, beckoning Ela's attention. "Look who's finally returned. Our little-girl prophet. Have you found the courage to face your people?"

She recognized the young man's arrogant, hard-featured bronzed face. Sius Chacen, the firstborn son of Zade Chacen, Parne's deposed chief priest. Understandable if Sius hated her. On her first day as Parne's prophet, she'd announced his father's downfall, as well as Sius's early death. He narrowed his eyes. "Why should we welcome you, when you've abandoned us to seek glory in other lands?"

Glory? Was this her enemies' plan? To greet her with instant accusations that dishonored her good name? "I've followed the will of the Infinite, which gives glory to Him alone—as it should! You allow vindictiveness and envy to warp your senses, son of Zade. You've weakened yourself and opened your thoughts to the Adversary's deceivers."

"There are no deceivers but you!" Sius spat at her feet and raised his voice. "You and your family are power seekers who use the Infinite's name to inspire fear. To coerce obedience from those who can't see the Roehs for the criminals they are!"

Behind him, deceivers' faces gloated and mocked Ela with twisted sneers. Pleased to be unrecognized by their prey. Pleased to set secret snares for anyone beloved to the Infinite.

Pet rumbled a low threat. Ela reached back to soothe the destroyer, grazing her knuckles against his big neck. But she stared Sius in the eyes and matched his harsh tone. Let everyone hear.

"The Infinite will defend my good name. But how can you defend yourself? Your friends sold lethal ores in other lands and accused my father of planning their crimes."

The young man's eyes widened. The branch's gleam intensified in her hands, its blue-white fire revealing the Infinite's fury. Wiser than mortals, the deceivers shrank away, then vanished. Ela accused Chacen, "Why have you betrayed your people, leading them toward eternal fire, while dealing with their enemies—mortal and immortal—as friends?"

"You have no idea what you're saying." And no proof, his look added in gloating silence. "It's known that prophets are unstable." Softly, he added, "Prone to early deaths."

Did he think she would answer him quietly? Wrong! Let everyone hear. "I will not be driven off by your threats and bullying!"

Sius neared. His smile faded and he muttered, "What will it take to banish you?"

Ela refused to mutter. "You've no power to exile me."

"Don't I? We'll see!"

She lifted the branch at him and their onlookers, warning, "I won't leave until the Infinite commands me to go. Do you think the Infinite hasn't seen your wrongdoings in your secret shrines and the way you've dragged so many others with you?"

Even as she spoke, the Infinite sent her a current of emotion—His longing for the people who had once loved Him. Pain knotted in Ela's throat, stopping her words, cutting to her heart. No doubt the onlookers could see her sorrow. Her tears. Just as she saw their guilt.

Sius Chacen leaned down, almost face-to-face with her, and feigned a smile. "Why the tears? Are you frightened?"

Behind Ela, Pet huffed and stomped. Vibrations rippled through the stones beneath their feet. Ela wished she could allow him to stamp out Sius. She glared at the young man through her tears. "Don't interpret my grief as weakness. I cry for the

Infinite's sake. And for the people who will die because you and your family have encouraged their rebellious impulses!"

"My father would like to meet you," Sius murmured.

Meet her and kill her, Ela knew. She dashed a hand over her eyes. "I will speak with your father. But not when he expects it. The Infinite will arrange the time and place. Until then, son of Zade, stay away from me and my family and friends. Unless you'd like to meet my father. He's coming."

She sensed Dan Roeh's approach even before he turned a corner and descended the high rooftop path beyond the now-wary Sius. The sight of her father's tall, cloak-clad form and toughened brown face made Ela long to run to him like a child.

His suddenly ferocious scowl stopped her cold.

Clearly targeting Sius Chacen, Dan Roeh stepped into the public square and wove his way through the crowd. Tzana's exultant squeal pierced the air. "Father!" She skittered past Ela and Pet, her small arms outstretched.

Dan bent and scooped up his tiny daughter, almost without breaking his stride. "Chacen!"

Sius Chacen retreated without answering the older man. But he glared at Ela, conveying such hatred that her stomach clenched. No doubt he was planning vicious retribution for her ousting of Zade Chacen as chief priest.

Father growled. Loudly. "He threatened you, didn't he?"

"He failed." Ela pitched herself at her father, willing aside all thoughts of the vengeful Chacen clan. "I'm so glad to see you!"

Dan kissed Tzana, then Ela. But he remained distracted, looking over Ela's head. "Are those . . . destroyers?"

Tzana chirped, "He's Pet—he loves us. They all love us."

Eyeing Pet, Savage, and Audacity's massive forms, Dan muttered, "I hope so."

"Father." Ela patted his arm, then nodded toward Jon and Beka. "These are our friends Jon and Beka Thel. They accompanied us here from the Tracelands."

His tension easing, Dan nodded at Jon and Beka. "Welcome.

Please, come eat with us. I'm sure we can find a place for you, and"—he flicked an uncertain glance toward the destroyers—"we'll feed them too."

Jon laughed. "We'll be honored to eat with you. But my staff and servants are camped outside, and we must return to them tonight with the destroyers. Until then, sir, where is your grain market? I ought to purchase bribes for our monsters."

The destroyers perked their ears at the word *grain*, obviously interested.

✦ ✦ ✦

Her fellow Parnians stared as Ela, Tzana, Jon, Beka, and the destroyers followed Father through the huge public square. Ela tried to ignore their whispers and prying looks. She wanted to be Dan and Kalme Roeh's daughter for now. Nothing more.

Just a few days to rest, Infinite, please . . .

While most Parnians seemed indifferent to their prophet, many threw dagger-looks or frowns of mistrust at Ela, making her cringe inwardly. The indifference was soul-endangering enough, but the hatred . . . Infinite? I grew up among these people. Why haven't I seen their rebelliousness and spiritual corruption before?

In silent response He sent her images—Ela Roeh as a girl, encircled by the Infinite's love but ever shunning all whose rebellious, malicious natures displeased or wounded her. Particularly after Tzana's incurable aging condition became known and the Roehs were considered cursed.

Such self-protecting walls she'd built around herself! Her own stubborn nature refused to permit others near. No wonder she'd never had many friends. No wonder Parne's true spiritual mire was hidden from her. No wonder so many found it easy to hate her now.

No wonder Parne would find it easy to kill her. Ela swallowed. Perhaps her own self-isolating walls must come down to enable her to touch Parne's spirit.

Seeming oblivious to the onlookers, Father walked onward.

Eventually the open public square narrowed and funneled into a smaller, less crowded public area, and Ela's distress eased.

As they walked, Tzana kissed Father's whiskered cheek and chattered happily. Beside Ela, Jon and Beka stared at Parne's simple whitewashed homes, stacked like terraced boxes within and against Parne's vast encompassing walls, with numerous stairs leading to rooftop walkways and countless tiny gardens tucked into all available alcoves.

"This is amazing," Jon murmured.

"The Tracelands is more beautiful," Ela said. "But Parne is home." Even now.

Beka breathed a sigh of admiration at Parne's temple, placed like a crown at the city's crest. "How lovely! Ela, everything looks so *clean*."

Choked by the thought, Ela said, "I wish it were truly as clean as it looks."

Parne was like one of its long-buried tomb houses. Pristine walls hiding decay within.

Evidently hearing their conversation, Father glanced over his shoulder and shifted Tzana in his arms. Ela feared he would question her. Instead, he nodded them toward the Roeh home, tucked into the far corner of the public square. "Your mother and brother are awake."

Her newborn baby brother. Jess! Ela restrained herself. Accompanied by Jon and Beka, she halted Pet, Savage, and Audacity before the house, offered bribes of grain cakes, and commanded them sternly to wait. Father eyed the proceedings with an air of mistrust. At last, evidently convinced the monster-horses would wait, he stepped over the raised threshold. "Kalme, the girls are home!"

Hearing her mother's joyful cry, Ela stepped inside.

Slender, youthfully pretty, her brown hair flowing down her back, Kalme Roeh kissed Tzana, then snatched Ela into a hug, trembling and laughing between sobs. "My girls! Oh, why did you wait so long to return? Come meet your brother. Jess . . . look who's here!"

Kalme lifted a plump little bundle from a basket near the low, whitewashed softly glowing hearth. Wide, dark eyes studied Ela from beneath a fluff of glossy black curls.

"Jess!" Ela seized her baby brother, stared at his perfect brown skin and his pudgy cheeks, and fell irretrievably in love.

Beside her, Beka breathed, "He's gorgeous! Oh, may I hold him?"

"Me next!" Tzana screeched.

"Not yet," Ela protested, "I'm holding him!"

Caught in the middle of his first sibling squabble, Jess sneezed.

✦ ✦ ✦

Ela knelt on the Roehs' small rooftop terrace and stared up at the stars. Tonight's joy faded beneath her fears. She tucked down her chin and shut her eyes, praising her Creator, then praying for Parne. For the least chance that her vision's terrors might be changed.

The Infinite's Spirit waited in perfect serenity, allowing her to finish despite the probable futility of her requests. Ela sighed. Infinite, won't You answer me?

She longed to hear His voice. Thirsted for His reassurance. How had she endured life without Him? She hadn't. Couldn't.

Deliberately, Ela allowed an excruciating memory to resurface. Her first test as a prophet. A fragment of total separation from the Infinite. The remembered instant gripped her. Breath-sucking agony seared Ela's throat. Fire burned downward into her lungs as her soul fell to pieces, screaming in torment. Needing death. Obliteration. Anything except life without Him.

On the Roeh terrace now, Ela pulled in chilling gasps of air and tried to still her frantic, hammering heartbeat. "Infinite?"

I am here.

Ela summoned her courage. "Wouldn't Zade Chacen and his sons be changed if they knew the torment of true separation from Your presence? Wouldn't all of Parne be brought to its senses—back to You?"

No. Infinite's rejection was firm. *Their choices are their own.*

"Infinite," Ela persisted, "losing You for that instant changed me. If Zade and his sons could experience it for themselves . . ." Her plea trailed into despair as she sensed His refusal.

You had already chosen My path, and I know your heart. You needed to understand what the Adversary steals from those he leads astray—for your own sake. Gently, His voice continued. *But evildoers respond to sufferings by hardening their hearts all the more.*

She crushed the need to cry. "How could they?"

Because they have refused My love. Therefore, they cannot understand their Creator.

Well, that hope was gone. Ela drooped, pressing her face into her hands. Mourning until the Infinite sent an image. Father, climbing toward the roof. Toward her.

To demand painful answers she'd rather not give . . . to the awful questions he must ask.

12

Ela studied her father as he sat on the terrace. Shadows and moonlight carved his face, and his grim silence only added to her dread. Never one to waste words, Dan cast down his first blade-sharp question. "Why have you returned?"

She pared her words to suit his. "Parne has been judged."

"For the shrines to Atea?"

"Among other things, yes."

Dan exhaled. "I've known about the shrines for years. Some existed in Eshtmoh's time."

Eshtmoh. Her legendary prophet predecessor. Remembering Eshtmoh's account in the Sacred Books, Ela nodded. "He spoke against the rebels and destroyed their shrines until Parne chased him off to Istgard."

But Eshtmoh died more than seventy years past. Had the secret shrines been immediately rebuilt and used by Parnians for all these years? Infinite?

Yes. I have given them time and prosperity to return to Me. Yet they have broken their pledges to Me, though I have loved them.

As Ela tried to absorb the Infinite's distress, Dan said, "Your mother and Matron Prill have been invited to join separate shrines for the women. They refused and scolded the rebels."

"Matron Prill?" Ela saw their most severe neighbor's stern,

keen-eyed face. Matron Prill was more inclined to reprimand wrongdoers than anyone in Parne.

Except Parne's prophet.

"She's helped your mother these past few months," Dan said. "Things have been difficult." Struggling, as if the words tormented him, he continued. "My business is failing."

"Because the Chacens' cohorts have smeared your good name?"

Father snapped a look toward her. Did he expect Ela's criticism? She waited. He glanced away. "I'm accused of smuggling deadly ores."

"To Istgard. I've heard the rumors."

"It wasn't me."

"I know, Father. The rebels are trying to discredit me—and the Infinite—through you."

He nodded. "After you became the prophet, I spoke out against the shrines. I should have said more. *Done* more to stop those Atea-worshipers. They've been unopposed for so long. . . ."

"They wouldn't have listened to you. Just as they probably won't listen to me."

"But you'll speak to them." Father sounded confident that she would correct the situation. "And bring them to right before something worse happens."

Something worse . . . A sick gnawing tore into Ela's stomach. "If Parne repents and destroys its shrines and returns to the Infinite, He will forgive them. If not . . ." She was going to cry. "Father, Parne *will* fall. From the temple downward."

He swayed slightly, his hands becoming fists on his knees. "You're saying Parne will be destroyed?"

"Yes. And soon. With many of its citizens—those who refuse to accept the Infinite's judgment."

Dan paused, then asked, "What of us? Your mother, Tzana, and Jess—your cousins?"

An ache tightened her throat. A knot of grief for a loss she couldn't yet name. "I haven't seen the Roehs escaping the city.

I'm not saying you won't. It's just that I haven't seen your escape. I only know that Parne will fall after a siege."

"A siege!" Father straightened now. "I thought you meant 'destroyed' as in a quake. A cavern opening beneath the city—or something like that. But a siege?"

"Belaal, Istgard, and Siphra will send their armies. . . ." Ela began.

"We must warn the city to prepare."

"No, Father. We must warn the city not to resist, but to surrender."

"Not to resist? Ela, we must!"

Even in the moonlight, Ela saw her father's shock. His impulse of defiance. Her heart sank. If it was this difficult to warn Dan Roeh, who was devoted to the Infinite, and who loved Parne's prophet . . . Ela swallowed. She would be killed.

She looked at the city's pale soon-to-tumble walls, which gleamed in the moonlight. Unbearable. The skies, the stars were easier to consider. More soothing.

Father stood, drawing her attention. "Why destroy the whole city?"

"What else can the Infinite do? Parne is ruined. Weakened like a rotting tree. Worm-eaten with shrines to the goddess Atea and her companions." Nauseated, Ela added, "Even the temple has been defiled by Chacen and his sons."

Father's footsteps thudded against the roof's pavings as he paced. "They beat Chacen's successor, Chief Priest Nesac. He dared to speak against them—he still dares. But most of the priests no longer listen to him."

"Which is why they no longer deserve the Infinite's Temple." She hesitated. "Father, won't you sit down? I'm sure Mother and Tzana can hear you pacing. Have you finished asking me questions?" She hoped he had.

Dan Roeh sat. For a time he was silent. At last he said, "I'll obey the Infinite. But it won't be unreasonable of me to warn our relatives, then prepare against the siege."

"I'm sure you'll pray about the matter. This must be between you and the Infinite."

He was so quiet for so long that Ela wondered if he was indeed praying. Until he shot more questions at her. "Why are you so vague about our escape? What aren't you saying?"

"I can't tell you what I don't know, Father," Ela said, a bit sharper than she meant. "I'm sorry." Was her fear of the coming days affecting her temper? Not that it took much to affect her temper. "I haven't seen everything that's about to happen. Only what's most critical to Parne."

"We'll make it through," Dan said. More to himself than to her. He held out a hand.

Ela scooted over to sit beside him and study the stars. If only she could confess her mortal heart's weakness. If only she could say, *Father, I love a Tracelander. His name is Kien Lantec—he's Beka's brother.*

It would be so easy to tell him now, if her life had been normal.

If she weren't going to die soon.

Father spoke into the darkness. "Short as it's been, your time as a prophet has changed you. When I saw you this afternoon, I almost didn't recognize you as my daughter." His voice softening, Dan said, "Your face is the same. But your eyes . . . your eyes are old."

She blinked hard at the stars, which glistened through her tears. Old eyes. "Well . . . that's something."

He hugged Ela and kissed her hair. "My girl. Whatever happens, I'm proud of you."

Ela concentrated on controlling her voice. On not crying like a child. "Father, whatever happens, I'm proud of you too."

Dan cleared his throat. "So. What's given you these old eyes? We've heard a few stories from traders, but they can't be true."

"I'm sure you've heard a bunch of exaggerations."

"Then, you didn't lead a revolution in Siphra?"

"Um . . . I didn't want to."

"But the Infinite sent you there."

"Yes. However, first I was in the borderlands. Then Istgard . . ."

She began to talk of other lands. Other adventures. Anything to forget that she was now in Parne.

✦ ✦ ✦

Huddled beneath his cloak in a rubbish-strewn alley, Kien opened his eyes to see murky dawnlight. And boots. Occupied boots. Standing directly in front of his face. Was he about to be stomped to death? Infinite!

Swiftly, he sat up. His head spun and his thoughts protested. Don't kick me! I'm civilized!

Though being civilized seemed to be an offense in Adar-iyr. At least the man hadn't robbed him.

You may speak to him.

Truly? Exulting at the chance to say more than the Infinite's twelve ordained words, Kien eyed the boot-owner's formal cloak, helmet, and sword. "Are you a soldier or a guard?"

"Chief guardsman. And you've at least half a wit." He snapped his fingers. "Stand. Now."

Kien dragged himself upright. "Are you throwing me out of Adar-iyr?" He almost hoped.

"No. If you're the vagabond we've been seeking, then you've been summoned by the king."

"Oh." Kings. Useless, all of them. Except Akabe of Siphra, who hadn't been raised a king. Kien yawned. Then remembered his duty. "I'm supposed to tell you that the Infinite will destroy Adar-iyr in seventeen days. Repent and be saved."

"We've heard. Obviously you're the vagabond we're seeking. Move."

Move? Easy for him to say. The chief guard wasn't half-starved or unsteady. Following the guard, his stomach growling, Kien asked, "Do you feed your prisoners?"

"You're not a prisoner. Yet."

Fine. Good. But that didn't resolve his concern for a morning meal.

The chief guard paused until Kien caught up to him. "How's your Infinite planning to destroy our city?"

"I don't know. Fire from heaven, maybe." His imagination taking hold, Kien added, "Or perhaps an earthquake with a tidal wave and a storm for good measure."

"Surprised you didn't throw in a plague," the man complained.

"Plagues are too slow."

Motioning aside a beggar, the guardsman asked, "Where are you from?"

"The Tracelands."

"Should've known." Kicking a cracked, abandoned jar out of his way, the chief guardsman elaborated. "You Tracelanders are all alike. Picky and judgmental. But your people aren't usually given to calling on the Infinite, are they?"

"I suppose I'm a peculiar Tracelander." A wave of depression descended on Kien. He almost wished Ela could be there, walking with him through this cloud-obscured city, ready to confound a potentially despotic king who might condemn them both to death. Almost.

The chief guardsman nudged Kien from the walking daydream, then motioned at a fetid open ditch in the next cross street. "Jump. And try to avoid splashing us. It won't do to stand before ol' royal Ninus while stinking like dog droppings."

"Kings usually need a whiff of reality," Kien argued. But he vaulted across the ditch. He'd already inhaled a lifetime's worth of reality in this putrid city—he didn't need additional pungency. At least the guard had expressed some concern, unlike the other inhabitants of Adar-iyr. Kien straightened himself, looked the man in the eyes, and nodded. "By the way, my name is Kien Lantec. And yours is . . ."

"Teos," the man said. "We've heard the gods are protecting you."

"You mean the Infinite."

"No, I mean the gods. We've got a witness who saw you spewed onto the beach by the ocean lord, Nereus himself, who took the form of a sea beast. He's told half the island."

Wonderful. Kien had prayed the living-vomit part of his journey would remain unknown. "The beast wasn't your god Nereus. It was a monster created and sent by the Infinite to convey me here, against my will." Abduction on a celestial level, guaranteed to humble and terrify reluctant messengers. Kien forced the unruly thought aside. Quashed it.

So someone had seen him spewed onto the beach. "A witness. Was his name Old Hal?"

"Pshhh . . . ! Not that sneaking wretch. His grandson—a smart boy. He saw you heaved up and ran for help. But all he had was Old Hal."

"And you're certain I'm the one the boy saw?"

"I don't see anyone else appearing cooked and peeled as the boy described. Not even the sailors in our harbor." Teos grimaced at Kien. "Now, why'd you deny being favored by the gods?"

"There are no gods, only the Infinite. As for favor—ha! You try surviving a beast's gullet, then walking into this accursed city. There's not one civilized soul here."

"Tracelander for sure," the soldier grunted, looking upward, as if addressing his complaint to the blackened sky. "Picky, judgmental, *and* foolhardy!"

"I'll amend that," Kien said. "You have behaved in a civilized manner. But you're the only person in this whole stinking city who's shown me the least courtesy."

"Well, I'll turn rude, Tracelander, if you keep blathering on about our stinking ways."

"Forgive me. Sleeping in alleys and eating rubbish has turned me testy."

"Just guard your words when you answer ol' royal Ninus."

Not reassuring. Kien tromped on through the filthy streets, tallying the citizens' legal infractions as he walked. A thief cutting a purse from an unwary man's belt, then fleeing down the street. Numerous people drunk in public. Prostitutes in residential doorways and shrine entrances, clamoring for his attentions. Not to mention assault. Two rough-clad men struggled in the street until one ended their brawl with a knife to the other's belly. Kien started toward the assailant. But Teos wrenched him back. Kien protested, "We must intercede! That man could be dying!"

"That's not my duty," the guard said. "Anyway, why stop one murder? There're thirty others equal to this today. And no one cares."

"They should! *This* is part of the reason your city's been condemned."

"Move!" Teos shoved him onward. "Don't make me bind you, Tracelander!"

The royal palace was grand. If garish red and black columns could be called grand. The gatehouse, a massive edifice of tasteless red stonework, manned by crimson-clad guardsmen, seemed more theatrical than royal. But Kien supposed it was best to not announce his opinion.

"Here." Teos led Kien through the gatehouse tunnel, following the lead of two gangly youths, who were evidently royal servants waiting for the chief guardsman's arrival. They straightened, bowed their heads, then led the way, remaining some ten paces ahead.

Kien noticed the curious, wary looks the young servants threw him over their shoulders as they walked through the palace's labyrinthine torch-lit corridors. Were they afraid of him? It seemed so. He tested them, meeting their stares with a frown. One servant stumbled, the other gasped, and they both looked straight ahead—not glancing at him again.

They *were* afraid of him. Kien suppressed a smile. Bad Tracelander. Ela would be more compassionate, he was sure. But he was glad she hadn't been forced to sleep in the trash-strewn, rat-infested alleys of Adar-iyr. And grateful she hadn't been subjected to such displays of moral degradation as he'd witnessed. Her heart would be broken, fearing for their souls.

Definitely an attitude he ought to cultivate more attentively. Dear Ela . . .

Voices in the palace corridors drew Kien's attention from

daydreams of Ela. Polished voices, different from the raucous cries of the rabble. Cultured, but no less brutal.

A woman's languishing drawl asked, "Is that the doomsayer?"

"It would seem so," a man answered.

A third sniffed. "Burn him. Now."

Kien gritted his teeth. Burn? He'd rather not.

Infinite?

✦ 13 ✦

Teos hauled Kien forward while placing one huge hand on the hilt of his own sword. Kien pondered the man's gesture. Why would a plain guard fend off surly courtiers for the sake of a mere doomsayer?

And what doomsayer had ever been popular? Certainly not Kien Lantec of the Tracelands. Indeed, the pack of courtiers seemed eager to attack him—if they'd been physically able. Thankfully, the nobility of Adar-iyr were swaying or leaning on each other, bleary-eyed: the men in their gold-belted tunics, with gold diadems and peacock feathers; the women with pearls cascading from their elaborate hairstyles down onto their stunningly emphasized bosoms.

Kien swiftly fixed his gaze above the diadems and peacock feathers. What was Adar-iyr's protocol for confronting debauched, half-undressed courtiers who wanted to burn him alive?

When in doubt, ignore them. And pray for their misguided souls to be enlightened.

He stared over their heads as Teos led him after the young servants, who bowed and scraped their respective ways through the crowd.

"Scruffy creature," one of the women complained.

A man answered, "What can you expect? He's mad."

"I still say we should burn him," the first instigator said. "A living torch."

One of the ladies giggled. "Perhaps we'll send a fiery offering over the waters to our god Nereus when the king is finished with him. That'll lift a few of these clouds over us!"

Kien focused on the arched doorway ahead, determined to ignore them. Wise men didn't argue with drunkards. Perhaps when these courtiers sobered, the Infinite would permit him to warn them. And yet, if violence threatened, he had to defend himself, didn't he?

If the courtiers were this decadent, what was King Ninus like?

Infinite? May I speak during this audience?

His Creator's answer was a silent affirming nudge that propelled him forward. Kien almost grinned.

Inside the lamplit royal audience chamber, the king lolled in a deeply cushioned chair, looking like a man who had been awake all night at a rather overwhelming party. His puffy, sagging face conveyed only tepid interest in the proceedings. He grunted as Kien approached, then motioned to a nearby clerk, ensconced on a massive floor cushion.

In response, the clerk dropped a wooden-spooled scroll into a basket beside him, then dismissed the two young servants with a careless wave. Licking a thumb, the clerk flipped through a stack of torn parchments, extricated one, and perused it. "Is it true you were heaved from the belly of a sea creature?"

"Yes. Don't I look it?" Kien asked. "Before the beast swallowed me, my clothes and boots were virtually new."

Ninus studied Kien's boots and clothes. "Mmph."

The clerk's thin nostrils flared. "What sort of beast? What name?"

Name? Was the man serious? Kien chuckled. "Being sucked down as a main course isn't exactly a social occasion. I didn't ask its name. But I've never seen such a beast before. I believe the Infinite created the beast for the singular purpose of failing to digest me."

Ninus sighed.

Obviously taking this as a signal, the clerk made a note, then proceeded. "What is your homeland?"

"The Tracelands. And believe me, I'd rather be there. Do you know how many laws I've seen broken in your streets? I've lost count! With all respect, King Ninus, your people are . . . feral!"

Eyes widening, Ninus sniffed. "Hmph—Tracelanders!"

The clerk mimicked his king's sniff. "Exactly, sir." He frowned at Kien. "What god cast you on our shores?"

"As I said: the Infinite. There is no other god."

"Eh?" Ninus shook his head.

"Disbelieve me if you like," Kien challenged. "But the Infinite brought down King Tek An of Istgard and King Segere of Siphra." Leaning forward, determined to convey his concern, Kien willed Ninus to pay heed. "Now it's your turn, sire, so I beg you to listen: You will perish and your people will go down with you if you can't be bothered to control them. Your island-realm is a stench in your Creator's nostrils! Unless you act, you have seventeen days to live. Then you, your kingdom, your people, even the rats in your streets will be obliterated!"

Ninus shifted in his chair. His clerk said, "What must we do to avoid . . . obliteration?"

"Pray to the Infinite. Believe, repent, and change your ways—you and all your subjects. Trust me, He hears you and will receive your prayers. He wishes to protect your souls."

The king slouched and closed his eyes, uttering, "Clouds."

"Ah." The clerk nodded. "Did your Infinite cast these unnatural clouds over our island?"

Kien blinked. Infinite? Are these ever-present clouds unnatural to Adar-iyr?

Yes. They are a warning of My coming judgment.

He should have known. "Yes. They are a warning of the Infinite's coming judgment."

Ninus winced. The clerk waved a hand. "You are dismissed." To Teos, he said, "Take this man to the kitchens and feed him. Offer him a bath and new clothes. Now depart."

Kien hesitated. That's all? What a bizarre royal audience. Was this a trap? He rested one hand on his sword as Teos led him out the opposite side of the king's chamber.

"You're a Tracelander for sure," the chief guardsman complained as they marched through a wan, overshadowed, grid-like garden. "No respect for royalty!"

✦ ✦ ✦

Ela tucked the last fold of her baby brother's swaddling linens together and smiled into his round, dark-eyed face. "Jess, you are so handsome!"

Jess pursed his baby lips, clearly unimpressed by the compliment.

Beside Ela, Beka scooped Jess from beneath Ela's hands. "Handsome? He's perfect!"

Jon looked up from the count-and-capture game he was sharing with Tzana. "Are you talking about me?"

"No, dear," Beka said. "But don't despair. I think you're perfect too. *And* handsome."

Kalme stepped over the plastered threshold into the main room, her soft brown eyes serene. "Girls, thank you for watching Jess. I'll take him now—it's nap time. Ela, I need some dried fruit and meat. Will you go to the market for me?"

Go, the Infinite prompted.

"Of course." She smiled. "I'll take Tzana. We'll visit Pet after our trip to the market."

"No, I think I want a nap," Tzana said. She pushed away the board game. "Mother, can I hold Jess until we fall asleep?"

Ela stared at her sister. Tzana, not wanting to visit Pet? Of course, she couldn't blame Tzana. Jess was irresistible. And Ela and Beka had been greedy, cuddling him most of the morning.

Besides, after ten days' rest, it seemed the Infinite had plans for His prophet. It might be best for Tzana to remain with Mother.

Jon pretended to complain to Tzana. "Fine. Take a nap. I'll try to not feel abandoned."

The little girl sighed. "But you yawned and made me sleepy, so it's your fault."

"Implying that I'm boring? Ow!" While gathering the game pieces, Jon told Beka, "I promised my men we'd return with supplies today, so I'll accompany you to the market."

"You presume I'm going?" Beka affected huffiness.

"Dear," Jon said, perfectly calm, "it's a market. If you're reluctant to go, then you must be ill."

As they grabbed their gear, Kalme handed Ela her coin purse. "Here's two-weight in coins."

"Two?" Ela protested, "Mother, you don't need so much for dried fruit and meat."

"No, but you need a new mantle and so does Tzana. Buy some fabric, please. Ten lengths."

"Yes, Mother." But marketplace fabric was so expensive! Ela stifled her objections and retrieved the branch. No doubt Mother was still celebrating her daughters' return with new garments, probably with Father's full approval. Ela blamed herself. She'd denied her parents the joy of a homecoming feast last week, reasoning that Parne's approaching destruction was no reason to celebrate. And Ela, as the prophet and bearer of such grievous news, shouldn't be given a new mantle. Tzana, however, was a different matter.

Ela crossed the crackling woven floor mats and bent to kiss Tzana's cheek. "Enjoy your rest. I'll give Pet a hug for you."

"He would understand if he could see Jess," Tzana explained, worry fretting her forehead. "Anyway, I'm really tired."

"Then you ought to nap," Ela agreed. "Come, let's tuck you in."

She rested the branch against the wall, then fluffed Tzana's sleeping pallet and its pillow. Tzana settled down with a sigh and a pleased smile, particularly as Beka nested the freshly swaddled Jess beside her.

Ela chuckled. "You two look so cozy, I'm jealous." She kissed her siblings, then stood and retrieved the branch.

"Don't forget the fabric." Kalme gave Ela a hug, then chased her outside with Jon and Beka.

Jon stretched in the sunlight, then yawned and shook himself. More alert, he grinned at Ela. "Your family's home is so quiet and peaceful that I almost fell asleep."

"It is. We've been blessed."

Beka gave her husband a fierce nudge. "Meaning our home isn't peaceful?"

Jon laughed and took her hand—after checking his sword. "*Our* home is exciting, and I wouldn't want it any other way."

As they walked, their boots and sandals clattering against the public courtyard's pale stones, Jon changed the subject, his voice turning grim. "Ela, it's been more than a week. When will Belaal's army arrive?"

"Soon. About two weeks." She caught Beka's gaze. "I know you promised Kien you'd keep watch over me, but you must leave before Belaal arrives."

"Ela," Beka protested, "I won't leave you here!"

Implacable as stone, Jon said, "Beka, we must. Otherwise, given Belaal's reputation, we'll be captured and enslaved, *if* we're blessed." His dark eyebrows drew together in a thoughtful frown. "However, we could travel to Istgard, then return with Tsir Aun's forces."

"The Infinite agrees," Ela said as her Creator's approval threaded into her thoughts.

Beka sighed. "Then we'll go. But not until the last possible instant."

"I concur." His serious expression brightening, Jon added, "That way, I'll be able to consolidate at least two reports of both Parne and Istgard into one scroll. The general will be pleased. Now . . . what do we need from the market?" He strode ahead.

They entered Parne's largest public square, which teemed with people. Quarreling men, laughing women, and the odd, high girlish voices of foreign eunuchs caught her attention as they bargained with Parne's renowned gem traders, purchasing treasures for their masters.

Evidently startled by the eunuchs' voices, Beka hesitated and whispered, "Oh, those poor men. Listen to them. . . ."

"Pray for them." Ela hurried Beka onward, hoping to distract her from asking questions. There were no eunuchs in the Tracelands, and Ela didn't want to repeat the horrifying, pity-inducing details she'd overheard from others in the marketplace whenever eunuchs visited Parne. "They're foreign servants, sent by their masters from the south and the west beyond the mountains—I'd hate to see them, or anyone, caught in the coming siege."

Thankfully, Beka grimaced at a passing manure cart. "Ugh! What a stench!"

Wrinkling her nose in sympathy, Ela focused on the bleating lambs sheltered along the walls in makeshift pens. Some of these same animals would be offered in sacrifices at the temple this evening—useless sacrifices, considering the rebellious souls who offered them. Heartsick, Ela breathed prayers to her cherished Creator.

Infinite, why don't these people, these hypocrites, see what they're doing?

A rush of images answered. Oh no. A vision. Ela leaned against a vendor's booth and shut her eyes—enduring the pain.

Beka gripped her arm. "Ela? Do you need to sit down?"

The vision ended as abruptly as it had begun. Ela drew in a deep breath and urged Beka, "Go ahead with Jon. I'm well."

"Are you sure?"

"Yes. Thank you." As Beka moved off, Ela opened her eyes . . . and stared directly at the first portion of her vision, an exquisite white linen sash. Ela turned to the vendor, who was frowning at her—probably because she'd leaned on his table. "How much for that sash?"

"One weight of silver."

"Sorry. I can't afford one weight," Ela countered. "What about a half?"

The man's expression hardened. "Three quarters. This is incomparable linen. My best! Meant for the temple's priests! I won't accept less than three-quarter weight of silver."

"Three quarters of a weight, then." The price was almost as much as all of Mother's remaining purchases combined, Ela was sure. Nauseated, she opened Kalme's coin purse and recited in her thoughts, *Mother, the Infinite commanded me to buy this sash instead of fabric for my mantle. . . .*

As she was paying, two young men ambled into her line of vision. Handsome. Dark-curled. Arrogant. Sius and Za'af Chacen . . . watching her. Ela lifted her chin, allowing the brothers to see her contempt for everything they'd done. All the souls they'd misled. All the evils they were now planning. Her stomach twisting, she knotted the sash at her waist, grabbed the branch, and marched off to find Beka, as well as dried fruit, meat, and a cheaper fabric vendor to provide material for Tzana's new mantle. The Chacens followed.

"Well." Beka turned from a spice merchant's stall and surveyed Ela's attire. "That's not *quite* the sash I would have chosen for you, but . . ."

"The Infinite chose it," Ela murmured, watching the Chacens eyeing her and Beka.

"Yes, but you can still tie it in a more fashionable manner."

"This has nothing to do with fashion, and everything to do with souls."

"Oh." Beka's lovely face skewed into a slight frown. "Well, I suppose you can wear it that way if you must, but at least let *me* choose the fabric for Tzana's new mantle."

"For half a weight of silver?"

Her friend hesitated. "And one dram is worth four weights of silver . . . so that leaves me with seven bits of a dram left from today's allowance. . . ."

"Yes." Guilt ate at Ela. Were her friends drained of money?

Finished with her calculations, Beka said, "My, but I'm still rich!"

Ela laughed. "And I'm blessed to have you as a friend."

"Yes, you are. Now, let's see. Tzana's color is a bright pink. Or at least bright blue."

Somehow, their laughter frustrated Sius and Za'af Chacen. The young men lingered a while longer, then stalked away—leaving Ela and Beka. With their arms full of fabrics and foodstuffs, the girls crossed the marketplace to the Murder Maze to meet Jon. He was leaning against a wall but straightened as they approached, clearly eager to return to camp for the night. Jon lifted his gear onto his back, then grumbled as he purchased a torch from a gate vendor. "I feel like a common foot soldier again. I should have brought one of my servants to help carry all this. Ela, who were those young men following you through the marketplace?"

"Sius and Za'af Chacen. Sons of the deposed high priest."

"They didn't look too friendly." Jon grimaced as the vendor lit the torch. "Tell us, Prophet, did you have something to do with their deposed father's downfall?"

"The Infinite did."

"Through you?"

"Of course. But don't worry—they're gone for now. Anyway, they won't trouble you or Beka because you're armed and a soldier. And the owner of a destroyer."

"Nevertheless, I ought to confront them," Jon argued as they entered the Murder Maze.

"Dearest," Beka soothed, her voice echoing lightly in the tunnel, "I'm sure we're safe."

"I'm not. Ela, does your father know those men are stalking you?"

"Yes. And so does the Infinite. Don't worry, Jon. I'm sure I'll be fine." From what she'd seen in her vision, she'd confront the Chacens later. For now, she wanted to enjoy her visit with her friends. As they turned the last corner of the Murder Maze, a deep rumble vibrated through the murky tunnel.

"A cave-in!" Beka gasped. "Or—"

Ela recognized the source of the commotion at the outer gate. "Pet!" She scooted forward and nuzzled his big face. "Sweet rascal! Now move back and let us through. Back up."

He whooshed a soggy, contented sigh into her hair. Ela frowned in the darkness. Really, much as she loved her destroyer, he had to move. Her packages were becoming heavy, and she needed to rest a bit before this evening's confrontation in Parne. "I know you've missed me—I've missed you. However, you must move back! *Obey!*"

✦ ✦ ✦

Branch in hand, Ela rushed through the sunlight's deepening glow, across Parne's public rooftop paths, taking her family's usual route toward the temple—the most direct way there. She must arrive before evening sacrifices to speak to Parne's worshipers.

"Let them hear," Ela begged the Infinite in a despairing whisper. "Let them return to You again, with the love they first knew for You!"

Still praying, she climbed the steps of Parne's highest roof path and turned, scurrying past a terraced garden and its shaded rooftop entry to the private home below. Her mantle snagged, halting her. Ela turned to free herself from whatever had caught her cloak—and walked directly into a young man. Not just any young man, but her former would-be husband. "Amar!"

He slapped a hand over Ela's mouth, swung her into the shadowed entry, and slammed the door behind them.

14

Amar, let go!" She tried to step away. But the rooftop entry, like most in Parne, was dimly lit and offered little maneuvering room. Unnerved, Ela wobbled between the wall and the rail of a small wooden landing that led to a narrow flight of stairs.

Amar laughed and gripped her forearms. "I *knew* you would come this way! Some things never change, do they?" He pressed Ela against the landing's wall. His voice turned coaxing, low and intense. "Ela, listen to me . . . we need to talk."

Listen? Talk? The warmth of his body and the nearness of his mouth to hers contradicted those words. Was he trying to seduce her? Struggling, turning her head away, she warned, "If you thought I'd be amused by this, you were mistaken. Let me *go!*"

"Why should I? You know, I'd forgotten how pretty you are." He bent to kiss her throat—a freedom she'd never allowed him when they were betrothed.

"Amar!" She shoved him with all her might and kicked his shins.

As he laughed and stepped backward, Ela noticed shadows flickering behind him, crowding the entry. Twisting shades of darkness coiled around Amar, then showed their faces, gloating at Ela as if to say, *We have him. You can do nothing.*

Deceivers! She lunged for the door.

Amar grabbed her waist, pulling her against him once more,

his bruising grip at odds with his lulling whisper. "Why are you trying to avoid me? Stay. Listen to me. We were mistaken to abandon our marriage plans, and we ought to go downstairs and discuss matters."

"No!" Her reputation would be ruined. Unable to free herself, Ela screamed and fought, trying to hit Amar with the branch.

"Hush!" He seized her wrist and smashed her hand against the wall. Pain stabbed through Ela's fingers. She cried out as her precious insignia clattered down the stairs into the room below. Amar lifted Ela off her feet and followed the branch's path, hauling her down the stairs.

Ela fought, screaming, tearing at Amar's hair with her uninjured hand.

Amar swore. "Shut up! Ow!" He lurched down the final steps and dropped her, feet first.

She tottered against a plastered wall, struggling for balance. If Amar was attempting reconciliation, he was failing! Ela turned from the wall, longing to wound him. Viciously. "Listen, you—!"

She gasped, now recognizing this room and its occupants. Sius and Za'af Chacen loomed behind Amar, smirking, their eyes flint-dark and hateful—just as she'd seen in this afternoon's vision. Sius asked, "Did you think we'd let you escape punishment for what you've done?"

Ela shrieked a frantic prayer. "Infinite!"

A heated blue-white gleam appeared in her palm, swift and brilliant as lightning, forming the branch. She swung a wide arc at her attackers and all three fell back, yelling and clutching their faces. The stench of seared flesh filled the room. The deceivers vanished like smoke blasted by a ferocious, cleansing wind.

Ela fled for the stairs, praying the young men wouldn't follow her.

They didn't.

She dashed up the stairs, shoved open the door, and staggered onto the high terrace, gasping for air. If she were a cursing sort, she'd curse Amar and the Chacens now. Her gasps became sobs, and she blinked at tears.

Despite her shakiness, Ela rushed along the path toward the temple. She should have been more watchful. She shouldn't have asked her parents to avoid the temple tonight. Yet her beloved Creator had protected her. . . . Her voice wavering, pathetic, she whispered, "Infinite."

I am here.

"I know." Tears slid down her face now. "Thank You." Hurried footsteps clattered on the paved path behind her. Were Amar and the Chacens planning to throw her off the wall? Ela turned, braced for battle. From now on, if she survived, she would take the street-level path to the temple. Winding and lengthy as it was, at least she couldn't be shoved off a ledge to her death. A gray-clad figure hesitated. A woman. Sharp brown eyes in a thin face. "Matron Prill."

"Yes." Ela's childhood foe approached, clearly concerned. "Why are you crying?"

Infinite, You sent her, didn't You?

Yes.

All right. For whatever reason, she would accept Prill's presence. Ela cast a nervous glance up the path, beyond the matron, toward the entry door. Stillness met her gaze. Only the leaves fluttered in the tiny terraced garden. Where were those three young men? Undoubtedly planning trouble. To Matron Prill, she said, "Pray for me, please."

"I'd like to walk with you," the woman said. She matched her steps to Ela's as they moved along. "I presume you are going to the temple."

"You know I am." Beyond doubt, the Roehs' habits were too predictable.

"But won't you tell me why you are crying?"

Did the matron have to sound so kind and concerned? Fresh tears welled, stinging Ela's eyes as she marched onward. "Amar and the Chacens were tormenting me." Really, she had to set aside thoughts of the attack before fear rendered her useless as a prophet. No doubt just as the Chacens intended.

"Huh. Those reprobates! The Chacen boys are married, yet they're seducing girls and leading them into Atean shrines. Forgive me for being blunt, Ela, but it's true. And evidently you're their next victim. Why there's no outcry about their shameless behavior, I don't know. It seems you need a chaperone."

Chaperone? The question Ela wanted to ask about the shrines was choked off by Prill's observation. Infinite? *She's* my new chaperone?

Behave.

"I'm trying," Ela muttered.

"Trying what?" the matron demanded.

"Nothing." While resigning herself to the situation, Ela felt obliged to warn the woman. "If you're seen with me, you'll become a target."

"I'm already a target." Amusement lightened Prill's words and her face, making her look more like a girl than a stern childless widow. "Do you think I'm so easily scared? Your parents and I have gathered enemies for speaking out against that so-called goddess Atea's shrines."

"I've heard. The Infinite sees your faithfulness, and He will bless you."

"I felt it was nothing but my duty." They turned a corner and trekked toward the temple's vast public courtyard. Prill said, "I must be honest. When you became prophet, Ela, I felt as if the Infinite had slapped me. Who would ever think that the Roehs' sassy, irritating little girl would be called by the Infinite? But you *have* become His prophet, and Parne needs you."

"Hmm." All right. That was a compliment. If Kien were here, he'd be laughing. Kien . . . Ela smiled. Perhaps enduring Prill wouldn't be awful as she'd imagined. And didn't her chaperone's honest observation deserve a truthful response? "Matron, when I was a little girl, I didn't understand you. I thought you were mean, interfering, and always tattling on me to my parents."

Matron Prill halted in her tracks and stared at Ela, obviously shocked. "Well . . ."

Ela hugged the woman as a peace offering, then nudged her onward. "Thank you. I understand now. Are you certain you want to be caught in my company?"

Prill took two stammering tries to respond. "Oh . . . well . . . of course. You do need a chaperone, and your parents are mightily overwhelmed with that new baby and your father's failing business. Besides, I'm convinced the Infinite sent me."

"You're right. He did." Meaning every word, Ela said, "I appreciate your kindness."

Her new chaperone's chin quivered as if she were about to cry. Ela linked arms with her. "Let's pray for courage. You know . . ." Ela studied Prill again. "You don't look as old as I remember. And nowhere near as . . . er . . . mean. Actually, you're quite sweet and kind."

The woman sniffled and worked up an ineffective scowl. "Nonsense. Obviously, you're the one who's aged, Ela Roeh. Though you're sassy as ever."

"I suppose I can't argue." As they entered the temple's courtyard, the branch glittered in Ela's hand. Her hand that ought to be broken. Or at least badly bruised and scraped. She'd been healed, and she hadn't noticed. *Infinite, You are amazing! Why . . . ?*

Beside Ela, Prill interrupted her thoughts. "What's about to happen?"

"Um." Ela blinked and looked away from her hand, pulling together her wits. "I suppose I'm about to become the least popular person in Parne."

"You are taking my role," her elder complained.

"You're not sorry, are you?"

"I suppose it's nice to have company." Prill pinched Ela's sleeve in the traditional Parnian-chaperone bid for attention. "Where are we going?"

"To the temple's door."

"And what, pray tell, are you about to do?"

Despite her distress, Ela smiled. A gentle current of words slipped through her mind, conveying some of Prill's past thoughts concerning the temple. "I'm about to do what you've longed to do for years."

In Ela's healed hand, the branch blazed, fueled by the Infinite's righteous wrath.

◆ ◆ ◆

Her heartbeat quickening, Ela called to the growing crowd, "Why are you here? Do you believe the Infinite wants your sacrifices after you've bowed before the altars of Atea? After you've offered your bodies and hearts to a nonexistent goddess?"

While some of the worshipers seemed indifferent, or merely curious, more than a few gave her scornful looks, as if to say, *Fool, what do you know?*

"Hypocrites! Liars!" Ela returned their scowls. "You're saying to yourselves, 'We're Parnians. We can worship as we please! We're safe because we obey our traditions.' But you're wrong! Do you think your Creator hasn't seen what you're doing? Or that He hasn't noticed the stains on your souls?"

Priests paraded down the temple's steps now, white-robed, their lips tight with irritation at her for delaying their work. Ela included them in a cold, sweeping gaze. "Do you believe the Infinite approves your offenses? By His own righteousness, He cannot! Parne has not obeyed its Creator or responded to correction. Truth has perished here. And Parne has been judged."

She had the crowd's attention. But not its support. How could they be so blind? Fresh tears threatened to fall. "Your ancestors wouldn't listen to the prophet Eshtmoh when he warned Parne of these offenses—just as you won't listen to me, but I'm warning you again! The Infinite has abandoned you! Belaal is assembling its army to invade Parne's lands, and other tribes will join Belaal before Parne's walls. Parne is about to be conquered. And those of you who stand by idly, thinking none of this matters—you're wrong! Your indifference has ensured Parne's death."

Numerous would-be worshipers laughed and shook their heads. Ela unknotted her white linen sash and then lifted it above the crowd. "You don't believe what I've told you! You think your souls are as pure as this linen. But you're lying to yourselves! Soon you'll see this belt is unfit for use, as you are unfit for your Creator."

The instant she'd spoken against their traditions, Ela felt loathing rise from the crowd and dash toward her like a wave rushing at a coastal shore. She gripped the pristine linen. "The next time you see this cloth, you will see your souls as the Infinite sees them! You've defiled yourselves and your temple by abandoning the Infinite. Therefore, He has abandoned you!"

A man stepped forward from the crowd, his dark brown eyes and majestic stance mocking Ela before he spoke. She recognized Zade Chacen, Parne's former chief priest, whom she'd ousted on the Infinite's orders. Chacen sneered. "*You* are a child. A mistaken child!"

Murmurs of approval greeted his sentiment. Ela studied Chacen and heard his thoughts plotting her downfall. Infinite, how could this man have been Parne's spiritual leader?

Emotions caught hold of Ela's soul, painful enough to make her wince. She fought down the urge to wail and tear her hair like a mourner preparing to seal off one of Parne's tomb houses.

"Chacen, you traitor! The Infinite asks you, and all those who follow your faithless ways, why have you angered Him by yielding to your desires and chasing after idols that don't exist? Do you think those little non-gods like Atea can help you?"

Zade Chacen laughed, gesturing broadly, as if to take in the crowd around him as kindred. "Do I look like someone who needs help? Do any of us need your help, little girl?"

Ela swallowed the lump forming in her throat and forced herself to speak past the pain. "You—all of you—believe you're strong. Whole. And healthy. But I see ashes where there was living flesh. I hear wailing from a distant land. And an outcry from heaven as your Creator mourns for His people, who refuse to be healed!"

She was crying again. So undignified. Weak! How could the Infinite have chosen her as His prophet? She was useless! Composing herself, she stared Chacen in the eyes. "Do you remember my first prophecy, Zade Chacen?"

He stared, maliciously unforgiving and silent.

Matching her fierceness to his, Ela said, "You believe it won't happen. You've told yourself that I'm a false prophet. But the Infinite hasn't forgotten. 'As a sign to you, your sons will die on the same day, during a terrible calamity.' That day is near, Chacen!"

The deposed chief priest climbed the steps. "We'll see, won't we, girl? Now step aside! The priests are waiting, and you have delayed Parne from fulfilling its duties."

To Chacen, and everyone, Ela cried, "Yes, enter the temple! Burn your sacrifices! But the Infinite won't attend your dead rituals. Instead, this temple will burn with this cursed city!"

Clutching the spotless sash, Ela descended the temple's steps. Beautiful white stone steps, leading false devotees to futile worship.

The priests marched past, some avoiding her gaze, others barely concealing their smirks.

A voice beside her hissed, "Stupid things! Fools!" Matron Prill wrapped a thin arm around Ela as if she could protect her from the crowd's animosity.

A young woman wearing an elaborate silver cuff, etched with the goddess Atea's serpentine coils, shoved Ela. Others added jabs and taunts as Ela wove a path through the temple's public courtyard. A young man, his hands clenched into fists, stepped in their way and didn't move. Ela looked up at him.

Sius Chacen. With a stark black slash seared like a brand into his right cheek. Around the black gash, the skin was puffed, blistered, and painfully crimson. His dark eyes glittering with hatred, he said, "We've decided how you will be repaid. Prophet."

"Young man, you are a disgrace." Prill sniffed.

Sius heard and muttered, "You're next, woman."

"Hmph!" The matron tugged Ela's sleeve. "Come along, Ela. Let's leave this trash on the pavings, shall we?"

Ela felt Sius watching her as they departed the temple's vast courtyard.

Infinite? Why couldn't I have been warned about Chacen's sons plotting with Amar?

What were you doing when Amar snatched you?

Running along the high path to the temple. And praying.

Praying for whom?

For the people of Parne to . . . Her thought faded as she sensed her Creator's response.

Do not pray for those faithless ones! Don't intercede for them, because I will not listen to you!

Ela's steps faltered. How could she cope with the Parnians if she couldn't pray for them? At least praying had given her some hope that Parne's situation might change. But now the hope was gone. Undoubtedly the Infinite knew her prayers were useless—wasting her strength. Now it seemed she must pray for the faithful alone. And yet . . . and yet . . . even Zade Chacen's soul—

"Watch where you're going," the matron scolded. "My, my, but you're distracted."

"Yes. Thank you." Giving herself an inward shake, Ela abandoned despairing thoughts of Parne's lost souls and focused on the homeward path—a different trek from her usual one. All the better. Amar would have to guess at her whereabouts from now on. But how could she completely avoid him? Or the Chacens? Reprobates! What were they planning now?

In despair, she sorted through possibilities until they descended into the small public square that fronted the Roeh home.

Father was waiting for Ela in the doorway. He met her gaze and crossed his arms. Not good. Behind him, Jon Thel stepped out of the house, one hand readied to draw his sword. Oh, a bad sign!

"Mercy," Prill murmured. "Your father looks *furious.* What do you suppose has upset him?"

✦ 15 ✦

Dan Roeh's gaze remained steadfast, fixed on Ela as if trying to wrest every thought from her mind. "What happened?"

"I . . ." Ela hesitated. How much should she say? Infinite, help! "I was going to ask you the same question. Why are you two waiting outside? What's wrong?" How could they know she'd been in trouble?

Jon seemed ready to lead a skirmish. "You tell us. Scythe went wild and tried to hammer down the city's gate. Were you hurt?"

Ela gulped. "Um, I'm fine now. Is Scythe all right?" Poor Pet! She'd forgotten about her destroyer's protective instincts.

"Yes," Jon grumbled. "He's settled down now. But I had to bribe the watchman to let us in to check on you."

"Us?" Heart sinking, Ela asked, "Did you bring Scythe?"

"I left him with Savage and Audacity. Beka insisted on coming with me."

Matron Prill's thin face reflected disapproval. "Who are Scythe, Savage, and Audacity? Are these some rough companions you've gathered, Ela?"

"Rough?" Ela smiled weakly, remembering the destroyers' irritable faces. "Yes, very."

Father cut the conversation short. "What happened? Did you provoke a riot at the temple?"

"No. Those Atea-lovers wouldn't listen to me. But before

that—" Ela fought a sudden fit of nerves. "The Chacens threatened me."

"As did Amar," Matron Prill added. "Dan, he's become incorrigible."

Father's brown eyes widened. "Did he dare to touch you?"

"Yes." Before Father could go storming off to beat Amar and add to the Roehs' difficulties, Ela added, "But I'm fine, Father, really. And thanks to the Infinite, I left Amar and the Chacen brothers with scars."

"Oh!" Prill clasped her hands together. "*You* branded Sius Chacen's cheek? Ela, that's perfect! I wondered what happened to him. Now, Dan Roeh, trust me, you needn't bash those miscreants further. Their marks are set for terrible infections, I'm sure."

Jon laughed, his militant stance easing. "I should have known! Ela, you *branded* them?"

"The Infinite did. I'm glad you're amused." Ela touched Dan Roeh's arm, the white sash fluttering between them. "Father, I know you're worried, but the Infinite will deal with Amar. Furthermore, Matron Prill has agreed to accompany me everywhere."

"Good," Dan said. "And if Prill is unable to accompany you in Parne, you *wait* for your mother or for me. Do you understand?"

"Yes, Father. Unless the Infinite wills otherwise." And neither her parents nor Prill were as strict with her as the Infinite, the Ordainer of parenthood.

Beka appeared in the doorway now, holding Jess. Naturally. She swept Ela with a head-to-toes glance. "You're safe? Ela, the way Scythe reacted, we thought you'd been knifed."

"Not yet." Remembering Zade Chacen's hatred, her breath snagged in her throat. She mustn't think about future attacks or she'd be incapacitated by terror. Think of something else. Think of others. "Beka, I know you want to stay to keep guard over me, but you must leave Parne soon." She glanced at Jon, adding, "When you go, please take Scythe. He can't protect me and neither can you. I don't want to see any of you hurt for my sake."

"We'll leave when we're ready," Jon said, an edge to his smile now. "In twelve days."

"Will your supplies last that long?"

"We're being frugal." Beka lifted her chin in something approaching smugness. "I'm an excellent household manager when I want to be."

Jon nodded, his gaze now on Jess. "In twelve days, we'll buy our supplies for the journey to Istgard. Once we've arrived there, if need be, I could arrange a loan." He lifted Jess from Beka's arms. "May I?"

"No!" Beka pouted.

Jess beamed at them, a toothless baby smile that wrung Ela's heart.

Twelve days until Jon and Beka departed. Thirteen days until Belaal.

Infinite, she implored silently, *protect those who love You!*

A waiting calm enfolded her.

Despite Father and Matron Prill's sharp-eyed stares.

✦ ✦ ✦

As Matron Prill stood guard, shielding her from the gazes of passersby, Ela tucked the white sash into a crevice at the base of one of Parne's public wells, wedged mud against it, then dusted it with sand to cover her fingermarks. Good enough.

Ela stood, rubbed her grimy hands together, then retrieved the branch from its resting place, set against the well's carved-stone sides. "Now we wait."

Obviously less than pleased, Prill waved her handbasket at Ela and whispered, "Did you really bury that lovely fabric there? Ela! What will your mother say?"

Keeping her voice low, Ela leaned toward her fussing chaperone. "What can she say? I'm obeying the Infinite's command. Mother would do the same in my place."

"It makes no sense."

"It'll be a sign to Parne," Ela explained. "Everyone saw me wearing it at the temple."

Prill exhaled a gusty disapproving breath. "Well. If the Infinite commanded it, then I suppose it must be endured. What now?" Lips primmed, the matron asked, "Will we be safe walking through the marketplace? I need some spices and dried fruit, and you'd best tell me now if we're going to be chased off before I can buy my food."

Go, the Infinite prompted.

To the marketplace again? Ela nodded to Prill. "Yes, I suppose I've reason to go."

As they entered the bustling public square, Ela looked for Amar and the Chacens. Where were they? Not that it mattered, Ela realized. She apparently had enough enemies in the marketplace to keep her on alert as Prill bargained for her modest pinches of spices and handfuls of fruit. Merchants' scowls met Ela's approach, and glares followed her as she trailed Prill through the market, perusing the wares. Many of these same merchants had gladly dealt with Ela before she'd become a prophet. This morning, however, they were turning their backs to her.

It seemed that telling the truth was an unofficial crime.

At last one of the spice merchants, Deuel, beckoned Ela. He'd traded with Mother in the past and spoke to her of the Infinite. Now his thick black eyebrows lifted like two crescents, as if he was eager to tell Ela a secret. Curious, she approached. Deuel grinned. "Prophet!"

As Deuel spoke, his face changed, his skin cracking and peeling back in murky layers that dissipated like smoke swept away in a breeze. In that same instant, the light in his eyes blazed, then faded to a normal, mortal gleam. His flesh, too, became normal within a breath. As if a deceiver had passed through him to taunt her. Ela froze. Was Deuel vulnerable to false worship? Infinite?

Look at his hands.

Ela glanced down at the token Deuel seemed prepared to give

her. A clay spice box, engraved with the triple coils of Atea. "Ugh!"

"What's wrong?" Deuel huffed. "All I wanted was to present you with a little peace offering, but you're behaving as if it's rubbish."

Ela looked from the box to Deuel. Why had she never noticed such signs of faithlessness before? The spiritual adultery in people she'd known her entire life?

Because now you see through eyes aided by My Spirit.

As Ela swallowed, Deuel's expression shifted to impatience. "Ela," he scolded, "you're going to shun my gift? Don't be so simple! So single-minded! Life is too complicated to be confined to one narrow little set of rules."

"Is it narrow?" Ela asked, aware of the branch's inner fire threading to the surface—strengthening her. "I've never felt confined." Her throat hurt. "Deuel, don't you understand the Infinite's sorrow? If you're playing a double-game spiritually, you're guaranteed to lose!"

"All you're doing is breaking your own heart and driving yourself mad."

"Breaking my heart, yes. Madness? No."

"If that's what you want to believe. So you won't take my gift?"

Give him your last tenth-weight for it.

What? Infinite! Those goddess-coils—

Imagery took form within her mind, hushing her. She slid the last bit of silver from her purse, placed it on Deuel's makeshift counter, and held out her hand. "Thank you, Deuel. But may I offer you some advice?"

"Of course."

"Reconsider the Infinite. He calls to you. Deny Him and you'll die within two months, though that's not His preference. Please."

The spice merchant's mouth twisted, but he nodded, as if indulging her foolishness.

Unseen pains of betrayal sliced at her, as if carved into her flesh. She looked around, surveying the marketplace. Spices.

Silver. Some fruits and vegetables. Oil. Wine. Various bags of grains. Meat. When she was a child, this marketplace had seemed so immense. So rich and full of good things. But not now. Had the marketplace shrunk? A prickling sensation crawled over Ela's arms, making her shiver. She stifled her new fear, unwilling to face it yet.

Measuring her surroundings against the image she'd just seen, Ela strode to the busiest section of the public square. Footsteps sounded just behind her, accompanied by Prill's breathless voice. "Ela! Goodness, where have you been? What's wrong?" She glanced at the clay storage box in Ela's hand. "Oh! *Why* would you carry such a thing?"

"I'm carrying it no farther. Stand back, Matron, please."

Wary, Prill stepped back, clutching her basket of fruit, grain, and spices. Ela looked around and recognized this place, this instant. Here were the merchants and market-goers she'd seen. And there was the contingent of priests, white-clad and proud, entering the market with Parne's wealthiest elders, eager to buy. And to be recognized and honored.

Ela raised her voice. "Parnians! This is what your Creator, the Infinite says! 'Listen! I am going to bring such disaster to this city that everyone who hears of it will shudder!'" All faces turned to her now, gaping. Staring.

Ela continued. "'You have forsaken Me and given yourselves to gods that Parne's first citizens never worshiped! You build shrines and burn incense and offer even your children to gods who don't exist—sacrifices I've never commanded of you!'"

Only the priests moved now, drawing near, their faces seeming carved as stone, cold and condemning. Ela lifted her chin at them. "The Infinite says, 'I will devastate Parne and make it a terror to travelers—an awful joke to foreigners! Your bodies will become carrion for birds and . . . '" Horror-struck by a final breath of imagery, she added, "' . . . those who survive will be so desperate for food that they will gnaw the flesh of the dead!'" Oh, Infinite, no!

You have warned them of the truth. An unseen nudge prompted her further. *The box*.

As commanded, Ela raised the clay goddess-box and smashed it on the marketplace's stone pavings. Shards of pottery flew toward the priests, who leaped away, shocked. Ela cried, "The Infinite will smash this city, just as this clay container is smashed and can't be repaired!"

One of the priests nudged a shard with his elaborate shoe and shook his head at Ela. "Tch-tch-tch!"

Her spirit almost failing, Ela turned away from the priests, lifted Prill's basket from her arms, and swept out of the marketplace. Twelve days until Belaal.

Father. She must speak to Father about her fears.

Kien called down the cold, bleak, echoing street. "In six days, the Infinite will destroy Adar-iyr. Repent and be saved!"

It was a wonder his voice hadn't given out—with his mind. Each morning, he cheered himself along, celebrating by changing one word in his predetermined litany. He'd begun at twenty-one days. Today was six. Tomorrow would be five!

Unless he was blessed enough to be stolen by pirates and rowed out to sea.

No . . . Forget anything to do with sailing. The sea beast would be waiting to gulp him down and heave him up again in Adar-iyr. Better to keep walking and watch where he was going—the clouds had darkened the daylight to twilight murkiness. He trudged into an alley and called out his obligatory twelve words. But why was he yelling down a deserted street?

Picking his way across a fly-swarmed rubbish heap, Kien turned wearily down the next street. Somewhere, a door slammed. Nearby, a shutter snicked closed. He bellowed his warning, then ambled to the next thoroughfare and frowned at the quiet marketplace.

Where were all the citizens this morning?

Kien sighed, raised his voice, howled the admonition, and

trudged onward. Something bashed into his chest, making him gasp. A loaf of bread dropped at his feet. What a waste.

Surely there were people starving in this city who would welcome this now-dusty bread.

Such as him.

Infinite? May I speak to these men, to return this bread and to warn them?

Yes.

Thank You. Kien looked around at the lifeless marketplace and its idle vendors. "Whose bread is this?"

"Yours now!" one of the vendors snapped. "No one else is around to eat it!"

Did he catch a whiff of blame in the man's words? Kien approached him. "Why are you so upset? Look—here's your bread." He set the bread on the edge of the vendor's stall. "I'm returning it."

The vendor shoved the loaf back at him. "Keep it! Everyone's fasting." The vendor's sculpted mustache twitched above his skewed lips as his tone and words accused, "Because of you! The king's ordered us all to pray to the Infinite and fast and mourn and repent with all our hearts."

The king had . . . what? Kien stared. Fast? Mourn? Repent? Seriously?

"Well, look at the bright side," another vendor called out in a cheery voice. "I haven't seen a murder all day. And the sackcloth merchants are earning their keep for once! Poor fools. Usually no one touches their wretched fabric."

Kien eyed the man's sleeve and noticed its coarse material. That stuff had to chafe. He winced. "Everyone's fasting and wearing sackcloth? And repenting?"

The cheery one grinned. "Isn't that what we just told you? Look here." He poured Kien a cup of liquid. "Purified fortified water. Help yourself. Go sit down and eat that bread. Have some meat. There's some fruit. No one's buying and it'll just rot." Quietly, he added, "With my thanks. The marketplace hasn't been this calm and safe in years! You need to keep up your strength while you continue to curse our city, eh? Blessings of our Creator as you go."

Dry-mouthed, Kien accepted the water. But he didn't consider eating the bread until he'd walked through half the marketplace with all the merchants handing him food—accompanied by their opinions of his mission's success. A marketplace cook slapped a heap of grilled meat into flatbread for Kien. "You've ruined us financially for now, but I haven't seen a theft in two days. I say, bless the Infinite!" He chased Kien onward with an encouraging nod and a wave of his sackcloth sleeve.

The entire city was fasting. And wearing sackcloth. And praying. Infinite . . . !

A slender, pretty girl with golden-brown hair stopped before him, hefting a roll of sackcloth. She smiled at Kien, elated. "If my arms weren't full, sir, I'd kiss you!"

He stared, then recognized the young prostitute who'd accosted him on his first day in Adar-iyr. Clean-scrubbed now, and the most radiant sight in the overcast marketplace, the girl hugged the sackcloth close. "My father has finally agreed to wear this stuff and bow to the Infinite! Furthermore, *I* am becoming a proper seamstress and determined to remain so—though I hope I'll progress from stitching only sackcloth robes." Lowering her voice, she added, "You frightened me to bits when I first saw you, but thank you for caring! Bless the Infinite and His monster that spat you onto the beach!"

Dazed, Kien watched the girl near dancing from the marketplace with all the giddiness of a freed soul. Surrounded by the Infinite's joy.

Infinite? I almost didn't recognize her.

An overwhelming whirlwind of jubilation spun Kien, as if his Creator had swept him into an impromptu dance of celebration. *She is new in My sight—My own precious child!*

Astounding . . . Kien staggered, laughed, scoffed at his own clumsiness, then gripped a marketplace stall to settle his euphoria-smacked mind. The young girl's fresh hopes, contrasted with the undoubted squalor of her previous life, chased his own miseries into nothingness.

Surely for her sake alone his task here *was* worthwhile.

His thoughts still spinning, Kien left the marketplace, too dazed to eat the food in his hands. After wandering down numerous streets, he noticed two rough-garbed men consistently turning after him at each corner. His senses sharpened. Were they following him?

Testing them, Kien turned another corner. When he was halfway down the street, they appeared. Definitely following him. Grim-faced. Swords readied.

Infinite? What now?

16

Before Father could step into the house, Ela grabbed his sleeve. "Father, do you know anything about Parne's provisions?"

Dan lifted an eyebrow. "Provisions? What do you mean?"

"I mean, the marketplace looks sparse. Doesn't Parne have food stored for emergencies?"

Covering her hand with his own, Dan said, "We've had no rain since the start of spring."

"Meaning . . . ?"

"There's been no harvest of any kind from our lands. Parne has been living on its reserves. We've sent traders to Siphra and Istgard for grain and fruit, but they haven't returned."

Ela pressed her knuckles against her mouth.

Father was talking, drawing her attention. "The fields flowered early this year—they were beautiful. Filled with blooms that even the elders had never seen in their lifetimes."

My last gift to Parne.

"Everyone believed we'd have a magnificent harvest this year, and the entire city celebrated."

They made offerings to Atea and gave themselves over to her.

Sensing the endless depths of her Creator's grief, Ela felt the blood drain from her face.

I will send no more rain to refresh Parne.

Instead, He sent her glimpses of forthcoming misery. Buckets lifted from Parne's wells. Dry. Grain bags emptied. Cattle, pets, and mice consumed. Emaciated faces staring at her. Accusing her. The trickle of imagery multiplied, pouring through her thoughts like an unleashed flood. Caught in the vision's current, Ela rocked on her feet, covering her eyes with her hands.

Father gripped Ela's shoulders and steadied her. "What are you seeing?"

"Famine," Ela whispered. "Disease . . . rotting flesh." Why couldn't she stop her arms and legs from trembling? The vision's pain increased. Multiplied to agony.

She dropped into darkness as Father yelled her name.

✦✦✦

"I suppose," Prill said, watching Ela dig out the linen sash from its hiding place at the public well, "if it's not too filthy, we could sun-bleach it."

"There'll be no bleaching this. Just as there's no bleaching Parne." Ela caught the sash's edge and drew it from the crevice at the well's base. The thick stink of mold clogged her nostrils even before she unfurled the fabric. She no longer recognized the exquisite sash. Gray. Not a hint of white anywhere. And the spots that weren't gray were mottled black. Or not there at all. Ela laced her fingers through a series of holes, amazed at how quickly the linen had rotted.

Prill knelt beside her now, lifting an edge of the ruined fabric. She looked from the sash to Ela, speechless at the ruin five days had wreaked on this linen.

Ela stood, raising the moldy fabric like a desolate banner in the dry, quiet air. Parne's women and children watched while waiting their turns to draw water from the well. As they smirked and scoffed at the useless cloth, Ela called out, "Parne, here is your soul!"

A violent wind blasted downward from Parne's walls, encircling the public square, startling some of the women to shrieks. Within a breath, the angry current whipped the rotted sash from Ela's hands and sent it skyward, toward the temple.

Ela watched until it vanished behind the temple's ornate walls.

And until she realized Prill was crying. The woman dabbed at her dark eyes. "That's how the Infinite sees Parne's soul? Oh, Ela! What can we do?" She covered her face with her hands.

"We pray." Ela hugged the sobbing matron. "And I need to go home."

To wait for her enemies.

✦ ✦ ✦

Before Mother noticed, Ela hurried outside in the evening light to prevent the unwelcomed visitors from entering the house.

Their features set in unforgiving lines, the delegation of priests glowered at Ela. The eldest priest enunciated each syllable. "We want that rotten fabric off our temple's banner pole!"

"Why?" Ela demanded. "That rotten, moldy priestly linen allows Parne to see its soul as the Infinite does! Parne's decisions—its faithlessness!—has caused its destruction. Just as priestly hoarding of gold and rare ores brings Parne's enemies to its gate!"

A younger priest stepped forward, his marvelously groomed and oiled beard twitching with agitation. "You're refusing? That fabric is an insult to us and to the temple!"

"Why don't you discuss your concerns with the Infinite?" Ela snapped. "He would love to hear from *you* for once!"

Before she could blink, the young priest struck her, his fist a hammer-blow that sent her crashing against the front wall of the Roehs' home. Metallic bitterness seeped through her mouth. Blood from her lower lip. As Ela straightened, the eldest priest also hit Ela, his elaborate gold cuff gouging her left cheek as he slammed her against the wall once more. A woman—Mother—screamed from the doorway. "Ela!"

The younger priest beat Ela until the sky dimmed to gray. A deep humming filled her ears—cut through by his sudden bellow. "Augh!"

A woman's scream revived Ela. "Unhand my daughter! Stop!"

From a distance, a man yelled, "Disperse, all of you!"

The priests scattered like an ostentation of startled peacocks. Mother was beside Ela now, holding her, crying, shaking her. "Why didn't you tell me! Ela! Next time, you warn me!"

Ela lowered her face into her hands, staving off a wave of faintness. The humming and grayness eased. From within the house, Jess began to squall. And Tzana's thin voice piped up, "Mother? Mother?"

Father was holding Ela now, but he shouted over her head, "Jon, stop! Let them go." To Ela, he said, "Can you walk? Let's get you inside."

She stood, stumbled over something, and nearly fell. Mother's big wooden laundry stick rolled away from her toes. Ela crooked a smile at Mother. "You were going to beat them."

"Well . . ." Kalme hesitated. "I . . . I hit one of them."

Despite her bruises and the renewed taste of blood, Ela laughed and mumbled, "Mother, you would've been a wonderful prophet."

"No I wouldn't! I wanted to kill them all!" Kalme's fingernails dug into Ela's arm, making her gasp. "Oh. Sorry!" Kalme relaxed her grip and urged Ela toward a mat.

The instant Ela sat down, Tzana was in her lap, touching Ela's cheek, peering into her eyes, then checking her lip. "Does it hurt too much? Can I help you?"

"I'll be fine."

Kalme hurriedly scooped up the wailing Jess, then snatched up a clean towel and crossed the room to the family's big golden-clay water jug. Father half knelt beside Ela.

Jon, standing guard at the door, stepped aside, allowing Beka to enter, her arms full of parcels. While Jon shut the door, Beka dumped the parcels on the floor and knelt. "Oh, Ela, what an awful cut! Your poor face! Who were all those men?"

"Priests." Ela accepted the damp towel from Mother and rested it against her lip. A sharp sting of pain made her flinch before the water's coolness soaked into the wound.

She looked from Beka to Jon, then to Father. "You were in the marketplace again?"

Father glanced up at Mother, then at Tzana, as if deciding whether or not to speak. He squared his shoulders. "I'm trying to gauge Parne's food supplies."

Mother sat down, with Jess tucked beneath her mantle, nursing. Dark eyes wary, Kalme asked, "What aren't you telling me?"

Dan sighed. "If Parne is besieged by Belaal within a week, as Ela says, then we're all in danger. Parne will be out of food as the siege begins, unless our traders arrive from Istgard and Siphra."

Ela braced herself, catching renewed glimpses of the beleaguered, sodden traders. "They won't." She licked her swelling lip again. "The rains that are bypassing Parne are delaying the traders."

"What will we do?" Kalme hugged Jess's bundled form closer.

Shifting the cloth from her lip to her bruised left cheek, Ela said, "We must urge everyone to not fight Belaal—or anyone."

Dan grunted. "They won't listen to us. We're in disgrace and untrustworthy."

Sounding a bit shamed, Beka said, "Jon and I think that perhaps we should stop buying supplies from the marketplace. We're taking food from Parne."

"You're obeying the Infinite," Ela soothed. "Both of you. And your attendants. You mustn't feel guilty."

"We'll protect anyone who comes with us," Jon promised. He looked at Kalme now. And Tzana, who was leaning against Ela in silent sympathy. "Perhaps you should accompany us to Istgard."

Kalme stiffened, clutching Jess beneath her mantle. "I'm not leaving unless my entire family does."

"I can't leave," Ela said. "But, Mother, Father, think of Jess and Tzana. You should go."

Father shook his head. "No. Those renegade priests will kill you, Ela, if you stay."

"If I'm meant to die, Father, we won't be able to prevent it."

Dan shot her a look of fierce disagreement. Ela shut her eyes, sending up a silent prayer for her family's safety. For the safety of Parne's remaining faithful ones. Tranquility answered, reassuring her, though she couldn't offer the answers her family and friends wanted. "All we can do is pray and know that He is here."

Quiet tapping sounded on the doorpost. Jon readied his sword, then nudged open the door, revealing a young couple, both draped in subdued mantles. The man's thin face was bruised, and the young woman's eyes were reddened and swollen from crying.

Ela had seen the young man only once, but she remembered him. Ishvah Nesac. Parne's new chief priest, whose heart ever longed for the Infinite. At their Creator's command, she'd declared Ishvah as Zade Chacen's successor. Now, obviously, Ishvah and his wife were suffering for their love of the Infinite. Aching, Ela murmured, "Jon, you can trust them."

Dan Roeh stood. "Come in. Both of you, please."

Balancing herself with the mantle-swathed Jess, Kalme stood beside her husband. "We're honored. Please sit down. Can you eat with us?"

While Ela pondered a way to stretch about five portions of bread and lentils to feed eight, Ishvah Nesac worked up a wry smile. When he spoke, his voice was bleak. "Honored? Thank you, but I don't deserve such kindness."

Tears slid down his wife's soft face. As she lifted her mantle to dab at her eyes, Ela realized the Nesacs were expecting a child. Soon. Oh, Infinite, not during a siege! Her heart skittered, caught mid-beat by a rush of compassion from their Creator.

Strengthened, Ela snuggled Tzana into her arms and hefted herself to her feet. "Chief Priest Nesac, you're mourning the Infinite's promise—that He would honor you as His chief priest. Why would you think He has forgotten you?"

Parne's chief priest fought for composure. When his wife reached for his hand to console him, he kissed her braid-crowned head. They exchanged looks. Nesac said, "Prophet, it seems you've heard something from the Infinite. Tell me. Tell *us*. We're feeling rather lost right now."

Dan Roeh interposed, his voice low. "Forgive me, everyone, but you're in my home, and I believe you've been invited to sit." He motioned to the mats.

"We ought to leave soon," Jon told Beka. "The destroyers were probably in fits when Ela was beaten."

"Surely they've settled down now that she's safe," Beka pleaded. "And I've brought enough food for the evening meal. We can eat while we wait to see if those brutes return."

One corner of Nesac's mouth twisted, revealing bitterness as he surveyed Ela. "Let me guess who beat you, Prophet. A few of my priests?"

"They beat you too," Ela realized aloud, studying his bruises.

"For daring to correct them," Nesac agreed. "They've gold on their garments, but none in their souls. Only a few remain faithful to the Infinite—may He bless them!"

Cuddling Tzana again, Ela smiled at the Nesacs. "The Infinite sees your souls and, though you believe you've failed, He treasures you both. Ishvah Nesac, whatever those renegade priests have sworn, you remain His chief priest."

Nesac shook his head. "I don't understand why He should notice me at all. But for as long as He wishes, I'm the Infinite's servant. Despite the beatings." He patted his wife's hand, seeming to relax a bit.

Kalme gave the now-drowsing Jess to Nesac's wife, then hurried to remove platters, bowls, and cups from a storage shelf. Beka opened her parcels, revealing flatbreads, olives, dried fruit, and smoked, lightly charred meats. Jon beamed at her. "You're brilliant."

Beka fluttered her long eyelashes. "Dearest, I've been telling you that for years."

Everyone laughed. Nesac offered prayers and blessings to the Infinite, and they ate.

Within a few bites, however, Tzana dozed off, a limp weight in Ela's lap. She'd been sleeping more since their return to Parne, as if still recovering from their journey. Ela tucked her little sister close by on the mat and covered her with the new blue mantle, which Tzana loved.

At the meal's end, Jon and Beka prepared to leave for the night. Nesac and his wife stood. The young priest asked Jon, "May we walk with you? Our home is along the way."

"Of course," Jon said. But Ela noticed him double-check his sword, as if prepared to use it. Was Jon sure they'd be attacked on the way? She longed for some hint.

As he bid Ela good-bye, Nesac lowered his voice to a whisper. "Don't go outside if you can help it, Prophet. If you must, then be cautious and remain with others. The rebel priests are planning to kill you."

17

Kien glanced over his shoulder at the men who'd been trailing him for the past five days. Stone-faced, they stared. He smiled and waved. Eventually, they might tell him who they were. Whenever he'd tried to approach them, they'd backed off. Not that it mattered.

Tomorrow the Infinite would destroy Adar-iyr.

Or would He? Was Adar-iyr's state of mourning and repentance sincere?

Kien looked up at the brooding gray-black sky. Infinite? Now what?

Go to the king.

A final farewell? Kien turned down the next street and stepped onto a main thoroughfare. His two dour-faced shadows followed—his only shadows on this dark day. Kien toyed with the idea of darting through a few alleys to torment the pair. No, it was best to not provoke the Infinite. He'd promised to be a good herald of doom and follow orders.

As he neared the palace, Kien noticed his stalkers closing in. And brightening, as if pleased by his choice of destination. He felt a prickle of unease. Was he being set up to become a corpse?

No. The Infinite answered Kien's fear. *You will not die. Instead, you may now speak freely. You must tell Ninus I have heard his prayers and the prayers of his people. They are forgiven, and I have relented. Adar-iyr will be spared.*

Relief nearly halted Kien in his tracks. Yet he couldn't imagine the ineloquent King Ninus mustering a coherent prayer.

He strode through the palace's massive crimson and black gatehouse tunnel, which was crested with a mournful banner of sackcloth. By now Kien's followers were almost on his heels like proper shadows. In the garish courtyard, one of the palace guards nodded to Kien's followers, asking, "No trouble keeping him alive?"

"Nah," one of the shadows answered, surprisingly amiable. "He's a chary mark. But dull."

Due to his twelve-word vocabulary, of course. In his own defense, Kien sighed and feigned absolute boredom with his shadows. The palace guard snickered.

So Ninus had sent these men to protect him, not to beat him, or imprison him. Unusual concept for royalty, if Kien judged by his own experience in the former kingdom of Istgard.

The palace resounded with Kien's footsteps—and those of his shadow guards—but almost no one else's. No half-naked, drunken, murder-minded courtiers lurked about today. He enjoyed imagining them all in their respective cloud-darkened homes, swathed in itch-inducing sackcloth.

A familiar guard stepped in front of him and bowed his head. "Sir. Come this way."

Kien grinned. "Teos!"

The chief guard scratched at his haircloth-draped arm. "You remember me?"

"Could I forget Adar-iyr's most civilized citizen? By the way, I'm commanded to speak to the king. Will you send word to him that I'm here?"

"'Course." He motioned toward Kien's face. "Ha! You're done molting. Now you seem only sunburned, though there's no sunlight."

"Thank you. That's reassuring."

"And," Teos added, raising a perturbed eyebrow, "with all the extra skin gone, it's plain you're younger than we'd thought." Before Kien could respond, the chief guard marched off.

He reappeared swiftly, almost running. "Hurry, Tracelander, the king's waiting!"

Kien rushed after the guard, suddenly aware of his own disheveled appearance and pungent air. Living in Adar-iyr's streets had certainly imbued him with their stench. Ah, well. He'd keep his distance from the king, then return to the beach this evening for another bath and a shave. This nest of a beard surely made him look like a wild man.

The haircloth-clad King Ninus paced in his lamplit audience chamber, agitated as a flea. No slouching in his chair today. And he was thinner. More alert. Because of the haircloth and fasting, Kien suspected. The instant Ninus saw Kien, he signaled to his clerk, who hopped up from his clerkly cushion.

As tense, jittery, and sackcloth-irritated as the king, the clerk asked, "What news, sir? Have you some word from the Infinite?"

Kien allowed them a smile. "The Infinite has heard your prayers, O King, and the prayers of your people. Your Creator has forgiven you and relented. Adar-iyr will be spared."

Sunlight flashed through the windows, as if signaling divine agreement, startling them all with its brilliance. Ninus exhaled loudly, flung his hands in the air, uttered a celebratory syllable, then dropped to the floor and rested his royal forehead on the ornate sunlit tiles.

Caught off-guard by a mirroring rush of gratitude for his Creator's mercy to offenders—himself included—Kien knelt as well, offering the Infinite praise in the dazzling morning light.

✦ ✦ ✦

The royal clerk walked with Kien through the sunlit gardens toward the palace kitchens. "We are profoundly thankful that you have come to Adar-iyr. For weeks beforehand, the king was troubled by such dreams of disaster that he was quite terrified and unable to sleep." He paused and smiled—a remarkably toothy, boyish grin for a clerk. "Last night, however, he slept so soundly that we dared to hope for blessings from the Infinite."

"It was no coincidence," Kien realized aloud, stunned.

Infinite, You planned for my mission here while I was still at home in East Guard?

A jab of humor edged the Infinite's response. *Do you think your choices in ToronSea surprised Me?*

Obviously not. Kien had to force himself to pay attention to the clerk, who was, of course, nowhere near as interesting as their Creator. The man was actually babbling. "You must allow us to reward you. Stay in Adar-iyr! What do you want? Gold? Manors? A title? The king is prepared to grant you anything you wish as payment for your services."

"No." Kien shook his head. "No-no. I'm not staying, and I won't accept payment for serving the Infinite."

The clerk faltered a bit and went gloomy, as if dismayed. "What will you do? Can you tell us your plans?"

Infinite?

Munra, Siphra.

Siphra. Kien caught his breath. Ela! He could speak to Akabe about Parne. Couldn't he?

Yes.

Stuttering with relief, Kien said, "S-Siphra. I'm going to Munra, Siphra."

Administrative once more, the clerk nodded. "I'll make arrangements at once. But first, sir . . ." His nostrils flared. "Might I recommend food and a bath? And—at the king's request—permission to replace your, er, befouled garments?"

Kien laughed, stepping out of the clerk's scent range. "Yes. Thank you."

Ela. Soon, if the Infinite willed it, he would see Ela.

✦ ✦ ✦

Kneeling on the protective floor tiles, Ela waved the stiff woven-grass fan, urging the Roehs' small domed oven's flames to burn more vigorously. As she worked, she prayed.

Infinite? What is about to happen? She could almost feel heaviness in the air. Unvoiced threats sent prickles of apprehension along her scalp and down her spine.

Behind her, the mats crackled in a footstep tempo. Ela jumped, then sagged, sighing. Mother knelt and pressed one slender finger to her lips, signaling that she'd settled Jess and Tzana for their afternoon naps. Kalme reached for her mending but nodded toward a small trough of dough and to the oven's raised baking tiles. Reminding Ela to prepare the bread.

Ela nodded. She slapped flat rounds of bread onto the baking tiles and waited. Praying. And fretting. Really, her imagination was running rampant again. She ought to be grateful for this afternoon's peace. As she shifted the final round of bread from the tiles to a basket, a flare of light appeared in her hand, solidifying into the branch. Ela gasped, nearly dropping her precious insignia.

Kalme lowered her mending and whispered, "Ela? What's wrong?"

"I don't know." Infinite?

Go up to the temple. Hurry.

"But . . ."

A gentle knock sounded at the doorpost. Ela rushed to peek outside. Matron Prill.

Opening the door, Ela pressed a shushing finger to her lips. "Matron, it's good to see you, but why are you here?"

Blinking, as if confused, the woman said, "Weren't you expecting me?"

"It seems I was." Turning to Kalme, Ela whispered, "Mother, I'm going up to the temple. Don't worry, please. I'm sure we'll be fine." Or almost sure. A sense of renewed fretfulness made her dash through the doorway and grab Prill's hand. "Matron, how fast can you run?"

✦ ✦ ✦

Ela allowed Prill enough time to straighten her tunic and catch her breath before they entered the temple's main court. Prill complained to herself in whispers, between gasps, " . . . knew she was going to be difficult! . . . had to say yes, didn't you, Prill? . . . jumbled and jostled to bits, and it serves you right! . . . Infinite protect you!"

"He will," Ela promised. "Protect you, I mean."

"I should hope so!" The matron checked her brown topknot, then glared at Ela. "I'm ready, and I must say, Ela Roeh, I pray you're not wasting my time with all these commotions!"

"You can decide that for yourself." She led Prill into the temple's bustling main courtyard.

When they'd crossed halfway, the Infinite said, *Wait here.*

Ela stopped. Why? What's wrong?

The priests have elected your successor.

My what?! Infinite? Is this where I die? I thought it was supposed to be—

Did I say, "This is where you will die"?

No, but—

Listen. Watch. He poured thoughts and images through her mind, making her clutch the branch in an attempt to remain upright amid the mental torrent's force.

The vision eased swiftly. And certainly not as she wanted. No, no, no. Infinite, please!

Sick with horror, Ela opened her eyes and looked around. Would-be worshipers stood at cautious distances, whispering to each other and staring at her. Many scowling. Why were they so hateful? Didn't the rebels know how much she longed for each of them to live? How much she wanted to avoid what was about to happen? Despair tightened her throat. But let her Creator's will be done.

The temple's huge gilded bronze doors opened, guided by two rows of white-robed priests, who greeted worshipers. The priests noticed her and swiftly conferred among themselves. One rushed inside the temple, then reemerged with Zade Chacen, who behaved for all of Parne as if he were still the chief priest. A tall, elegant man walked behind Zade. Both men wore opulent gold-embroidered robes, and Zade's follower wielded an intricate silvered staff.

At an exaggerated gesture of courtesy from Zade, the elegant man descended the steps, smiling at Ela. She watched, nauseated, as he said, "I am Mikial Tavek, Parne's chosen prophet."

"Are you?" Ela called out. "If so, tell us about the vision the Infinite shared with you!"

Tavek lifted his chin, offended, his stiffly combed and waxed beard moving oddly with the motion. But his voice rang out, persuasive and authoritative as Ela imagined a prophet's voice should sound. "Listen to me, everyone! The Infinite promises you His protection! His love! His continued favor!" He deigned to glance at Ela. "Do not listen to those who try to frighten you with false warnings of death and Parne's destruction. They seek power through fear!"

Power through fear? Ela argued, "If only you knew how little I care for power! My concern is for you, and Parne. Mikial Tavek, if you value your life, please proclaim the Infinite's will, not your own. Don't rebel! You're a genuine prophet *only* if your predictions come true!"

"Indeed they shall," he said in an authoritative tone. "For I speak the Infinite's truth!"

"Tavek," Ela pleaded, desperation welling, "don't soothe listeners with lies and lead them into soul-ruining rebellion. Honor your Creator, or you'll die!"

He shot her a smirk, as if to say, *Poor deluded creature.* "I honor Him with every word."

Liar! He honored only himself. No deceivers needed to add to Tavek's personal love of evil. The branch gleamed now, sending out spirals of light that made the elegant Tavek squint. To counter the false prophet's prediction, Ela called out, "Parnians, listen to me! In five days Belaal's army will arrive in Parne! Within two months, the Infinite will bring down this temple and our city! To survive, you must surrender to the armies sent by your Creator! On the last day of besiegement, you must peacefully abandon Parne!"

"How dare you!" Tavek yelled, waving his ornately carved staff—his elaborate gilded mockery of the branch.

"Tavek, don't!"

"We are Parnians!" the false prophet proclaimed. "Beloved to the Infinite. He will protect us against our enemies! Yet you proclaim these insufferable disasters! Ela Roeh, how dare you!"

No! Couldn't she close her eyes and shut herself away from what was about to happen? Tears burning, Ela pronounced the Infinite's will. "Tavek, because you've lied and rebelled against your Creator, and because you tempt others to their destruction, He will remove His presence from you! Now!"

The branch flared, sun-brilliant, casting the temple's occupants into fiery silhouettes, making Ela gasp at its white-hot glow.

18

Ela burst into tears as Tavek's magnificent voice became a piercing shriek. A whirlwind swept above him, then vanished. Screaming, the false prophet staggered in the temple's public courtyard, his body becoming a grayed corpse before it crumbled on the white paving stones. Even his gold ornaments turned to dust, falling into tiny shimmering heaps where he'd stood.

As for his soul . . . "Oh no!" Ela remembered the agony of separation from her Creator. The endless fire. The overwhelming need for an absolute death to blot her soul from its searing existence. Her own torment had lasted a few useless breaths. But Tavek's agony was eternal.

Ela leaned on her vinewood staff and sobbed, stooped with the Infinite's grief.

Someone was clutching her, trembling. Matron Prill squeaked, "Ela! What have you done?"

Straightening, Ela cried, "Matron, why wouldn't he listen!" As if Prill had the answers. But the woman's terror brought Ela back from memories of eternal torment into this instant again. This existence. With worshipers screaming, retching, and fainting in the temple's open square. Priests dropping to their knees, stunned. And Chacen, backing away into the temple once more, though his face looked frozen in gaping wide-eyed shock.

Go home.

Home? Ela sniffled, then froze. Oh, Father and Mother were going to hear about this! She needed to tell them first. Ela snatched at one of Prill's cold hands. "Can you walk? We must go home. Come on, don't be afraid. I'm not the one who turned that false prophet to dust!"

"No?"

"Would you wish that on *anyone*, Prill? Tavek's Creator doesn't, but Tavek would have destroyed others' souls!"

"I'm going to be sick."

"Hurry and heave, then," Ela pleaded. "We must go. The Infinite commands it!"

Instead of doubling over, the matron straightened. Pale. Wobbly. And indignant. "Really! Turning ignorant men into screaming piles of dust was *not* part of our bargain."

Ela almost nudged Prill along with the branch like a sheepherder. The onlookers were stirring. Once they'd recovered, surely someone would mention the idea of stoning a certain dust-inducing prophet. "I'm sorry, but there's nothing I could have done about the situation. I tried to warn Tavek. You're free to un-chaperone me. Until then—home!"

"How, for the life of me, am I going to explain this to your parents?"

Let Matron Prill tell Mother and Father. Good idea.

✦ ✦ ✦

Crowds lined the sunlit streets, cheering and celebrating as Kien took his final walk through Adar-iyr, led by Teos and a glittering, armor-clad honor guard. Kien bit down a grin. No doubt Adar-iyr was glad to be rid of him. Yet the city's air of celebration was real, reflecting the Infinite's own joy. From all that Kien had seen and heard, the island-kingdom's citizens were celebrating freedom from years of terror induced by the violence and spiritual weakness of its own citizens.

"Infinite? Help Adar-iyr to remember its joy on this day and to remain resolute when faced with future temptations!" Praying, Kien followed Teos, turning down a magnificent white stone wharf that had obviously been swept and scrubbed clean.

A delegation waited for Kien beside the crimson-sailed ship hired to take him to Munra. Ordinary citizens and merchants, clad in summer-bright clothes, beamed at him, bowing as he approached. A small boy, prompted by one of the merchants, stepped forward. His eyes shining, the boy bowed to Kien. "Sir, thank you! I always feared for my life when I entered the city, but no more." A dimpled smile lit his tanned young face. "The day I saw you spit from that sea beast's mouth . . . Aw! It was amazing!"

Kien laughed, even as he felt a shaming blush. Oh, perfect. *This* was the boy who'd witnessed one of his most mortifying circumstances. "You're Old Hal's grandson?"

The little boy returned Kien's grin. "Yes, sir! And I told everyone what I saw—even the king! I had to let them know you weren't just some crazy man yelling in the streets."

Well, that explained a lot. Kien knelt, humbled that this vulnerable child had braved Adar-iyr's streets despite his terrors to warn others of the truth. "That took a soldier's courage, sir. A prophet's courage. Thank you—and I pray the Infinite blesses you!"

Old Hal crept forward now—nearly unrecognizable in fresh robes, with his silver hair trimmed and clean. Solemn as any dignitary, he nodded to Kien. "Pray for us, sir, as we pray for you, knowin' the Infinite's set you on another course. Long as mortals are breathin', there's never sure peace beneath these skies."

Teos stepped near and coughed. "Sir, the captain asks you aboard so as to not miss the tide."

Kien gave the boy a hearty hug of thanks, then stood and thumped Hal's shoulder, surprised by his own inability to speak. And his brief reluctance to board the waiting vessel.

Soon the ship retreated from the shoreline. Kien watched as sparkling blue-green waves broke against the ship's sides, foaming, then angling away with the current as the square-rigged ship lifted and fell in the waters. Ela would enjoy being in a ship on the ocean. However, the ocean's luster had vanished for him.

He now watched for sea beasts. His new lifelong fear.

To survive this voyage, he must banish all thoughts of monsters. Contemplate his work in Siphra, for Ela.

Ela . . . He ached to see her face. To tease her and laugh with her. Ela wouldn't have failed in ToronSea. But if she had, Kien suspected she would have had a better attitude about Adar-iyr. Yet despite Kien's own failings, the Infinite had forgiven the citizens of Adar-iyr. Cleared their grubby wax tablets—it seemed—of their moral and spiritual crimes. So, considering all the murders, violence, and immoralities of Adar-iyr, how was justice served?

Do you have the answer?

Kien's scalp tingled. How uncomfortable, realizing one's Creator could hear every thought. Bracing himself, he said, "You know my initial answer, sight unseen, would have been to destroy the entire city. Yet, I know Your answer is far superior to mine. Might You . . ." he felt uneasy asking, " . . . explain a bit of Your reasoning?"

You judged their outward forms. I judge hearts.

True.

I see what Adar-iyr's children will become. My desire is to save them for My own sake. After an eloquent silence, the Infinite added, *In this same way, I judged you.*

Sobering thought. Well, the sentence for his failure in ToronSea had certainly been life-changing. "Thank You. I didn't deserve Your mercy."

Yet mercy had been granted. To him, and to Adar-iyr . . .

"Sir?" The captain approached respectfully. Thus far, the entire crew had been appallingly obsequious, despite Kien's attempts to put them at ease. Now the captain extended a brass-bound sealed wooden box. "The king's clerk asked me to give you this once we were beyond the harbor. He said the king wishes to assure himself of his own peace."

Kien grasped the heavy box and eyed the seal. The captain offered him a knife.

"Thank you." He pried off the seal and lifted the box's gilded latch. A leather bag rested within, accompanied by a weighty gold pin embossed with what must be the king's personal insignia—a crown resting on the ocean's waves.

Despite the captain's obvious curiosity, Kien shut the box. He didn't have to open the bag to know it contained coins. Whether it was Adar-iyr's gold ninus, the Tracelands' silver drams and bits, or Siphra's gilded silver noble, Kien didn't care. Accepting and keeping money for warning Adar-iyr seemed dishonest somehow. Although he could now purchase courier birds and some parchment and ink to inform his parents and General Rol that he was alive and in Siphra.

And he could afford to eat during his last two weeks of military leave.

Fine. He would seek a worthy cause to donate the remainder to.

No . . . he had to pay the stables in ToronSea for boarding Father's puny horse. And the inn might charge him a watch-fee when he retrieved his gear. Which brought up the thought of renting a room somewhere in Munra.

"Infinite, thank You for making King Ninus a practical man."

Likewise, focusing on practicalities, Kien decided the first thing he must do in Munra was to send King Akabe a request to discuss Parne.

For Ela.

✦ ✦ ✦

Akabe of Siphra looked more civilized and much younger than Kien remembered. Hair trimmed, beard gone . . .

His gold-edged robes and mantle lifting with the swiftness of his walk, Akabe strode into the ornate room as if he were still uncrowned. Not as Siphra's Infinite-chosen king, anointed by Ela. Merely a wild hunter-rebel chasing prey through Siphra's Snake Mountains.

In his usual genial, lilting accents, Akabe said, "Ambassador! Or is it 'Commander'?" He laughed at Kien and gripped his hand in greeting. "What *are* you now? And why do you wear one of King Ninus's highest courtier's badges?"

Kien grinned and removed the gold pin. "Forgive me, Majesty. I decided your clerks and attendants would take me more seriously if I wore the gold."

"Is the badge yours?" Akabe asked, not a trace of suspicion weighing the question.

"Indeed it's mine, sir. I've just arrived from Adar-iyr."

Akabe made a face and sat in a chair. He motioned Kien to a nearby bench. "I've heard that Adar-iyr is a cesspit. Why would you go there?"

"To help clean things up a bit."

Akabe chuckled. "I do not see you emptying cesspits, Tracelander. No doubt your work in Adar-iyr was more than that. You will tell me everything, Ambassador. I demand it."

"Forgive me, O King, but I'm no longer an ambassador. I'm training to be a military judge-advocate for General Rol of the Tracelands, specializing in treaties." Before sitting, Kien slipped the gold pin into his coin pouch and eased his sword out of the way.

Akabe leaned forward, elbows on knees, his light brown eyes suddenly intense. "Is that your military sword?"

"It is."

"Azurnite?"

Was it acceptable to share knowledge of the military's Azurnite swords? Unsure, Kien smiled. And said nothing.

Akabe bounded from his chair. "May I see it?"

"Respectfully, sir, I must refuse until I've received clarification."

Growling, Siphra's king dropped into his chair once more. But a prankster's smile played over his face. "I'll see it before you leave Munra, Tracelander. You know I will. Now—" he shifted, relaxing—"tell me, how is the instigator of our revolution? My people speak of her often—your sister's friend, Ela of Parne."

Sister's friend. The description made Ela sound so remote. As if Kien had nothing to do with her. Yet it would be presumptuous of him to say that Ela was anything more than Beka's friend, or his own.

"You hesitate." Akabe leaned forward again. "Why? Is she dead?"

"No, but she is in danger. Which is why I wanted to talk with you."

All ease faded from Akabe's expression, replaced by a cool-eyed hunter's stare. "Talk then. I promise I am listening."

In rapid, sparse sentences, Kien described Ela's vision, her journey to Parne, and Belaal's impending attack incited by Parne's gold, gems, and its destructive ores, which could strengthen Belaal's military beyond imagining. "Have you heard anything of the ores she described, sir?"

Still serious, Akabe said, "I have heard rumors of Parne's ores, just as I have heard rumors of the Tracelands' Azurnite swords. Until my people obtain proof, how can we take action? Parne is no ally to Siphra; therefore, my people will not be interested in sending our army into Parne's territories. We'd be considered a hostile force." Scowling slightly, Akabe added, "Parne has nothing to recommend itself but its isolation, its temple, its wealth, and its prophet. Therefore, you must help me obtain proof that Parne possesses such dangerous ores, and that Belaal is determined to control them. Then I can persuade my council to fund this campaign. Meanwhile, I'll alert my commanders."

Kien groaned inwardly. As if he had solid proof of Belaal's treachery to present to Siphra! What Akabe required would take days. Perhaps weeks! He must send another message to General Rol and to Father, asking for information and indulgence for Akabe's Azurnite obsession. But these delays could cost him the chance to reach Ela before the siege. Kien's stomach clenched at the thought. He could only trust the Infinite's timing.

Infinite, protect Ela, please. Help me to reach her and save her from Parne!

✦ ✦ ✦

While Dan and Kalme retired to their secluded room, Ela snuggled Jess in her lap and tucked Tzana's blankets closer as the little girl rested in her puffy sleeping pallet. Though she was exhausted, Tzana didn't seem quite ready to shut her eyes. She tweaked Ela's dark, heavy braid and wound its end-curls around her small, gnarled fingers. "Jess and I want to hear a story," she pleaded. "Tell us one!"

Ela smoothed her baby brother's black curls as he gazed up at her. Adorable, plump . . . and obviously unaware that he wanted to hear anything. "Which story? You decide."

Tzana worked her thin eyebrows together in a wrinkly, pondering frown. Then her forehead smoothed and she lapsed into a blissful half-dreaming reverie. "Remember the tree, Ela? Before we went to visit Syb and Warden Ter?"

The tree. Syb. Warden Ter. Ela smiled, remembering the difficult journey to Istgard. And their imprisonment, with Warden Ter and Matron Syb guarding them. But before their imprisonment, the Infinite had blessed them with a haven in the desert. A stream. And the branch, transformed into a colossal tree with shimmering leaves and jewel-like fruits too beautiful to belong to their ordinary world. Ela brushed a knuckle against Tzana's soft cheek. "Do you miss the tree?"

Tzana nodded. "Jess needs to see it too."

Ela caught her infant brother's lustrous gaze and nuzzled him. "You would miss the tree if you'd seen it, Jess! Yes, you would!" As he smiled and wriggled within his swaddling linens, Ela crooned, describing the tree. "You would climb the big twisty trunk with Tzana! And you would pick the red fruit first—"

"The purple fruit," Tzana mumbled, drowsily. "I want the purple fruit with the green top . . . and the . . ."

" . . . the white centers," Ela agreed, finishing the description. "Then we would chase all the little animals. . . ."

By the time she'd detailed the tree and its inhabitants, Jess and

Tzana were dozing off. Ela kissed them both and tucked Jess into his vinewood basket. Precious baby. A good little sleeper despite his infrequent squeaks and sighs.

Really, she needed to tell stories more often. They were so relaxing, particularly when told to tired children. Ela shifted their single oil lamp to a sheltered alcove, then padded over to her pallet. She settled down, sighing, treasuring the peace.

Perhaps she would sleep better tonight. The past two nights had been nightmarish, filled with Tavek's disintegration. And threatened by Belaal's army surrounding Parne, demanding ores, gold, and blood. She tried to shake off the images.

As she rested her head on the pillow, a sudden chill ran through Ela. She tugged her blankets closer. The chill didn't leave. Was she ill? Infinite?

I am here.

What do You wish to tell me?

His words a severe warning, He said, *You will not mourn.*

The coldness settled into Ela's limbs. Into her heart. Even her mind. He gave Ela time to absorb the vision. Small. Hushed. More agonizing than she could ever have believed. The chill deepened, freezing her tears to stillness. Halting the screams and wails building in her throat.

She must not mourn.

Despite the icy composure, Ela warred within herself. One crack—the slightest—and she would break completely.

Infinite, give me strength! I cannot survive this on my own.

I am here.

19

Mother found her when the first glimmers of morning's light sieved beneath the doorway.

Seated between Jess's and Tzana's sleeping forms, Ela held Tzana's little hand and watched the slow rise and fall of her breaths.

Kalme kneeled with her. "Ela? What's wrong?" She checked Tzana and whispered, "Let her rest."

"We have to stay with her this morning. Father too. He shouldn't even go to prayers."

"Why?" Mother leaned down to study Tzana more closely. As she did, Tzana's breathing pattern changed, becoming more labored. "Tzana?" Kalme shook her gently. Tzana didn't stir.

"Tzana!"

"Mother." Ela wrapped her arms around Kalme. "She's too weak to endure anything more. The Infinite will remove her today. And I'm not supposed to mourn."

Jess began to stir. Kalme wailed.

✦ ✦ ✦

Amid the mourners and onlooking neighbors, Ela kissed Tzana's delicate face one last time, memorizing its sweet scent. Its tenderness. Such a fragile form had sheltered Tzana's bright soul—both too sensitive to survive Parne's siege. Better to release her now. In peace.

Pain threatened to claw Ela's throat and slash her soul to pieces. The coldness kept her anguish at a distance.

Ela hugged her dazed parents and touched Jess's soft chin with a light caress. Flinging on her best mantle—a faded embroidered crimson—she grabbed two rounds of bread and the branch, then walked outside.

He is right, and He is good.

And she must persevere as His prophet.

Prill's scolding voice called after her. "Ela Roeh!" Ela turned to face the matron's outrage. Approaching, Prill flicked at the worn, too-short crimson mantle. "Old though this is, you cannot wear it—you need a mourning cloak! Come inside and change."

"I'm not mourning."

Her words left the woman unmistakably aghast, openmouthed and speechless. For an instant. "What do you mean? Of course you're mourning. How can you not? Everyone knows Tzana was your dearest friend! Your only sister, whom you've adored!"

Don't, Ela begged from beyond her icy distance. Oh, Prill, don't make me think of her too deeply. "Yes. But her death and my reactions are signs to Parne. The temple, Parne's pride, is about to be destroyed with the city. We'll have no chance to formally mourn our losses." She smiled at the matron. "Will you walk with me?"

"Certainly not! I'm staying with your parents, as you should."

"Tell them what I've said. Tell everyone what I've said. Tzana wouldn't have survived the siege." Ela turned and walked through the modest public square, into the wider square beyond. No one else stopped her. Indeed, everyone retreated. The terrors surrounding the false prophet's death remained too fresh in their minds for comfort.

She passed through the marketplace and entered the Murder Maze. The tunnel's tomb-like closeness and darkness would have suited Ela perfectly this morning. But the branch answered the gloom with a gleaming light. And Parne's gateway opened before her at the last turn, spilling sunshine through the entrance like a tribute to life.

Outside Parne's walls, Jon and Beka's modest encampment bustled with a turmoil focused on one object. Scythe. Tzana's dear Pet lay on his side in the dust, groaning. His destroyer comrades, Savage and Audacity, lingered nearby, also groaning, their heads down, both obviously distressed by Pet's misery, aware of his loss and their own.

Beka saw Ela first and stood. "Ela! Oh, I'm so sorry—Pet's dying! Jon was about to send for you."

"He's not dying." Ela set down the branch and the bread and draped her arms over the destroyer's neck. To Pet alone, she whispered, "Remember her! Don't ever forget that you made her very happy."

Pet shut his eyes.

Jon said, "Ela, I don't know what happened to him. He was a bit nervous this morning, then he went down, groaning and thrashing as if he'd been hit with colic."

"It's not colic." She looked up from Pet to meet Jon and Beka's respective stares. "The Infinite removed Tzana while she slept, so Pet is grieving. I'm forbidden to mourn, however, as a sign to Parne."

Beka paled. "What? Tzana?"

"Yes." Ela nodded. "We'll place her body in the tomb tomorrow."

"Oh . . ." Beka reeled against Jon, then hid her face in his shoulder and cried.

Holding his wife, his expression shocked, Jon said, "Tzana? Ela, we're so sorry."

"I know." Could he see past her cold façade? Surely he knew she would miss Tzana for the rest of her life.

Gulping down a sob, wiping her tears, Beka asked, "Is there anything you need?"

"There is." Some of the chill eased. She stroked Pet's glossy black neck, then smiled at her friends. "I need you all to survive.

Tomorrow morning, you must leave for Istgard and take Pet with you. Return him to Kien. Promise me."

"We will," Jon said. "I'll send a messenger to General Rol today, telling him of Tzana."

"Thank you both. For everything you've done. I don't deserve such dear friends."

"You do!" Beka argued, swiping at fresh tears. She fumbled through her long sleeves and money purse, as if digging for a cloth to blow her nose. "We're the ones who ought to thank you for blessing us."

Jon added, "Furthermore, Kien loves you. Consider yourself as our adopted sister."

She was going to cry. And if she started, she'd be unable to stop. Instead, Ela hugged her miserable warhorse. "Here." She offered her bread to the destroyer. "Eat this. Obey."

Pet obeyed, but without a bit of spirit. When he'd finished, Ela scrambled onto his back. "Stand. Let's circle the whole city. Obey."

Moaning, his sides heaving, Pet hauled himself upright, though his big head still drooped. Ela hugged his huge neck again, rubbed her face into his flowing mane, and wove her fingers into its warmth. "Go!"

The destroyer drew in a rushing breath, then burst into a full-out gallop, so swift that Parne's walls blurred and his hoofbeats echoed in immense, booming drumbeats of sound, loud enough to shatter the wall's stones. Or at least enough to rouse the whole city, Ela was sure.

Let Parne see itself encircled by a grieving destroyer. Surely this was another sign.

Her home would greet one more sunrise of peace.

Then Belaal would come slavering at Parne's gate like the Adversary, craving mortal blood and immortal souls.

Eventually, the destroyer slowed. At the long ride's end, Pet knelt and Ela slid off his back. He grunted, still miserable, but not behaving as if he sought death. Ela smoothed his handsome monster-horse face and whispered, "Go with Jon and Beka to Kien. Do you hear me? Kien. You will go to Kien. Obey."

Pet grumbled, refusing to look at her.

Red-eyed, Beka gave Ela a hug. "Are we allowed to be with you during Tzana's interment tomorrow?"

"Yes. But I'd rather you leave as soon as possible. I want a full day's distance between you and Belaal's army." Beka's face turned mutinous. Ela persisted, "Please, Beka. For my sake. For Kien's."

"If you insist. I'll tell Kien you love him."

Kien. Ela's heart constricted, pained. Wasn't she supposed to be numbed to all emotion?

Infinite, I wish I could see him again before I die.

Unable to deny the truth, Ela nodded, affirming Beka's plan. What could it hurt? Let Kien Lantec know that Parne's prophet loved him. To her last breath.

✦ ✦ ✦

As Mother held Jess and wept, Ela clasped Tzana's new blue mantle about her small body. So still. So quiet. She stepped back, allowing Father to close the white shroud. Dan's face tightened, suppressing grief as he tied the final knots, then lifted Tzana from the pallet.

Working a path among the mourners in their modest home, Father entered a lamplit room at the back of the house. There, he tenderly placed Tzana's body within an open stone-block crypt that had been hurriedly mortared and fitted to her diminutive form.

Waiting Roeh cousins lifted a flat stonework lid and rested it over the crypt.

Leaving one clay lamp inside to symbolically burn itself out, they shut Tzana in the family's tomb. The instant the door was closed, the mourners lifted trowels of mud and plaster, sealing the door and smoothing it over until the entry seemed to be nothing more than a recessed section of wall. Separating death from life.

After a year, traditionally, this door would have been opened again, and the sarcophagus would be formally plastered, then dried and painted in tribute by loved ones.

But there would be no paintings for Tzana's resting place. Only the ashes of Parne. Ela watched the mourners. Most were relatives, yet all seemed impatient and uninvolved. Clearly begrudging the Roehs their time.

Because of me, Ela thought to the Infinite. Or, rather, because of You?

Yes. Distress subdued His response.

The mourners also failed to mourn because Tzana was Tzana. An Unfortunate. A curse.

A hand rested on Ela's shoulder. Prill's remorseful voice said, "Ela, I considered what you'd said about Tzana's death being a sign . . . and about that Tavek-man's death."

Ela looked her wary chaperone in the eyes. Prill swallowed and continued. "I was wrong. I was paying attention to legalities more than to the Infinite. Will you forgive me?"

"Of course. The Infinite's ways aren't Parnian." Ela smiled. "Actually, His ways aren't even mortals' ways, and sometimes it's a struggle to accept them."

Straightening, as if fortifying herself against an expected blow, the matron asked, "Do you still accept me as your chaperone?"

"Yes. Unless you'd rather not."

"Well . . ." Prill sniffled. "You do need a chaperone with those boys chasing you."

Ela sighed. Truly, there was only one "boy" she'd want to have chasing her. If the Infinite willed any to chase her at all. Kien's face, lit with a charming smile, filled Ela's thoughts. What a mercy he wasn't here. His sympathy and grief for Tzana would have shattered Ela into unprophet-like pieces. To distract herself from thoughts of Kien, Ela asked, "Matron, will you walk with me through the marketplace tomorrow morning?"

"Why? What's going to happen this time?"

* * *

Sitting on her pallet, Ela closed her eyes and walked the city in her vision. Parne's citizens stared at her. By now it was known that Parne's prophet had lost her cherished little sister. By now it was said that Ela of Parne was cursed—unable to protect one of the people she'd loved the most. Clearly the Infinite had abandoned her. Surely she was no one to be heeded.

Ela heard the whispers.

The lies.

Opening her eyes, Ela jammed her feet into a pair of old boots, swept the worn crimson mantle over her shoulders, and picked up the branch.

Kalme, face swollen from crying, looked up from her cushion where she was nursing Jess. "Where are you going?"

"Out with Matron Prill."

"Your father will be home from prayers soon. What should I tell him?"

"I'm obeying the Infinite's command. Stay inside, all of you. Don't go up to the wall when Belaal arrives."

"What?" Her voice rising in desperation, Kalme cried, "Ela . . . !" She shifted Jess and stood, looking so frantic that Ela crossed the room to soothe her.

"Mother." Ela wrapped her arms around Kalme and Jess, hugging them both with all the warmth she could allow herself to feel. "I'll be as safe as a prophet can ever be. Until then, rest and pray. And, please, tell Father my warning is serious. Don't go up to the wall this morning."

Kalme burst into tears. "You're going to die! I'm losing both of my girls!"

The hairs lifted at the back of Ela's neck. The Infinite once asked Mother to become His prophet. Could Kalme turn prophet even now? Suppressing the thought, Ela kissed her mother, scolding gently. "We both knew what it meant when I agreed to become the Infinite's prophet. I'm willing to face death, Mother. I *have* faced it. But today I'll survive."

"Give me your word!" Kalme clutched Ela so fiercely that Jess mewed in protest.

Ela nodded. "You have my word. Today I will survive."

Others wouldn't. But she wasn't about to tell Mother so. Ela stepped outside into the morning light. Matron Prill's home sat above the Roehs', but farther back, and to the east, behind a modest alcove garden. Prill was already descending the steps, surefooted and quick, with a large basket on her arm. Ready for battle, Ela hoped.

Greeting her with a nod, Prill asked, "Marketplace first?"

"Yes. We'll start there."

And end on the wall.

20

Sibilant hisses sliced through the air as Ela and Prill entered the marketplace. Prill muttered, "Someone's offended that you're not wearing mourning."

"Quite a few someones. And they're more than offended." Ela watched a half-eaten pastry spatter near her feet, followed by a bit of dried fruit. "They wish me dead." She nudged her short boot at the largest piece of pastry and watched the sweet delicacy crumble. A meat vendor laughed as one of his patrons cast greasy, gnawed poultry bones toward Ela's face. She stepped back and watched the insulting tribute fall. Only a few nips of meat and skin remained on the carcass. "Within seven days the ones who threw these things will be longing to eat them."

Almost serene behind her icy spiritual shield, Ela studied the faces of her accusers. The guilty ones looked away. Others, who'd evidently prepared additional missiles, lowered their hands as she eyed them.

"Why are we here?" Prill's thin face turned strict, demanding an answer.

"You need supplies," Ela said. "Buy as much as you can carry. And I'm waiting for Zade Chacen."

"Chacen? Huh!" The matron looked near to spitting with contempt.

"His followers are now running to tell him and his sons I'm here—and that I'm a disgrace for my lack of mourning."

A deep, stern voice beckoned. "Ela!"

Deuel, the spice merchant, motioned her toward him. Ela nudged her chaperone. "Buy everything you can carry, then hide it inside Deuel's booth until our return."

Shaking her topknotted head, Matron Prill stomped off.

"Ela," Deuel chided as she approached. "What are all these stories I've been hearing of you?"

"You've heard a bit of truth mixed with a great deal of exaggeration." Ela stared at the merchant's small, keen eyes. "Deuel, you have been kind to my family in the past, despite your impatience with our 'narrow' views. I'm concerned for you—as is your Creator."

"I'm surprised," he admitted, his thick brows lifting, then knitting together. "After you broke that box I sold you, I doubted you'd speak to me again, much less be concerned."

"Today you will either listen to me or ignore my advice. Belaal approaches. The Infinite will save you, if you call to Him. Meanwhile, close your booth today, and—"

"What!" Deuel snorted. "Close my booth?"

"The 'prophet' Tavek ignored my warnings," Ela reminded the man. "I hope you listen. Share my counsel with others. Close your booth. Buy supplies and hide in your home. Now."

Deuel bit at his lower lip, then asked, "Did you really turn Tavek to dust?"

"I didn't. The Infinite did because Tavek would have destroyed others."

"And little Tzana . . ."

"Rests with the Infinite. But I'm forbidden to mourn her departure." Protected by her numbness, Ela forced out words. "You saw me with my sister often enough. You know I loved her. Believe me, I'm not scornful of tradition. My lack of sorrow is a sign to Parne. We'll have no time to formally mourn after the siege."

Silent, he organized his boxes and spices. Ela persisted, "Prove the Infinite to yourself, Deuel. Give up on the Ateans. They're a lure to the flesh that will cost you eternally if you ignore your Creator's call—His love!"

His hands stilled. "How would you know of Atean rites? Did you attend a gathering?"

"No. The Infinite told me. And His word is enough." Ela straightened, shifting the branch, seeing its iridescence, its inward light. "The Chacens are coming for me as we speak. Allow yourself a serious discussion with the Infinite. Now. Tell others what I've said. *Don't* go up to the wall."

She left his booth and surveyed the marketplace. Prill moved from vendor to vendor, lugging her basket with both arms, while a now-weighty cloth sack hung heavily from her shoulders. Obviously Prill was taking Ela's advice and buying everything she could afford. Though there was far less food to buy today. As if answering a similar observation from one of his buyers, a grain merchant to Ela's left declared cheerily, "We've received word through a courier. Our supplies will arrive any day now."

Supplies from the traders, who'd gone to Istgard and Siphra. Ela shut her eyes, watching their approach in her vision.

Until someone jostled her and a light girlish voice said, "Why don't you move on? You're not wanted here."

Ela steadied herself and looked at the voice's source: a pretty young woman her own age. Beautifully clothed, with elaborately braided brown hair, showy goddess-coil ornaments, and artful face paint. An exquisite exterior, masking corruption within. "Go home," Ela told her.

The painted face sneered, less lovely now. "I'm not the one causing trouble, Prophet." As she spoke, the young woman glanced beyond Ela and her eyes brightened. Pouting provocatively, she swept past Ela and joined the Chacens, who now approached Ela—all three wearing swords. As if they expected her to fight. As if they hoped to win.

Zade Chacen brushed off the flirtatious young woman. Cold-eyed, fixated on Ela, he spoke, his resonant, dignified voice carrying to all the booths. "You will come with us. We are bringing you to the courts, to be charged with Mikial Tavek's murder."

"You've finally summoned the courage?" Ela asked. "Or did you lose a draw of lots?"

The eldest Chacen grabbed Ela's arm, digging his fingers in hard enough to leave bruises. Despite herself, Ela winced. Sius Chacen shoved her. "Cooperate and we'll be merciful—a swift death rather than lingering torture."

"The Infinite offers you true mercy," Ela countered. "Even now, it's not too late."

Shifting his hand, Sius Chacen wrenched Ela's braided hair, forcing her to look up at him. His scar, inflicted by the branch, showed black as ashes against his puffy, infected skin, marring his handsome face. "Do anything, try anything, and we'll cut you to pieces!"

A pulsebeat of fear thudded behind Ela's protective, emotionless barricade. Particularly as Sius slipped a dagger from beneath his cloak and pressed it against her ribs. Just a bit more pressure and he would draw blood. A bit more force and he would inflict a lethal wound. As she stared into his eyes, Ela saw his desire to cut out her heart.

Za'af closed in behind them, his swollen, hateful face mirroring his brother's threat.

Matron Prill's agitated voice summoned her attention from a distance. "Ela?"

"Stay near!" Ela called to her chaperone. "Prill, don't run. Stay near as my witness. The Infinite will protect you!"

Zade snarled at Prill, "Don't interfere, woman! We're taking her to meet justice."

Ela's hidden pulsebeat quickened in terror. She prayed. Willed her fear to submerge once more. "If only you would listen! Even now your Creator longs for harmony with you—He loves you!"

High above them on the wall walk, the watchman signaled a warning blast with his trumpet as another man yelled, "Soldiers! An army! Seal the city!"

Wielding the branch and raising her voice to match the watchman's, Ela cried, "Parne, you've been warned—Belaal approaches! Lock yourselves inside your homes!" To the Chacens, she said, "Belaal will capture Parne's traders."

Sius pulled away his dagger. Zade's grip on her arm went slack. He looked around the marketplace at his fellow citizens, whose faces reflected his own shock. The watchman sent up another warning trumpet blare. A war call.

Gouging his fingers into Ela's arm again, Zade shoved her toward the stairs nearest the wall walk. "Move! Hurry!"

"Zade, no! If you go up to the wall—"

He spoke through gritted teeth. "You've said enough! Move!"

Sius pressed his dagger into Ela's side once more. "Go."

"Remember my first day as prophet, Zade! Here is your calamity. Don't go up to the wall!"

The dagger moved. Stinging. Making her gasp as it scratched through her clothes. Zade was dragging her now, adding his bellowed orders to the watchman's call. "Parnians! Gather your weapons!"

"No!" Ela screamed over her shoulder at the marketplace while the Chacens dragged her up the stairs. "No weapons! Parnians, go to your homes and pray!"

Zade shook her. "You stupid girl! Shut up! If our enemy approaches, we have the right to defend ourselves! And we will show them we intend to fight!"

Thrown off balance, Ela slipped on a step and caught herself with the branch. Chacen yanked Ela to her feet again, then shoved her along.

Following them up to the wall walk, Matron Prill cried, "Ela, what should I do?"

"Prill, stay close!" Ela prayed for her chaperone and mourned for the Chacens. As well as for the other Parnians who were rushing up to the wall walk, against her warnings, brandishing their swords and bows and arrows. Infinite? Why won't they listen?!

✦ ✦ ✦

At the wall's crest, beside the watchman's stone shelter, Ela sucked in a breath.

From north to south, all along the mountains rimming its southern plains, Parne's western fields teemed with approaching soldiers. Banners of gold and sapphire shone against the arid blue sky. And the midmorning sun reflected a harsh glare off the approaching soldiers' shields.

As Zade Chacen and his sons stared, Ela said, "It's not too late. Leave the wall and pray to the Infinite for mercy."

"Traitor!" Sius accused, still squinting at the nearing army.

Za'af said, "We should throw you from the wall."

Not yet, Ela pleaded to her Creator. Save me!

A form moved behind Ela, casting a shadow over her. Fingers touched the nape of her neck, making her shiver. Someone twisted her braid. To Ela's left, Matron Prill scolded, "Amar, take your hands off her!"

Amar snapped, "Stop squawking, hen!" He leaned so close to Ela that she felt his breath against her cheek. "Not so courageous in the sunlight, are you, my love?"

Love. He'd failed there. "You're brave now because you believe I'm defenseless."

"Aren't you?" Amar questioned.

Zade Chacen spoke, his voice low with dismay. "There are the traders with our supplies."

A long line of horses and carts emerged from a stone pass in the northern borderlands which separated Parne from Istgard. Even as Ela recognized them, she saw the next fragment of her vision unfold. While the main army continued its relentless pace toward Parne's walls, horsemen rode out from Belaal's lines and charged the traders, surrounding them.

Zade called to the watchman, "Belaal's taken our supplies! There's no hope that we'll retrieve them. Tell everyone below to form a line and fill the Murder Maze with stones and mortar! Tear down homes for materials! Command it done!"

As the watchman elbowed his way through the crowd to issue Chacen's orders, Amar asked, "How long can we hold off such an army?"

The former chief priest grimaced. "For as long as our food and water hold out. We'll send courier birds to Istgard, the Tracelands, and Siphra requesting their help."

"They will not come as allies, but in their own defense," Ela warned.

Sius shook Ela. "Shouldn't we just toss her from the wall and kill her?"

Zade ran one hand over his tensed brown face, seeming lost in thought as he stared at the army. "No." He studied Ela now, suspicious, as if considering her poison. "Hasn't Belaal's army arrived as she said? I believe we should imprison her. She may yet be useful."

"Useful? Not when you won't heed the Infinite's warnings." Ela gazed out at Parne's drought-dried western fields. Seeing Belaal's first contingent of horsemen approach, her own terrified scream—locked deep inside—persuaded her to try once more. She looked up at Chacen. "Tell everyone to put down their weapons, please. It means their lives."

Though he didn't seem ready to kill her now, Chacen was clearly none too pleased by her words. "You speak like a traitor, not a true Parnian. Our best tactic now is to gain the enemy's respect. We must show that we can defend ourselves!"

Why wouldn't these rebels listen? As Belaal's preliminary ranks neared, Ela forced her voice to carry, to convey strength. "Parnians! Lower your weapons! Do not resist the will of your Creator, the Infinite!" The branch glowed in her hands now, dazzling, beckoning attention from every direction. "Do not defy Him—you won't win! Instead, you'll die!"

Mutters lifted along the wall. Rebellious growls. A man to

Ela's left cursed her in vicious, hard-clipped syllables. Prill said, "How dare he!"

"I don't care if he curses me," Ela murmured, "as long as he doesn't curse his Creator."

The commander of Belaal's lead delegation drew his horse to a standstill. Thickset and older than his men, he waited before speaking, as if wondering whether Ela would say more. When she remained silent, he urged his wearied horse forward and shouted in a deep, accented voice, "Parne! I am General Siyrsun. In the glorious name of King Bel-Tygeon of Belaal, we require your surrender. Open your gates! Clear our path and do not resist us! Thus you will survive!"

Again the man to Ela's left cursed, this time invoking the Infinite's name. Before she could rebuke him, he aimed his bow and shot one of the general's men.

The soldier fell from his horse and writhed in the dust.

Siyrsun and his men rescued their comrade, then turned their horses, swiftly rejoining the main army, which neared.

Triumphant laughter spread along Parne's wall walk.

Undeceived, Ela reached for Matron Prill, tugging her within the circle of the vinewood's glow. "Kneel with me and pray." Prill obeyed.

Trumpets blared from the army below. And a sickeningly familiar sight threatened to shatter Ela's icy core.

A volley of gold and blue arrows arced upward from Belaal's army, then sliced down, perfectly aimed at everyone standing on Parne's wall walk, drawing blood and screams. Chacen bellowed and dropped inside the watchman's stone shelter to his right.

Prill shrieked and clung to Ela.

Ela held her chaperone within the branch's light and prayed.

✦ 21 ✦

Within a breath's span of the first, a second volley of arrows fell. Fresh screams and wails echoed along the wall walk. Prill huddled within Ela's arms crying, "Oh, Infinite, save us!"

Beside Ela, Sius Chacen slumped on the stones beside Za'af, who howled in agony. Za'af attempted to wrench an arrow from his chest, then fainted.

Behind Ela, Amar clawed at her mantle, his voice rough. "Ela . . ."

She turned and saw what had not been within her first glimpse of this vision. The young man she'd almost married, downed by an arrow just below his left collarbone. His scar showing ink-black against his inflamed cheek, Amar clutched Ela's wrist, muttering, "Help me . . . stand."

Quavering, Prill told Ela, "I-I'll support him to the left, if you'll t-take the right. But . . . what about the arrow?"

With a glance at the stilled Za'af Chacen, Ela said, "Leave the arrow. It may be that we'll injure him further by removing it."

They managed to haul Amar to his feet. But as they picked a path along the wall walk, between the wounded and dead, Amar gasped. "Stop!" He dropped to one knee, a hand fumbling to touch the paving stones for support.

Heartsick, Ela knelt with him. He would never descend this wall. Perhaps now Amar would finally listen. She pressed a hand to his whiskered cheek, making him look at her. "Amar, I'm going to find your father. Listen, it's not too late. Speak to your Creator, *please*. He loves you! You need only call His Name and—"

Amar shoved at her weakly, unwilling to listen. Clearly signaling her to go.

He eased himself onto the pavings and shut his eyes.

Opposite Ela, Prill shook her head and pressed a hand to her mouth, shaking, as if suppressing sobs.

Supporting herself with the branch, Ela stood. Amar didn't stir. He rested on his side, his breaths shallow and rapid. Was he dying? She was afraid to petition their Creator for details. Helping the matron to stand, Ela said, "Prill, if I could cry now, I would. And I'd welcome it. But this is only the beginning."

Prill sobbed, "For me, this is enough! More than enough."

"Let's hurry." Ela gripped her weeping chaperone's arm and propelled her toward the nearest public path leading down into the city. Parnians, dead and dying, were scattered in every direction. It seemed that few arrows had missed striking someone.

How could this be real? Infinite? Let it still be a vision—an image not yet lethal.

"Why are we alive?" Prill demanded. "So many others have fallen."

"Because His plans for us are not yet finished, and you are my witness." With each sight of fresh blood from a corpse or of a weeping, bereaved citizen, Ela drew more deeply into herself, sheltering behind the terrible, protective coldness. "Go retrieve your supplies from Deuel's booth, Matron. I'll come back to help you once I've spoken to Amar's father."

Surely even the shielding numbness wouldn't protect her from this next task. Bracing herself, Ela hurried past the marketplace, into the public square beyond, then up a flight of stairs tucked between the structures of several houses. Hadn't Amar's parents heard the commotion? She rapped on the door, waited, and rapped again. Amar's father, Shekar, answered the door, tousled and groggy, as if she'd summoned him from sleep. Fumes, like the afterwash of heavy drinking, surrounded the man. Ela sighed. "You must go through the marketplace, then up to the wall. Amar was struck by an arrow from Belaal's army. We tried to bring him down, but he couldn't continue."

Shekar squinted, then blinked. "What?"

Pitying him, and Amar, Ela repeated her message. Shekar stumbled inside again, evidently seeking his cloak.

Ela hurried toward the marketplace once more. She would find Prill, lead Shekar to Amar, then alert Father. Perhaps they could assist some of the survivors.

She found the matron just entering the wide public square adjoining the marketplace. Behind the matron was Deuel. The merchant's rounded face was ashen, and his sturdy legs wavered as he shifted a large basket on his shoulders. The instant he saw Ela, Deuel stopped and stared. As if she were frightful.

He lowered the basket and knelt beside it. Bowing, hiding his face in his hands, the vendor cried, "The Infinite is God, and Parne is cursed!"

His words struck Ela with an almost physical impact. Deuel might have been a prophet. She wished he were.

✦ ✦ ✦

Hiding behind an intricately carved white column in Siphra's throne room, Kien read General Rol's letter.

It seems Prophet Ela's prediction has come to pass. This morning, a courier bird arrived in East Guard from Parne. Now, after shunning their neighbors for generations, the Parnians are appealing to us all for rescue from Belaal, which is now encamped before their city. Furthermore, Commander Thel's reports indicate a deeper disaster. Parne's wells are drying, and their crops have failed this year, due to a severe drought. Thel believes that unless Parne receives substantial rains within the next few weeks, thirst alone will force Parne's surrender to Belaal within eight weeks—unless we intercede.

Furthermore, Istgard's prime minister has sent word to the Grand Assembly that certain ores have been recently confiscated from Parnian traders and Tsir Aun himself has personally witnessed their destructive effects. Because Tsir Aun's courier-note corroborates Commander Thel's written testimonies, the Grand Assembly has approved the measures I have recommended. Our army is alerted and the campaign planned. We must ensure Belaal does not gain control of those ores, lest that god-king Bel-Tygeon rule us all!

In light of these concerns, the remainder of your leave is rescinded. You are, by default and preference, the Tracelands' envoy to Siphra in this matter. We order you to request Siphra's aid in neutralizing Belaal. We will send further instructions as decisions are reached. You will treat this communication as confidential, to be shared with only the king and his closest advisors.

On a separate parchment scrap, Rol added:

Regarding the king's curiosity concerning the Azurnite sword, allow him one bout in strictest isolation. You will also allow his advisors to inspect the sword. Soon, however, if Belaal emerges victorious with Parne's spoils, then the Tracelands, Istgard, and Siphra must join forces for battle. Further secrecy concerning the swords will be, to twist words, pointless.

Kien refolded the general's missive and hid it within his money purse. General Rol wrote this a week ago, yet Kien had received it only this morning due to a tardy messenger. At most, Parne would fall in seven weeks. He must persuade Siphra to act today! Wasn't the king's audience finished? Aggravated, Kien leaned around the carved pillar and studied the last of the petitioners.

A thin, dark-clad nobleman was now speaking to the king. Why did he seem so familiar? Kien frowned at the nobleman's arrogant bearing, his black swept-back hair and his embroidered cloak. Could it be . . . ? Kien slipped from behind the pillar and joined the crowd of bored Siphran courtiers. Unable to see the noble petitioner's face, he listened intently.

"Majesty," the nobleman was saying, "for the sake of my family, I ask you to mercifully restore my family's long-held estates to our care."

Suitably cautious, Akabe watched the nobleman. "Which estates?"

"Here is the written legal description, just as it has existed for two hundred years, concerning my family's honors." When the nobleman turned, offering a parchment to the king's clerk, his proud profile removed all doubt of his identity.

Kien muttered beneath his breath, "Ruestock!" The scheming, duplicitous Siphran lord who'd stolen Ela from Jon and Beka last year! On instinct, Kien gripped his dagger. So the man was begging for the return of confiscated lands? No! Kien moved forward. Surely Akabe, as Siphra's king, knew of Ruestock's past deceits.

Akabe smiled, pleasant but noncommittal. "We will consider your request and answer in due time."

"Thank you, Majesty." Ruestock bowed with marvelous elegance. "My family and I are your most humble servants."

Humble? Ha! Kien nearly scoffed aloud.

Ruestock backed away gracefully, until he caught sight of Kien. For an instant, the oily nobleman froze. Then, shifting his gaze briefly toward the king, Ruestock gave Kien a courtier's bow, pointedly equal to the one he'd just offered Akabe. "Majesty! What a pleasure to see you in your fellow king's court, sir! I wish you a good day—and a good visit."

He continued his smooth retreat, though with such a secretive, calculating smile that Kien wanted to lock him in a choke hold and squeeze the truth from his immoral soul. What game was the man playing? Every courtier within earshot was now staring at Kien.

Akabe frowned. "Wait."

Ruestock paused, the image of sublime patience. "Yes, Majesty?"

"Explain what you just said to former ambassador Lantec."

Kien growled. He saw where this conversation was going. As soon as he could isolate Ruestock, Kien would flay the man. *Infinite, give me patience, please!*

In his most unctuous manner, Ruestock said, "Forgive me, Majesty—and Majesty." He bowed to Akabe, then Kien. "I did not realize that former ambassador Lantec has concealed the matter. He is the rightful king of Istgard. He refused the honor following the battle of Ytar."

Akabe stared at Kien, incredulous. "Is this true?"

"In Istgard's best interests." Kien fumed. He would beat Ruestock bloody! Why create this scene?

Siphra's king straightened on his throne, an eyebrow lifted at Kien, not altogether pleased. "We must talk."

Kien offered with an envoy's bow. "Of course, sir."

While Akabe was distracted by the final petitioner, Kien wove his way through the crowd to Ruestock. All courtesy and grace, the rogue nobleman bowed and straightened. "Majesty."

Kien spoke through gritted teeth. "What game are you playing?"

"My favorite game," Ruestock murmured. "Realms and kings. And the more kings the better, as far as I'm concerned. I've done you a favor by speaking the truth, sir. All the honors of Siphra are now yours. One day, I'm sure you'll be glad of it and, perhaps, consider me less of an enemy."

"Unlikely. On all counts."

"Oh, more than likely. In time. Majesty." Eyes glittering, Ruestock bowed and backed away.

✦ ✦ ✦

The instant Akabe's royal audience ended, Akabe descended from his dais and faced Kien, his displeasure unmistakably driven by envy. "Majesty," he said to Kien in carrying accents, "May I request a bit of your royal time?"

"Gladly." Lowering his voice, Kien warned, "We need to speak in an isolated place. Wholly secure and free of prying courtiers. With plenty of room." He deliberately rested a hand on the white-metaled hilt of his Azurnite sword. "Do you have such a chamber, sir?"

"Better than a chamber. A sanctuary." Akabe nodded to his gold-and-crimson clad council members. "Our meeting will be slightly delayed."

More than a few of the council members looked grateful.

Courtiers bowed as Akabe and Kien left the throne room. Before Kien could speak, Akabe said, "You received a message this morning from the Tracelands. What has happened?"

Kien grimaced. So the palace spies had been set upon him. Aware that they were being followed by Akabe's personal guards, he said, "My leave is canceled. I'll tell you more when we reach this sanctuary you've promised."

Akabe quickened their pace. "Are we using weapons, Majesty?"

"Yes, sir. And, please, stop calling me that."

"But I enjoy inflicting the title on an equally unwilling wretch. What else haven't you told me?" Akabe demanded. "You deserve to be beaten!"

"You may try."

Guards stood at attention on either side of the doorway to Akabe's apartments. Servants awaited their king inside. Akabe motioned everyone to leave. None too happy, they obeyed. The instant the door closed, Akabe fastened its bolt with a resounding thump.

Alarmed yells echoed from outside. Akabe roared, "Hush, all of you! I'm in no danger."

He removed his gold crown and plopped it on the huge royal bed, then yanked the gold clasps off his robes. While flinging his dazzling royal trimmings over ornate chairs, he complained, "It's a mighty injustice when I, a fugitive *almost*-nobody, am forced to become king, while you—with royal blood!—have escaped the same fate!"

Kien looked around the glittering apartment. Not a window to be seen. "I imagine you're feeling trapped."

"*Trapped* is not a sufficient word!" Akabe darted a wary glance at the door and said more softly, "I am suffocating!"

"I regret your sufferings."

"You smirk!"

Well, yes, a little. But he was too worried about Ela to truly enjoy himself. "Let's have our bout and talk."

Now clad in his plain tunic and leggings, Akabe flung a golden vest at Kien like a weapon. "At least with you, I can expect a fair bout of swords. No throwing me the victory because I am king."

"I will never throw you a victory," Kien pledged. To emphasize his point, he pitched the golden vest back at Akabe.

The young king dashed aside the garment and grinned. Rummaging in a storage chest, he removed two swords and some gear, then sat on the floor. With a sigh of relief, he shed his gold-embellished shoes and yanked on some scuffed, still-dirty boots. He donned one of the swords, then snatched the second. "Now, O King who escaped your country, I am ready to crush you!"

"Again, you may try."

"I will. But don't worry. My surgeons will stitch you up."

"After they stitch you!"

Akabe led Kien to a far wall and slid a superbly carved, golden-winged aeryon-beast to the right. A narrow panel shifted, then turned like a small ship's sail aligned to the wind. Akabe grinned. "I hope you deal well with complete darkness and little breathing room, Majesty. Beware."

Kien stepped forward. As he studied the darkness behind the panel, his heart took a sickening plunge.

22

Akabe's warning was entirely justified. A tight-coiled set of spiraling stone stairs twisted upward within near-airless darkness. Blinded at the first turn, Kien paused and nudged at the steps with his boots to find his way. Several steps above him, Akabe said, "We could have brought lamps, but that would have meant calling the servants. I didn't want them to interfere."

"I don't blame you." The higher they climbed, however, the more the darkness pressed in like a strangling force. Kien pushed at his growing agitation. Since when had darkness and confinement affected him so badly?

His stomach muscles tightened as he remembered being inside the sea beast's gullet after ToronSea. The stairs' stifling, twisting blackness evidently bore enough of a resemblance to the sea beast's innards to rattle him. Severely. *Infinite? Will this be a lifetime affliction?*

No words met Kien's unspoken plea. Praying, he fought his panic and continued up the stairs. He must control himself and convince Akabe to hurry Siphra's army to Parne.

At last, Akabe said, "Wait."

Kien paused, gripping the stone wall, listening to the clink of metal bolts and locks in the stifling blackness. Akabe exulted as the door opened. "Ha! It worked!"

"You led me up here without being certain you could open the door?"

"I believed I could, so I did." Akabe stepped up into the sunlight, then squinted down at Kien. "Majesty, you look like something dug from a grave. Why? Does darkness alarm you?"

"You wouldn't believe me if I told you."

"Another mystery?" Akabe retreated, allowing Kien out of the stairwell. "Never fear, I will learn your secret soon enough."

Kien hoped he wouldn't. The truth was too mortifying. Sucking in huge, reviving breaths of fresh air, he looked around. They stood within the rim of an encircling stone wall, which was garnished with elaborate bow loops. Surrounded by brilliant blue sky. Curious, Kien peered out a bow loop. More sky. With the palace courtyards below. Too far below.

Too sickeningly much like the cliffs of ToronSea.

Kien shut his eyes. Wonderful. Now he was afraid of heights, as well as closed, dark places? Not good for anyone in the military. Infinite, help?

"What is wrong?" Akabe demanded. He shut the stairwell door with a thud. Sounding impatient, he asked, "Is this part of the mystery?"

Kien saw how this would end. Akabe would have him investigated. Probably send servants to make inquiries in Adar-iyr. It might be best to confess the truth now. He turned and eyed the king. "Swear you'll never tell anyone what I'm about to tell you. Your word of honor. On your sword."

"Is it such a secret?"

Kien hoped it would remain one. He frowned at Akabe, silent, until the young man lifted his sword. "You have my word, my friend. Now tell me."

"The Infinite threw me off a cliff in ToronSea. I was swallowed by a sea monster."

"You are not serious."

"I am. By the Infinite's will, it's true."

Akabe stared. "And you lived."

"Barely." Kien pulled in another deep breath, then exhaled through his nose. Be calm. Here, surrounded by sunlight and solid stone walls, he had nothing to fear. "The beast heaved me up on the beach at Adar-iyr. I spoke to King Ninus and his people, as the Infinite commanded, and then I journeyed here. It seems my adventures have left me with a few troubling symptoms."

"Perhaps time will ease them." Akabe shifted the sword loosely in his hands, a disappointed gesture. "I suppose you are now too ill for a bout."

"No. I'm not." He couldn't allow himself any weakness. For Ela's sake, he must win this bout and prove to Siphra's king and royal council that, because of their Azurnite, the Tracelands had reason to fear an invasion from Belaal. And that Siphra would be overrun in the conflict. Fortified by another deep breath, Kien unfastened his cloak, dropped it, then walked to the center of the tower's wall-encircled crest. This was a perfect practice area for a king. Isolated. Reasonably level. Open, yet hidden and secure. Kien prayed for an instant, took a few calming breaths, and felt better. "Let's have a bout, sir. Then we must talk."

"Akabe," the king insisted. "Someone has to call me Akabe, and you seem to be the approved someone."

"Fine." Kien swept his Azurnite sword from its scabbard and saluted Siphra's reluctant king with the glistening blue-silver blade.

Akabe's attention fixed on the sword. "May I test it?"

"No."

"If I win?"

"You won't."

"Tracelanders!" Akabe grumbled, unsheathed his spare sword and tossed its scabbard to the foot of a wall. Then he advanced, cold-eyed, his mouth set. Obviously determined to fight close-in, hoping to seize Kien's sword.

Kien answered with an attack, a lunge and a feint, forcing Akabe to step back. Akabe swung away and threw him a taunt. "You're nothing but a dance master!"

"You don't want to cross swords with me," Kien warned.

"But I do!" Akabe countered, bringing his sword downward—a falcon's guard, stooping for prey.

Kien parried with the flat of his sword and shifted, putting more distance between them. Akabe attacked again with a swift thrust. Kien stepped back to lull him, then lunged, sliding his blade along Akabe's sword until the Azurnite rested at Akabe's throat. "See it?"

Akabe grinned. "If my guards could see this they would have convulsions."

They unlocked blades, circled, then traded strikes until Akabe became impatient. He advanced energetically and swung at Kien in a wide, ferocious arc.

Kien instinctively met the strike with such force that Akabe's blade snapped beneath the Azurnite.

Akabe whooped, waving his broken sword. "This is what I wanted to see!"

He darted to the wall and returned with his second sword, a two-handed blade. "Once more, then I must attend my council."

The council. Kien nodded. He would plead for their intercession on Parne's behalf. "If I win, I attend with you."

"Do you believe my counselors will discuss our country's affairs while you listen?"

Kien smiled. "Perhaps they'll be the ones listening." He advanced, forcing Akabe to defend himself, parrying each strike. At last, Akabe charged through an attack, swung around, then brought his blade crashing high against Kien's uplifted Azurnite sword.

Sparks flew, and so did the tip of Akabe's longsword. Over the tower's edge. "Infinite!" Akabe gasped. "Let no one be standing beneath!"

They ran for the nearest bow loop, jostling each other to see the courtyard below. Empty. Akabe heaved a grateful sigh, then laughed. "That was worth ruining two swords!" He backhanded Kien's arm. "Let's hurry. My council waits. Now, why must they listen to you?"

Queasy, Kien dug General Rol's note from his money purse and handed it to the king.

Akabe read it, his elation fading. His gaze went distant. "May I share this with the council?"

"The sooner the better. As it is, half of Parne might be dead before the Tracelands arrives." With Ela among them.

Siphra's king gathered his broken swords and led Kien to the tower's door. While they edged down the spiraling stairs in the unrelenting darkness, Akabe asked, "Why should you have escaped ruling Istgard, when I was not permitted to escape ruling Siphra?"

Concentrating on finding the stairs, and on quelling his panic, Kien took another step downward. "By the Infinite's advice, I knew I would best serve Istgard by refusing the throne. Just as He knows you will best serve Siphra by ruling. A king must always consider his people's welfare before his own. Besides, I've no wish to become a king."

"Nor have I," Akabe muttered. "Yet here I am, wishing I were you—free to travel about with an Azurnite sword and a . . ." He hesitated, as if realizing something. "Where is your destroyer? The one I saw you riding last year?"

"In Parne with my sister and brother-in-law, and Parne's prophet."

Akabe released a gusty sigh. For a few more steps he was quiet. Then he said, "If Parne is conquered and Belaal removes their treasures and particularly their ores, then nothing will prevent Bel-Tygeon from marching across Siphra into the Tracelands for its Azurnite and destroyers."

"Exactly!" Kien hesitated. "Siphra is undoubtedly considered vulnerable."

"Meaning Belaal considers me inexperienced and weak? No doubt, but I will prove Belaal wrong. You must show your sword to my council. And I will show them mine, newly broken. They will not be pleased."

Reason to celebrate. Once he escaped this panic-inducing

darkness. Breathing, praying, Kien edged the toe of his boot forward. Downward.

✦ ✦ ✦

One by one, Siphra's royal council members read General Rol's note, stared at the swords strewn across the polished stone table, then frowned.

Kien pinched the bridge of his nose hard, wishing his queasiness would end. Infinite? How do I convince these noblemen to fight for Parne?

They are pledged to Me, the Infinite murmured into Kien's thoughts. *Yet they have not asked My advice.*

Kien caught his breath at the realization. Too loudly. The entire council and its king turned to him. Trying to sound rational despite his mutinous stomach, Kien said, "You should not listen to me."

Their surprise, a unified chorus of uplifted eyebrows, was really quite amusing. Kien wished he weren't too nauseous to laugh. He looked at Akabe. "Doesn't Siphra have prophets? Call them. Ask them for the Infinite's will."

"Of course!" Akabe started in his chair, then paused as if reminding himself he was the king, not some minion who ought to run to the door and summon Siphra's prophets. The arguably youngest council member stood, bowed to Akabe, then swept grandly toward the council chamber's door to beckon a servant.

While they waited, the noble council members passed around General Rol's message and Kien's Azurnite sword. A furtive scratching sounded at the door. A scrap of parchment was passed through to the council. The youngest nobleman cleared his throat and read, "'From the citizens of Parne to Siphra's king and his people. Belaal's armies have besieged our city and killed our young men who defend us. We beg your army to rescue us before we are overrun and slaughtered by our mutual enemy.'"

Akabe sat back. "This, then, is our tardy plea from Parne. What—"

He was interrupted by another rap at the door. Two men entered, one weathered, lean, and rough-clothed, the other younger and well dressed. The weathered one nodded to Akabe. "Your servant met us as we were coming to speak to you, Majesty."

Straightening, Akabe asked, "The Infinite has already sent you, His prophets?"

"He has," the younger one agreed.

The weathered one nodded. "Your Creator commands you, O King, to lead Siphra's army against Belaal at Parne."

Akabe eyed his silent council. "I agree. Will you also obey the Infinite?"

The eldest council member ruffled his elaborately waxed gray beard. "How can we not, sir? It seems Siphra is at war. May the Infinite spare our lives and take Belaal's."

Kien's nausea vanished. "The Tracelands thanks you, sirs."

Now, Infinite—I beg You—let us arrive in time to save Ela!

✦ ✦ ✦

Ela jolted awake, seeing the branch's blue-white fire before she opened her eyes. Senses screaming, she gripped her precious insignia and looked around the Roehs' night-stilled home.

Infinite?

Stand!

She scrambled to her feet. A thud hammered the door with an alarming crack of splintering wood. Outside, a man raged, "Prophet! We're going to kill you!"

23

The entry door dangled on its hinges. Ela expected a mob to rush inside. Instead, someone threw an oil lamp, followed by a blazing torch. Instantly a pool of flames spread across the floor, lapping at the woven grass mat.

Ela gasped, then choked on the heated smoke. Father's sleep-roughened voice called to Ela from the direction of her parents' secluded room. "Ela! What's that noise?"

Unable to reply, Ela screamed an inward plea. Infinite!

An image flashed through her thoughts. Following its silent direction, Ela tapped the branch into the fire's midst.

The blaze vanished, as if snuffed out by a giant hand. Fearing her attackers would throw another lamp and more torches, she rushed to the door. "All of you, back away!"

When Ela stepped outside, a man snarled, "Prophet, listen to what you've done!"

Distant, keening wails lifted off Parne's walls and echoed toward her in mourning. Who had died? True, after two weeks of besiegement everyone was hungry, but surely no one had yet starved. Surely their rations would last a bit longer. As for the drying wells . . .

"Ela!" Her antagonist's voice spat the word like a curse.

Ela recognized the man. One of her father's cousins, Abiyr, stood before the house, backed by four other men. Abiyr's face was similar to Father's. Even his voice conveyed Dan's low tones. Yet this cousin possessed none of Dan Roeh's love. "My wife's brother has died, poisoned by his wounds from the first attack. Tell me you don't hear my family's screams!"

"I hear." How could she not?

Father called to her from inside the house, but she didn't dare turn from her accusers.

Another man lunged past Abiyr, equally furious, yet weeping. Heedless of the branch, he struck Ela, then grabbed her by the arms and shook her. "This was my son! My son who died—and you're to blame! You spoke these curses. You brought Belaal! You killed my son!"

Father charged from the house and shoved her assailant away. "Ranek, my daughter did not kill your son! An enemy arrow felled him because he didn't listen to her warnings, so you keep your curses and your hands to yourself!"

The grieving father swung at Dan and missed. Dan walloped the man and sent him sprawling on the paving stones.

Cousin Abiyr grabbed Father's arm and threatened, "Kindred or not, Roeh, we've agreed to repay you and your family for every death we suffer! Every blow we endure, we'll inflict upon you and your wife and children and anyone who defends you! We're going to turn your house into a tomb and seal you inside!"

Dan shook him off. "You should be accusing yourselves! If you were the honorable, *faithful* men you've pretended to be, none of us would be in danger now."

Ranek hissed, "Say what you want, but I swear we'll kill you all!"

Pressing a hand to her burning face, Ela watched Abiyr and Ranek curse and threaten Father. If these men had their way, Father and Mother and Jess would die. Because she was the Infinite's prophet. No. She couldn't allow it. "If someone must die to compensate for your loss, then kill me. Leave my family out of your schemes."

"No." Father stepped in front of Ela and faced their assailants.

"If you attack her again, you might all die! Do you want to become instant dust, like Tavek?"

The men backed away, but the bereaved Ranek spat at Ela. "You are responsible for every death in this city!"

What good would it do to argue against such single-minded hatred? Anyway, for Father's sake, perhaps for the sake of these men's souls, she had to diffuse the situation. Gently, Ela set the branch before Dan and herself. The branch's glow intensified in the darkness. "Leave. Now."

Her enemies squinted, then turned and fled, their footsteps echoing and fading with distance. The branch dimmed to plain vinewood.

Dan put an arm around Ela and swung her into the house, past the broken door. "Even if we mend that door, we cannot stay here."

True. Ela sensed the Infinite's silent affirmation of Father's statement. She relaxed and waited as Dan pondered options.

Kalme's voice whispered from the darkness, "Who was it?"

Ela heard her father pacing, his footsteps crackling on the grass mat's remains. Finally, he spoke. "My own relatives. Abiyr and Ranek wanted to kill Ela, and all of us, because one of Ranek's sons finally died of wounds from Belaal's attack."

Mother exhaled shakily in the darkness. Father paused and spoke tenderly. "Kalme, we must hide. I know of a possible refuge."

"But . . . Tzana . . ." Kalme protested.

"Tzana is at peace," Ela promised her mother. "Nothing can happen to her now. But Father is right. For your sake—and for Jess's—it's time to hide."

Kalme sniffled, yet her voice strengthened as if she'd made a decision. "All right. I'll gather what we can carry and we'll go. But where?"

A tentative knock at the door startled Ela. Prill's silhouetted form and soft words calmed her immediately. "Is everyone safe?"

"Yes." Ela motioned her chaperone into the house. Not that

Prill would be more secure within the Roeh home. Which reminded her . . . "Father? What about Matron Prill? And Deuel and the Nesacs?"

Dan approached Ela and Prill. "Matron, it's clear we must abandon our home. Come with us. I know where we might hide, but you cannot breathe a word to anyone. Just gather your things and meet us here promptly. We must steal away before dawn."

Prill huffed, sounding taken aback. "Dan Roeh, is this really necessary?"

"We won't compel you," Dan said. "But you ought to hide as well."

"Goodness, no," the matron objected, "I can't simply leave my—"

Ela interposed. "Prill, if my enemies cannot find me, you'll become a target. You know it's true. You've been seen with me too often."

The matron's sigh acknowledged Ela's warning. "You're right. I'll hurry and gather my things. Not that there's much left worth gathering."

"Things can be replaced," Ela murmured. "You cannot. Hurry, Prill. And don't tell anyone."

Dan grunted. "Except Deuel, the Nesacs, and a handful of others. Ela, gather the food while your mother prepares Jess."

✦ ✦ ✦

Tzana?

Kien lowered the general's latest note, and a sealed bag of coins, which had been delivered from East Guard by a horseback messenger. It couldn't be true. How could Tzana be dead? Dazed, he stared at tonight's feast, set before him by Akabe's servants in the palace's crowded, regal central hall. Tender quail, baked in clay, perfumed the air with a spicy, smoke-scented sauce. Impossible to eat now.

Seated beside him, Akabe rested his carving knife on a platter's golden rim. "Bad news, my friend?"

"Yes. And quite delayed." Unable to say more, Kien handed Akabe the parchment. He could almost see the words Akabe was now reading.

Thel's latest news, much delayed, is grievous. Tzana Roeh is dead. Moreover, the Parnians have beaten their chief priest and threatened Ela Roeh's life for prophesying that Parne will fall. Parne's infighting can only hasten Belaal's triumph and assure us of our worst fears. I am sending you a month's military pay with this messenger. . . .

Finished, Akabe snapped a glance at Kien. "Do you consider this note to be confidential?"

"No."

"Good. Time to kick the hornet's nest. The army is prepared, yet my people dawdle, dragged down by legalities. It's been two weeks—I'm sick of waiting!" Akabe stood, grabbed an ornate silver salt cellar and hurled it across his table. Salt and silver fell with a ringing crash onto the hall's elaborately tiled floor. Everyone, nobles and servants, turned to stare at their king.

Lifting General Rol's note, Akabe bellowed, "News from the Tracelands! Ungrateful Parne has beaten its chief priest and threatens their honored prophet with death because she has foretold Parne's defeat. Already, Parne carves itself to pieces as a feast to strengthen Belaal's armies with gold and weapons! I give Parne less than a month to survive!"

Formidable as any general, Akabe glared at his courtiers. "And when the monster Belaal has consumed Parne, it will stalk its next victim, its nearest foe—Siphra! Yet, like fools, we delay over trivial official concerns! Whoever loves Siphra will fight to protect it *now*!"

Akabe shoved the note at his nearest advisor, then muttered to Kien, "Walk with me."

"To where?"

"Anywhere. Let everyone see that I'm too upset to eat. In fact—" As they departed from the great hall, Akabe yelled, "Where is my fightmaster? Bring me my swords!"

"Admirable show," Kien said beneath his breath. Almost enough to distract him from grieving for Tzana and Ela.

Akabe hissed, "Who said it was show? I am serious and *done* with waiting. Now let's see if my advisors' rumps are stung enough that they move!" Brooding, he added, "Even if our armies begin the march tomorrow—which I doubt—it'll take us two weeks or more to make the journey and assure our supply lines. We cannot allow Belaal to take Parne!"

"Call a meeting," Kien urged, forcing off his grief. "Keep your council awake until they finish preparations. We *must* go!"

With Your blessings, Infinite. . . .

✦ ✦ ✦

Deuel glanced up and down the dark street before answering Ela in a conspirator's hushed whisper. "Are you sure?"

"Yes," Ela murmured. "My father knows of a reasonably safe place. Gather your supplies and be ready to go with us. He's speaking to Chief Priest Nesac this instant."

Deuel's eyes widened in the dim light. "How long do I have to decide?"

"Now."

He nodded. "I'm coming."

✦ ✦ ✦

"I've packed lamps and some oil and wicks," Kalme whispered, adjusting a basket slung from her elbow. "And we have all our food. There's not much left. What will we do when it's gone?"

"Mother, we mustn't fret." Ela shouldered one parcel, threaded her free arm through the straps of Father's oldest knapsack, then grabbed the branch. She eyed Mother's burden. Kalme had rolled numerous garments into tight fabric cylinders and fitted them snugly into Jess's emptied carrying pouch. After shifting the sagging pouch onto her back, Kalme tucked the dozing Jess into the crook of one arm. When she reached for a bundle of foodstuffs double-knotted within the Roehs' largest coverlet, Ela grabbed it instead. "I'll carry this. You're holding Jess."

"I'm not helpless," Kalme argued.

"Neither am I."

Father, loaded with tools and supplies, motioned to them from the doorway. Joined by Prill, they followed Dan through the small public square that fronted their home. Moonlight slanted silver-pale over the city's white plastered edges, lending an appearance of false serenity to the night. Ela could almost pretend Parne was at peace, tranquil beneath the starry skies.

Abiyr Roeh's family had long since quieted. Ela hoped they were sleeping. Her face still burned from Ranek's blow. Not that it mattered. Worse would follow.

They crept through the silent marketplace. Near the heavily barricaded Murder Maze, Nesac and his wife stepped out from the shadows. Both were cloaked and holding all they could carry. Footsteps sounded nearby, muffled, yet rushed.

Deuel met them, shifting several large bundles and whispering, "I've begged others of the faithful to accompany me, but they're frightened."

"Perhaps we can help them later," Ela murmured. She turned to Father. "Which way?"

Dan nodded them toward the oldest, least prosperous section of Parne, along its ancient southern wall. They crept through a labyrinth of old courtyards, worn street paths, and overgrown alcove gardens. At last Dan herded them inside a murky courtyard tucked against Parne's southern wall and obscured by several other houses built above.

An overgrown tangle of parasitic plants and dead-limbed snags discouraged any thoughts of welcome. Musty heaps of leaves and weeds lumped beneath Ela's feet. Nesac's wife gasped and

Deuel grumbled as they ducked beneath a rustling curtain of dry vines. Kalme stifled a sneeze.

Finally, Dan halted before a sealed door.

Ela winced. A tomb house. They were taking refuge in a tomb house?

Matron Prill sucked in an audible breath. Mother protested softly, "Oh, Dan . . ."

"Trust me."

While they waited in silence, Dan kindled a small taper with his flint and metal kit. Obviously comprehending his plans, Mother offered him a lamp. He lit the wick, then removed a slender chisel from his tools and slid it behind the seals, quietly loosening them. Finished, Dan stood. "Inside. Hurry, but don't touch the seals. The sky will lighten soon."

One by one, they eased through the doorway, cautious of the seals, which still lined the doorframe. Father stepped inside, shut the door, and carried the lamp to a far wall.

Dark-painted plaster had crumbled away from the wall, revealing pale ancient rockwork. Ela imagined she'd glimpsed a bit of the city's skeleton through its decaying plaster-flesh. She shuddered.

Father slid a wider chisel along the wall, swiftly prying off more crumbling plaster.

He outlined the door traditional to most of Parne's tombs, and shouldered it open. Dry cold air wafted from the room beyond. Dan exhaled. "Move inside. It's safe, believe me."

Prill spoke now, squeamish. "We're staying in here? All of us in this one little tomb?"

"No." He smiled at the matron, suddenly mischievous as a boy. "Tomb houses shelter more than corpses. I visited this place as a child, with my father. He had business dealings with the old man who rests here."

Jess squeaked in the darkness, evidently waking up. Kalme set a kiss on her son's small head. "Be patient."

Lifting the lamp, Dan surveyed the inner chamber. Ela joined her father and looked around at the rows of sarcophagi. Dan inspected the tombs, touching their sides. "One of these hides a stairway."

Oh. Ela set down her parcels, keeping only the branch. "What are you looking for?"

"An air current. I remember feeling an air current from the false tomb."

A false tomb? Ela copied her father's motions, checking each sarcophagus. Deuel and Nesac joined their search. In the second-to-last row from the wall, a chill slid past Ela's hands as she touched a tomb's lid. "Father?"

The branch took fire, gleaming beside the false sarcophagus.

24

Father made no move to lift the sarcophagus lid. Instead, he knelt at the base of the tomb and pried at the narrow slab until a small door rasped open in the gloom. Soft-voiced, Dan exulted, "They thought I'd be too young to remember anything!"

Apparently not. Despite herself, Ela almost smiled. Trying to see, she held the shining branch near the small door, which shifted downward, shelflike.

Dan looked up at her. "Will you go first?"

No! "Why?"

"You're carrying the prophet's branch for light."

Ela's hands went cold and sweaty. Her mouth dried. Why did it have to be a tomb—even a false one? Was this where she would die? Infinite?

His answer was an unseen parental nudge. *Go.*

"All right." Offering inward prayers, she knelt, slid the branch through the narrow entry, and looked inside. Three stone steps led down into a tawny dirt tunnel, its rough walls clawed through by gnarled, moisture-seeking roots.

As she hesitated, Father nudged her. "Go."

Augh! Yes, both of you! I'm going. She scooted into the tunnel feet-first.

Dan shoved his old knapsack after her, followed by the two bundles she'd been carrying. "Take your parcels."

Balanced on the stone steps, Ela set the supplies in the dirt below. When she looked up again, Father was holding Jess. "Take him before he yells. Your mother's next."

Jess blinked at the branch and at Ela, then whimpered. She tucked the branch into the crook of her arm, then cuddled Jess close. He nuzzled at her, making noises of complaint. "Mother's coming," Ela promised. Jess squirmed, adorable despite being hungry. If only . . . Ela tried to force down the hopeless longing.

If only she could hold Kien's baby. *Their* baby. No, no, no. She couldn't torment herself with thoughts of what might have been.

Kalme was on the steps now, Jess's heavy carrying sling in her hands. "I'll trade you," she told Ela. Jess squalled the instant she spoke, his patience clearly outdone by hunger. Ela kissed his tender cheek and gave him to Kalme.

As Kalme settled Jess beneath her mantle, Ella tried to pull her thoughts away from babies and Kien. She slung Father's old knapsack over her shoulders, then juggled the remainder of their belongings and the branch and cleared the narrow steps.

Prill descended next. Then Nesac climbed down and helped his wife. Deuel passed his gear through the entry and scrambled after it. By the time Dan edged inside and pulled the slab door shut, they were crowded within the dirt walls, the men uncomfortably hunched down. As the designated lightkeeper, Ela moved farther into the darkness.

Her feet slipped a bit on the sloping yellow dirt path. After several turns, the walls were nothing but barren-looking rock and soil, too deep for roots to penetrate. She called back to Dan, "Did your father dig this tunnel?"

"Some of it," Dan admitted. "In secret. But it was hard work, with little reward. And if the authorities had caught him, he would have suffered heavy fines for illegal digging. Which is why he gave it up in favor of repairing Parne's walls. His old friend continued to dig down here until he was too crippled to proceed. It's amazing they were never caught."

As they walked on, Deuel asked, "Were they looking for gems?"

"Yes. But as I've said, they earned almost nothing."

Bitterness lacing his words, Chief Priest Nesac said, "They had no chance of earning anything. The priests control the most profitable mines. Greed and self-indulgence have been their downfall."

"You've escaped them," Nesac's wife soothed.

"I pray so."

Prill asked, "Where will we find water down here?"

Deuel gave a mirthless chuckle. "We might have to dig for it."

Equally unamused, Dan said, "I haven't explored much beyond the entrance. If we can't find an underground stream, we'll be forced to return to the city each night and go to the wells."

A worrisome option. The few productive wells were guarded and dwindling rapidly. Ela bit her lip. They needed to find an underground stream. Infinite?

She moved on in the darkness. Kalme called, "Ela, slow down. We're depending on you for most of our light."

"Sorry." Ela glanced back over her shoulder and promptly fell, sliding down an incline. A chorus of yells lifted in the cave above. Sprawled faceup in the dirt, Ela caught her breath and the still-glowing branch. Nothing hurt except her dignity, her elbows, and her rump. To reassure the others, she called out, "I'm safe." Maybe.

She tried to see beyond the branch into the darkness. And failed, of course. Except . . . chilling liquid seeped into her short boots. "I've found water!"

✦ ✦ ✦

Hunger gnawed into Ela's sleep. She tried to ignore it, taking refuge in her dreams. Really, three days of strict rationing should have accustomed her to a growling stomach. And it would be unprophet-like to grumble. Hadn't she fasted in the desert for longer than three days? Scolding herself, she reached for the branch. Gone.

Jolted wide awake, she sat up. Not only was the branch missing, but something in the cavern had changed. A shift in light and air. Shadows, large shadows, spread throughout the subterranean landscape. And large shadows meant a large light. Behind her. Had they been discovered? Infinite!

Turn and see.

Wary, she looked over her shoulder. A tree. *The* tree. Broad, spiraling vinewood trunk. Shimmering fruits, glorious flowers, and leaves all jewel-like in the darkness. Just as she remembered. Ela stared, dazzled and distressed. If only Tzana could be here.

Tzana.

Pain sliced through the numbness that had sheltered Ela since Tzana's death. Tears burned and glistened, blurring in the vinewood tree's glow. And sobs shattered her breath. Lowering her face into the dirt, Ela worshiped her Creator and cried.

Someone knelt beside Ela and held her. Mother.

Kalme cried with her. But she kissed Ela and snuggled her as if she were a child again. Ela hugged Mother tight. At long last, she sniffled and straightened. Tears, hers and Mother's, dripped off her face.

"Better?" Kalme sounded congested from crying.

No. "A little." She would miss Tzana for the rest of her short mortal life. Sucking in a shaky breath, Ela wiped at the tears. Father and the others were staring at her. Even Jess was watching. Though he did turn within Father's arms to gaze at the tree.

Ela tugged off her short boots and reached for her baby brother. "May I?"

Dan handed over Jess, then stood. Clearly astounded by the tree, Father said, "Tell us about this . . . miracle."

"I will. But, first, everyone, remove your boots and sandals."

As he wrenched off his boots, Chief Priest Nesac recited, "'From dirt we were created, to dirt we will return. Bless the Infinite!'"

While she waited, Ela kissed Jess and comforted herself by smoothing his curls. When everyone stood near, barefoot, she said, "The tree is the branch, transformed by the Infinite's mercy.

He has chosen this way to provide for us." Fresh tears threatened as she said, "Tzana loved this tree!"

Reverent, Ela carried Jess over to the sacred ground. Grass sprang soft, cool, and rich green beneath her bare feet. And so sweetly scented that she felt fed just inhaling its fragrance. After unwrapping Jess from his swaddling clothes, she leaned against the tree's broad spiraling trunk, lifted her brother's tiny hand, and rested it on the gleaming vinewood. The baby gripped an iridescent twist of bark and stared, frowning, as if trying to decipher the purity of its inward light.

She wished he were old enough to remember this instant. To remember Tzana. And her.

Followed by Sara Nesac, Prill neared, her slim face scared, yet elated. "Are we permitted to touch the tree?"

"Yes. And we can eat the fruit."

Deuel halted at the verdant edge of the subterranean oasis and shook his head. "I don't deserve to approach it!"

Nesac pulled at the merchant's sleeve. "It's not a matter of you deserving the Infinite's gift. What matters is His perfect love in offering it to you. Will you abandon your pride and self-absorbed ways and accept His gift? Or will you shun it and Him?"

Deuel covered his face with his hands and sat down on the cavern's barren rocks, clearly overwhelmed. Casting a longing glance at the tree, Nesac sat with him, ready to counsel this new and profoundly distressed follower of the Infinite.

Dan and Kalme approached the tree cautiously. For a long time, they simply stood beneath the branches, admiring it. At last, Dan asked, "Tzana saw this tree?"

"Yes. While I was in the desert, after I first became a prophet, she obeyed the Infinite and guarded the branch in my absence. In return, He protected her, sheltering her and feeding her by changing the branch to a tree. While she was here, where you now stand, she was free of her illness. She was beautiful. . . ." Remembering her little sister's joy, her vivid lovely face, Ela's throat tightened.

Kalme rested her face against the tree, tears sliding down her cheeks. Dan said, "I wonder why the Infinite allowed her to accompany you on such a dangerous journey."

Why, indeed? Ela sent her thoughts upward. Infinite? Why did you allow Tzana to face such dangers with me?

Because she loves you. And because she fulfilled her work for My glory.

Warring for composure, Ela repeated the Infinite's answer to her father.

Dan sat in the lush grass and tender flowers and covered his face with his big, work-toughened hands. "It's more than I'd ever hoped for her." His shoulders shook with sobs.

✦ ✦ ✦

In Akabe's tower-top arena, Lorteus, the royal fightmaster, glowered at Kien, then spoke, his voice as harsh as metal raking over stone. "On your journey to Parne, your role as the king's friend—his near equal—has great importance. At all times, you must be ready to defend his life as well as your own."

And Ela's, Kien added silently, determined to best this arrogant brute of a fightmaster. For Ela's sake, he must be battle ready. Whatever it took. Even enduring Lorteus.

Strutting about, chin lifted and big nostrils flaring, Lorteus said, "Danger surrounds every king and those nearest him. My task is to ensure you both survive any sort of attack." With a disdainful frown, he added, "The problem now is that you Tracelanders can be duped by your own reflections! You're too confident in your Azurnite! But pretty blades will not defend a dismal swordsman." Smug, he lifted two wooden longswords—wasters—from a nearby stand and slapped one at Kien. "Believe me, Tracelander, I can bring you down despite your weapon!"

Kien eyed the hair curling from the man's ear canals. And his distorted, oft-broken nose and battle-ravaged skin. Understandable that Lorteus needed some reason to boast.

The man shifted his weapon into a plowman's waist-level stance. "Strike when ready."

Kien lunged, cutting his waster toward Lorteus with all his might.

The fightmaster received the strike flat on the lower portion of his blade and deflected Kien's weapon, hammering it upward with his sword's crossguard. Just before he sliced down to Kien's shoulder. "You've lost your arm," he taunted Kien. "Yet, even now, mortally wounded, you can kill!"

The words became a cadence, drilled into Kien's thoughts with each defeat.

Even now. Mortally wounded. You can kill!

Sweat stinging his skin and eyes, Kien fought. For Ela. At last, he forced the fightmaster to a pause, their swords crossed at throat level.

Lorteus snarled, "Your grip is weak, girl."

Silence, Kien warned himself. Feeble taunts don't merit response. He glared into the fightmaster's beast-grim eyes. When the man shoved him, Kien locked his foot behind Lorteus's and threw him to the pavings amid the clatter of wooden blades. Instantly, as Kien aimed for the kill, Lorteus swung out a leg and toppled Kien. His blade touched Kien's throat within a blink.

Amazing. Must be the man's ear hair. Kien affected a threatening glare. "Again."

Lorteus growled and stood. "Why? You won't learn. I'd be wasting my time just teaching a Tracelander to spit properly."

"Are you saying I ought to spit like you—with every word I speak?"

Kien rolled aside to avoid Lorteus' retaliatory strike, then leaped to his feet.

Before Kien raised his own waster, Lorteus pressed the tip of his weapon against Kien's heart. "Tracelander, I don't care if you are king, ambassador, or envoy. I will make every step of your journey to Parne a living torment! Beginning at dawn, you will eat what I feed you, drink what I give you, and sleep when I allow you ten breaths to do so!" His eyes fixed on Kien, seeming wholly malignant. "You will learn. Otherwise, when Belaal kills you in battle, you will be grateful!"

This animal would control his meals? Kien regretted mentioning the spit.

✦ ✦ ✦

Amid the evening meal, shared with her family and friends in the cavern, images called to Ela. Faces, some familiar, some new, sought her in the city above. And words, Sacred Words, beckoned her from their neglected shelter in a now-dead house. Ela hastily set down her food as emotions slid into her thoughts. Spinning . . .

Trying to contain the vision's momentum, she rocked forward on her knees and gripped her head. Amid the escalating tempest of words, fear, and pleading faces, Ela felt Kalme's arms encircle her. Mother's embrace stilled her. A sanctuary.

Released from the vision, Ela straightened and pulled in a breath. Infinite . . . truly?

Yes.

Seated beside Ela, Prill asked, "What are you seeing?"

"The Infinite's faithful ones."

Nesac approached, his thin face furrowed in concern. Dan crouched beside Ela. "Tell us."

Ela motioned toward Nesac. "He must return to the temple for the Books of the Infinite—they cannot be taken as spoils of war by any king. And I'm sent to find others for the Infinite."

"Others?" Kalme's lovely eyebrows lifted. "Who?"

"The faithful ones who must join us to survive."

Dan grunted. "It seems the Infinite will feed them." He looked up at the tree. After a reluctant pause, he said, "You'll need to take the branch."

"The branch stays here. I've faced danger without it before, Father. Don't worry. The Infinite is my Protector." Though she would be seen as vulnerable when she entered Parne without her insignia. The branch was the symbol of Parne's prophet and her

Creator's care. Ela's enemies, *His* enemies, would believe they could more easily capture her. And soon a particular enemy would succeed, Ela knew. Where, when, she couldn't tell. But this cavern obviously wasn't the place of darkness she'd experienced in her vision. There was no fear in this underground sanctuary. No pain. No stench of death. Unlike the place she'd envisioned.

Ela rested a hand on Prill's arm. "I'm sorry, but you must accompany me, with Nesac."

The matron blanched.

25

Stars flecked the purpled predawn sky above Parne. Beautiful and peaceful. A serene contrast to the city below. Ela, followed by Prill and Ishvah Nesac, hurried over the rooftop paths, praying and listening to varied cries of distress and broken weeping from the homes beneath their feet.

Had most of Parne consumed its supplies?

Behind Ela, Prill breathed, "I feel guilty, being well fed."

"All were warned," Ela reminded her. "This disaster could have been avoided."

Nesac drew nearer, obviously sickened, and worried. "The temple's doors are sure to be locked! How can I get inside?"

Ela almost smiled. "Whose house are we discussing? You'll find He's opened the door for you."

The chief priest grinned in the first light. "Of course!" But just as quickly, a frown returned, casting shadows across his lean features while he turned, evidently distracted by a piercing wail from the city below.

Prill tucked her hand into the crook of Ela's arm. "What will we be doing while he's in the temple?"

"Causing commotion." Which would be fun if matters weren't so deathly serious. She longed for Kien to walk this path with her. Here. Now. Thoughts of Kien weakened Ela, slowing her pace. He'd accompanied Ela on some of her first forays as a prophet.

It only seemed right that he should be here. Surely he was on his way to Parne. She'd see him before her entombment, wouldn't she? Was it right for a prophet to long for another mortal so much? She prayed . . . not only to see Kien one last time, but to protect the Infinite's faithful remnant in Parne. As well as her parents. Prill. And Deuel and the Nesacs.

Ishvah Nesac's voice murmured again, "I know this is all His will, but I wish the siege long gone. With all of us looking back upon this from a distance in time."

"Because you fear what you don't know," Ela said. His fears touched her prayers. Infinite, how could this young chief priest be reassured?

A sensation poured over her, and a rush of light built around them all like a clear golden wall. Ela looked over her shoulder and trembled. Three silent warriors were walking with them, calm, watchful. And so filled with the Infinite's radiance and power that she almost wept with gratitude. Thank You!

Prill grasped Ela's arm, staring at her oddly. "What's wrong?"

"Nothing." Ela gathered her senses. She'd stopped walking. And her friends were watching her as if she'd lost her mind. All right. Aloud, she prayed, "Infinite, who is like You? Please, allow Nesac and Prill to see the watch-care You've set over them."

Beside her, the matron gasped and flung her arms around Ela. Nesac missed a step and fell against a wall, clearly too shocked to make a sound. No doubt they saw the Infinite's warriors.

One of the Infinite's servants slid a powerful glowing hand through the air, as if closing a curtain around himself and his two comrades. Shielding mortals from their fear-inducing presence.

Prill squeaked into Ela's ear, "Are they still there? Were they sent by the Infinite?"

"Yes, yes. And we must hurry. Nesac, when you've retrieved the Sacred Words, return to the hidden courtyard. We'll meet you there. Nesac?"

Mute, the chief priest nodded. He shoved himself away from the wall and then ran ahead as if being chased to Parne's temple.

Ela shook the matron. "The others are approaching the temple to pray."

Like Nesac, Prill nodded. Unlike Nesac, she managed to speak. "If-if *they* are here, why would you need the branch for protection?"

Infinite? Ela resumed walking, tugging Prill alongside her as she listened to His answer. When they reached a high and level rooftop path, which seemed only an arm's length from the fading stars, Ela said, "The branch is more than mere protection. It serves the Infinite, and is a symbol of His pledge to us." She shook her head. How could she express what she didn't understand? "One day the Infinite will send a truly righteous priest to rule us and to intercede for our mortal wrongdoings. Everyone who accepts Him will be spiritually cleansed."

Nudging the matron along the steps toward the temple, Ela added, "Our Creator will walk among us, and we won't need to be shielded from His holy presence."

Prill shook her head. "I thought I would die at the sight of those . . . those guards! It would kill me to see the Infinite Himself."

"All you need to do, Prill, is accept Him, and obey Him as your Sovereign." She quickened their pace, reaching the temple's gate just as the first true rays of dawnlight pierced the horizon.

Her heart aching, Ela watched a straggling flock of Parnians and several priests approach the temple. All these faithful ones looked so broken, despairing beneath their separate burdens of hunger and fear. An icy hand clutched Ela's wrist. Prill.

Her expression squeamish, the matron pleaded, "Promise me there'll be no screaming heaps of ashes today."

"No screaming heaps of ashes today," Ela agreed beneath her breath.

"What aren't you telling me?"

"You're going on a little errand, but don't worry. You'll be perfectly safe."

"You'd best be right. But what about you?"

As Ela tried to collect words to describe what was about to happen, Prill said, "Ela Roeh, if you die and I'm forced to tell your parents, I . . . I'm sure I'll never forgive you!"

"Yes, you will. And you might even miss me." She pried her chaperone's cold fingers from her wrist. "Now. I was serious about the errand. These people are about to speak to me. You're going to lead them to the hidden courtyard and wait quietly. Nesac will arrive soon after. Then I'll follow." In one piece, she hoped.

The first of Parne's faithful reached the gate. An older man and his wife. He recognized Ela and gasped aloud. "Prophet! We'd heard you were dead!"

Hmm. She could imagine who'd spread that little rumor. The others, perhaps eighty Parnian men, women, and children, gathered around her, eyes huge, as if seeing an apparition.

Evidently perceiving that she was safe and well, they nudged each other, whispering. "She's alive! Chacen was wrong!"

Before they created an uproar, Ela lifted her hands. "Listen. This is important. My chaperone, Matron Prill, will lead you to a safe place. Don't stop for anything and don't talk to anyone. Just go with her. Be quiet, and trust the Infinite. Hurry!"

She weakened a bit, watching them rush after Prill. If only she could go with them. But she had to be sure Ishvah Nesac wouldn't be trapped while rescuing Parne's Sacred Books.

Closing her eyes, she breathed a prayer. Calm. This wouldn't be too sickening, would it? Infinite?

Look.

Ela opened her eyes. A man descended from a nearby stairway, his pace slow as if pained, his shoulders stooped beneath the weight of his cloak. He started through the temple's gate, glanced at her, then halted.

Swallowing her nervousness, trying not to consider her death, Ela said, "Chacen."

Zade Chacen choked as if the air in his throat had become a solid lump. But even as he fought for breath, he clawed toward her, his expression murderous.

Alert for any signs of daggers in her foe's hands, Ela darted away. To the wall.

Chacen followed.

✦ ✦ ✦

Catching her breath, Ela stared down at the fields beyond the wall. Belaal's army spread before her in the dawnlight like an uneasy sea of dark tents and rippling sapphire and gold banners. Here was her vision brought to life. The seething cauldron poured out against Parne. Yet it was only the first wave. She glanced up at the sky. Almost time.

A warning, like a tap on the shoulder, alerted her to Chacen's approach. She turned and saw him ascend to the wall walk, one hand clasping the right side of his chest as if warring with hurts from his wounds.

The former chief priest lumbered toward her, his dark eyes wild with hatred. His body might be weakened, but his voice, now recovered from the shock of seeing her, was sonorous as ever. Surely everyone in Parne and in the army below could hear him raving. "Traitor! My sons died! They had wives and children, yet you showed no pity!"

Before the first pang of remorse could slash Ela with guilt, the Infinite sent her threads of emotion from the Chacens' entire Atea-worshiping clan. All raged against her. And against the Infinite, because she'd obeyed and spoken the truth. Ela suppressed a shiver, focusing instead upon the Chacen patriarch.

Why bother to hide her frustration with this grasping, rebellious, destructive man? He was the physical representation of Parne gone astray! Ela squared her shoulders. "I warned you and your sons! Remember what I said!" Deliberately, Ela rephrased her younger self—the scared girl-prophet voicing her very first prediction from the Infinite.

"Your sons refused to even acknowledge the Infinite, yet you favored them over Him! Therefore, you were removed from your place of power. As a sign to you, your sons died on the same day during that terrible calamity. Your descendants will never be priests again, though they will beg for the lowest priestly office, asking for nothing but bread to eat!"

He remembered. Hatred of the truth burned heat into his face, fire into his eyes. "How easily you curse us! You are not fit to—"

"Easily?" How could he be so deluded? Ela cried, "Do you believe I delight in your agony and your eternal destruction? No!" Shards of pain sliced through her like fragments of the Infinite's own broken heart. "Your Creator bleeds for *you*, Chacen! He weeps for you, and you reject Him! If you could comprehend an instant of His sorrow for you and your family, you'd never think those words! 'Easily'—how dare you!"

Rage shook her. "I'm leaving before I truly curse you now! Do you wish to test the Infinite's prophet in wrath?" Ela hoped not. She didn't want to learn what could happen.

Leaving the silenced, still-furious Chacen, Ela stormed along the wall walk. She needed to calm herself. She looked again at the army below. Not that there was anything calming there. But Belaal was her second reason for visiting the wall.

Praying the Infinite's Spirit would strengthen her words, Ela lifted her voice once more. "Belaal! I am Ela Roeh, prophet of Parne! Our Creator, the Infinite, has allowed you to lay siege to His people as punishment for their rebellion! But unless you offer Him the honor He is due, this victory will be given to another king!"

Ela paused, allowing her words to sink in to the army below. Men were hurrying from their tents, weapons readied. Raising her voice again, she cried to Belaal's king, "Bel-Tygeon!" She watched him emerge from his blue royal pavilion, golden-robed, elegant and impressive, a hand on his sword, a scowl on his handsome face. Ela exhaled a prayer, willing Bel-Tygeon to take her seriously. "Listen to your Creator. You are not a god! Bow or He will bring you down! This is your first warning! If you fail to heed Him, the Infinite will punish you for your arrogance!"

As Ela spoke, Zade Chacen crept toward her from the right.

To shove her from the wall, she knew. He'd learned nothing. Despair weighing her very soul, she turned. "Chacen, do you think the Infinite hasn't seen you?"

Before Chacen was within arm's reach, air blasted between them, throwing him back. The invisible current circled Ela, becoming a whirlwind, whipping her robes and mantle tight around her body. Remembering her vision, she stood still, begging in silence for composure.

The whirlwind surrounded her completely, removing all other sounds. Blurring her senses. Dizzied, she shut her eyes.

Just as nausea twisted her stomach and threatened to overwhelm her, the air calmed.

Brain spinning, Ela opened her eyes, managed to focus, and saw Prill's shocked face as the matron waited in the hidden courtyard.

Infinite, don't let me be sick on Prill!

✦ ✦ ✦

A wild clatter woke Kien from his first sound rest in a week's travel. Eleven days until they reached Parne! Frowning, he looked around his tent. What had awakened him? The clatter resumed, shaking his tent's central pole. Attacking the whole structure. Kien rolled from his cot.

A shadow rushed along outside the tent, and someone muttered, "Hurry! Kill it!"

Kill what? Kien swept his sword from its scabbard and ran outside.

Siphran soldiers were flinging weighted nets at the tent's crest. An errant woodpecker flitted from the central pole, too late to save itself from being enmeshed.

"Breakfast!" one netter bellowed. He bowed as others roared approval.

One bug-ridden bird had caused all this commotion? Kien laughed and shook his head. Then realized he was barefoot and wearing only an undertunic. Not naked, at least. Already the soldiers were snickering. Best to ease into his tent. Had half the camp seen him? He swept a glance around—scanning Akabe's tent in particular.

Yes, there was Akabe, properly dressed and laughing at him. However, Akabe's nearest servant wasn't laughing. Indeed, the man hadn't noticed Kien's inappropriate attire. His attention was fixed on the king. Kien frowned. Actually, he'd never seen this particular servant before. Odd. The man's uniform fit him poorly. . . .

A blade flashed from beneath the servant's long sleeve.

"Infinite! No!" Wielding his Azurnite sword in a two-handed grip, Kien raced toward Akabe's would-be assassin.

26

Kien charged Akabe's attacker, rage deepening his bellow. "Save the king!"

Eyes widening, Akabe turned just as his intended killer slashed toward him. The blade stuck, angled behind Akabe's right shoulder. The young king yelled and knocked aside the assailant's wrist with his forearm.

Before the man could produce another weapon, Kien shifted his sword to the left and flung his right arm around the criminal's throat, tightening the hold with all his might. The impact threw him to the ground with the assailant, who fell against the Azurnite blade. A garbled scream told Kien the man could still breathe. He cinched his right arm tighter and anchored the miscreant to the ground with his own weight.

Just as Akabe's laggard bodyguards fell on them.

Crushed, smothering, and hit with punches and kicks from every direction, Kien yelled, "Ow! Grab him! Help the king!"

From a distance, Akabe bellowed, "Don't kill him!"

Don't kill who? The rescuer or the assailant? Kien gulped for air, then coughed at the taste of blood. He was trapped beneath the brawl, unable to move, and afraid to release his hold on Akabe's attacker. The man wheezed hoarse threats and clawed shreds of pain into Kien's bare forearm.

Someone roared in Kien's ear, "We've got him, sir! Let go!"

Ears ringing, Kien released his captive, and the bodyguards dragged them apart. The Azurnite sword escaped Kien's numbed left hand as he was hauled away. "Stop!"

Three bodyguards, pummeling the failed assassin, froze. "Not you," Kien told them. "The ones holding me." He twisted to glare up at two fight-riled soldiers. "Unhand me *now*."

They dropped him. Every fresh bruise on his beaten body screamed. Kien gritted his teeth. He couldn't very well snarl at them for obeying him, could he? He staggered to his feet and bent slightly to test a deep breath. Good. No broken ribs, just bruises. But blood splashed down the front of his undertunic. Crimson splotches on white. A bashed nose. And likely—from the grinding stabs in his feet—broken toes. Kien scowled and retrieved his sword. Blood oozed from the flesh-shredded scratches on his forearm. He hoped the assassin hadn't loaded his fingernails with poison.

But what about the knife blade he'd used on Akabe? Horrific thought. Sword in hand, Kien faced the bodyguards who'd dropped him. "The king! Is he well?"

A call echoed from Akabe's royal tent. "Bring His Majesty to the king!"

Kien hesitated. "Who?"

The bodyguards answered Kien's question by gripping his arms. Supportive now. "Majesty, are you well? You've blood everywhere. The king will be alarmed."

Majesty. Wonderful. More than a month of politely arguing with the entire Siphran court had accomplished nothing. He *had* to break Akabe's people of their insistence upon calling him *Majesty* as well as referring to him as *the other king*.

Tsir Aun, current prime minister of Istgard, might misunderstand if he heard that Kien was being addressed as Istgard's uncrowned sovereign. Bad for international relations.

The bodyguards jostled Kien, evidently concerned. "Majesty?"

Forcing himself to sound courteous, Kien said, "Do *not* call me that! I am Kien Lantec, special envoy from the Tracelands, and a judge-advocate. Either designation will suffice."

"Yes, um . . . sir." The man hesitated. "But are you well?"

"Yes, thank you. And thanks to the Infinite. Please unhand me. I'm capable of walking on my own." Or limping, at least. Yet it would be rude of him to point out that the bodyguards had inflicted most of his injuries. Blood dripped steadily from his nose. Was it broken, not merely bashed? Perhaps Ela wouldn't mind his altered profile. Actually, she'd be appalled and quite sympathetic. Liable to fuss over him. He smiled at the thought.

The king's fightmaster, Lorteus, stood guard at the entry to the royal tent. He surveyed Kien from head to toe, clearly hiding a grin. Lorteus bowed his ugly head to Kien, then warned, "Do not think you are excused from practice today, sir. Even now, bloodied and injured, you can fight!"

Cheering beast of a fightmaster.

Kien entered Akabe's pavilion and halted. Akabe was seated on an x-framed chair in the midst of the oversized tent, his big hands on his knees, his feet braced on the floor. The splendid red tunic hung in shreds around him, evidently cut away by his surgeon, who was now dabbing at the wound with a drenched, blood-tinged cloth. The pavilion reeked of sharp-scented medications. Akabe grimaced as the surgeon splashed more liquid on the gash. At Akabe's worktable, a clerk poured thick blood-red liquid onto a parchment. Jolted by the sight, Kien reminded himself that all official documents were sealed with Akabe's signature dark red wax.

Too worried to offer formal greetings, Kien asked, "Was the blade poisoned?"

Akabe shot him a sidelong look. "Trust you to consider a worse possibility, my friend." He glanced over his shoulder at his military surgeon. "Well, Riddig? Am I poisoned?"

While arranging a series of delicate tools, the surgeon tilted his silvered head, birdlike, contemplating the damage. "It appears a clean wound, sire, more aligned beneath the skin than piercing the muscle. Therefore, if you are poisoned, which I doubt, it will likely be treatable. Odd angled wound, and a lucky one."

"A blessed one," Akabe corrected kindly. "The Infinite and my friend protected me." He nodded to Kien. "I say you have received more injuries than I, Majesty."

"Respectfully, please, don't call me *Majesty*."

Akabe's mouth tightened briefly as the surgeon jabbed him, suturing the wound. Between stitches, Siphra's ruler said, "What you wish . . . does not signify with . . . my people. Now that . . . your heritage is known . . . in their thoughts . . . you are a king. Nevertheless . . ." He took a deep breath, then exhaled as the surgeon paused. "If you forbid us to address you so, then you need an official Siphran title." Eyeing his hovering advisors, Akabe asked, "Suggestions?"

One of the graybeards snatched a document from the heap on Akabe's worktable. "Aeyrievale has just brought a petition requesting Your Majesty's personal selection of their next lord."

Title? Lord? They were serious! Kien snapped, "No!"

"Aeyrievale." A second graybeard nodded. "Perfect! The income is appropriate to—"

The king of Siphra flexed his hands, then removed one of his rings and tossed it to his clerk. "Approved, chosen, and commanded. Sign and seal the document."

Summoning absolute sternness, Kien said, "No. I'm a Tracelander, not a Siphran! It's inappropriate for me to hold any sort of title!"

"Might I also declare him Siphran?" Akabe asked his advisors, who hovered over the petition, scribbling on it. "A dual citizenship?"

"Certainly, sire," graybeard number one assured Akabe while pouring a blood-red pool onto the document and pressing Akabe's signet into the liquid. "We'll see to it immediately."

Were they *trying* to be irksome, disregarding his protests? "With all respect, sirs, I refuse the title."

Akabe grinned at him. "Impossible. Your name was signed with my seal added. The document cannot be unsealed."

"It's done?" Kien stared. "That's ludicrous! What sort of government conducts business so swiftly?"

"An efficient one," the graybeard muttered. "With much catching up to do."

"Undo it!" Kien commanded. "I've refused the title. Doesn't that count for something?" In desperation, he said, "Burn the document."

Graybeard's eyes widened, alarmed. "Majesty, uh, my lord, tampering with the royal seal is a criminal offense, punished by death."

"I'll burn it," Kien offered. Then he would run for his life.

While the clerks hastily locked the document in a wooden chest, Akabe spoke to Kien. "You're injured and too distraught to think calmly. Don't worry, my friend. Aeyrievale, from what I've heard, is not all gold and joy. Aeryon nests fill its most remote areas, and you're obligated to clear at least a few of the beasts using your own resources. They tend to prey upon your subjects and their animals."

Aeryon hunting? Well, he'd enjoy the chance to take down one of those golden monster-bird, feline-tailed raptors. What a trophy to . . . No. What was he thinking? The Tracelands was his concern, not Aeyrievale. Kien growled, "There must be some way I can set aside this title."

"Short of killing me, you cannot. It's a royal bequest. An honor." Siphra's king motioned to his surgeon. "You're finished stitching me? Good. Work on my noble friend. He's out of his mind with pain. Meanwhile, where is my misguided assailant? If he's still alive, we must interrogate him."

✦ ✦ ✦

Following the trail of a vision, Ela lifted the lamp higher, watching its flame sway amid the tunnel's darkness. Beside her, Father smiled in the fragile, flickering light. "There *is* a definite current of air flowing from here. Are you sure about this, Ela?"

"Very sure. This tunnel is what I saw in my vision. For everyone's sake, we must find a way to escape Parne without going through the city." Everyone's sake but her own. Shoving aside her fears, she studied the nearest wall. Golden handlike formations of crystals glinted at her in the darkness. Beautiful crystals. "Father? Have you seen these?"

Dan stared at the glittering yellow stones. "Don't touch them. These are the caustic ores I was accused of selling to others. We must warn everyone not to touch the walls here."

Footsteps and Deuel's voice echoed through the tunnel. "Are you there?"

Ela turned. Father called, "Deuel? We're here—don't touch the walls!"

Helpful-sounding, Deuel answered, "I've a torch, a lamp, and tools." His words faded, though his footsteps approached. At last, Ela heard him mutter, "Stars and sunsets! What I wouldn't give for a proper light when we're away from the tree." He appeared, his face a play of shadows and creases. "How did you two cross this distance with only one lamp?"

"I've been here in a vision," Ela told him. "It's only a bit farther. Do you mind climbing?"

Father's eyes flickered in the lamplight. "*Now* you mention climbing? Ela, you must warn us in advance of risks."

"Hmm. Well, this is a risk. I'm praying no one from Belaal or in Parne hears us creating this escape."

Deuel chuckled. "Using metal tools against stone walls? Bah! Who would hear us? Now . . . where is this escape route?"

Ela led the way, pondering each turn, measuring everything against her latest vision. At last, she held the lamp against an oddly angled wall. "Up there."

As if to verify her statement, the lamp's flames and the torch drew upward, fluttering, seeming pulled by a current that led to the surface above. No doubt there was a break somewhere, slight and hidden from their eyes.

Father tested the angled wall. "Stone. But workable. We'll have to carve steps first and be sure they're safe for the women and children." He opened his leather knapsack and began removing tools.

Deuel grabbed one of the chisels and a hammer, then hesitated. "Oh. I forgot to tell you, Ela, Nesac's wife is having pains. Her child is coming."

"Oh!" Ela breathed a prayer for the young woman, but envy ate at her. Infinite? Is there the least chance I'll survive? That I might—

She left the thought dangling. The hope must be buried with her in the darkness of an unlived desire. Why allow herself to dream of Kien? Of marrying him, loving him, and bearing his children? She was supposed to die young, somehow entombed beneath Parne. . . .

Parne's departed sages whispered at her. *A silver-haired prophet has failed. All prophets die young.* And horribly.

Alone. Entombed. Surrounded by the stench of death. Ela's throat dried.

As if sensing Ela's fears, Father gave her a brief hug. "Let's get busy cutting the steps."

✦ ✦ ✦

Properly clothed now, Kien stared down at the failed assassin.

Bound and unwillingly kneeling before Akabe, the wiry, swollen-jawed man darted a look of hatred at Kien through puffy, bruised eyelids. A slice, evidently inflicted by landing on Kien's sword, created a bloody vertical wound along his left cheekbone.

Akabe spoke to his attacker in low, pondering tones, weighed with reluctance. "Will you say nothing to mitigate your circumstances? To possibly save your life?"

The man refused to meet Akabe's gaze. Refused to speak. Akabe tried again, actually pleading now. "Will you at least tell us your name? Should your family be left to wonder at your departure from their lives? Do they deserve the agony of endless uncertainty?"

Kien saw the condemned one flinch and suck in a breath as if

Akabe had found a weakness. Bracing himself visibly, the failed assassin shook his head, silent.

"Sire," an advisor murmured to Akabe, "we can gain nothing from him. By his markings only have we learned anything of this man." The advisor nodded to one of the guards, who pulled up the assailant's sleeves. "Observe the goddess coils. He is an entrenched Atean who has participated in their deepest rites."

Kien stared at the permanent etchings curving thick and black around the man's biceps. These were goddess coils? Infinite? How may I serve You here?

Speak to him.

Stilled, Kien listened to the flow of words through his thoughts. Fighting down his own vengeful impulses, he obeyed and spoke quietly to Akabe's attacker. "Your Creator calls to you. He bears the scars of your hatred, yet He loves you as His own son. *Maseth.*"

The condemned one, Maseth, widened his swollen eyes at Kien. "How did you know?"

It was impossible to hate or resent the man now, realizing how desperately the Infinite cared for Maseth. A rush of emotion swept Kien like a wind from the heavens, permeating his soul. Humbling him. And granting the same elation he'd experienced in Adar-iyr. Was this outpouring of the Infinite's Spirit the source of Ela's strength? Shaken, Kien said, "I know your name, Maseth, because the Infinite told me when I saw your markings. He asks you to call His name. To trust Him with your whole being. If you do, all will be forgiven."

Infinite? All?

All.

"All," Kien repeated. "Your Creator mourns separation from you—He loves you."

Seeming hit by Kien's words, Maseth rocked on his knees, back and forth, as if fighting to make a decision. The man's struggle was visible. Agonizing. Kien coerced himself to watch.

At last, Maseth's rocking stilled. He gasped, "You must kill me! I must die. To protect my family I can say nothing more, except . . . except what you already know." He looked Akabe in the eyes. "They want you dead. They *will* have you dead because of the Infinite!"

Akabe sagged in his chair and covered his face with one large hand. When he didn't speak, Maseth said, "You must order me killed! You have no choice! I have no choice! I've been caught, and I mustn't survive! Order my death!" Tears rimmed the man's eyes. "Please. You don't know them. Please . . ."

Akabe nodded and motioned to his guards. Rough-voiced, he said, "Be swift and merciful."

Truly condemned now, Maseth wavered in obvious relief. While the bodyguards wrenched him to his feet, Maseth appealed to Kien. "Walk with me?"

Sickened by the thought, Kien started to shake his head.

You are a judge, and he is condemned. Prove My compassion. Walk with him.

Kien stood, motioned one of the guards aside, and gripped Maseth's arm.

27

Their booted feet trampled the autumn-dried grass beyond the encampment's edge. For a time, Kien fixated on the brittle rustlings of the faded meadow. On his own broken-toed limp. And on the guards around them who were armed with short spades, picks, and long knives. Implements for digging Maseth's grave, then executing him. Was the condemned man frightened? To distract him, Kien asked, "Why did you request that I accompany you?"

A pained half smile twisted in Maseth's gashed face. "Because I have not been called Maseth since my mother died. I was six."

"I'm sorry." Kien winced inwardly. By his lowered, reverent tone, Maseth remembered his mother tenderly.

His smile fading, Maseth added, "She would weep to see me now."

"Tell me about her."

"You know enough."

"I respect your sentiment. Did the Ateans threaten your family in order to convince you to assassinate your king?"

Silence. Beneath his breath, Kien said, "I'm taking that as a yes." Turning the topic slightly, he added, "I glimpsed an Atean rite not long ago. Understandable that such . . . festivals . . . would attract many." It wouldn't do to mention that revulsion had overwhelmed his fascination. He didn't want Maseth to become defensive.

Maseth's swollen eyes widened slightly. "You, one of the Infinite's believers, witnessed a hidden gathering?"

"Yes. I'd been tracking a young miscreant and supposed I was following orders. When I realized what was happening, I retreated."

Dry voiced, Maseth said, "No doubt." After a pause, he asked "Did the Ateans bear marks? Coils, like these on my arms?"

"Not that I noticed within that brief look."

"Hatchlings." Bitterness laced Maseth's words. "Nothing but foolishness and false freedom."

"Yes, and I admit I was startled by the, er, revelry. I'd heard rumors of ritual strangulations."

"In the highest order only. Not among the hatchlings."

So the ritual strangulations weren't mere rumor? Kien scarcely heard his own whisper, "Where do they acquire the victims?"

"Stolen from the most vulnerable hatchlings. The Infinite's followers are blamed for disappearances."

Infinite?

Pained, brooding stillness met Kien's question.

They walked until the guards agreed upon a spot where the sunlit field met the shadows of a nearby wood. One of the guards wrenched at Maseth's bound arms. "Sit. Pray if you've a brain."

Maseth's answering snort was suspiciously close to a chuckle. But after he'd managed to sit, he bowed his head. And his lips moved silently as if in prayer.

Cautious of his broken toes, Kien sat beside the man and prayed for him. Maseth, beyond doubt, was acutely aware of the guards slamming their picks and spades into the soil before them. He twitched whenever the picks struck the ground near his feet. Surely the man would be honest to his very soul during his final mortal breaths. At long last, Maseth opened his puffed eyes, staring at his dark, deepening grave.

Kien asked, "To whom did you pray?"

Without lifting his gaze from the widening hole, Maseth said, "When you have been told, since age seven, that you are expendable, and that the one *being* you must love and worship can replace you . . . And you believe it until the last day of your life . . . Until a stranger, who knows your first, most secret and cherished name, says your Creator is calling you, your Creator loves you despite your evils . . ." He looked at Kien now, wearied, bruised, and bloodied. "Who would receive your prayers?"

Some of Kien's distress eased. He gave Maseth a celebratory thump on the shoulder and apparently struck an injured place. Maseth flinched and growled. "Ow!"

"Apologies."

When the grave was nearly finished, one of the guards paused, untied a waterskin, and took a long drink. Kien saw Maseth's gaze following the guard's motions and avidly watching excess drops of water falling into the grave's depths. On impulse, Kien reached toward the guard. "May I request a drink?"

"Certainly, my lord." Obviously considering himself honored, the guard offered the waterskin to Kien.

"Thank you." Kien held the skin's spout toward the startled Maseth. "Here."

The man drank as if he hadn't touched water in days. Finished, he licked his lips. "My last wish granted, and by a lord." He sighed, his tensed posture easing. "Truly, it's time for me to die."

Clearly offended, the guard snapped at Maseth, "He's no plain lord! He's Istgard's rightful uncrowned king."

Maseth stared at Kien, incredulous. "Are you?"

What could the truth hurt? "Yes. However, with the Infinite's counsel, I refused Istgard."

While Maseth absorbed this and shook his head, Kien said, "Your King Akabe wishes he'd been given a similar option. He would have refused the Siphran crown."

"He seems a good man," Maseth confessed. Sighing heavily, he added, "I'm glad I failed to kill him."

"My lord," one of the guards prompted Kien and cast a meaningful look at the grave.

Before Kien could respond, Maseth heaved himself to his

knees, scooted toward the grave's edge, then looked up at the sky. Sweating, he addressed the guards. "I'm ready."

✦ ✦ ✦

Kien frowned, watching Akabe as they rode beneath Siphra's red banners. It had been seven days since the attack. Four days yet until Parne, and the young king was a marvel. Always busy: Praising his commanders and his men. Enforcing order. Overseeing the army's provisions. Gathering additional troops, horses, and wagons garrisoned along the way through Siphra toward Parne. Moreover, he unfailingly beguiled citizens in every town with his brief good-natured speeches and his remarkable kingly appeal.

But when would he talk of Maseth?

The king waved off his general, who'd described where they'd make camp for the night. Kien glanced about to be sure no one else was within earshot and said, "Akabe."

Akabe lifted an eyebrow at him. "What?"

"Maseth. He died well."

Shifting his gaze to the dusty road ahead, the king said, "Our couriers were remarkably efficient in alerting the rural commanders to muster their troops at specific intervals."

"He was glad he didn't succeed in killing you."

Akabe adjusted his horse's reins, shifted uncomfortably, and then, finally, gusted out a sigh of apparent resignation. "Tell me why I want to think of the first man I condemned to death."

Good question. With at least one obvious answer. "Because, inevitably, you'll have to condemn others."

The king snapped a glance at him now, hurt and anger merging over his features. "Well enough! You wish to know? I see Maseth every day. In my sleep, I hear his voice pleading for death. I wake up and say to myself, 'Never again! Infinite, I beg You, never again!' And now you say I'll condemn others to haunt my dreams? Ones who will be less eager to die? What sort of friend have I found in you?" Almost surly, he added, "When I think of Maseth, I long to be wild, free in the Snake Mountains, hunting with my men."

"*I* think of Maseth and I'm grateful."

Another look. A truly royal scowl. "Why?"

"Because, through Maseth, I experienced the Infinite's mercy and justice. His mercy in calling to Maseth and comforting him. While showing His justice in protecting you, Maseth's family, and your kingdom, despite the assassination attempt."

Akabe grunted, seeming a bit calmer.

Curious, Kien asked, "During your time as an outlaw, you never killed anyone?"

"Yes," Akabe admitted. "But in self-defense. And that is justifiable, as is war."

"How was Maseth's death different? It was justifiable. He *was* trying to kill you."

"Perhaps because I was forced to order another to execute him, knowing there were . . ."

"Possible extenuating circumstances that partially absolved the offender's culpability?" Kien offered.

"Yes, Judge." Akabe grimaced. "Might we speak of other matters?"

"Such as Parne?" Kien's whole being tensed, listening.

"We have two days yet to the border. Forces from Istgard and the Tracelands will meet with us, south of the city called Ytar. We must discuss our strategy."

Yes! Time to pry Parne from Belaal's claws and save Ela! By now, according to reports, Parne had been under siege for over a month. Was Ela starving? Dead? Infinite, let me see Ela when we reach Parne. Let me know she's safe!

Do you not trust Me to know what is best for My prophet—including her death?

Kien's stomach twisted. Here was something he did not want to surrender. His love for Ela. His fears for her life. Yet Ela desired Her Creator's will, as Kien must.

Infinite? Strengthen me and teach me to trust You. I know I am weak!

"Lord Aeyrievale!" Akabe's use of that frustrating, unwanted title made Kien turn. Akabe scowled. "I asked, 'What do you know of Parne?'"

"Not enough, sir." Only that Parne held Ela in its grasp.

And Kien must trust the Infinite for her life.

✦ ✦ ✦

Kneeling in the spring-bright grass, Ela combed her clean hair while looking around the cavern. Every contour of this space, warmly lit by the tree's radiance, reflected peace. A tranquility that soothed Parne's exiled faithful despite their fears. Only the Infinite could have inspired such calm.

Ela tucked her comb into her knapsack, then crept over to a nest of quilts and kissed her sleeping baby brother's softly rounded face. Jess didn't wake, but a blissful smile played over his sweet mouth. The most perfect little boy alive.

Thank You, Infinite!

Seated nearby among the other women, Nesac's wife, Sara, drew Ela's attention by rewrapping her newborn daughter, Adania. When she noticed Ela's glance, Sara beckoned her with raised eyebrows and an I-want-to-tell-you-something tilt of the chin.

Ela crept over to Sara Nesac and sat between her and Prill. Sara had left Adania's delicate hands free of the swaddling clothes. Captivated, Ela stroked the tiny girl's fingers, admiring her blooming complexion. She willed herself to set aside her envy of Sara. To repress mournful thoughts of the children she and Kien would never have.

Her gentle brown eyes solemn, Sara said, "We've been praying for you."

"Thank you," Ela whispered. She would need every prayer. Every possible blessing that might see her through these last few days. To prevent herself from remembering her death, Ela began to braid her hair. "Is there a specific reason you've prayed?"

"I can't be certain," Sara murmured. "I just need to pray for you, and it's easier to pray here than it was up in the city."

To Ela's left, Prill said, "I agree." She frowned at Ela's hair. "You'd best let me rework that braid, Ela Roeh."

Ela looked down at her handiwork. All right. So the braid was uneven. Ragged, actually. But should a prophet worry about such trivialities? However, if it made her chaperone happy to tidy up the braid . . . "Thank you. I'll fetch my comb."

As she returned, Ela glanced around. Most of the women were clustered in groups, chatting and tending children, as placid as brooding hens. Kalme, however, was perched within the tree's branches, picking gem-bright fruits and tossing them to the children and matrons who were too frail or timid to climb. Satisfied, Ela settled between Sara and Prill once more.

While Prill unraveled Ela's braid, Ela murmured. "I'll tell only you two. I don't want my parents to be unnecessarily frightened. If I vanish within the next few days and fail to return, please pray for me. Reassure everyone that I'm fulfilling the Infinite's will."

Prill's nimble fingers stilled. "Doing what?"

"I'm not quite sure."

"Without me?"

"Yes."

"I think I don't approve." Prill resumed braiding, but tugged at Ela's hair. Hard.

"Ouch!" Ela rubbed her stinging scalp. "Trust me, you do approve."

Additional braid tugging accompanied the matron's scolding tone. "Ela Roeh, what aren't you telling us?"

"Something you'd rather not know. Augh!" Fussy biddy of a chaperone!

Instantly, Ela regretted her rebellion. She turned and hugged Prill. "Just pray!"

The woman sniffled. Moisture, suspiciously tear-like, brimmed in her stern brown eyes. "I'm sorry for being so short-tempered. It's because I'm concerned. You just be safe."

Not likely. "I'll try."

✦ ✦ ✦

A waking vision.

A breath of a breeze. An invisible separation from her fellow refugee-Parnians, who were sleeping in niches throughout the cavern. Ela stood and exhaled, bowing her head as a twist of nausea built in her stomach.

Infinite? As You will.

The silent, invisible whirlwind closed about her, tightening its hold like an indomitable fist. Removing her from the underground sanctuary.

28

Parne was night-haunted. And she, Ela Roeh, was the unseen being who flitted across its refuse-strewn rooftops after dusk, her voice breaking into the city's tattered stillness. Into the wretched, sleepless weakness of disease and starvation. "Parne, call to your Creator! Pray to Him—allow Him to spare you from the beasts who gather at your gates. Surrender and live!"

Most often, silence met her pleas. But now and then, a doorway creaked in the darkness, followed by whispers and footsteps in the courtyards below. And weeping, mingled with cries of despair that wrung Ela's heart.

The stench of death permeated every street. All avoidable losses!

Pray, she urged the starving mourners. Listen to the Infinite and escape with your lives!

The Infinite whispered, *If they call to Me, I will save them!*

They would survive famine, sword, and flames.

Oh, Parne, listen to your Creator. . . .

In the highest sector of the city, just below the temple, Ela paused on the roof of Zade Chacen's house. "Chacen! Even now, He will spare you if you call to Him."

The rooftop door creaked open and Chacen lunged toward her from the darkness. But not fast enough—and unarmed.

Ela skittered away into the deepening night. "Surrender and live!"

✦ ✦ ✦

At dawn, she stood on the wall and stared out at the sea of crested tents and rippling banners. Banners, bearing badges of writhing reptiles and a golden flower—delicately incongruous in life as in her vision—heralded two western tribes, the Agocii and the Eosyths, who'd allied with Belaal and merged their small armies to King Bel-Tygeon's, hoping to share Parne's treasures.

No doubt they'd feasted on Parne's captured supplies.

And, obviously, they'd seen her standing here, looking down on them. A number of Belaal's gold-and-blue clad soldiers clustered together in the wall's shadow watching her, their infrequent glances over their shoulders telling her that they were awaiting someone else's arrival.

She watched, remembering her vision.

Bel-Tygeon, striking, self-assured, and filled with the arrogance of spoiled royalty, strode toward the gathering. His men bowed, but the king ignored them, calling to Ela, "Now, Prophet! Am I shamed? Have you come to curse me again?"

"You bring curses and shame to yourself, O King, by allowing yourself to be worshiped as a god. Only the Infinite rules in the heavens."

He laughed and yelled, "Is it so? I've seen nothing to persuade me of your words—your idle threats! What will you do to convince me Belaal's ways are wrong?"

Prill would not like his tone. Or his manner. The confidence of a man used to treating all women as his own. Handsome as he was, his soul was nothing like Kien's. Unmoved, Ela said, "Within seven days, Bel-Tygeon, another king will take Parne, and you will know you are not a god."

The king's amusement faded. "By what means?"

"By the Infinite's Word. Until then, know that He watches you!"

She felt the sweep of air against her cheek. The unseen current encircled Ela, removing her from the sight of Parne and its enemies.

✦ ✦ ✦

For Ela! Two days until they reached Parne!

Kien gritted his teeth as Lorteus struck his arm with the flat of a sword. The fightmaster snarled in a chant, "Always moving, always moving! Expect every foe to deliver you a fatal strike at any instant!"

What about a mortally beastly fightmaster? Kien scowled into his opponent's battered face. How were his broken toes going to finish mending if this man kept hounding him? While Kien tried to move without reinjuring his toes, a thunderous cadence shook the ground. Recognizing its rage-inspired pace, Kien nearly howled, sensing imminent victory over his ruthless trainer.

Lorteus clearly felt the same fearsome beats, which sent vibrations upward from the very soil, shaking Siphra's whole encampment. Lorteus shifted his gaze toward the sound, distracted just long enough for Kien to lunge and grab him in the same stranglehold he'd used to bring down Maseth.

They dropped like two felled trees. The fightmaster spit syllables of outrage until a massive black monster-horse snapped him up by his thick tunic. Lorteus screamed.

Kien released his howl of laughter, then yelled, "No, don't hurt him! Scythe! Drop the fightmaster!"

Scythe grumbled in supreme disapproval. But he dropped Lorteus like a rejected snack, then bent to lift Kien instead.

Dangling midair, Kien warned, "Careful of my toes, you lummox." The instant he was on his feet, Kien stroked the monster's glossy black neck. "How are you?"

The destroyer groaned tellingly and sighed unmistakable noises of sorrow.

Kien smoothed what he could reach of Scythe's mane. He could almost feel the beast's grief for Tzana, his longing to see Ela. "I understand. Believe me. The wait is killing me too!"

Scythe shifted and exhaled a moisture-laden gust of breath into Kien's hair. It was all Kien could do to refrain from checking for slobber.

By now, Lorteus had scrambled to his feet. He started to reach for his sword. But Scythe bit toward his hand. To his credit, the fightmaster didn't retreat, though his complexion went ghastly in evident alarm. He muttered to Kien, "You've a . . . destroyer?"

"Yes." He grinned at the shocked man. "Why? Is this important?"

"It is in-indeed." Lorteus scraped together something resembling an air of command. He studied Scythe and his eyes lit like an eager boy's. "You must learn new fighting tactics!"

Scythe rumbled a threat. Lorteus's fight-scarred face tightened, but he didn't step back.

Kien felt obligated to say, "Again, Scythe, don't hurt him. He's a fightmaster. We're supposed to quarrel. It's his job to swat me with swords."

The destroyer curled his equine lips back from his big teeth in obvious disgust.

Lorteus bowed and said, "We'll delay the remainder of today's lesson."

Good. "Thank you, Lorteus. Most likely my sister and her husband are on their way into camp." When the man left, Kien gave Scythe a fond cuff. "Have you behaved for Jon and Beka?"

The monster warhorse sniffed and looked away.

Not good. That sort of avoidance behavior guaranteed some costly mischief. "Did you eat someone's garden?"

The black monster grazed near Kien's booted feet. Feigning innocence, Kien suspected. Wonderful. Scythe had probably chomped down several estates somewhere.

More thunderous hoofbeats shook the encampment. Kien waited, certain Jon and Beka's destroyers would bring them directly to him. Or, more accurately, to Scythe.

Jon rode into the open space first, splendid in his black commander's uniform. He saw Kien and called over his shoulder to a yet unseen person, "He's here and in one piece!"

"Were you wagering I'd lost a limb?"

"Not precisely." Jon reined in Savage, then descended to the ground. "Beka's been fretting over you. Particularly now."

"Why particularly now?"

Jon grinned. "You'll hear why soon enough."

Looking thoroughly aggravated, Beka rode up and commanded Audacity to stand with Savage. The female destroyer obeyed but fussed and huffed as if certain Beka was making a terrible mistake. Beka stormed in turn, "Really, Aud! Will you just behave?"

Kien laughed. "Now, girls—"

Audacity snapped at him and so did Beka. "Oh hush, Kien!"

Scythe tugged Kien backward. Gently. Kien muttered to the beast, "Obviously, you know something I don't. So what is it?"

The destroyer sighed. Humid monster-horse breath saturated Kien's hair. He suppressed a shudder.

After Jon had helped Beka dismount, and after she'd stretched and shaken the wrinkles from her gown, Beka offered him an apologetic look. "Kien, I'm sorry. I didn't mean to sound testy. It's just that I feel awful!"

She looked awful too, but Kien wasn't about to mention her sickly coloring or the circles beneath her eyes. Before he could ask if she'd contracted an exotic fever, which he intended to run from, Beka beamed. She patted Jon's arm in obvious delight and said, "I'm pregnant!"

Kien hesitated. "This is good news, right? You won't bite me if I congratulate you? And Audacity won't bite me if I hug you?"

"No! Here." Beka rushed to hug him. Kien gave her a gentle squeeze and kissed the top of her braided, veiled hair. Beka sighed. "Oh, Kien, I'm so tired! And I'm hungry and swelling like—"

"Stop!" Kien raised a hand in warning. "I want to be the proud and ignorant uncle, remember? I don't want to hear your symptoms."

"If you know how miserable I feel, you'll be more sympathetic. Really, I have to tell you . . ." She continued to talk as if she'd mistaken him for one of her friends. Xiana Iscove, for example. Kien shot a squeamish look at his brother-in-law.

Jon smiled and deliberately looked away.

Coward!

"Oh." Midstream, Beka stopped complaining. She patted Kien's hand. "I told Ela that I would tell you she loves you."

What? Trust Beka to confuse him with something that ought to be simple. "Can you rephrase that?"

As if Kien were a toddler, Beka carefully enunciated, "I said to Ela, 'I'll tell Kien you love him.' And she agreed I should."

"She didn't argue?"

"No. Why should she? It's the truth."

Kien laughed and lightly jostled his sister. "*You* are my favorite meddler. Thank you."

"You're welcome. Now, please, can we eat?"

"Of course. If you don't mind rations." Two days. He sent up a silent, fierce prayer.

Infinite, I beg You, let me see Ela soon!

Even as Kien finished the prayer, a young crimson-clad royal servant scurried toward him. Breathless, the scrawny servant bowed. "My lord, the king requests your presence. The prime minister of Istgard waits with him."

Aware of Beka's questioning look and Jon's sudden frown, Kien nodded to the boy. "Yes, thank you. Tell the king I'm on my way."

The youth turned and ran, his movements so uncoordinated that his official red cloak swung precariously, becoming awkwardly misaligned about his neck. Obviously new at his job. Kien shook his head, then realized Beka and Jon were both staring.

Beka said, "'*My lord?*' What's this about, Kien?"

He grimaced. "Akabe, the king, has declared me Lord of Aeyrievale, against my will, because I saved his life. He's also declared me Siphran."

Jon's frown deepened. "Is this sanctioned by the Tracelands' Grand Assembly?"

"The Grand Assembly isn't aware of my situation, and I'm told it's irrevocable in Siphra. Imagine being a king unable to rescind an order! I've sent General Rol a message, requesting his advice and asking him to speak to the Assembly."

Somber, Beka gripped Kien's sleeve. "You don't suppose the Tracelands will censure you . . . do you?"

Her words mirrored Kien's growing fears. Censure was a possibility, particularly if certain anti-Lantec factions took control of any official debates regarding Kien's Siphran status and his unwanted title. What if his homeland did condemn him? What if he was stripped of martial authority mid-campaign as he tried to save Ela and Parne? He'd be rendered powerless. "We'll find out soon enough. Meanwhile, the king and the prime minister are waiting."

"Well," Beka said, a gleam of mischief and inspiration brightening her face, "while the prime minister's wife and I are here, waiting for the siege to end, we'll wage our own battle. I'll write letters to the wives of every possible sympathetic member of the Grand Assembly. I'll humbly explain your dilemma and beg the ladies, in their wisdom, to speak on your behalf to their husbands and anyone else who might question your devotion to the Tracelands."

Despite himself, Kien laughed. "As I said, you're my favorite meddler."

"Of course I am."

✦ ✦ ✦

Ela set the flickering lamps into niches within the tunnel walls, then stepped back, trying to gauge the men's progress in finishing the stairs.

Wearing scarves tied over their noses and mouths, Father, Deuel, Ishvah, and half a dozen others worked together, chiseling at the stone and passing rocks down the steps in an unspoken communication forged through long days of joint labor. Their mutual masterpiece, the stairs, resembled one of Parne's ascending paths, though it approached the crest of a cavern rather than the edge of a roof. Surely they were within days of completion. Then, once Father and the others were certain they could safely reach Siphran or Istgardian forces, they would escape Parne's destruction.

Ela wished she could escape with them. Yet, somehow, that would become impossible.

Infinite, guard them, please.

A sense of His waiting patience answered. With something like an unspoken rebuke. All right. Ela frowned, sifting through her thoughts. Her emotions. Her attitude. How had she erred? Infinite?

Do you not yet trust Me with those you love?

Ow. Yes, there it was. She still doubted His provision for her family and friends. Hadn't she conquered this weakness? Would she struggle with it until she died, all too soon? Dejection made her droop like some sort of wilting plant. Infinite, forgive me, please. I'm thinking and behaving like someone who doesn't understand You. Help me.

I am here.

Something in His words alerted her. Nudged her. Ela shook off her feelings of dejection, then looked around the tunnel. Now that she'd replenished the lamps and brought a cache of fruit from the tree, she wasn't needed here. She called up to Father, "I'm leaving!"

Dan grunted. "Take a torch."

"Thank you, I will." She lifted one of the crudely fashioned, resin-soaked torches from a pile near the steps, then cautiously lit it with a lamp's flame. Torches didn't burn nearly as long as lamps, but their glow was brighter. Just holding this torch made her long for her prophet's insignia, the branch. She hadn't realized how much she'd depended upon the branch's light and its surrounding sense of protection. Was this part of the reason the Infinite had removed it from her? Had she been using the branch as a spiritual crutch? She hoped not.

Such a prophet she'd proven to be. An absolute failure. Ela shoved away her self-accusations before they took hold of her thoughts. Why was she feeling so dismal today? What was wrong?

Praying silently, she lifted the flaring torch high and hurried through the tunnel, her boots crunching over stray bits of rock and dust. Here and there along the walls, the poisonous golden crystals glinted from the shadows like claws. Delicate yet lethal talons clutching rocks throughout this passageway. Just waiting to attack and carve toxic furrows into her flesh. No. Not yet. She must contemplate greater things and consider her blessings. She shivered.

Just as she reached the end of the tunnel, a low, ominous reverberation shuddered through the cavern beyond, permeating Ela's body and rattling her to the core. She froze in her tracks. What was that? A rockfall? Infinite?

His answer was a whisper of images sent to rest uneasily within her thoughts, provoking a pounding headache. She saw Chacen, gaunt, hateful, and armed with a yellow blade, storming a home in the city above, accompanied by his equally furious weapon-wielding followers. They were invading Parne's innermost locales, placing oily cakes within walls and igniting trailing wicks. Destroying hidden tomb houses within Parne.

"He's trying to find me?" Ela nearly choked on the insight. "He's destroying tomb houses and shrines to uncover our hiding place?"

Yes.

"Oh no!" Still seeing the weapons in her enemies' hands, she dashed from the tunnel and turned, her focus drawn to the tree's luminous presence. Toward the precious souls sheltered beneath its branches. Men, women, and children. Mother. Jess. "Infinite, is Chacen very near?"

Yes.

She approached the tree, breathless, not daring to speak aloud. Can I stop him?

Yes.

By surrendering to Chacen, she realized.

Then he would kill her. Sweat filmed Ela's palms. She quivered, causing the torch to waver in her grasp. To give herself time to pray and overcome the panic, Ela knelt and rolled the torch over the cavern's floor, extinguishing its flickering light.

Infinite? If I surrender to Chacen by dawn tomorrow, will it be soon enough?

An unspoken affirmation settled her. Ela breathed a sigh. Thank You.

She mustn't cry. She wouldn't. She needed to trust her Creator and think instead of a blessing. Her family and His faithful ones would be spared.

Still trembling inwardly, Ela found her mother.

Sheltered in the tree's glow with Jess in her lap, Kalme lifted her dark brows, eyes wide with fear. "What was that noise? That quaking?"

"The Infinite showed me it was a tomb house collapsing in the city. Rather close, but everyone will be safe enough down here."

Kalme's distress eased visibly. "How is your father?"

"He's fine. They'll finish the stairs in a day or two. May I hold Jess?"

"Of course." Mother looked down at Jess, clearly doting over his plump little form, his sweet face and bright brown eyes. "He's getting heavy."

Ela snatched her baby brother and kissed him, mumbling into his warm little cheek until he rewarded her with a toothless, soul-soothing grin.

Another more ominous boom rumbled through the vast cavern, shaking everyone. And shaking the walls. Ela huddled over her brother, shielding Jess from a spattering rain of clods and dust. Was Chacen bringing down the whole city?

Around her, she heard the other women and children shrieking. Jess cried, evidently resentful of Ela's protective grip. When the dustfall stopped, Ela sat up, jostling her infant brother to soothe him. He scrunched his tiny face at her and put out his lower lip, Tzana-like. Yes, beyond doubt offended. "If only you knew," she told him.

Kalme reached for Jess. "That one was closer! You're sure we're safe here?"

"Yes, Mother. Don't worry."

Though the attacks would succeed if she didn't surrender. Everyone here would be condemned as traitors to Parne. Ela shivered, almost seeing the bloodied swords and knives wielded by Chacen and his followers, exacting revenge on the Infinite's faithful without reason or pity.

Infinite? I'm ready. I'll go.

29

Kien shifted on Scythe's back, settling his feet into place along the destroyer's war collar.

His broken toes felt better today. It helped that the army's determined march toward Parne had consumed most of the past two days, preventing Fightmaster Lorteus from commanding him to practice.

Prime Minister Aun of Istgard rode up beside Kien now, matching his destroyer's pace to Scythe's. Kien nodded a greeting, marveling that this honorable man had, only last year, been his captor-guard—repeatedly dragging him to and from one of Istgard's prisons to face his accuser, Istgard's deceased king, Tek An.

His severe face outlined in the lowering sun, the prime minister nodded, a corner of his mouth lifting. "Lord Aeyrievale."

Kien grimaced. "Sir, no offense intended, but I believe you're secretly laughing at me."

Tsir Aun smiled. Just a bit. "Yes, I admit I'm amused. You, the most patriotic of Tracelanders, have had a second noble title forced upon you in less than a year. And this time the title's proponents were successful. One way or another, you'll have men bowing to you."

"Please, let's not even joke about it."

"Nevertheless, whatever the Tracelands might think, you *are* a Siphran lord." Tsir Aun eyed their destroyers, who were huffing low threats at each other. "I've heard your new lands and your tenants are beleaguered by Aeryons."

"So I've been told." Kien growled at Scythe, who was snapping at Tsir Aun's steed. "Aeryon hunting is the only appealing aspect of this whole disaster."

"What about protecting those who depend upon you?"

"What are you trying to say, Prime Minister?"

"You will be compelled to accept responsibility for your people."

A certain bleakness in Tsir Aun's tone made Kien stare. "You didn't want to become Istgard's prime minister, did you?"

"No. Yet I am. And I'll remain so for as long as I'm needed." He spoke sternly to his destroyer, who'd fitfully flattened his equine ears. "Wrath! Straighten those ears! *Now.*"

Wrath obeyed, but both destroyers grumbled as if the prime minister had ruined their game. Tsir Aun eyed Kien again, still severe. "Your people could suffer the rule of a far worse lord."

They are not my people. Kien almost said the words aloud, but stopped himself. According to the Siphrans, he was wrong. Officially. The inhabitants of Aeyrievale *were* his people, and Akabe couldn't rescind the order.

Infinite, I don't want people!

And to think that less than two months ago, he'd had the effrontery to lecture Akabe on a king's responsibilities and obligations. He had less to whine about than Akabe. "The inhabitants of Aeyrievale might have to live without me. I'm a military judge-advocate. The Tracelands will inflict penalties upon me if I officially accept this honor."

"It would be a terrible loss for Aeyrievale." The prime minister surveyed Kien now, clearly undeceived. "You are reluctant to accept responsibility for leading others. Not in a military setting, but in a personal realm. May I ask why?"

Kien hid a scowl. Tsir Aun was entirely too perceptive. "I know what it is to have others depend upon my decisions. And to fail them."

The prime minister's expression became faraway. And self-blaming. "You're thinking of the massacre at Ytar. And the attack in Riyan, the day you were arrested."

"The day I was ambushed and my servants were slaughtered? Yes." He'd never be able to speak of that day without self-loathing. And hatred for the tyrant who'd ordered the attacks. "I failed my men. They begged me to leave the night before, but no! I thought I knew better. I believed I should tell that butcher king, Tek An, what I thought of him for attacking Ytar."

His tone harsh, the words of a soldier who knew the truth, Tsir Aun said, "Undeserved as the charge was, you'd been condemned as a conspirator. Had you heeded your servants, you would have been caught and attacked anyway. In the wilderness, no doubt. And if I know you, sir, you would have died with them."

Yes. That was true. The massacre at Ytar had been too fresh and raw in Kien's thoughts. He would have fought any Istgardians to the death. "I'm sure you're right."

"I know I am." Tsir Aun didn't smile. Nor did his mood lighten. But he shifted the subject as if trying to distract Kien. "My wife and I visited Ytar recently. We were nearly ambushed, though it was clear we were visiting as a private household."

Hit with surprise, Kien stared. "The Ytarians are still thirsting for revenge?"

"I cannot blame them. However, thankfully, the Infinite sent a certain prophet to Ytar in advance of our visit, and she interceded."

"Ela." Kien almost sighed over her name. "How was she?"

"Well enough." Tsir Aun grunted. "She and the Thels were beset by robbers the day before. I've heard you've had dealings with the robbers' leader."

What? "I have nothing to do with robbers, sir!"

"An exiled Siphran lord. Ruestock."

The thin, arrogant Siphran lord's face smirked within Kien's thoughts, making him seethe. "Well, he's no longer exiled—though I wish he were! I should have allowed Scythe to kill the man last year. He's partially to blame for this Aeyrievale debacle."

"Perhaps it's not a disaster, but the Infinite's plan for you and for Aeyrievale. Do not be hasty in abandoning them, Lord Aeyrievale."

A chill slid over Kien's scalp and down his neck and arms. How could he escape this burden? Infinite?

Tsir Aun spoke again. "I take it you've no regrets in refusing the Istgardian crown."

"None. Particularly knowing it was the Infinite's will that I refuse." Kien wished his Creator would answer as decisively regarding Aeyrievale.

Tsir Aun didn't reply. Instead, he studied the horizon.

Kien followed his stare and saw a haze of smoke rising over what appeared to be a distant, pale hill. "Parne! Finally! And, it seems, the campfires of an army." Ela . . .

"Belaal," Tsir Aun observed. "Our timing is perfect. We'll approach Parne under the cover of darkness. By the way . . ." The prime minister of Istgard nodded toward Scythe. "Your destroyer ate half of a former palace garden."

"Only half?"

"It was a large garden. We are waiting to see if any life returns."

Kien scowled at his destroyer's twitching, listening black ears. "Have you no sense of restraint?"

Scythe grunted an unconvincing noise of disregard.

Tsir Aun said, "He was improperly leashed by government servants while Lara and I were meeting with the Thels. We accepted the blame."

"Thank you. But I still feel responsible."

"No need." The prime minister half smiled. "Actually, it was quite impressive. Your destroyer deserves his name."

Scythe tossed his head, betraying definite pride with the gesture.

✦ ✦ ✦

Moving softly to avoid waking anyone, Ela tucked the strap of Father's old waterskin beneath her mantle. Its podgy water-filled outlines sloshed against the small hoard of fruit she'd hidden within the belted, layered folds of her tunics.

Ready, she allowed herself to glance at her parents, who slept beneath a quilt with Jess snug in a nest under Kalme's hand. If only she could kiss them good-bye. But she didn't dare. Forcing herself to turn away, she smiled toward Prill instead. Even in sleep, her redoubtable chaperone was on guard. She'd evidently bundled three of the busiest little girls together and whispered them to sleep with stories. Then she'd fallen asleep herself, her thin hands turned toward the children even in slumber, as if—at the slightest stir—to prevent them from wandering.

Ela didn't know the little girls' names. She'd been too busy warning Parne at night and sleeping during the day to visit with many of the refugees. Well, though she'd had no time to play and teach the little ones, at least Prill did. Infinite, bless her.

Prill, don't forget! Tell my parents I've been called away by the Infinite.

Her heart hammered at the thought, so hard that she shook with its violence. If she stayed any longer, she'd weaken. She'd collapse. Infinite? Ela looked up at the tree, trying to calm herself in its gentle light, worshiping its Creator despite her panic. Help me!

A spiral of air steadied Ela, then swept her from the hushed cavern.

For an instant she blinked, disoriented by darkness until she looked up at the nighttime sky. Stars glittered amid sapphire and violet heavens, so lovely that she could almost forget she was standing in a dying city. Then she took a breath, and her nostrils filled with the thick, foul-sweet odor of disease and rotting flesh.

She hugged herself, fighting the need to retch. How many had died? The overpowering stench of decay testified that the living had given up on entombing the dead. Yet some still lived. In a darkened house to her left, someone was sobbing, low and harsh. Giving voice to a despair so profound that Ela couldn't escape its depths. Another soul lost!

Tears welled, almost choking her with grief. She clawed at

her braid and unraveled it, then arranged it as a tangled cloak of mourning. Dust from the street offered the only adornment she needed. As she sifted a handful of grit over her hair, sobs shook her, refusing to be contained.

She drew in a tormented breath, then wailed, "Paaarne! Will you die in your faithlessness? Why won't you call to your Creator, Who has always loved you? Why did you reject Him? Now you must drink from the cup you poisoned for yourselves!"

Infinite? Why was *I* so blind to their transgressions? Why won't they hear You?

Driven by desperation, she ran up a public stairway. At the top, she looked over the city and wept. Through her tears she cried, "Listen to the Infinite and live!" A vision overtook her then, and she reeled against its impact, falling to her knees.

Though she huddled beneath a nighttime sky, she saw the coming day's terror. Parne's secret would be revealed. Sickened, she scrambled to her feet and ran along the rooftops, toward the temple. "Chacen! You've weakened Parne's walls! Tomorrow your enemies will laugh, believing you've given them a way into the city!" Ela paused, listening. A scuffling sounded below, punctuated by harsh whispers that prickled the fine hairs along her arms. Who was coming for her?

Robes fluttering, she ran up flight after flight of steps until she couldn't breathe. At last, she sagged against a wall and listened, muffling her harsh, hurting gasps within the folds of her mantle. No footsteps sounded from the stairs below.

Safe. For now.

Regaining her breath, she cried, "Parne, you must surrender to the conquerors who will enter your streets! Listen! The Infinite commands you, 'Surrender and live!' If you fight, you will die by the sword!"

A man's voice bellowed, "Traitor!"

Footsteps again. Clattering up stairs. Coming toward her.

No! Not yet. Infinite, please, give me one last night to warn them! Praying, she ran.

✦ ✦ ✦

A tug wrenched Kien from his cot. "Hey!" He tumbled to the rough carpet, trying to see in the darkness as he sought his sword. Destroyer breath whooshed into his face, reassuring him instantly, but not calming him. How had the monster unleashed himself? Fearing Scythe would bring down his tent, Kien slung his sword over his back, then grabbed his boots and eased them on, wary of his toes. "I'm awake. And you'd best have an excellent reason for dragging me from a sound sleep!"

Scythe grunted and eased his head and front hooves out of the tent.

"My lord?" a sleep-roughened voice called out, accompanied by the unmistakable ring of metal—a blade drawn from its scabbard. "Are you well?"

"Yes . . ." Kien hesitated. What was the man's name? He'd followed the army to deliver that pestilent petition from Aeyrievale. And he was now so politely determined to serve Kien that chasing him off was impossible. Bryce. Yes. That was his name. Kien flung on a cloak. "Go back to sleep, Bryce. There's nothing to fear. My destroyer is being annoying."

"Yes, sir."

Scythe's breath gusted against the tent, shivering its thick fabric. A deep, indignant thud sent vibrations into the soles of Kien's boots. Kien hissed. "Stop that, you wretch! I'm coming!"

He ducked through the tent's entry and glared at the destroyer's huge form. "What?"

Scythe hunkered down and exhaled an imploring huff.

Kien growled. "I'm not running you in the middle of the night!" He studied the stars to the west and the faint glow in the east. Fine. It *was* nearly dawn. "Still, it's too early."

The monster opened his big mouth and stretched, as if to snap up Kien. "*Stop.* No kidnapping your master." Scythe groaned, pathetic as any destroyer could ever be.

"There's no escaping you, is there?" Kien flung himself over the warhorse's bare back and grabbed handfuls of thick black mane. "Well then, go. This had better be worth lost sleep!"

✦ ✦ ✦

"Surrender and live!" Ela's feet ached. Her throat hurt. And lack of sleep muzzied her thoughts. To the east, the sky was brightening. Almost time. If she had any tears left, she would have cried in despair. Soon she would die, taunted by memories of tonight's failure. Infinite?

Silence answered.

Broken by an unmistakably articulated destroyer-call. A rumble she'd thought to never hear again. "Pet?" A delusion, surely. Ela ran along the nearest path to Parne's wall walk.

✦ 30 ✦

Scythe halted and faced Parne's wall, releasing another throaty destroyer-call that rippled through Kien as if his body were water. The eagerness in the warhorse's tone made Kien straighten and stare upward. Did he dare to hope? He refused to even think her name lest disappointment shred his most heartfelt desire. Was she there? Infinite?

A woman appeared on the wall above, outlined in the first hints of dawn. Pale robes, long, dark, wild hair . . . delicately sculpted form. Ela! Kien stifled a shout of celebration.

Obviously in agreement, Scythe curveted, his unexpected leap nearly tossing Kien to the ground.

Kien grabbed another fistful of mane, secured his seat, then hissed in the destroyer's ear, "Shh! Everyone'll come running." He intended to be selfish, not sharing this encounter with anyone—except a capering, joy-maddened warhorse. "Hush. Not a sound!"

Sides heaving in an unmistakable and valiant effort to obey, the monster-horse settled. But he kept tilting his dark head to and fro, staring up at Ela.

Understandable. Kien stared up at her, longing to climb that huge wall. He'd steal Ela, and then he and Scythe would run away with her—never mind if she argued. Actually, she appeared to harbor the same thought. She was climbing higher on the wall, tucking herself into a stone embrasure, never once looking away from him. Adorable prophet! Kien craved a chance to hold her, to console her for Tzana's sake, and to breathe in the scent of her unbound hair. Her hair . . .

A sudden memory unnerved him. Ela, her black hair unbound and wild the night before battle. Before Istgard's final defeat in the bloody fields beyond Ytar.

Had she spent the entire night trying to warn Parne, as she'd warned Istgard? And he noticed one more oddity, too unusual to be ignored. Why wasn't Ela carrying the branch?

Infinite? What's happening?

✦ ✦ ✦

Pet! Dear monster. And Kien . . . safe! Oh, thank You, Infinite!

Kien's smile enticed her, warm as sunlight. If only she could descend from this wall and run away with him. Or, at least, if she could hold Kien one last time. She'd take refuge in his embrace. It was impossible, of course. And for the best, because once she was in Kien's arms, she'd be unable to leave him and fulfill her work as prophet. For her family and friends' sake, Chacen must have no doubt where she was, living or dead. Dead. Her empty stomach constricted.

Enough. Deliberately, Ela set aside thoughts of death and Chacen. She'd been granted one last glimpse of Kien and Pet. Wasn't this exactly what she'd begged from her Creator? A dream answered.

But how could she see Kien or Pet if she was crying? Foolish tears! Ela swiped at her eyes. She needed to celebrate this last fragment of their time together. First, Pet deserved a treat.

She dug her booted toes into a mortared line of the wall and climbed into an embrasure crowning the wall. Settling as best she could within the snug space, Ela reached into a fold of her mantle and retrieved a piece of the fruit she'd picked from the tree. What was the use of keeping it? A few bites of fruit wouldn't save her.

Waving a plump violet and green fruit that gleamed in the first hints of dawnlight, she whispered to Pet, "Here. Catch!"

The destroyer pranced beneath the wall, like a child in a game. Ela pitched the fruit and laughed silently when Pet caught it. Nimble monster! He took his time munching her gift, obviously savoring it. Happy.

Unlike Kien, who suddenly looked older. And as somber as . . . well . . . a judge.

What was wrong?

Was he concerned about the upcoming battle? Ela scanned the fields of tents behind him—banners of Istgard, the Tracelands, and most numerous of all, Siphra, marking the forces loyal to the Infinite. And surely the Infinite would protect them. Did Kien have doubts?

Before she could try to question him or reassure him, a breeze whisked past her face. Her signal to leave.

Aching, she gazed down at Kien, then blew him a kiss, love mingling with longing and regret. He answered, sending her a kiss in turn. And another smile, radiant with delight. How could one man be so captivating? Some of Ela's distress eased.

Infinite, thank You!

The invisible whirlwind answered, sweeping her away, stealing her breath as only her Creator could.

✦ ✦ ✦

Ela collected her spinning senses and tried to focus. A good thing her stomach was empty; otherwise she'd be violently ill with this unexpected shift. Where was she now? Another sea of tents swam before her. Ela blinked. She was on the opposite side of the city, facing Belaal's army and its allies' forces.

More numerous than Istgard's, the Tracelands', and Siphra's.

Swallowing her fears, Ela asked silently, Infinite? Why did You bring me here? What is Your will?

The answer came, brief and mostly bearable. Even so, she had to lean against the wall to absorb the vision. Belaal was saddled with the most prideful king alive!

Belaal's sentries had seen her. Already, foot soldiers were racing toward the royal pavilion to alert their king to her presence.

Bel-Tygeon appeared almost at once. He strode from his yellow pavilion into the early morning shadows, poised, bareheaded and casually robed—an apparent fault his servants were trying to remedy. Even as he walked toward Ela amid his prostrated subjects, one servant flung a glittering cloak over the king's shoulders while another rushed after him with a gold sword and its matching belts. Others brought torches, lighting their god-king's path within the gloom. And illuminating his face, which was handsome, cold, and nowhere near as amused by Ela as he'd been before.

Ela drew in a breath. "Bel-Tygeon, this is your Creator's last warning! You are not a god, yet you persist in requiring your people to worship you. Therefore, in five days, the Infinite will bring His hand against you, a mere mortal. Stop Him if you can!"

"Where is He?" Bel-Tygeon demanded, lifting his own hands, spreading out his arms as if he'd searched the skies and found nothing. "If He is Lord above me, let Him appear! Why does He send a girl to taunt me? Is He so weak? I demand to see Him now!"

"Who are you to command the Infinite? Your pride is too great, O King! Punishment of your own making stalks you like a predator. Before you glimpse a hint of His glory, your Creator will bring you low. Your face will be in the dust! And, yes, I am His prophet—a mere girl, daring to scold you! This is the first indignity you've suffered as king. But only the first. He has warned you!"

A clatter of footsteps and weapons sounded from the stairs behind her.

Ela exhaled. Time to surrender to Chacen. She turned from the wall and hurried down the nearest path toward the stairs.

If only her heartbeat would slow. Her hands were shaking, chilled with the sweat of fear. Infinite!

I am here.

Thank You. She clung to His words. The assurance of His presence and strength. He sheltered her within that strength now, so comforting that she wanted to cry. Yet she wouldn't.

She had every reason to be grateful.

He'd allowed her one last glimpse of Kien and Pet.

He'd saved her family, friends, and His faithful ones.

He walked with her now. Unseen, yet so present she almost felt His hand rest on her shoulder in a gesture of protection. Infinite, who is like You?

Her heart's frantic racing eased. She stood at the top of the stairs and waited.

✦ ✦ ✦

Ela watched Chacen lead his men onto the rooftop path, his face hollowed by hunger and hatred. Yet he looked healthier than most of his zealot-followers. No doubt he'd been rationing a secret cache of food, saving himself while more vulnerable citizens starved and died of disease in Parne's streets.

Even in this high place, on the wall walk above the city, Ela inhaled the heavy sickly sweet odors of decaying flesh. Her stomach clenched in revolt.

You added to their deaths, Ela told Chacen in her thoughts. You wielded such power! Everyone trusted you. Instead, you followed your desires into secret shrines and yielded your soul to deceivers. You've killed your people as surely as you intend to kill me.

Zade Chacen stood before her now, breathless with the effort of running up the stairs, and triumphant, yet wary. "I see the Infinite has abandoned you."

"No. He hasn't."

"You say so, but your hands are empty. The branch is gone."

"By His will." Ela clasped her hands and extended them. Surrendering. "Here I am."

Zade didn't question his sudden victory, or her evident weakness. Gloating, he ripped cordage from his own mantle and bound her hands with savage motions, pulling the cord so fiercely that she gasped and staggered for balance. Chacen wrenched Ela upright and shook her hard. "Tonight we'll have peace! No footsteps waking the weary. No traitor screaming foolish, weak-minded warnings!"

"You've declared the Infinite's warnings traitorous."

The deposed chief priest slapped her so sharply that her senses spun.

The taste of blood, thick and metallic, welled within her stinging mouth. Chacen shook her again. "I want to hear nothing from you but curses against your Creator as you die!"

If he thought such a thing would happen, he was truly mad. Ela clenched her hurting jaw.

The former chief priest and his zealots led her across Parne's open rooftop paths, toward the temple. Past bodies, bloated heaps. So many bodies . . . Unable to restrain herself, Ela snapped at Chacen, "Look at them! If you were the leader you should have been, they'd be alive now!"

Zade's gaunt face contorted with rage. He threw Ela onto a path, then kicked her back and ribs, provoking her shrieks as he bellowed, "Don't make me kill you here and now—I could!"

Ela tried to think past the pain in her sides and a myriad of hurts along her arms and face. Did she want to die quickly? No. Despite all her resolutions, an anguished, terrified part of her soul begged to live. If only she could. Infinite . . .

At last Chacen turned away and two of the zealots, with the smooth hands and fine robes of priests, hauled Ela to her feet. Her slapped, scraped face burned with the rawness of its torn flesh. And a shiver-inducing trickle that could only be blood worked down her right cheek. Her eyesight dimmed and her hearing buzzed unpleasantly. Ela lowered her head, trying to concentrate on breathing. On remaining conscious.

She revived in the temple's outer courtyard, aware, in her first slight breath, of nothing but peace. Bliss. And the overwhelming need for sleep.

Until a slap stung her face and a man's voice snarled, "Wake up!"

Dazed, Ela remembered what was happening. Particularly as Zade Chacen shoved her with his booted foot, provoking fresh pain. "Stand up."

Could she? Ela eased to one side, forcing herself upright a bit at a time. Chacen remained composed as she stood and steadied herself. Disturbing, that composure. He clamped a hand on the back of her neck and guided her toward the open well usually reserved for the priests and their families. Zade pointed at a step adjoining the well's low, encircling stone wall.

Wary, Ela obeyed and mounted the step. By now a small crowd had gathered. Mostly priests and a few of their wives, all of them emaciated, and none sympathetic to her plight. Indeed several were gloating.

Shifting her gaze from the priests to the well's darkness, Ela confronted what she'd been trying to ignore. Zade intended to wound her and drop her into the well to die. Useless to beg . . . His expression, when she dared a glance at his face, chilled her with fear. As did the knife he removed from a scabbard at his waist. The blade glistened in the morning's first light. A crystal knife. Yellow crystals. Caustic ores. Wounds that failed to heal. . . .

Zade smiled. "Your expression, *Prophet*, is laughable. You know what this blade is carved from."

"Yes," she mumbled, her swollen mouth making it difficult to speak. "The poisoned ore you accused my father of selling."

Don't touch them, Father cautioned in her thoughts.

Chacen was talking. "When I thought of killing you, I decided you must have time to think while dying. To repent of your guilt. You've betrayed us all. My sons died because of you!"

"Parne is dead because of rebels like you!" she retorted, speaking through the pain. "Yet the Infinite will forgive you if—"

Zade shook her. "Be silent!"

He slashed at her left arm, the blade leaving a burning wake in the flesh over her bicep. Even as she gasped at its searing torment, Chacen sliced the skin over her right bicep. Ela clenched her teeth against the fiery cut and watched blood ooze from her wounds. Sweat stung her skin from scalp to toes.

Zade pushed her forward. "Climb up. Hurry, or I'll carve your pretty little prophet-face!"

She climbed. If only she had the courage to provoke him to stab her through the heart. It would be swifter. More merciful. However, mercy and Chacen obviously weren't compatible. At least where Ela Roeh was concerned. Praying she could endure the poison without going mad, she sat on the well's edge, feet dangling. Chacen shoved her in.

She gasped and dropped endlessly into the blackness. At last, her feet struck the well's muddy bottom. Stabs of pain shot upward through both legs. "Augh!"

Ela fell backward in the well's dank interior and consciousness vanished.

✦ ✦ ✦

Kien pivoted away from the impromptu meeting before Akabe's royal pavilion, watching as Scythe galloped beyond the Siphran army's encampment. The destroyer's giant hooves hammered tremors through the ground, unnerving all the encampment's occupants—himself included. Kien's heartbeat raced. "Ela . . ."

Infinite? What's happened to her?

Followed by Jon, Akabe, and Tsir Aun, Kien ran for the destroyer. Scythe flung himself at Parne's walls, slamming his massive hooves against its stones in a futile attempt to break into the city. "Scythe, stop! *Obey!*"

Scythe huffed, then stomped, managing to sound offended and distraught in the same gust. But he held still, glaring and seething as Kien and the others approached. "Calm yourself," Kien urged, trying to take his own advice. "If pounding on those walls would help matters, I'd join you!"

Akabe, Tsir Aun, Jon, and a handful of guards closed ranks around Kien. Jon said, "This is how he behaved when Ela's enemies attacked her before the siege. No doubt something's happened to her!"

Tsir Aun exhaled, his stern face tense as he watched Scythe. "Whatever's happened, it concerns more than Ela, I'm sure. The last time I knew of Parne's prophet walking throughout the night, as Kien said, Istgard was defeated and our king was cut down in combat."

"I thought of that same night," Kien agreed.

Akabe stood to Kien's left now, wary of the destroyer. "We *are* at risk for combat today. Belaal's certain to find us now that the sun's up."

Tsir Aun grunted. "Given his reputation, Bel-Tygeon is likely to send negotiators first, without honor, to gather information."

"Undoubtedly," Akabe agreed. "Everyone spread the word. We must fully arm ourselves. Now."

"Thank you, Majesty." Kien grabbed Scythe's halter, willing to face anything to free Ela from Parne. Infinite? When?!

31

Inside his tent, busy with his military cloak's gilded clasps, Kien glanced at Bryce, who stood before him. Infinite? Is this man always so serious? "How may I help you, Bryce?"

Bryce stood even straighter if such a thing was possible. Sharp-eyed, his brown face strictly controlled, his voice cool, he said, "My lord, I offer myself to be a spy for Siphra."

Bryce was offering himself as a spy? No. Kien scowled at the thought of sending another servant into probable death. "My name is Kien."

"It is indeed, my lord."

"May I bribe you to stop calling me *my lord*?"

"I cannot be bought for any reason, my lord—particularly in failing to honor you."

Fine! And Siphrans called Tracelanders stubborn. "How will you spy for Siphra?"

"By infiltrating enemy ranks. I'll walk in quietly by night, observe Belaal's forces by day, then walk out quietly, again, by night."

Kien stared. The man was serious. "You intend to just walk into the enemy's camp?"

"Unarmed, sir," Bryce added.

Unarmed . . . "Have you done such a thing before?"

"Rather, sir. I'm unrivaled at remaining unnoticed, when I wish to be."

Scanning Bryce's subdued apparel, his calm brown eyes, silver-brown hair, and unmoving stance, Kien believed him. *Infinite? What sort of servant have You sent me?*

Wait. He didn't actually want an answer. The question was badly worded and presumed the Infinite had indeed sent him a servant. Kien wanted no verification of his suspicion. He didn't want servants. Already he admired Bryce. Liked him. Not good. Kien ran one hand over his face. "Do you realize you'll die if you're caught?"

"Yes, sir. Death would conclude all the details of being caught. Yet I'll survive."

Kien heard *torture* and *interrogation* unspoken within those words. Despite Bryce's cryptic acknowledgment, the man seemed confident. And determined to go. Kien exhaled, realizing the decision had been made. "You'd best survive, Bryce—and in one piece. Before you leave, we'll speak to the king. And Istgard's prime minister."

"Yes, sir."

✦ ✦ ✦

Ela returned to consciousness, then wished she hadn't. Trembling in the absolute darkness, her arms burning with the poison, she pressed her back against the curved, slimy wall. Yes, this was her death-scented burial place. *Infinite, I don't want to be here!*

Could she stand? "Infinite, please . . ." Ela tensed, willing her legs to support her within the sticky mire. Mud oozed cold into her boots, slathering her nearly numbed feet, causing her to slip, half burying her, and provoking renewed spikes of pain in her legs. She fought sobs and the sludge for an instant, then stopped. Must she fear drowning in this mud? Biting her lip against tormenting pain, she pushed a heel into the gooey depths. There was a base. A nearly solid foundation to the mud.

This well was drying, of course. Useless to Parne. Had all the wells run dry? Was this why so many Parnians were dying so swiftly? For lack of water?

Water. Did she still have her own supply?

Ela fumbled at her mud-slopped garments, seeking the podgy contours of the old water bag she'd appropriated from Father. Gone. Obviously, someone had taken it while she was unconscious. Proof that Parne was dying of thirst.

As she would die. Unless the poison killed her first. Her arms felt swollen, burning as if she'd been set afire from shoulders to fingertips. Could she untie herself?

Moving cautiously, Ela eased her body along the mud's surface, trying to spread out her weight and rest. Satisfied that she wasn't sinking too much, she raised her bound wrists to her cheek, testing the cords in the darkness. Where were the knots? If only she could see! There. The small, hard edge of a knot. Ela clamped her teeth over the muddy bond. Sludgy grit coated her tongue and crunched between her teeth. She spat into the darkness and lost track of the knot. All right . . . be calm. It wasn't as if she could leave this well. Nothing remained for her except to pray and die. Or might she be wrong? Was there more she ought to do?

Infinite? What now?

Ela found the knot again and tugged at it cautiously, feeling it slip as she listened.

Infinite?

Silence pressed around her, upsetting as the chilling, unseen mud. Ela lowered her hands, trying not to give way to fear. Was He testing her? Allowing her to die alone?

Waiting for her to curse Him?

No! "Infinite!"

✦ ✦ ✦

In Akabe's royal pavilion, Kien accepted a leather-wrapped packet from the young messenger, a Tracelander. His censure? So soon? Without a trial? Would he be forced to resign his commission? He would fight the decision!

Aware of Akabe, Jon, and the others watching him, Kien opened the packet and glimpsed a blue wax seal, embossed with a military shield. General Rol. Kien released a breath he didn't know he'd been holding. A message from the general, not the Grand Assembly. Good. Kien slid the note into his coin pouch. Akabe and a number of the courtiers seemed disappointed. Regrettable, but Kien wasn't about to read potentially bad news amid a crowd.

Akabe, however, was already addressing his men, Jon, Kien, and Tsir Aun. "No sign of Belaal's approach?"

"None, sir," one of his advisors said, distinctly pleased.

Istgard's prime minister, Tsir Aun, frowned. "They have no reason to miss seeing our fires, as we've seen theirs. Have you noticed that almost no smoke rises from within the city? Parne has run out of fuel."

Kien nodded. True. He'd seen none of a typical city's household cooking fires this morning. "It seems Belaal is occupied by other matters."

Akabe said, "What these other matters might be, we hope to learn soon enough." Akabe had agreed with Bryce's plan only after Bryce had insisted. Even now, Siphra's king seemed unhappy. "And until we know Belaal's plans, we can only guess at our own strategies."

At Kien's right, Jon observed, "By now Parne's water supplies must be dwindling. When I was here more than six weeks past, we were told that this region has suffered a severe drought. The wells I visited were low enough to alarm me, and I'm not Parnian." He glanced around the tent. "What's the longest anyone's heard of a city enduring if there's no water? A week?"

"If the weather remains mild, perhaps ten days," Tsir Aun said. "If plagues are present and if the citizens have had little food from the start of the siege, they have less than a week."

His voice low, uneasy, Akabe said, "Siphra's prophets declared Parne will become a tomb if we allow Belaal to take the city. Everyone will be slaughtered. Slaves will not be taken."

Kien listened, appalled at the enormity of such a potential butchery. Ela would die. As would her family. Infinite . . . "Then our role is clear. We must save the remaining Parnians. Have your prophets told you how we're to accomplish the task?"

"No. However, two of Siphra's prophets are traveling with us. I'll send them word and ask them to pray—as should we all. Perhaps the Infinite will have some answer for us soon. Meanwhile, those who are not keeping watch should rest." Akabe targeted Bryce with a swift, rueful glance. Was the young king already questioning his conscience in sending an unarmed Siphran into the enemy's camp?

If so, it didn't matter. Bryce would not be talked out of going. Kien prayed the man's life wasn't about to be squandered.

✦ ✦ ✦

In his tent, with Bryce dozing and Jon lurking, Kien pried open the blue seal and scanned the pale note. General Rol's handwriting covered the parchment in a chopped, concise script.

News of your honor, Lord Aeyrievale, has unleashed a tempest within the Grand Assembly. Be prepared. Undeniable jealousy now inspires your father's enemies to do their worst, and East Guard's Lantec supporters have already suffered for championing this excursion to Parne. Those with shortsighted views now call us warmongers, naming your father as the chief instigator and you as his singular reason for risking the lives of our soldiers.

Kien growled, almost hearing Father raging from this distance. Yet a gnawing guilt bit at the edge of his thoughts. Was he partially responsible for this confrontation? Infinite? Have I judged wrongly in this? Have I acted impetuously instead of trusting You?

Silence answered. Not reassuring. Gloomily, Kien continued reading Rol's message.

As a result, when you are summoned, you must, unfortunately, defend yourself from a point of weakness. Your personal integrity and your continued good standing with the military are vital. If you give Belaal the slightest concession—much less a victory—you will be condemned.

Truth is, we are all condemned. For speaking my mind in the Parnian matter, my home was defaced by vandals. Insult enough to make one consider invading the swamp of politics. . . .

General Rol, a politician? Not a bad idea, except that the Tracelands would lose its finest general.

After a lengthy political digression, Rol concluded:

I advise you to set aside, unopened, any official communications from the Grand Assembly, should they arrive before the Parnian conflict is finished. If the communication is hand-delivered, do not accept it, but return to East Guard as soon as Belaal is defeated. I order you to burn this parchment.

Kien dropped the parchment into his tent's low, fiery brazier and watched it burn.

Jon muttered, "Bad news?"

"Unwelcomed, but not dire yet. I pray your wife writes convincing letters to the wives of those assemblymen."

"She's your sister. She'll charm them."

Yes. But charm had its limits. Kien sat on his cot and stared up at the tent's sloping, oiled canopy. *Was* he guilty of helping to set this invasion in motion for his own purposes? Was his love for Ela—despite his honorable intentions—against his Creator's will?

Infinite, please guide me!

✦ ✦ ✦

Ela woke, startled, as the well's cover scraped and echoed high above her. Zade Chacen's distinctive, resonant voice called, "You are forsaken! Cursed as you cursed me! Dead, as you killed my sons! Do you still praise the Infinite?"

She squinted at the light above. Working her dry tongue from the roof of her mouth, she called upward, "Yes!" Her teeth chattered as she said the word. So hard that Ela clenched her jaw, not daring to say more. Yes. Should she abandon Him because He was silent?

Infinite? Will You remain quiet while I die, thirsting for You?

She blinked at the scanty tears stinging the edges of her eyes, craving His voice. The reason she'd become a prophet was for the joy of hearing Him. Yet now He seemed absent.

Was He testing her?

She repeated the verses of praise that had lulled her to sleep. You are like no other. There is no god beside You. . . .

Chacen's gloating laughter summoned her attention once more. He overturned a bucket, dumping its contents into the well. A brittle clatter resounded against the stone walls. Dark fragments descended toward her. Ela ducked her head into her arms, shut her eyes, and screamed. Searing pains sliced into her scalp and shoulders, and fiery slashes cut along her already wounded biceps.

She sobbed through her clenched jaw. Hearing the cover thud above her, she was entombed in thick blackness once more. What had Chacen tossed at her?

Ela worked her chilled fingers through her hair, feeling warm bloodied gashes. Finding shards in her scalp.

Broken pottery. No doubt Parne's former chief priest meant to inflict fresh wounds. Well, he'd succeeded. Blood slithered down Ela's face, neck, and arms. Trembling with the pain, she dug for any shards remaining in her flesh, throwing them clumsily to the opposite side of the well. Why couldn't she stop shivering? She was warmer now. Too warm, considering her continual bath in the mud. Why?

When the answer occurred to her, Ela's shivering redoubled.

Fever. From the poisonous yellow ore.

Dying was going to be harder than she'd imagined.

Infinite.

32

Fighting impatience, Kien sat on a low stool in the royal pavilion and studied Siphra's prophets. Lean, sharp-eyed men in plain, layered robes.

As composed as Ela when facing royalty, the eldest prophet told Akabe, "The Infinite, your Creator, commands you and your allies to obey in this. If you enter Parne, spare no one who lifts any sort of weapon against you. Whatever their appearance, do not pity them, for they will carry deceit and death, corrupting others for as long as they live."

Prime Minister Aun frowned, pondering this order in silence. Beside Kien, Jon whispered, "This could easily go wrong for us! You know how this will be presented in the Grand Assembly. Certain parties will scream that we lifted weapons against vulnerable citizens in their own homes!"

"Yes," Kien agreed beneath his breath. "But, remember, Belaal will butcher *everyone* in Parne, not just those bearing weapons. Moreover, we have the right to defend ourselves. Even a dying foe can inflict a fatal wound." Good of Lorteus to beat this idea into him.

Akabe's face settled in grim, unwilling lines. "What of those who do not lift weapons against us?"

The second prophet's eyes gleamed as if pleased. "Lead them from Parne, Majesty. They are given to your care."

Finally—an acceptable answer! Kien exhaled, relieved. Jon nodded mute agreement.

"And Parne?" the young king demanded, leaning forward in his chair. "What is the Infinite's will for the city itself?"

"You must burn the city—it is corrupted as rotten wood."

Kien's stomach tightened. An understandable command. The city and its ores must be destroyed. However . . . Kien frowned. Jon spoke the truth. This whole situation could easily turn into a political mire when the dust settled. Too much didn't align with the Tracelands' ideals of warfare. Burn, not rebuild a beleaguered city? Kill, not subdue and assist resident civilians who'd survived a siege? Certain factions of the Grand Assembly would surely demand punishment for the Tracelands' commanders.

Infinite? Is such destruction necessary?

The response struck Kien, so physical and immediate that he flinched.

Have you seen rebel Parnian hearts, Judge Kien? Do you comprehend their thoughts and see what they have done—what they will do, corrupting the future souls they encounter? Souls I love even now?

He managed a whisper. "No."

Jon stared as if fearing for Kien's wits. But the eldest prophet almost smiled. His dark eyes glittering with understanding, the prophet said, "Therefore, you must obey."

Kien looked away from the man. One of Akabe's advisors spoke, his voice rough. Agitated. "What of Belaal and its allies?"

The younger prophet said, "You will wait upon Belaal and attack at the given time."

More waiting—ugh! Kien gritted his teeth, wrestling irritation and his fear for Ela.

Another advisor, thin and fussy in elaborate robes, argued from Kien's left, "All well and good, but why has the Infinite allowed such destruction upon a city—a people—He loves?"

The elder Siphran prophet whirled upon the advisor, ferocious. "Do not think your Creator is pleased by this! He *mourns*! He allows these events not because He cannot prevent disaster, but because He granted mortals dominion over this realm of dust when they rebelled and strayed from His love, according to their own hearts. Now He has revealed His will to save His faithful ones. Make your choices, all of you."

The prophet's keen-eyed stare cut through Kien once more, raising unnerving chills. "You must live with the consequences of your decisions. Yet He will bring good from evil."

Was there a promise within those words? Kien hoped so. Unable to restrain himself, Kien asked, "What has happened to Parne's prophet?"

Both prophets stilled. The youngest shook his head. The elder said, "We've been told nothing. We pray she survives."

✦ ✦ ✦

Had two days passed? Three? Chills shook Ela like a dried reed in a windstorm. Her parched lips seeped metal-tasting blood where they'd split. All her wounds trickled ooze, while her swollen arms felt laden with weights. And her head pounded. An absolute battlefield of pain, but not from a vision.

She'd welcome a vision's agony now. Anything to indicate her Creator's presence. If she had the strength, she'd scream. Beat her fists bloody on these dark walls, demanding answers. But her voice was the barest whisper. "Infinite." Unable to continue aloud, she thought, Where are You? I'm in torment! Haven't I been faithful? Remember me! I've been mocked by my enemies. Abused by a man who once claimed to love me. Beaten by priests and my own relatives! Now I suffer alone. Day and night I've called Your Name. . . .

Dry heaves crushed her efforts, causing her to struggle against the hardening mud. When she could finally summon a coherent thought, Ela pleaded in silence: How have I failed?

Incandescent mist shimmered before her sleep-deprived eyes now. Green-blue in the darkness. Real? Or another hallucination offered by her fevered mind? She licked more blood from her lips and stared as the haze took exquisite form. An otherworldly masklike face. Whispering.

"Do you yet believe? Do you serve Him still? Here in your tomb . . ."

The beautiful mask multiplied, becoming many. Each questioning her softly, mirroring her terrors in an all-encompassing chorus. "Why do you wait on Him? Where is your Lord?"

She blinked at the faces. Tried to comprehend them. Not mortal. "Who . . ." Who are you?

Fevered imaginings? Deceivers taking advantage of her weakened state, trying to draw her into their realm? No. Ela recoiled inwardly. If the faces were nothing but her fever, then what would resistance matter? Yet if they existed beyond her mortal realm, becoming present to tempt her, she must fight. Snatches of verses worked through her thoughts.

"My—" Her dry mouth refused to recite. She poured the verses from her heart instead: My soul weeps for Your presence, my Lord. O Infinite, hear my cry! Deliver me from my enemies . . . scatter them with Your mighty hand. . . . I trust in You. . . .

Empty nausea seized her again. When she was able to lift her head once more, only blackness met her gaze. Tears Ela could no longer shed burned at the edges of her eyes. Infinite? Remember me—

Before she finished her unspoken prayer, fatigue took hold. Elusive sleep finally wrapped around her like a cloak, removing her from misery.

✦ ✦ ✦

Kien sat up on his cot, shaking off sleep, a hand to his sword. What was that noise? He blinked at the day's first gray hints of light. Bryce staggered into Kien's tent, so unsteady that Kien jumped, an edge of horror threatening. Had he lost another servant? "Are you wounded?"

"No, my lord. Just wearied." The man swayed.

"Sit, before you fall!" Before Kien could reach him, Bryce

dropped to the floor. Kien crouched beside the man. "Are you sure you're well?"

"Quite sure." The servant sighed, then mumbled, "And we're safe enough fer now."

"You're certain?"

"As I live, m'lord. Wouldn't risk . . . otherwise . . ." Whatever explanation the man tried to make faded as he lost consciousness on the rough carpet.

Feeling Bryce's pulse, Kien relaxed. Steady. The man was sound asleep. Probably sleepwalked his way here. Fine. Kien covered Bryce with a quilt, then gathered his gear. Outside, he tied his tent's entry flaps. First, he would check Scythe. Then he would tell the king that their volunteer spy had returned.

✦ ✦ ✦

Kien stepped back from Akabe's worktable as Bryce strode into the royal pavilion. Garbed in clean clothes—and hopefully more coherent after a morning's sleep—Bryce bowed to Tsir Aun and Akabe, who was seated at the table, elbow deep in official documents. Bryce also bowed to Kien, who shook his head. The servant grimaced, then half knelt before the king, offering a leather scroll. "Your enemies' encampments, Majesty."

A map! Would it show some Parnian failing, or a lack of oversight from Belaal—offering a way to reach Ela?

Kien crowded alongside the prime minister and Jon as Akabe unfurled the scroll over his table. Studying the map's outlines, Akabe laughed. "Perfect! You'll be rewarded for this, Bryce. Now, explain your map, and tell us if you have any other good news."

"Rather, sir." Bryce's calm brown eyes gleamed as he pointed to details on the map. "You've heard nothing from the enemy because Belaal has found a weakness in Parne's wall—here—and they've fixed all their attention upon sapping its foundations. Belaal is building giant catapults—here, and there. Parne's defenders are resisting the attack on its wall, but not strongly enough." Bryce's elation faded, becoming solemn. "It's clear

Parne's citizens are weakened. Their movements and defensive strategies are almost nonexistent. Once Belaal has undermined the wall's foundation, their catapults will bring down the whole section as a rockslide. We should hear a sound like thunder when the section crumbles."

"But then Belaal must deal with Parne's inner walls," Jon pointed out. Tracing the main wall's stark line, he said, "Homes are stacked all along here, one upon another like staggered bricks."

"Perhaps we should allow Belaal to clear some of those too." Akabe stood and brought his big fists down on either side of the map—a triumphant, crushing gesture that shook the table. "Knowing this, we wait. Let them finish our gateway, then we attack. Within the Infinite's will." Settling a bit, he grinned at Bryce. "What else? Surely they know we're here."

"They do, sir. I heard their talk. All three camps scorn our numbers. Their forces far exceed our own, and they believe you are here to plunder Parne. They await your messenger."

The king shrugged. "No need to distract them. Let them send the first messenger to us."

Bryce allowed himself to smile. "I believe they will, sir. Most likely to spy about for provisions. Belaal's supply lines are failing. While I was there, the soldiers were ordered to observe strict food rations using provisions confiscated from Parnian traders."

Kien leaned toward the map. "If they're rationing so severely, then we should remain battle ready and double our watchmen. It's likely they'd attack us for food."

Jon asked, "What about their water supplies?"

"Much as ours, sir. They've dug wells and every drop is measured. Drought has dried the streams. We could use a good rain."

Curious, Kien asked, "You weren't questioned at all?"

"Not much, sir," Bryce said. "Belaal thought I belonged to the Eosyths. The Agocii believed I'd arrived with Belaal. None deemed me worthy of interest once they'd decided my origin. My one difficulty was lack of sleep."

Settling into his chair once more, Akabe grinned. "You were blessed, and we are grateful for your return. Do you require anything else? More sleep?"

"No, sir. Thank you."

Aware of the king's counselors twitching with their impatience to return to official procedures and documents, Kien stood and nodded in correct Tracelander form. "With your permission, sir, we'll depart."

"Trade me, Aeyrievale," Akabe offered with a grim smile. "I'll run the destroyer. You sign documents."

"A worthy try, O King." Kien bowed his head and departed, feeling half-wild with the enforced wait. But even an all-out run on Scythe wouldn't help. When might they save Ela?

Outside the royal pavilion, Bryce said, "Thank you, my lord, for your concern."

"I'm not a lord, Bryce," Kien told him. "You need not bow and treat me as one."

"There you're wrong, sir, and we prefer it so."

"We?"

"Aeyrievale. And the king."

Fightmaster Lorteus marched up, halting their conversation. Perfect.

Kien drew his sword and scowled at the man, glad for the chance to thrash someone while enduring the frustrations of waiting.

✦ ✦ ✦

Sweat poured off Kien's face and slithered down his chest, back, and arms, stinging his fresh waster-inflicted welts and bruises. Evade. Attack. No mercy! He feinted a lunge. Lorteus threw a low strike and betrayed an opening, chest height. Kien charged, hammered down the fightmaster's waster, stomped it flat to the ground, and then whipped his own waster into the hollow behind Lorteus's chin. "Swallow!" he commanded, knowing Lorteus couldn't without difficulty.

The fightmaster bared his teeth. "Finished."

Finally! Kien kicked the waster from beneath his feet, then lowered his own weapon just enough to allow Lorteus to step backward.

"Very good," Lorteus approved. "Now we eat."

Obviously nothing wholesome, by his tone. Kien braced. "What now?" A putrid stew? Rotting bread?

"Specialties from your own people."

I have no people. Kien bit down the words, suddenly aware of Bryce at his side. Bearing a tray of brown cubed . . . cheese? And dried meat that looked as if it had been aged for several hundred years. In pig slop.

Bryce, the traitor, smiled secretively. Kien glared at the man. "Did Lorteus pay you?"

"No, sir."

"Do I pay you?"

"Yes, sir."

I do? "How?"

"With your revenues, my lord," Bryce said, again with the hidden smile. "Or you will when you formally accept your place as Aeyrievale's lord. I'm your steward and sometimes-marshal, among my other duties."

"And, obviously, you're displeased with the king's choice of a potential lord if you're offering me this . . . food."

Lorteus chuckled, exceedingly pleased. "Enjoy your evening meal."

Kien snapped a look at the fightmaster. Until Bryce interposed. "I dare you, sir."

A challenge to his courage. Kien sighed at the vile-looking cubes. "What is it you're trying to feed me?"

"Dried Aeryon meat and Bannulk cheese."

Helpful for once, Lorteus offered, "*Ulk* is the sound you'll make just before you puke up the cheese."

Perhaps. But Lorteus had never swallowed sea-beast bile while inside the beast. Surrounded by rotting fish, no less. Kien deliberately recalled the taste and smell of bile, then chewed a cube of the acrid cheese. Close enough. He swallowed. And waited. Unpleasant, but not threatening a digestive revolt either. Surprising. He bit off an edge of the Aeryon meat. Harsh. Salty and leathern. With a tongue-grating mineral aftertaste. Only slightly better than the cheese. He frowned at Bryce. "You've eaten this?"

"All my life, sir."

"No wonder you volunteer to invade enemy camps alone. You're trying to kill yourself to avoid Aeyrievale's food."

Bryce laughed. "No, my lord. I'm fond of Bannulk cheese. And of Aeryon meat when we kill one of the beasts. But Aeyrievale is not a typical fief. Takes a bit of courage to live there."

"Which is why they've had no lord for years," Lorteus said. Helpful again.

Kien scowled but asked Bryce the next, most logical question. "What happened to your last lord?"

"The last true one? Murdered, my lord. By King Segere and Queen Raenna—may they rot forever."

It was the first time Kien had seen Bryce's air of calm disrupted. Hatred of Siphra's former king and queen glittered in his eyes. "*Their* designated lord—an idle, pretty man and no true lord—died within a week of his arrival. Of a fall."

"A fall?"

"Yes, sir." Calm again, Bryce said, "The designated lord disregarded my advice and fell off a cliff trying to escape an aeryon." As if to reassure Kien, Bryce said, "You seem more level-headed, my lord."

Comforting. "Bryce, you and Aeyrievale cannot depend upon me to become your lord. I'm a Tracelander. We do not accept titles or honors of nobility."

"We ask you to not set aside this bequest lightly, sir. We need you. Without a lord, our revenues are divided up by the former favorites of Segere and his queen. You would put a stop to such abuse. You would also command the funds to control the aeryons."

Not asking for much, were they? Only his heritage, his future, and possibly his life. Unable to disappoint Bryce immediately, Kien sighed. "I'll consider what you've said. Meanwhile . . ." He nodded toward Parne and lowered his voice so Lorteus couldn't hear. "The woman I love is trapped behind those walls. Until she's safe, we won't discuss this again."

"Understandable, sir."

"Bryce, how close is Belaal to bringing down the wall?"

"Mere days, unless the Parnians muster better defense tactics. So those walls and a battle stand between you and your love." Bryce sighed. "May she survive."

Survive. The very word he'd say to Ela if he could. Just *survive*.

While he risked his own future to reach her.

33

Standing outside his tent, Kien drew in a slow breath. Moisture imbued the nighttime air. "There's a scent of rain," he called over his shoulder to Bryce. Moreover, the stars above them were vanishing. Clouds. Kien's thoughts soared as a raindrop splashed against his face. Infinite! Be merciful—send us a downpour! Perhaps some of Parne's misery would be eased. "We should set out every possible container to catch the rainwater. It'll ease our rationing!"

"I'll tell others as soon as we've finished here, sir." Bryce immediately snatched cooking pots, pitchers, cups, even tarps and fabric. Kien helped him arrange everything in front of the tent. As they set out the last utensils, a torrent of rain splatted onto Kien's scalp. Thank You! He tore off his cloak, boots, and outer tunics and stashed them with his weapons inside his tent. A shower would be worth running around half-clad.

Bryce laughed at him but followed his example, then darted off to alert others.

Kien hurried to Jon's tent. "If you're sleeping, brother, you'd best wake up and bathe!"

After an instant, Jon emerged, his shadowed outline disheveled. His voice sleepy. Disgruntled. "What *are* you talking about?" He halted, put out a hand, felt rain, and whooped. Kien helped him place every available container and tarp in front of his tent. Then they raced off to alert Akabe.

Seeing them, Akabe chuckled, obviously glad to interrupt his late-night council meeting. "You Tracelanders are insane. Armies are supposed to reek!" But he followed their example, horrifying his loitering council members by stripping off his royal insignias and grabbing potential water vessels. The dignified men argued until Akabe said, "Don't expect me to share my water with you later! And if you stink, but I do not, you're forbidden to approach me with any documents whatsoever."

Threatened with the halt of formalities, Akabe's council members rushed off to their tents. The young king ordered all empty water barrels to be opened and set throughout the camp, then he marched into the rain. "May it fall only on us!"

The words sounded like a prayer. Kien echoed the plea silently. This rain was a blessing, unless it fortified their enemies. Infinite, as You will.

The entire army was now alerted. Tracelanders, Siphrans, and Istgardians were all enjoying the downpour as they worked to fill the army's barrels and vessels, giving up sleep for the gift of water.

Halfway through the night, Scythe was unleashed and trailing Kien, nudging his shoulders, exhaling soggy-destroyer sighs into Kien's hair. Worrying him. At last, certain all available barrels stood filled, Kien retrieved cloths and wiped down the monster-horse in the darkness, hoping to soothe him. "What are you sensing?" he asked the beast. "Is Ela in pain?"

Scythe's answering rumble sounded like the beginning of a groan.

"We'll find her," Kien said, trying to reassure himself as much as his destroyer. Unable to endure the thought that Ela must be injured, Kien changed the subject as he swept streams of undoubtedly dirty water off Scythe's back. "Tomorrow, if the weather's cleared, I'll comb your mane and tail, then polish your hooves. And you'd better cooperate."

The beast whooshed out a mournful breath that would have drenched Kien if he weren't already soaked. A shadow appeared at his elbow now. A talking shadow. Bryce.

"Sir. We've visitors in the camp, asking for Commander Thel and the king."

"Visitors?" Kien's wet skin crawled with alarm. "From Belaal?"

"No, my lord. From Parne. Refugees—men, women, children. I thought you'd wish to greet them. Here is your cloak."

"Yes. Thank you, Bryce." Refugees. Perhaps Ela was here! Kien flung the cloak over his shoulders and buckled the clasp. At least it made him look slightly less sodden and disreputable. "Where are they?"

As they walked, Kien shook out his hair and pushed it back from his face. Scythe immediately rumpled his hair with a fretful shove that made Kien's heart sink. If Ela had arrived with these refugees, the destroyer would be exultant. Obviously not. He reached up and gave the beast's wet mane a futile smoothing. "No biting anyone."

Scythe snuffed.

Bryce led Kien to Jon's tent. Scythe bumped his shoulder as if to follow. Kien rubbed his neck. "Wait."

Inside, Jon's tent was humid with a crowd of rain-drenched refugees. Unable to see his brother-in-law, Kien called, "Jon?"

"Kien!" A hand lifted above the refugees, who stared at Kien, curious despite their obvious fatigue. "Here."

Sidling through the crowd, Kien found Jon. At once, Jon gripped his shoulder as if to brace him. "Kien, these are Ela's parents and her baby brother."

Her parents. Naturally, he'd meet them while looking half-drowned. However, they seemed equally waterlogged. As Jon introduced them, Kien noted glimpses of Ela in Kalme Roeh's delicate face and in Dan Roeh's forthright, searching gaze. Even Ela's infant brother reflected hints of Ela with those dark curls and big brown eyes. If only Tzana were with them.

Kien extended his hand to Dan Roeh. "Sir. I'm honored to meet you." Would the man consider it forward of Kien to ask about Ela immediately? Kien suspected so. Better to ask his second most pressing question. And his third and fourth. "How did you escape Parne? Might Belaal invade your city by the same route? Might we go inside?"

"Too dangerous—despite my wish to return." Dan Roeh studied Kien as if trying to pick his soul to bits. "We waited until dark, covered our tunnel with dead bushes and brush, then hurried away. It's a miracle we weren't seen—we emerged within sight of Belaal's encampment." He exhaled. "Believe me, we were grateful to find Siphra's army beyond our eastern wall—as we'd been told."

"Though it was a long walk," another man grumbled behind Roeh.

His complaint alerted Kien to their distress. "I'll find food. And, sir," he said, nodding to Dan, "you and your family and friends may use my tent as your own. I'll shelter with my brother-in-law. I'll see if I can arrange for other tents as well."

The man's face relaxed visibly, and his wife managed a tremulous smile. Roeh said, "May the Infinite bless you for your kindness."

May He bless me with Ela's safety, Kien added silently. He would gladly chance entering Parne alone through the secret tunnel. However, he would not risk Ela's life bringing her out the same way. Better to wait until he could ride Scythe into the city.

Better to wait until the Infinite's designated time.

Infinite? When?

✦ ✦ ✦

Ela saw Tzana playing on the floor of their stone chamber on East Guard's Temple Hill. Delighted, she scooped up her tiny sister and hugged her within the comfort of their cherished Traceland sanctuary. Smiling, Tzana snuggled against Ela. And Tamri Het—dear fussing chaperone!—enfolded them both within her arms. Abruptly, the stone floor and walls warped around them. Tzana vanished from Ela's embrace. *No!* She looked at Tamri, who dissolved into darkness, surrounded by agonized screams.

Pain jolted Ela from the Traceland refuge. And her own screams. Oh no! Awake again.

Her leg muscles were cramping. Hard. If only she could rub them. Shivering, she opened her eyes to blackness. To hostile solitude and misery. In desperation, she squeezed her eyes shut and reached for the consolation of her dream. For Tzana's joyous giggles. So much better than the ravening hollow within her stomach. The feverish drumbeats within her skull. And the weighted torment of her arms and legs. Ela worked her dry tongue from the roof of her mouth.

"Infinite . . . ?" How much longer?

She drifted, imagining herself outside this tomb-well. In sunlight. Trailed by Pet. Walking with Kien, hearing his laughter and basking in the bright warmth of his gray eyes. So good to see him, even in this poison-induced delirium. Infinite? Thank You.

Surely her Creator waited with her now, through the silence. If only she could hear His voice! Better than water, His voice. Worth dying young for. Part of the bargain. He'd warned her that she would face an early death. She couldn't complain that He'd been dishonest.

No regrets. Not for loving Kien. Nor for loving the Infinite. Though she wished her death could be easier. Chacen's fault. Where was he? The daily taunting must be near. She'd almost be glad to see him. Someone real. "Hmm." What was she thinking?

Her muscles twitched and cramped anew, making her whimper, while the hollow in her stomach growled as if threatening to consume her from the inside out. Yet starvation wouldn't come soon enough. Thirst, the poison, and her fever would devour her long before.

Unable to move or escape the pain, Ela retreated inward. Listening.

✦ ✦ ✦

On the infuriatingly slow fourth morning of their encampment at Parne, Kien watched three horsemen ride alongside the wall.

Their dust-besmirched yellow surcoats and the gold-garnished blue banner proclaimed their origin and their status as messengers.

"Belaal," Bryce muttered, turning aside—Kien suspected—to avoid being seen and recognized.

"To spy, no doubt." Kien pivoted about-face. "Return to Commander Thel's tent and stay hidden. I'll go wait on the king." He'd learn what he could. Then act as needed.

"Sir," Bryce cautioned, "the oldest man is General Siyrsun. Twice, I was ordered—with other foot soldiers—to move from his path. He is one of the few enemies who looked directly into my face."

"And you believe he's particularly keen-eyed?"

"I was reminded of an aeryon, my lord. He's cruel and enjoys his own power. Though he's not wearing symbols of his rank, which concerns me. Have care."

"Thank you, Bryce."

Kien hurried toward the royal pavilion. A general posing as a nobody? Interesting. Were the other two representatives false as well? Spies? Assassins?

Quickening his pace, Kien gripped his sword. Outside the pavilion, Kien paused to catch his breath and survey the gathering crowd. Peaceable enough. Encouraged, Kien strode inside.

Akabe stood in the tent's center, semicircled by his counselors, allies, prophets, and men-at-arms—all listening to a visitor's extravagant opening speech. Akabe acknowledged Kien with a swift, tense glance that conveyed his mistrust of the situation. Had the prophets warned their king of some danger?

Deliberately, Kien stood with the prophets, causing Jon and the other Tracelanders on the opposite side of the pavilion to raise their eyebrows. Beside Jon, Tsir Aun frowned, then gave his attention to the messengers. One of the younger representatives was speaking, complimenting Akabe in flowing accents. "Our king, the noble Bel-Tygeon—prized of the heavens!—is eager to greet Siphra's lord. He sends his regards and asks what you wish to gain from your venture to Parne."

Akabe smiled slightly. "I defend my people and their interests. Belaal's recent actions toward its neighbors have been unpredictable. We prefer certainty. Parne, isolated as it is, has never been our ally, yet its location merits Siphra's interest."

"And Istgard's," Tsir Aun added.

Jon nodded formal agreement. "As well as the Tracelands'."

The smooth-voiced messenger's face betrayed nothing but a placid acceptance of their replies. But Kien noticed General Siyrsun's gaze cutting about the pavilion while his mouth puckered like the drawn strings of a money purse.

Beside Kien, the eldest prophet exhaled a command beneath his breath. "Speak what you've learned. Your Creator commands you."

"You could speak it," Kien muttered, amused despite his aggravation, remembering his earliest conversations with Ela. "You're a prophet."

"*I* haven't been told what you've learned." Despite his whisper, the prophet sounded disgruntled. "I was told only that you must not conceal what you know!"

"Fine." Were all prophets bad-tempered while on duty? At least Siphran prophets didn't carry insignias like Ela's branch. Otherwise, Kien suspected, he would've been thumped on the head for tormenting this particular servant of the Infinite. If only it could be Ela standing with him, ready to demand truth from their enemy. If . . . No. He couldn't risk daydreams of Ela now. Kien focused on the representatives and waited for an opportunity to confront the general.

" . . . surprised," another of the representatives was saying to Akabe. "We observed you received rain."

"We were blessed with rain," Akabe agreed, quiet. He would refuse to discuss water supplies, Kien was sure.

Before Belaal's loquacious representative could respond, the testy prophet beside Kien called out, "The Infinite, your Creator, sent a downpour to Siphra and its allies. For Belaal and its supporters, however, there will be no blessings until your king acknowledges he is not god."

General Siyrsun's mouth pursed again. He scowled at the prophets and Kien.

Deliberately resting one hand on his sword's hilt, Kien asked, "General Siyrsun, have you nothing to say to Siphra's king or its allies?"

Siyrsun gaped. As did everyone. One of Akabe's more nervous council members stuttered into the shocked hush, "A-an enemy's general? Here? Unannounced before our king? *Why?*"

Reflecting the council member's suspicion, Akabe's guards unsheathed their swords and closed the gap between their king and Belaal's general.

Akabe said, "You three *messengers*, disrobe to your undergarments and discard your weapons. If you resist and my men must disarm you, we'll confiscate your garments and return you to Belaal naked. Attack anyone, and we'll kill you at once."

When the general hesitated, Tsir Aun half drew his sword and glared, clearly ready to fight. Kien followed suit, his heartbeat quickening. Jon and his subordinate-commander echoed his motion, though the subordinate looked displeased.

Siyrsun hissed something to his Belaal inferiors. They removed their surcoats and outer tunics, flinging them into a pile before Akabe's guards. Weaponry followed in a clattering heap. Sheathed daggers were unlaced from forearms. Short-swords were unbuckled from belts girded to their waists, thighs, and inside their boots.

As Belaal's general tossed down his final dagger—and no doubt felt a draft through his short tunic—he cut a look at Kien's insignias. "Tracelander, how did you recognize me?"

It wouldn't do to taunt the man. "I was granted the knowledge, sir."

The general's nostrils flared. "Who are you?"

"No one you've met. I'm a military judge, specializing in treaties." How much should he say? Could he persuade these men to open negotiations toward Belaal's withdrawal from Parne?

Siyrsun's hostility sundered the notion at once. "However you came by such knowledge, Tracelander, you have insulted me and my men, and caused us to suffer this indignity! By the name of my king who is my god, I will seek you in battle!"

"You'll regret finding me, sir." Scythe would be sure of it. "May I advise immediate talks between our countries instead? Negotiation will be preferable to your army's annihilation."

"I'll cut out your tongue first!" Siyrsun sneered. "Then I will flay and gut you!"

Not a peaceable image. Kien nodded. "Fairly warned. But, remember, I also warned you. Negotiation would serve you, your country, and your king far better." Huh. He was sounding almost prophet-like.

Siyrsun hacked up a gob of mucous and spat it toward Kien. "That's for your negotiations! My god-king would never submit to the shame of compromise!"

"The choice was yours. And his." Frustrated, Kien shot a look at Akabe.

Siphra's king grumbled something beneath his breath, then motioned to his guards. "Take these men outside. Give them their robes, their boots, and their horses, then immediately chase them from camp."

Belaal's general snarled, "I'll have my sword!"

Akabe's voice was pure ice. "No. You've lost all honor by concealing your weapons in my presence and by threatening my men." To his guards, the king of Siphra snapped, "Take them outside at once! And from now on, you will search everyone who approaches my tent and my council."

The guards obeyed as if haste could make up for their failure.

When General Siyrsun and his subordinates were secured and marched from the tent, Jon hurried over to Kien. "How did you know?"

"Bryce, may the Infinite bless him."

Akabe approached, his expression suddenly older. "Aeyrievale, thank you. Again."

To Kien's left, the elder prophet spoke abruptly, as if repeating a message. "Tomorrow, midmorning, you will attack Belaal and its allies. The Infinite commands it."

Finally! Infinite, thank You!

Exultant, Kien turned to his comrades, ready to plan their attack. Tomorrow, if the Infinite willed it, he would bring Ela out of Parne!

34

Battle ready, Kien stood outside his relinquished tent, arguing with Dan Roeh. "Respectfully, sir, you cannot accompany me."

"I can and will." Dan turned and started inside the tent, beyond doubt the parent who'd bequeathed Ela her stubbornness.

Kien pushed an arm in front of the man, halting him. Not good, being rude to his beloved's father. "Again, respectfully, sir, you *will* wait here and protect your family. Please. Otherwise, you'll be a distraction to me in the coming battle, and we'll both die."

Roeh shifted. Scowled. Kien could see his emotions warring in the lines of his hard-edged face. The longing to rescue his daughter. The desire to protect his wife and infant son, with their friends. Looking away, Dan nodded. "Thank you. We'll watch and pray. And guard the camp."

"Thank you, sir. But if the worst happens, save yourselves. Flee north to the Tracelands."

A whistle summoned Kien's attention. Jon motioned to him. Time to form ranks and leave. Kien waved acknowledgment at his brother-in-law, then told Dan, "We appreciate your prayers."

By now, Kalme Roeh was standing beside her husband. And, obviously, she'd been listening to their argument. Her soft face revealed distress, unlike the bright-eyed baby in her arms, who stared at Kien as if enthralled by his gold clasps and armor—particularly his gilded arm guards. Fine little boy. Kien swiped a light teasing touch along the small face. The infant turned his head, open-mouthed, as if trying to bite Kien's fingers. Grinning, Kien pulled back. "We'll bring your sister to you," he told the baby.

Kalme Roeh sounded half-choked. "Thank you!"

Was she going to cry? Offering her a parting smile and a nod, Kien retreated, his weaponry clinking with every step.

Bryce, standing at a discreet distance, quickly joined him. "Sir, if I may, I'll follow the army just long enough to witness the battle's outcome. If all fails, I'll return to warn her family and friends to escape."

"Thank you, Bryce." Kien sighed, relieved by the offer. Amazing of Bryce to anticipate a worry that he himself hadn't yet considered. And aggravating. Really, Bryce was much too easy to depend upon. How could he free the man of feeling so obligated to serve the non-lord of Aeyrievale? Kien asked, "What if we defeat Belaal? What'll you do then?"

Bryce straightened. "May I act as I believe most needful?"

"Of course. But don't ask me. You're a free man, Bryce—I'm not your lord. Remember?"

"I know you prefer to think so, sir."

Giving up temporarily, Kien hurried to meet Jon, who grimaced. "Took you long enough. Scythe's been snapping at everyone."

"He's hungry, no doubt." Destroyers never appreciated rations. "He will be happier after the battle." If they survived the battle.

Glossy black, Scythe stomped his massive polished hooves as if to urge Kien along. "Steady," Kien ordered. He unleashed the monster and climbed the footholds. "We're leaving."

The destroyer groused, shoulder and neck muscles shimmering and twitching in barely controlled fury. Bryce, evidently unimpressed, approached and offered Kien his shield.

"Thank you, Bryce, for everything. Guard yourself and stay alive."

"I will, sir—and I'll pray the Infinite guards you all."

Kien guided Scythe into the Tracelands' destroyer ranks, which were combined with Istgard's. All the monster-horses seemed testier than usual—stomping, huffing, and biting toward each other.

Reassuring, Kien decided. Scythe must be eager for the battle and incited by the natural rivalries among the destroyers. Most important, Scythe showed no signs of overwhelming grief. Meaning Ela was still alive. Grateful, Kien dug his booted feet more securely into the footholds of Scythe's war collar. Survive the battle. Subdue all enemies. Find Ela and remove her from Parne. A single day's work, he hoped.

The leader of the allied destroyer-force, Tsir Aun, nodded to Jon and Kien, then surveyed their troops coldly, ever the soldier. "I pray we finish matters today." He raised his voice to everyone under his command. "Your task is to terrify Belaal's troops. Break their formations and send them running in panic! While doing so, you will maintain close ranks throughout the charge. Do not allow the enemy to individually isolate you. For those who've never ridden into battle, trust your destroyer to do its work. If your steed argues with you in battle, there's good reason—so pay attention!"

"I'm still the master," Kien muttered.

Scythe tossed his head.

After a final sweeping check of his destroyer-battalion, Tsir Aun goaded his beast, Wrath, into formation after Akabe's personal battalion. The armies merged and then traveled along Parne's seemingly endless northern wall, heading west. While their forces entered the dry open fields beyond the western wall, Kien straightened, studying the opposition.

As Bryce depicted in his leather map, the Agocii forces, with the Eosyths, held the northern sectors of the plain, reinforcing Belaal's army, which was encamped nearer Parne.

Full-bearded Agocii scouts spied Siphra's forces first. They scrambled, signaling the alarm with trumpet blasts to alert Belaal and its allies.

Belaal, caught up in working its giant catapults against Parne's weakened wall, failed to immediately heed the Agocii trump calls. During their approach, Kien admired Belaal's powerful siege weapons. As soldiers released heavy chains, each catapult's massive counterweight dropped toward the ground, sending its opposing beam hurtling skyward, launching a huge boulder toward the wall. How many missiles had Belaal launched this morning? Kien eyed the wall as a boulder fell, swiftly followed by a second.

The huge stones crushed into the wall, collapsing the section in pieces. A deep, thunderous vibration shook the ground, causing Scythe to flatten his ears. But the destroyer's huff of challenge vanished amid a second blast of noise. Evidently too damaged to withstand continued shocks, an adjoining section of Parne's wall crumbled to its foundations, spewing out a vast cloud of grit.

The cloud failed to settle. Instead, a ferocious wind swept the dirt upward.

Kien watched, stunned, as the mighty current of air built the pulverized wall fragments into a vast curtain of debris that swept southward, slashing into Belaal's forces. Devastating them. "Infinite!"

Belaal's allies scattered in obvious terror. Beneath his breath, Kien muttered, "A rout!" With this one storm blast, the battle's odds evened. "Strike," he urged the distant Akabe. "Now!"

At the head of the joint army, Akabe shouted orders lost to Kien over the commotion. But trumpets echoed reassuringly in Siphra's prearranged signal, directing a charge against their chief target—Belaal.

Tsir Aun bellowed, "Forward!"

Unsheathing his Azurnite sword, Kien braced himself. Scythe charged across the field with the other destroyers, not into an army, but into a fray of screaming, bloodied, panicked soldiers. Bodies, hideously broken and gashed by the storm's onslaught, littered the landscape. Belaal's able-bodied soldiers ran.

From a distance, more trumpets blared. Yells lifted from among Belaal's forces. "Turn and fight! Stand your ground!"

Several of Belaal's men tried to attack Kien. Scythe mowed them down before they could take proper aim. Kien had to close his thoughts to their agonized screams. Equally pitiable, Belaal's horses fled in terror before the destroyers, who bit them bloody and tore their Belaal masters from their backs.

Kien glimpsed a blade's flash as one unseated soldier lifted his short-sword against Scythe. The destroyer shifted away, but not quickly enough—the soldier swung wide to gut Scythe.

"No!" Kien slashed the Azurnite sword down against the man's arm and left him screaming, clutching at spilling blood as Scythe charged ahead.

Just as the destroyers' attack seemed near its end, a sudden lurch jolted Kien. Scythe broke ranks, pulling back. Why? Kien scanned the battleground and saw a chariot manned by an archer. Aiming at him. He raised his shield just in time to feel the arrow's thud. Huffing furiously, Scythe charged the offending chariot and its bleeding archer—General Siyrsun.

The general's horse squealed as Scythe barreled past it to get at Siyrsun. The general screamed, his arm caught in the destroyer's grip. Scythe flung the man away. Kien lost sight of his body in the clash and press of shields, destroyers, and chariots.

Twice Belaal and its allies attempted to regroup. Twice, Akabe's forces and his allies scattered their foes. By midday Belaal's men had fled, routed toward the distant hills. Soon after, their allies retreated to their respective encampments.

A bleak calm overtook the field. Kien turned Scythe about and surveyed the landscape. Most of Belaal's tents littered the former encampment as scraps of gaudy rags and splinters of wood—abandoned. And a detachment of Siphran soldiers now guarded the breach in Parne's wall. Before Kien could rejoice at the sight and plot Ela's rescue, Jon rode up, his face smeared with blood.

Kien winced. "You're injured."

Bewildered, Jon rubbed at his jaw and studied the crimson stain on his hand. "Oh. Savage and I disagreed with each other, didn't we?" He nudged his destroyer.

Savage huffed, hesitated, and then became restless.

Scythe hesitated as well, an uneasy noise sounding low in his throat.

Ela! Kien was sure both beasts sensed her suffering. Savage had been briefly pledged to Ela after the battle of Ytar and no doubt still held some devotion for her. And Scythe frankly loved Ela above Kien. Above life.

As did Kien. Agitation quickening his motions, Kien dismounted, removed his cloak, and began to unlace the change of clothes he'd tied to the destroyer's war collar. "Jon, I'm going after Ela!" While Kien wrenched at the knots, he glanced over at Parne's breached wall.

At his elbow now, Jon said, "Huh. It seems Belaal destroyed the buildings inside as well. I'm sure anyone could ride through that gap, but—"

"I'm sure we can," Kien interrupted. "Jon, come with me to find her."

Uncertainty shadowed Jon's face. "Given our instructions, Kien, we'd best wait until Siphra clears the way."

Kien nodded at his brother-in-law, remembering the Infinite's command. *If you enter Parne, spare no one who lifts any sort of weapon against you*. Fine. He would go in alone.

Tsir Aun rode up to join them, drawing the huffing Wrath alongside Scythe.

Not dismounting, Istgard's prime minister said, "The allies wish to negotiate the terms of their surrender. Separately, because they've been fighting among themselves. I've agreed. The sooner we settle matters with Belaal's allies, the better. We cannot risk them taking up weapons again while we're inside the city." Tsir Aun hesitated, clearly reluctant to ask for Kien's help. "The king is meeting with the Eosyths. We need you to talk with the Agocii. They're the most difficult, and negotiations are your field of expertise. Meanwhile, I'm leading half of our forces in pursuit of Belaal's soldiers to be sure they don't return. Only the Agocii remain."

Your duty. Kien heard the unspoken words. No! There was nothing to negotiate. Belaal and its allies lost. *Lost.* And he needed to ride into Parne and find Ela.

Duty, Kien reminded himself. His responsibilities as a military judge-in-training took precedence above personal commitments. Even above finding Ela. Kien growled and immediately felt ashamed. Souls would be lost if the Agocii decided to take offense and attack. And, if she knew, Ela would insist Kien deal with his obligations first. Scythe's twitching had increased. The beast stomped now. And groaned. Ela. Kien shut his eyes. Infinite?

Silence pressed in around him. Duty versus rescuing Ela. Infinite? Is this a test? Sickened, Kien said, "I'll go."

"I'll accompany you," Jon told Kien. "Just allow me to wash my face first."

Kien nodded, then warned Istgard's prime minister, "As soon as we've concluded the terms of surrender, I'm riding into Parne to find Ela."

Tsir Aun frowned at Parne's collapsed wall. "I'm sorry. I'd prefer you bring her out immediately, as you do. My wife would also be distressed at the delay. I'll be praying."

"I know. Thank you."

Jon returned, still in battle gear but minus the blood, accompanied by his taciturn, battle-bruised subordinate, Selwin. They rode to the Agocii camp, dismounted a safe distance from the tents, and commanded their destroyers to wait.

At the entry to the largest tent, thick-bearded Agocii guards sneered at their arrival, as if greeting defeated foes instead of the battle's victors. Haughty wretches—still armed with swords and bad tempers. Kien exchanged a wary glance with Jon as they entered the tent.

Infinite, protect us, please. And make the Agocii chieftains conciliatory! Speed along these negotiations for Ela's sake. Truly, he had to cease thinking of her for now. Duty.

Arrogant in gold-etched armor and elaborately detailed robes and cloaks, the pale Agocii chieftains sat in a semicircle on a cushioned mat within the tent. An evidently symbolic tray of bread rested before them, with writing implements arranged on a low table nearby. All seemed ready for immediate talks. Until the Agocii leaders saw Kien, Jon, and Selwin.

The chieftain wearing the most gold tugged at his elaborately braided beard in obvious agitation. "Has Istgard's prime minister considered us so unworthy that he sends three raw-green youths to bargain in his stead?"

The tribal chiefs' motions reflected his own nervousness—all three unraveling and rebraiding sections of their silvered beards. Kien suppressed a frown. Really, the Agocii seemed inordinately obsessed with their beards. A true mania. Likely denoting . . . status. . . .

Oh, wonderful. Kien's empty stomach sank as he cast a sidelong glance at Jon and Selwin's recently shaven faces—each showing variants of afternoon-whiskered shadows. No beards and certainly nothing braided.

Wild with frustration, Kien muttered to Jon, "Unless we find some other Agocii-recognized claim to status, apart from beards, these talks are going to take all week!"

Jon hissed beneath his breath. "Beards? What about beards?"

He was going to shove his brother-in-law, then flee the tent. Now! Gritting his teeth, Kien knelt on one of the unoccupied cushions. Be patient. Placate all parties. Begin from a point of agreement. Bargain through differences and conclude terms of surrender, allowing the defeated to retreat with honor. Without bloodshed. Then find Ela. Infinite, help me!

He smiled at the unhappy fray-bearded chieftain-losers, planning his strategy.

✦ ✦ ✦

Her eyelids too heavy to open, Ela returned to consciousness, surrounded by the stench of decay. Still alive. Why?

Her heartbeat wavered uncertainly, rapid and feeble with

distress. And her breath rattled painfully in her throat. Harsh to her ears. She could do nothing except breathe. Hurt. And wait.

Thoughts flickered. Tremulous as near-extinguished lamp flames.

Summoning the last wisps of her strength, she sought her Creator. His voice. She needed to hear His voice. Infinite? I'm dying. . . .

I am here.

35

As they left the negotiations and hurried through the late afternoon sunlight, Kien muttered to Jon, "Remind me to beat you later, when we're both off duty!" After he'd found Ela.

Wholly without remorse, Jon said, "You implied that, victory notwithstanding, we had no status as far as the Agocii were concerned. We had to do something to improve our bargaining position. You *are* regarded as a Siphran lord, and as Istgard's rightful king. Even the Agocii honor royalty—beards or no beards—so why not mention it?"

Kien cast a wary over-the-shoulder look at Selwin, who was likely listening. "Your comments were recorded."

"My comments accomplished our objective—to swiftly facilitate negotiations for terms of surrender that wouldn't offend the Agocii. What better way to raise the status of a beardless 'raw-green youth' than to introduce him as an uncrowned king?"

"You're right." And he was. "However, you've almost guaranteed my censure before the Grand Assembly. I'd intended to persuade the Agocii of my previous ambassadorial rank."

"Ah!" Jon tugged at his cloak. "I forgot about the censure. I apologize."

Too worried about Ela to remain upset with his brother-in-law, Kien nodded. "I hope quite a few of the representatives will agree with your point of view simply because we succeeded. The

Agocii are breaking camp." Indeed, around them, their bearded former enemies were bellowing threats at each other while packing gear—and casting them renewed looks of scorn. Kien shook his head. Fine. At least he was freed.

As they approached the destroyers, Scythe whickered deep, plaintive vocalizations of distress. "I'm hurrying." Kien tore off his outer garments, lashing his military gear onto the war collar, then swiftly draping himself with plain non-military attire. When he lifted Scythe's chain-leash and fastened it to the war collar, Scythe trembled with the unspoken indication that they were about to leave the Agocii camp. Grabbing his agitated destroyer's reins, Kien said, "Commander Thel, with your permission, I'm going to search for Ela. Off duty. Will you tell the king and the prime minister?"

"You don't need my permission. But you're going alone?"

"Yes. I'll have Scythe," Kien pointed out.

Selwin stepped up now, his face unreadable. Glancing from Kien to Jon, he asked, "Permission to speak, sir?" At Jon's nod, the subordinate-commander addressed Kien, each syllable so sharply clipped that Kien had no trouble reading condemnation in the man's words. "Sir, the city is not secured. Siphran orders, which might be considered reprehensible in the Tracelands, are still in effect. It is advisable for all Tracelanders to remain outside the city."

Selwin's warning verged on a threat. Kien stared. This man would report his actions. Before Kien could snarl a reply, Jon said, "Your point is taken, Selwin. But Judge Lantec is entering the city, off duty, to locate a friend who might be in danger."

"Thank you, Selwin, for your concern." Kien turned away and mounted Scythe. The destroyer quivered, a gigantic heap of monster-anxiety. Kien shoved his feet into the collar rungs. "Go—no trampling anyone!"

Scythe bolted for Parne, gusting irritated breaths of warning, as he cut around Siphrans, Tracelanders, and Istgardians too slow to flee from his path. Kien yelled, "Clear the way! Move!"

Just as Scythe neared the breach in Parne's wall, Kien saw a horseman charge toward them. "Bryce!" Reluctantly, Kien reined in the agitated Scythe. "What are you doing?"

"Waiting for you, sir." Even as Kien started to send him away, Bryce said, "I'm a free Siphran, and I believe you might need my help. Lead and I'll follow."

From this vantage point, Kien heard screams lifting above the breach. Smoke billowed high and thick beyond the rubble. Had the Parnians decided to set fire to their city? Kien argued, "You could die in there!"

Bryce smiled. "I could just as easily die at home, my lord. Lead on. You won't change my mind."

"I am not your lord!"

Bryce waited in silent disagreement.

Scythe exhaled a tormented destroyer complaint, so distressed that Kien couldn't ignore it. Ela was surely dying. "Stay alive, Bryce!"

"You also, sir."

Kien unsheathed his sword and turned Scythe into the rubble-strewn breach. "Go! Carefully—"

The destroyer thundered through debris. Splintering timbers. Sending stones flying. Confronting sheer mounds of rubble. Scythe scattered everything in his desperation to reach Ela. Looking behind him, Kien saw Bryce's little horse doing its valiant best to keep up. But Bryce was forced to choose his path more carefully and eventually disappeared from sight amid the wreckage.

Kien hesitated and pulled Scythe to a walk, the decision clawing his thoughts like a live beast. He couldn't leave Bryce behind. He'd lost servants before—friends, all—and it seemed he'd still not recovered from their deaths.

The instant Bryce rode out of the rubble, his sword readied, Kien goaded Scythe ahead. Infinite! Spare Ela, please. Protect her—

Spare no one who lifts any sort of weapon against you!

The reminder poured into Kien's thoughts like burning oil,

making him gasp. He could not afford a mistake here. Kill one innocent citizen by accident, and he'd be forever condemned in the Tracelands.

He saw the Parnians now. Wraithlike shells of mortals peering from windows and doorways, and over the edges of walls. Frail creatures with haunted dark eyes—some despairing, some furious.

To fend them off, Kien yelled down each street, "Parnians, obey your Creator! Go to the wall! Surrender and live! Put down your weapons!" Why did they stare at him so oddly? Didn't they want to escape Parne? The streets stank of putrid flesh at every turn—so overwhelming that Kien was grateful he'd eaten nothing since dawn. Worse, some of the bodies looked . . . hacked. Had the Parnians resorted to cannibalism? Kien shuddered.

Bryce echoed his cry. "Put down your weapons! Go to the wall! Surrender and live!"

The tactic worked. Scythe rushed through the city as if he knew each turn within the twisting paved streets and courtyards. His wall-shaking hoofbeats caused the Parnians to retreat in panic. "Obey your Creator! Go to the wall! Surrender and live! Put down your weapons!" The Parnians who dared to remain seemed transfixed by Kien's words.

Why?

By now, Scythe was thundering toward the highest point of the city—a magnificent building that could only be Parne's temple. Kien glimpsed echoes of East Guard's fallen temple in those glorious columns. Had East Guard's temple looked like this—gilded and shining in the sunlight on Temple Hill? Drawing all eyes to itself?

Scythe charged through the open gate, scattering the few souls within the temple's court. Kien yelled, "Obey the Infinite! Put down your weapons and go to the wall! Surrender and live!"

They gaped at him, but Scythe was already turning, charging along a stone street that led beyond the temple toward a maze of whitewashed homes, larger than most, built against Parne's wall. Hooves thudding against pavings, the monster warhorse entered a stone courtyard, which was framed by ravaged gardens and decorative stone alcoves. But the destroyer paid no heed to the gardens' remains. He circled a stone-rimmed well in the center of the courtyard and whickered in distress. Kien was about to turn and look for Bryce. Until he realized that Scythe had reached their goal.

She's in the well? Oh, Infinite . . . no . . . not a well!

Sickened, Kien tugged Scythe's mane. "Are you sure? She *cannot* be down there."

The destroyer tightened his circle, then halted. Bending his huge dark head, Scythe nosed at the well's wooden cover, shoved it partially aside, then leaned into the well and released a destroyer-cry. Just as he'd summoned Ela to the wall the last time they'd seen her.

"She's in the well. . . ." Merely looking into that confining darkness brought Kien's memories back in a nauseating rush. Swallowed alive. Trapped in darkness.

He descended the war-collar rungs, almost screaming at Parne's citizens, "Why a well? Why not a prison? Why not a barred hole in the wall?"

Swallowing hard, Kien leaned over the encircling stone rim and yelled down into the musty blackness, "Ela?"

Did he hear a faint sound? A cry? Scythe bumped him, clearly distraught. Kien straightened and sucked in a deep, hopefully calming breath.

He was going down into a black, probably slimy pit. Let it be dry. It *had* to be dry. No need to panic. "Fine!" Fine. If he repeated the word often enough, perhaps it would be fine. Kien sheathed his sword, dragged the wooden cover completely away from the well, and reached for the ropes built into the windlass above. Were they strong enough to support him? And long enough to pull up Ela? Where was Bryce? He should have been here by now.

A scuffling on the nearby stones raised every hair on Kien's head. As he whipped out his sword again and turned, Scythe verified the threat by rumbling a furious warning.

Kien watched a man approach—gaunt but not quite as scrawny as the wraiths in Parne's lower streets. "Are you the owner of this well?"

"Leave!" the Parnian commanded, his voice resonant—the tone of authority. "You have no business here!"

"Indeed I do!" Kien snapped. "Parne's prophet, Ela Roeh, is in that well, and I—"

To his horror, the man unsheathed a sword and charged him.

Scythe swung about, bent his big head in an arc, grabbed Kien's assailant, and flung him away. Screaming but still alive.

Spare no one who lifts any sort of weapon against you!

The words cut through Kien again, a warning this time. Kien called to Scythe, "Stop!"

The destroyer groaned, but halted. Azurnite blade glittering deep blue in the afternoon sunlight, Kien approached the Parnian. "Who are you? Why should it matter if I free your prophet?"

"She's no prophet!" the man cried. "She's a traitor, cursed by the Infinite!"

Cursed by the— Seething, Kien left the thought unfinished. He shifted the Azurnite sword and beckoned his enemy. "Stand. You'll have to stop me from saving her."

"My lord!" Bryce yelled from the courtyard's edge.

His eyes still fixed on the hostile Parnian, Kien called, "I'm here, Bryce! Stay back."

In Kien's thoughts, Fightmaster Lorteus snarled from a past lesson, "Any foe, however weak, however wounded, can *kill*!"

Thank you, Lorteus. I haven't forgotten.

Deliberately, Kien taunted his opponent with the truth. "I'm going to save her. If you want to stop me, you'll have to kill me."

The Parnian charged, sword lifted, clumsy and undisciplined as any civilian would be.

Kien braced himself and swung the Azurnite blade flat against the man's sword to deflect it without breaking the blade.

Then, as ordered, he put the man to death, stabbing the Azurnite through his heart. The Parnian gasped and dropped like a stone.

Kien paused to be sure his opponent was truly dead. Military judge or not, the necessity sickened him. Yet there'd been no doubt this man was an enemy. Infinite, bless You for removing all uncertainty! Kien swiped his sword on the dead man's robe, then turned away.

Bryce met him and muttered, "Parne's priests are a savage lot. I had to kill two, sir. We'd best be alert for more."

Priests? Kien stared back at the dead man's bloodied elaborate blue and white robes. Had Parne's priests turned against Ela? He hurried to the well. "She's in there," Kien told Bryce. "Scythe is sure of it, and I thought I heard her. But she might be unable to help us pull her out. I'm going down after her."

Even as Kien spoke, Bryce hurried to his horse, planning aloud. "We'll tie a cradle, sir, then I'll keep watch while you go down."

"A cradle?"

Bryce unfastened a leather-wrapped roll from his doughty little horse. "With Aeyrievale's cliffs and chasms, all officials carry and use rope cradles."

"My thanks to Aeyrievale," Kien murmured. Blessing the Infinite for Bryce, he helped unroll mesh and ropes, following Bryce's lead in tying knots.

Bryce tested the ropes and wound an end around the windlass, then hesitated, eyeing the mournful Scythe. "I presume your destroyer will cooperate? He'd speed matters."

"He will gladly speed matters." Kien seized the end of the rope and tied it to Scythe's collar with quick, fierce knots. "Don't eat this!"

Scythe made a pathetic noise of complaint and bumped Kien as if to hurry him all the more. At least the destroyer wasn't prostrate with grief, signifying Ela's death. Kien rushed Scythe to the edge of the courtyard, unfurling the rope and tightening it along the way. "Stop."

As Scythe groaned, Kien ran back to the well. "How do I use the cradle?"

"Sit in it as a deep chair, my lord. We'll lower you in. Tell us when your feet hit bottom."

No water. Please. Kien sat on the well's edge, wrapped within the mesh. "Scythe, walk!"

The mesh tightened about Kien and he was lifted off the stones with a sickening sway. "Stop!" Gripping the ropes, dangling in the cradle, Kien stared down into the well's center. He could do this. He must. Shutting his eyes, he yelled, "Scythe, back—slow!"

Scythe's "slow" pace dropped Kien with a rush. "Easy!" The descent eased. Kien opened his eyes in darkness and immediately needed to talk to himself. "This is not a monster. It's a well. A *dried* well." The cradle's mesh wasn't a sea-beast's gullet, and he would not heave. . . .

At last, his booted feet hit soil at the well's edge. "Stop!" Kien's breath nearly halted with the word. The well's decaying stench seemed to clot in his nostrils and lungs. "Ugh!"

"Sir?" Bryce called from above, "Are you injured?"

"No!" But he would be if he had to breathe again. Where was Ela? Cautious, trying to avoid shifting from the mesh cradle, Kien reached into the darkness, touching damp soil. Then fabric. Finally, matted hair. He followed the knotted strand's length and touched a face. "Ela?"

Her skin was cold. Did he feel her breath against his hand? He couldn't be sure. Kien scooped Ela into his arms and rocked backward into the mesh. She felt so frail. Impossibly light, though her mantle and robes were clumped with dirt. And . . . she stank. Horribly. "Infinite!"

Shuddering, Kien settled Ela's limp body in his lap and held her close. A small sound escaped her. Not a word, nor even a cry. More like an exhalation. He mustn't think that it was her last breath. "Scythe! Walk!"

Above him, the ropes tensed, then creaked. The mesh closed around him. Sea beast-like. And throughout the tortuous ascent,

Ela remained lifeless in his arms. Kien prayed all the way up to the well's mouth. At last, the early evening sun made him squint. Bryce grabbed the cradle. "Steady, sir. Swing your legs over here."

Bryce lifted Ela from Kien's arms and placed her on the ground. Kien freed himself from the mesh, knelt beside Ela, and stared, horrified, at the gashes on her scalp, the dried blood streaking her hollowed lifeless face. And her arms . . . He wouldn't have dared to hold her if he'd seen them. Her hands and wrists were swollen and dark, while huge open wounds gaped over her upper arms, the flesh eaten away, exposing bare muscles. "Oh, Ela . . ." How could she live?

Bryce gulped audibly. And when he looked at Kien, his eyes reflected pity. Sympathy.

Scythe approached them now, groaning. Kneeling. Mourning.

Kien stood, fury lending him strength. Allowing him denial. "No!" He'd neither give nor receive futile condolences. Not when there was the least hope she'd survive. He cut the rope from Scythe, then untied his military cloak from the destroyer's back. "Stop your groaning! We're taking Ela to her parents. *Now.*"

36

How many tears had he swallowed on their journey back to camp? They hardly merited counting. Kien fought to harden himself against the grief. Against Scythe's despairing moans. Against the concerned voices of comrades calling his name.

Nonetheless he must admit the truth. He'd lost everything.

Ela, wrapped in his black military cloak, never moved in his arms. If she breathed at all, he couldn't feel it. Moreover, he'd found no pulse at her throat, and he was afraid to test her darkened, swollen wrists and hands. She'd known Parne would take her life. She'd warned him.

In my vision, I was entombed. Surrounded by the stench of death.

A silver-haired prophet has failed.

Biting his lip, blinking against fresh tears, Kien smoothed Ela's dark tangled hair, then dared another look at her face. So serene. Beautiful beneath the dried trails of blood. What had she suffered? Brave little prophet. He whispered, "I love you!" Always.

He hoped he'd killed the Parnian who did this to her.

The Siphran encampment hushed as he approached on Scythe. Kien refused to look at anyone. Instead, he rode straight to his tent and commanded the destroyer quietly, "Kneel."

Scythe, Ela's cherished Pet, sank to the ground and heaved another groan. Balancing Ela in his arms, Kien cautiously slid off the destroyer's big back and braced himself as Ela's parents rushed to meet him.

Kalme Roeh was already crying. And Dan Roeh halted an arm's length away, staring, as if too stunned by the sight of his daughter's bloodied, lacerated scalp to take Ela from Kien.

Kneeling, Kien placed Ela on the ground with a tenderness she'd never feel. And he studied her, trying to memorize her face before the Roehs finally carried her away. They knelt with him.

Dan touched Ela's throat now, obviously testing for a pulse. When he spoke, his voice sounded raw with pain. "What did they do to her?" He reached for the edges of the cloak. Kien moved to stop him, but Roeh was too quick—his expression fierce as he opened the cloak, despite the tears in his eyes.

Kalme screamed at the wounds, "Oh, Ela! Oh, my baby . . ."

Weeping, Dan Roeh released the cloak and held his wife, preventing her from clutching Ela. Inside the tent, Ela's infant brother began to howl.

By now, Jon, Bryce, and Selwin were hovering next to Kien. Akabe knelt with him and grasped Kien's shoulder, clearly speechless as he stared at Ela's flayed arms and the dried rivulets of blood marking her face and throat. And other Parnians drew near, staring, aghast.

Unable to look at Ela's injuries any longer, Kien reached for the edges of his cloak to fold them over her.

A blue-white flash appeared in Ela's swollen right hand, taking the shape of a thin, iridescent, weathered vinewood staff. Ela's insignia, the branch.

Ela's fingers twitched, healing the instant she clasped the vinewood. Kien saw her gasp for air. The gaping wounds closed within that breath. And her eyelids flickered. He leaned forward. "Ela?"

Behind Kien, Scythe scrambled to stand, huffing.

✦ ✦ ✦

She drew a breath. Alive. Why? Infinite, no! Hadn't she suffered enough? Wasn't her work finished? Tears seeped beneath her eyelids—real tears. And light glimmered through the edges of her lashes. Unfair! Her pain had ended. She didn't want to endure more.

"Ela?"

Kien? Before she could turn—to see nothing but another hallucination, she was sure—a tickling, nuzzling warmth grazed softly over her face. A breathing, tickling, nuzzling warmth, with hints of slobber. Alarmed, Ela lifted a defensive hand. "Pet! No . . ."

Voices lifted around her now, laughing, cheering as if celebrating. But somewhere, Jess was crying. Or was she imagining him? Ela opened her eyes.

Kien was staring down at her, too perfect to be a fever-wrought hallucination.

Really, this was a very crowded, bright hallucination. Or was it? Unnerved, she glanced around. Oh, how awful! She seemed to be the center of everyone's attention. And . . . she was holding the branch. Ela clenched her precious insignia tight. Yes, it was real. The vinewood gleamed at her, bathing her with blessed warmth and yet-unspoken promises for the future. "Infinite?"

A woman clutched Ela now, sobbing. Mother.

And someone was wiping her face with a blessedly cool, wet cloth. "Prill? Where am I?"

"You're safe now," the matron soothed, ridiculously teary-eyed.

Kalme snatched Prill's cloth and scrubbed at Ela's face, exultant. "Look at you! We thought you were dead! Oh, my girl! You had us fooled!"

Truly?

Father's low voice cut into Mother's happy hysterics. "How do you feel? Any pain?"

"No." But Kalme was smothering her. Ela protested, "Mother! I can't breathe. And Jess is crying—"

"Let's go to him. Can you stand?" Kalme continued to fuss as she and Father helped Ela to her feet. "Your clothes stink, your hair is a mess, and you look starved—ugh! You need a bath!"

Oh, lovely. This was not prophet-like, having Mother behave as if Ela were three again—amid a crowd, no less.

And yet . . . and yet . . . While Father paused to speak to Kien, Ela hugged her mother hard. Fighting sobs. Infinite, thank You. I love You!

Evidently oblivious to Ela's tears, Kalme patted her shoulder and resumed fussing. "We also need to clean and air this cloak. Oh, dear . . . look at it."

Ela looked. Why was she wearing Kien's military cloak—dirtied and stinking like the well?

Realization sank in, and she stared at him. Finished talking with Father, Kien sought her with a glance as Scythe loomed over his shoulder.

Had they removed her from the well? Ela whispered, "Thank you!"

Kien grinned and retreated as her parents coaxed her away.

✦ ✦ ✦

"The Eosyths requested access to the city," Akabe told Kien as they walked through the sunset-reddened camp, accompanied by Tsir Aun, Jon, and the ever-present Selwin. "I refused their petition, of course."

Kien nodded. "The Agocii requested access as well, claiming they'd been promised shares of the gold and gems. We reminded them, politely, that they'd lost. Belaal offered them rights that are no longer defensible."

Grim-faced, Tsir Aun said, "Yet Belaal and its allies might return. We cannot leave Parne unguarded. However, Istgard cannot afford the expense of protecting the site indefinitely."

Akabe spoke, sounding reluctant, though his expression was determined. "Mine is the commanding army here. Does anyone disagree with this?"

Jon shook his head. "No. The Tracelands sees its role here as supportive. We're not the prevailing force."

"Nor is Istgard." Tsir Aun shot Siphra's young king a questioning look. "Why do you ask? What are you planning?"

"The plans aren't mine," Akabe reminded them. "The Infinite commanded that Parne be destroyed and left a burned waste."

Kien heard Jon's subordinate-commander, Selwin, make a stifled sound of protest. Akabe stopped, then turned, his royal crimson and gold robes fiery in the setting sun. The young king's easy lilt didn't hide his coldness. "If you have objections, sir, I wish to hear them."

"No, sir." Selwin bowed his head in apparent acquiescence. Kien saw rebellion beneath Selwin's outward humility.

Obviously, Akabe saw the same. He folded his arms and waited, destroyer-stubborn. "I request you voice your objections. A Tracelander's view interests me exceedingly."

Selwin remained silent.

Jon said, "Selwin, perhaps you don't give way to kings, but I am your superior, and you will voice your objections freely—and immediately! You're delaying us!"

Selwin straightened. "Sirs, you know what will be said if the city is burned. That we had no compassion for the Parnians. That we failed to protect them and show mercy. That, instead, we bow to the cruel whims of their Infinite."

Even as Kien clenched his jaw to silence himself, the Infinite filled his thoughts with a stream of questions, ending with a command. *Ask him!*

Ask Selwin. And, in the process, give him an arsenal of verbal weapons to use in the future. Watching his career evaporate, Kien obeyed. "Commander Selwin, are you all-seeing? Can you prophesy the future before time's beginning? Do you see how many souls will be lost in the coming generations if the Infinite's judgments are not obeyed here?"

"No, Judge, on all counts, I cannot. Nor do I care to."

Kien persisted. "You stood with us this evening and watched a young woman, by the will of the Infinite, healed of fatal wounds. Do you doubt what you witnessed?"

"There's an explanation for everything, Judge."

"I said the same thing a year ago, while trying to dismiss the Infinite." Kien smiled at the memory of Ela's reply. Rephrasing her words, he said, "But the Infinite is the explanation, and you don't want to hear Him."

"Your conclusion, sir."

Kien nodded. "Of course. You are dismissed from this meeting, Commander Selwin."

The man's mouth twitched as if longing to defy the order. Outranked, he bowed and departed. Kien's enemy, no doubt.

Beneath his breath, Jon said, "You deliberately provoked him! Why?"

"Orders." He raised an eyebrow at Akabe and changed the subject. "How will you proceed against Parne, sir?"

Akabe studied the vast expanse of wall darkening before them in the dusk. "We empty the city and the temple. Remove the survivors to safety, then use Parne's ores and fire to destroy every standing wall. If Parne was selling the ores in Istgard and Belaal, there must be a cache somewhere. We'll find it and use it to take down every possible structure."

Prepared to bargain, Kien asked, "What are your plans for the survivors?"

The Siphran king's tension eased. "We remove them to safety. Restore their health, then—hopefully before the winter storms begin—we bring them to Siphra, where they're needed." Bemused he said, "I'm told Parne's chief priest has escaped with the Infinite's Sacred Books. Most of our copies were destroyed, but Parne's is more ancient."

"Do you intend to make the Parnians Siphran?"

"Of course."

Not so hasty, my royal friend. "What if they prefer to emigrate to Istgard or the Tracelands? Will you allow them to depart?" Particularly Ela.

After a breath of silence, Akabe said, "Yes. But I hope they will not." His gaze turned distant. Joyous. "The Parnians can help Siphra rebuild its temple! Parne's chief priest has the learning and devotion many of our priests lack. And Parne's prophet . . . is unrivaled."

The soft inflection in the king's words, and that reverent pause, set Kien on edge. Akabe admired Ela? In what manner?

Kien vanquished his jealousy. Or, to be honest, he caged it like a snarling beast, then mentally retreated to a safe distance. Infinite, don't let me rush to judgment! Help me.

He must speak to Ela.

✦ ✦ ✦

Four days after the battle, as they tried to walk Jess to sleep in the shadow of Parne's wall, Kien complained to Ela in a whisper, "Where *do* you find your chaperones?" Matron Prill, marching a strict three paces behind them, was more cold-eyed and vigilant than Tamri Het in East Guard.

Beatific, a near-perfect image while cuddling her baby brother in her arms, Ela murmured, "My chaperones find me. The Infinite sends them."

Of course You do, Kien grumbled to his Creator. And, I confess, You are right to have me watched. Won't You answer me concerning my wish to marry Ela? Is this Your will or not?

He could only presume that the Infinite's silence meant neutrality. And if their Creator was impartial in the matter, then Kien meant to pursue Ela until he was certain that his pursuit was hopeless. Really, his self-control was being severely tested right now, being this close to Ela. He wanted nothing more than to snatch up his little prophet and run away with her.

The idea prompted a swarm of improper thoughts, difficult to fight off. Kien put his hands behind his back and kept them clasped there as he continued to walk with Ela. He almost heard Prill's silent wish to tie his wrists together. Wise woman.

"Anyway," Ela continued, a bit louder, "I love Prill. We've been through so much."

There. His opportunity. "Speaking of love, my sister said that you admitted you love me."

"Not in so many words!" Ela hissed, delightfully feisty.

"Oh? Then deny you love me."

She opened her mouth, then shut it and sighed. In her arms, little Jess hiccoughed, still awake.

Kien grinned at the baby, but spoke to Ela. "You love me, yet you still refuse to marry me."

"Nothing's changed." Ela patted her brother's back, a bit too quickly. "I can't marry you or anyone. I'm too distracted by my responsibilities as a prophet to be a proper wife—too busy almost dying every time I turn around!"

She released a frustrated puff of a breath and nodded toward the thin, violet-red slash on her left bicep. "I'm amazed I've escaped with so few scars. Kien, Parne hated me enough to threaten anyone who befriended me. I can't ask that of you."

"You asked it of Prill," Kien pointed out.

"I didn't ask her. The Infinite sent Prill, and she offered—"

"I'm offering," he countered gently. "And if the Infinite didn't send me your way, then I'm seriously deluded, and you need to pray for me. You must admit that He introduced us." He leaned toward Ela, determined to coax agreement from her. Behind them, Matron Prill cleared her throat. Killjoy. Kien straightened. "Will you go to Siphra?"

"Yes. My family and friends have decided to settle there."

Beneath his breath, Kien argued, "Marry me! Come with me to the Tracelands instead!"

"Kien, please don't make this so difficult for me. I've given you my answer. I can't—"

"There!" he interposed, smiling, keeping his plea low to prevent Chaperone Prill from overhearing. "If it's difficult for you to dispute marrying me, then my case has merit. Quite promising, actually! Pray, as I have been praying, and I'll ask again later."

She breathed out a sound of exasperation, but didn't seem wholly irritated with him. Watching her bite her lip, he was sure she'd covered a smile. A small victory. Even so, best to not risk his advantage. Changing tactics, he whispered, "Please. Just consider what I've said. Meanwhile I'll write you a long letter—as soon as I've thought of new arguments to wear you down."

"I'd rather you not . . ." She stopped. A tiny frown etched between her eyebrows. "Letter? You mean to say you're leaving immediately?"

"See? You already miss me." Before she could reply, he said, "I'm leaving for East Guard as soon as possible to turn myself in before I'm summoned like a criminal. It's to be a nonverbal proclamation of my good intentions and, hopefully, my blamelessness."

"What!" Her openmouthed shock delighted him and startled the baby.

Unable to hold back his smile, Kien said, "I'm elated by your obvious concern."

Ela jostled her brother lightly, soothing him. "Of course I'm concerned! What do you mean—before you're summoned like a criminal?"

"I've had a few adventures while you were in Parne, and the Tracelands is about to demand explanations."

"Adventures? In ToronSea?"

"ToronSea was the beginning. I failed, dear prophet. Completely." It was a relief to tell her every unexaggerated, wretchedly honest detail. His condemnation. Becoming sea-beast bait. The Infinite's mercy. And his endless warnings in Adar-iyr, followed by that city's submission. While Ela stared, Kien asked, "It's all rather prophet-like, don't you think?"

Ela's pace slowed. When she finally spoke, her words were laced with the threat of tears. "Adar-iyr listened to you. . . . Think of all the souls saved! Why couldn't Parne have reacted the same way?"

He should have realized Ela would compare Adar-iyr's repentance with Parne's defiance and see herself as a failure. Stupid, Lantec! "I'm sorry."

"Don't be." She sniffled, wringing his heart in the process. "I'm glad for Adar-iyr."

He wanted to distract her. Tell her about Akabe, Maseth, and the disastrous royal bequest of Aeyrievale. But now the baby was dozing in Ela's arms. And Bryce was walking toward them from the encampment, carrying what appeared to be an official packet, which Kien guessed he should ignore. Moreover, Scythe had somehow escaped his leash. The destroyer merged behind Kien and Ela now, breathing on them. Clearly, their walk was at an end.

Beyond Scythe, blocked from sight by the destroyer's massive body, Matron Prill grumbled, "Shoo! Go away!"

Kien smoothed Scythe's gleaming black neck. "Don't listen to her. You stand right there like a good monster-horse." Matron Prill couldn't see anything but Scythe's formidable self, Kien was sure. And neither could anyone else. He wiped Ela's tears, then slid his arms around her. Mindful of the baby, Kien bent and kissed Ela, his self-control endangered by desire. Her lips against his were delectably tender, her skin so petal-soft and sweet that he could linger with her forever.

Before Ela could work up a protest, Kien stepped back. But he caressed one last tear from her cheek and whispered, "I love you! We've been through so much together! And, perhaps more than any other man alive, Prophet, I understand your role and honor it. Pray! Think about what I've said, and wait for my letter. Please."

Dazed, Ela watched Kien lead Scythe away. How dare he be so . . . persuasive? She licked her lips—just a hint—still tasting his kiss and longing for another.

Forget being a prophet! She twitched, ready to hand Jess to Matron Prill, then run after Kien.

But Prill caught her sleeve now, furious. Ready, Ela hoped, to talk angry chaperone-sense until these unprophetly thoughts dispersed.

"You'd best never allow that man such liberties again," Prill huffed. "Or you'll have to marry him, Ela Roeh, mark my words!"

Oh, Prill. Not helpful in the least. Ela adjusted the drowsing Jess in her arms and kissed his curls. She must stop thinking of Kien.

Destroyer hoofbeats echoed off Parne's wall. She looked toward the sound and felt a hit of disappointment. Jon. Not that Jon was dreadful, but he wasn't Kien.

Jon dismounted from Savage and fell into step beside Prill, though he spoke to Ela. "How are you feeling?"

Ela shrugged. "All right." She was about to ask Jon why Kien would be summoned to East Guard, but Jon was already talking.

Gently, as if fearing he'd hurt her, he said, "Ela, you ladies must return to camp. We're pulling everyone back for their own safety. Parne is empty. Everything's set and the Siphrans are preparing to destroy the city."

37

Standing at a distance from Parne with the other survivors, clutching both the branch and Jess, Ela watched vast gaps open in the wall. Parne was being shattered by its own ores, reducing the traitorous Atean shrines to dust.

Pain tightened around Ela's throat like a noose and tears spilled down her cheeks, but she forced herself to watch. To face her sentence.

She, Parne's prophet, stood as guilty as the Atea-lovers for failing to recognize her city-state's fatal corruption. Verses from the Book of Praises slid into her thoughts.

Declare them guilty, Infinite, for their intrigues have ruined them. . . .

The temple, now cleared of its treasures—she would not think the word *looted*—fell amid billowing towers of smoke. Explosions shattered its white columns, then brought down the temple's gilded dome. Parne's crown.

By Your love, my Creator, I may approach Your house. . . .

Never again. "Oh, Infinite!" She couldn't prevent the tears. "What will happen to Your people who love You?"

Kalme hugged Ela now, crying quietly. Behind her, Prill sobbed aloud.

As Ela watched the clouds of smoke and the walls of flames consuming homes, His voice whispered in her thoughts.

I consider the exiles sent from this place as righteous. For their good, I watch over My people. Tell them to build homes in their new land and be content. I remember and love them still.

She willed herself to rest in His words. And in the temple she now saw in her thoughts, yet unbuilt, above the white-arcaded homes of Siphra.

Bowing her head over Jess's soft black curls, Ela prayed.

And the branch gleamed in her hand, offering its silent promise of reconciliation.

✦ ✦ ✦

General Rol stood as Kien entered his residential meeting chamber. "You received the summons."

"Yes." Kien opened his money pouch and removed the small parcel Bryce had given him outside Parne. "I haven't unsealed it, but that hardly matters. I'd hoped to leave Parne before it arrived."

Rol glared at the formal blue-wax-sealed parchment. "Recessed or not, they've wasted no time in sending it." Concerned, he asked, "What are your plans, my boy?"

"To defend myself before the Grand Assembly, then deal with the aftermath."

The general turned and looked out the nearest window. "Yesterday, I received a missive from Thel's subordinate-commander, Selwin."

"I'm sure you did, sir."

"You will tell me every detail," Rol ordered. "However slight, I want to hear it. But first, we'll take a walk."

"A walk, sir?"

Rol turned from the window, suddenly testy. "Yes, Lantec. A walk. Fetch your destroyer to my front courtyard."

Why? Kien restrained himself and went outside. He unleashed Scythe from the chaining block in front of the general's residence and led him through the gate, into the main courtyard. "Best manners," Kien reminded the monster. "No biting, no licking, no eating. Do you hear me?"

Scythe grunted.

Rol waited in the courtyard, clad in muddy boots and an old cloak. "Out to the pasture." He marched alongside Kien as if on a mission. What was wrong?

"How is Ela?" the general demanded. "Tell me she survived."

"She survived, sir. I believe she's now traveling to Siphra with the other Parnian refugees."

"Good." Rol sounded grimly pleased. "I'll send word to her chaperone. Tamri Het will be glad to return to Siphra and resume her duties, I'm sure."

"Yes, sir. But Ela is already surrounded by chaperones." Her parents and Prill were enough.

"Hmph! Chaperones aren't fail-safe, and I have proof." The general halted at a stone-arched reinforced gate leading into his private pasture. He motioned Kien and Scythe inside, closed the gate behind himself, then released a sharp, impressive whistle. "Flame, come here!"

The general's destroyer was already approaching from the opposite side of the pasture. Dark and elegant as a destroyer could be, she nickered a low greeting.

Scythe answered her—a summoning call.

General Rol scowled at Kien. "Well? Notice anything different about my destroyer?"

Unnerved, Kien studied Flame. Well. "She's, um . . . larger." Bulging at the middle, actually. Kien eyed Scythe. "Is there something you'd care to confess?"

Scythe moseyed off to greet Flame with a nudge. She responded with a nip to his neck, then stood with him. Together, they appeared for all the world like a settled married couple.

The general cried, "I knew it!"

Kien coughed, trying to disguise a laugh.

Rol seemed almost sincerely disgruntled. Almost.

✦ ✦ ✦

Father stormed through Kien's tower room, shaking his head. "I blame myself. My enemies are trying to attack me by destroying your career!"

"You weren't in Siphra or Parne, sir," Kien argued, wishing Father would sit with him at the writing table and calm down. "You've no need to condemn yourself for my actions."

"And you've not been in East Guard!" Rade Lantec snapped. "Now, I've already submitted a formal request to delay your trial. You'll meet with my advisors next week, and . . ."

No! He didn't want a delay. Kien abandoned his writing table, hoping to conceal his frustration. Father meant well. But the more Rade talked, the more Kien realized he would be battling political maneuverings as much as legal charges. Not good.

Infinite, give me patience!

By the time Father left Kien alone in the tower, Kien was too unsettled to continue preparations for the trial. He dropped into the chair before his writing table, deciding to finish his letter to Ela instead. He would send it to Jon to give to Ela. He'd already detailed Siphra's former ambassador Ruestock's meddling in the Siphran royal court. And Maseth's assassination attempt and death. Then Akabe's disastrous gift of gratitude—Aeyrievale. And Selwin's official disapproval.

Onward. Kien picked up his reed pen, tapped it within the ink jar, and continued.

To present my case before the Grand Assembly, I've gathered evidence against myself. Matters do not look promising.

Too dramatic? No, it was the truth. And if the truth inspired Ela's sympathy for him, why not?

If I am condemned and censured— Never mind, the thought is too worrisome to consider. Therefore, I'll ignore it until later.

Another more critical cause concerns me. Before you left East Guard last spring, you observed that I would never give up pursuing you.

Who am I to argue with the Infinite's prophet? Particularly the most adorable prophet ever to live? You are correct.

Again, the truth—and surely no surprise to Ela. Why argue? He must challenge her instead.

For as long as we both draw breath—and if I am allowed to walk free, or walk at all, after my trial—I will persist until you change your mind. Unless, of course, the Infinite wills otherwise.

My love, don't fear a future you cannot see. Instead, we ought to meet life together! By the way, I still ascribe to my theory that you cannot see my future because it is too intimately entwined with your own.

Let her blush as she had the last time he'd suggested this thought. Kien grinned and continued.

In closing, remember: The first trait I admired when meeting you—apart from your lovely face and form—was your courage. And your courage never fails you in anything but this, dear Prophet. Therefore, reconsider. And pray!

I dare you.

Please write to me! I'll need your wisdom in the months to come.

She'd be unable to resist that plea, he was sure.

Kien signed his name without a flourish, sealed the note, then looked around his boyhood room. Still restless. Disturbed, actually.

Infinite? What if I lose? What if I'm condemned?

He could almost feel amusement in the Infinite's response.

Who are you?

Basic question, but loaded with snares. Kien stood and paced until the most basic answer struck him. Could it be so simple? "I am Your servant."

Who am I?

"My Creator."

What will change if you are condemned by mortals?

"My mortal circumstances." But not his eternal one—the undeserved favor he'd found with his Creator. And, if the Infinite was speaking to him now . . . "Won't You tell me Your will regarding my possible marriage with Ela?"

Silence. But comforting neutral silence. Giving Kien reason to hope.

Kien sat at the table again, staring at the heap of legal documents. "I wish You were my Judge in this coming trial. You know my heart." You love me.

He couldn't speak those last three words aloud. Too overwhelming. Particularly remembering all his failures.

Humbled by the Infinite's mercy, His love, Kien said, "So whatever happens, I will continue, despite my faults, as Your obedient servant. In everything."

He removed fresh parchment from his writing box and checked his ink.

Reliving every word, Kien wrote,

In the third month before the fall of Parne, the Infinite spoke to His servant and said, "You will go to ToronSea. . . ."

ACKNOWLEDGMENTS

This story would not be in your hands, dear reader, if I hadn't received invaluable help from a multitude of remarkable people.

First, my wonderful husband, Jerry, and our sons, Larson and Robert, who have endured my daydreaming and years of obsessive writing. Love you guys! Also, Robert and Sharon Barnett, my dear parents, who first encouraged my love for books. Donita K. Paul—dear friend and amazing author. May we always drag each other into marketing mischief. Tamela Hancock Murray, my ever-fun and patient agent, who agreed to present this series to publishers. And to Katharin Fiscaletti, who meticulously hand-copied the map in parchment and ink.

Bethany House editors-extraordinaire David Long, Sarah Long, and David Horton, who—intrepid adventurers all—welcomed Books of the Infinite into their realm. Thank you, everyone, for bringing Ela's story to published life. I'm enjoying the whole process and still pinching myself.

Thanks and serious heartfelt applause to:

The Bethany House Marketing Team: Steve Oates, Noelle Buss, and Debra Larsen.

Bethany House Marketing Support Team: Chris Dykstra, Stacey Theesfield, and Brittany Higdon.

Bethany House staff, including Jolene Steffer, Carra Carr, Elisa Tally, Whitney Daberkow, and Donna Carpenter.

The Bethany House Design Team, and to Wes and Steve for their epic cover art!

Baker Publishing Group Sales Team: David Lewis, Scott Hurm, Bill Shady, Nathan Henrion, Max Eerdmans, Rod Jantzen, Rob Teigen, and the Noble Marketing Group.

Above all, dear reader, thank *you* for bringing this series to life in your imagination! Please feel free to visit me at my website: www.rjlarsonbooks.com. I'd love to hear from you!

DISCUSSION QUESTIONS

1. In chapter 1, Kien is startled by the Infinite's voice. What emotions do you see in Kien's response to his Creator? How would you react in a similar situation?

2. In chapter 3, Ela tells Kien to obey the Infinite's orders. Do you believe Kien takes this warning seriously? Why or why not?

3. What aspects of Kien's personality and his role as a military judge cause difficulties in ToronSea? How does he justify or excuse his actions and judgments? Is Kien truly justified by doing what is right in his own opinion?

4. How does the Infinite ultimately reveal His love and concern for Kien despite Kien's failures? Do you sense your Creator's love and concern for you as you face difficult situations or spiritual struggles?

5. What signs does the Infinite give to Adar-iyr's citizens to warn them of their impending destruction? Why does He warn them? How would you react if you were a citizen of Adar-iyr?

6. What is Kien's main spiritual obstacle in Adar-iyr? Does the Infinite give Kien guidelines or encouragement to successfully complete his mission?

7. Throughout the book, Ela repeatedly faces enemies and situations requiring forgiveness. Do you believe she models the Infinite's love and mercy as she confronts these situations?

8. What spiritual differences between Adar-iyr and Parne determine the differing outcomes in each city? If you were a prophet, which situation would you rather face, and why?

9. Do Kien and Ela sacrifice personal goals or passions to fulfill their work? Why? What do your own personal sacrifices reveal about you spiritually?

10. Has Kien's spiritual outlook changed by the time he returns home? Has his relationship with the Infinite changed? What does he now believe about his Creator and his own life?

11. What do you believe is the Infinite's prime motivation in *Judge*? In our own lives?

ABOUT THE AUTHOR

R. J. Larson is the author of numerous devotionals featured in publications such as *Women's Devotional Bible* and *Seasons of a Woman's Heart*. She lives in Colorado Springs, Colorado, with her husband and their two sons. *Prophet* and *Judge* mark her debut in the fantasy genre.

An excerpt from

KING

BOOKS OF THE INFINITE #3

Poison? Yes, it must be. Blisters bubbled in Ela's mouth. Searing pain scorched its way down her throat. Courtiers and guards closed about them now, some calling for physicians, others kneeling beside the king, whose usually healthy complexion turned waxen. Little Barth cried out and writhed against her. Prill and Tamri supported each other, gasping as if burning alive, and no wonder. Her own stomach seemed on fire.

Ela snatched the branch from the mat, pleading, "Infinite, what must we do?"

An image flashed within her thoughts, sped by a ferocious mental nudge from her Creator. *Hurry!*

Battling faintness, Ela grabbed a round of flatbread from Tamri's dish. The instant she lifted the bread, Ela saw the branch flare, its blue-white fire spreading through her and into the loaf. Frantic, Ela tore the still-glowing bread in two and thrust one half at Akabe. "Eat! Quickly!"

The king obeyed.

Ela dropped the branch and ripped off pieces of bread for Barth, Tamri, Prill, and herself.

In obvious pain, her chaperones snatched the bits of bread and crammed them into their mouths.

While Ela lifted Barth, she swallowed her own bite of bread. It went down her raw throat, quenching the poison's fire. Ela shoved a piece of bread into Barth's mouth. He squirmed and fought. "Chew!" Ela ordered. "Barth, swallow the bread—please!"

The little boy wailed. Ela covered his mouth to prevent the bread from falling out. Holding him, she begged, "Eat the bread. Barth! Swallow the bread, and the Infinite will save you!"

She felt his jaw clench. Barth gulped audibly, opened his eyes, and chirped, "I feel better!"

As the onlooking courtiers laughed and exclaimed their relief, Ela hugged Barth and kissed his soft cheek. Infinite, thank You! But she trembled inwardly. Someone had tried to kill the king. With four of his subjects—one a child. Infinite? Who would do such a thing?

No answer.

Ela turned to the king. Thankfully, Akabe's complexion was no longer ashen. He shook off his fussing attendants. "I'm well. I give you my word. Step back, all of you." To Ela he said, "Prophet, thank you."

She rocked Barth. "Thanks to the Infinite, sir. I'm grateful you're alive—that we've all survived."

Barth snuggled into Ela's arms, seeming content. Until the king commanded him, "On your feet, young sir. We must return to the palace. Your lord-father ought to see you're well before rumors reach him that you were . . . ill."

"He won't mind," Barth argued. But he stood. A grim-faced official in sweeping crimson robes nudged the child toward the steps, to the royal cavalcade of horses in the street below. Akabe departed as well, surrounded by his anxious men.

As the crowd around them thinned, Ela grabbed Tamri and Prill's hands. "You're not too shaken?"

"Oh, no." Prill's mouth pursed testily. "Just another day tending our little prophet!"

"Sorry," Ela muttered.

Tamri's grandmotherly face crinkled as she smiled. "Well, we're alive for now, my girl. Do you suppose it's safe to finish our food?"

"Yes. I'm certain only that single pitcher was poisoned."

"The king's men took it with them," Prill observed. "No doubt they mean to test it."

"Yes, no doubt." Ela reached for her dish. Someone had kicked it, spilling half her food on the mat. She picked up scattered bits of bread and vegetables until a gruff voice stopped her.

"Prophet?"

Ela looked up. Two crimson-badged officials stared down at her, their expressions as unmoving as masks. The gruff-voiced one said, "Will you answer a few questions?"

She nodded and set down her dish. So much for eating.

✦ ✦ ✦

"Huh." Akabe studied the dead flies floating in the gold bowl on his council table. "It's the most effective fly poison *I've* ever seen."

Unamused, his counselors stared at him, then at the bowl again. Lord Faine rested his broad, ring-garnished hands on the table. "How did your enemies know so quickly you'd be at the site today?"

"How indeed?" Akabe sat back in his chair. The celebration and his appearance were planned only this week after he'd signed the land contract. "Is there a spy in my household?"

Faine sighed. "We must redouble our surveillance and your guards. Majesty, this is the second attempt on your life within the past seven months."

"I'm well aware of that fact, my lord. My knife-wound from last year *and* this morning's blisters have made the dangers abundantly clear. What are you suggesting?"

Faine hesitated, his delicacy at odds with his blunt face. "You need an heir. We've agreed you must marry."

"But have I agreed?" Akabe studied his council member's faces. To a man, they were nodding, deathly serious.

"Yes, sir, you must." Faine harrumphed, adding with an awkward cough, "Duty."

"Ah." Duty. Perfect reason to marry. Nothing could be less inspiring to a prospective wife, Akabe was sure. "Do you believe there's a young lady somewhere in Siphra who is brave enough to live in this marble inconvenience of a palace—with a man who is clearly marked for death by assassins?" While they blinked at his acidity, Akabe continued, "Should we also warn her that she'd be sentenced to a life of cold food, perpetual gossip, and endless ceremonies? Surrounded—forgive me, my lords—by packs of staring royal courtiers who'd follow her to the privy to discuss business?"

His council members shifted guilty glances here and there. Faine attempted a joke. "Majesty, you make life in the royal court sound so *uncomfortable.*"

"It is."

Lord Trillcliff broke their awkward silence. Stout and earnest, his eyebrows moved in thick, upstanding silver fringes over his ocher owl-eyes. "Being the king, Majesty, you will have no lack of young ladies willing to share your . . . interesting circumstances."

Squelching further complaints, Akabe sat back in his carved, gilded chair and stared at the dead flies. Poor creatures. A pity they'd suffered what he'd escaped. With as much grace as he could muster, Akabe conceded defeat. "As you say, then. Have you a list of courageous candidates, my lords?"

Faine sighed as if relieved. "Not yet, sir."

No? Good! Akabe straightened. "Am I permitted to suggest a possibility?"

Trillcliff said, "Any young lady of some social standing and good reputation may be considered. However, sir, a foreign princess might bring—"

Princess? Akabe stopped Trillcliff with an upraised hand. Here, he must declare his personal battle lines. "No foreign princesses. And no Siphran ones either—if any exist."

His tone approving, Faine agreed, "Indeed, sir. Foreign brides bring foreign gods, and we've enough to deal with, trying to protect ourselves from the Atea lovers. One of those goddess-smitten fools is likely your failed poisoner from this morning."

Glad to shift the subject toward ardent worshipers of the fertility goddess Atea—and away from his future bride's pitiable fate—Akabe asked, "Has the man been found who served us the poison?"

Faine snapped a look at Lord Piton, the youngest council

member with the fewest silver hairs. Caught off guard, Piton stammered, "Um, not yet, sir. Your men are questioning everyone at the temple site, including the priests and the prophet."

"They're questioning Ela?" Akabe kept his outrage in check. "Do they suspect her?"

Piton moistened his lips. "Er, no, sir. But perhaps she saw some detail about the intended assassin that others have missed. And she could petition the Infinite for the man's identity."

Ela. He must speak of her before the opportunity was lost. Akabe pressed his fingertips together. "What I am about to say will not leave this room—does everyone understand?"

"Of course, sir," Faine said as the others nodded agreement. "We hope you may trust us."

Watching their faces carefully, Akabe said, "Ela Roeh is now Siphran. She's highly regarded by our people and used to dealing with extraordinary circumstances. Not least, she's more dedicated to the Infinite than any lady I've ever met. I'd prefer to marry her."

His council showed surprise, but no opposition. Trillcliff, ever aware of rank, lifted his silver-spiked brows. "The prophet's place is unique in Siphra. Difficult to dispute, should anyone mention her status. Though she's not highborn, she's quite presentable."

"And," Piton quipped, "considering her swift actions this morning, sir, no doubt you'd be marrying your antidote to future poisonings."

Even Trillcliff laughed. But as Akabe enjoyed the joke, it distressed him. Ela deserved better than to be considered a living antidote to future assassination attempts. Would she agree to wed a king?

Tomorrow, he would seek information from someone well-acquainted with Ela.

Then he would visit with his favorite prophet and persuade her to marry him.

Don't Miss the First in the Books of the Infinite Series!

To learn more about R. J. and her books, visit rjlarsonbooks.com.

No girl has ever become a prophet of the Infinite. The elders warn that she will die young, but Ela heeds the call of her beloved Creator and is sent to bring the Infinite's word to a nation torn asunder by war. There she meets a young ambassador determined to bring justice. Can she balance the leading of her heart with the leading of the Infinite?

Prophet by R. J. Larson
Books of the Infinite #1

"This tale captured me and held me hostage to the very last page. Breathlessly waiting for the next book."
—Donita K. Paul, author of The DragonKeeper Chronicles and The Chiril Chronicles